EMMA HINDS

THE KNOWING

EMMA HINDS

Bedford
Square
Publishers

First published in the UK in 2024 by Bedford Square Publishers Ltd,
London, UK

bedfordsquarepublishers.co.uk
@bedsqpublishers

ISBN
978-1-915798-13-8 (Hardback)
978-1-915798-65-7 (Trade paperback)
978-1-915798-15-2 (eBook)

Typeset in Garamond MT Pro by Palimpsest Book Production Limited,
Falkirk, Stirlingshire

Printed in Great Britain by CPI Group (UK) Ltd, Croydon CR0 4YY

To Rachel

Please note, *THE KNOWING* contains themes of sexual violence which some readers may find challenging.

Chapter One

Five Points, New York, 1866

I dipped the needle into the pot of dark-brown ink and pressed its tip against my ankle, spreading the skin taut as a drum. My hand followed the line of the star, the familiar sharp prick followed by the smallest tap of ink settling, letting me know I had gone deep enough and could remove it with a pulling sting. This was the soothing rhythm of my days; pain and blood and ink mixed together.

'How's it coming?'

I winced. Just hearing his voice made me punch the skin too deep and red blood mingled with the ink. I wiped it clean, the brown pigment staining the palest skin on the inside of my ankle. I looked up at Jordan.

'Nearly done.'

'Hurry up,' he grunted. 'He wants his cards done after.'

He nodded to the man sat shirtless in front of him, receiving a sailor's tattoo on his shoulder. He looked like a side of beef on the turn, red sunburnt skin curdling with pale sweats as his fingers dug into the splintering arm rests of the chair. A first-timer, that much was clear, but like all navy lads he'd not said a word of complaint.

I turned back to my foot. The star wasn't my favourite, but it wasn't my worst. My self-made marks were still shaky, but at least they were mine. Jordan had the run of my back, my chest and neck, my legs, my arms and my ass but he had little interest in my stomach (said the skin was too flabby) or my feet. He didn't like working on bony crevices. If someone requested these delicate nooks he'd set me to it, saying it was 'a woman's work'. As far as I knew, I was the only woman tattooist in New York City, so what he really meant was it was work he was too lazy to do.

'Now, Florence.'

I knew a warning tone when I heard it. I wiped once again, applying my handmade witch hazel balm, and dropped my needle in a pot of rum for cleaning. I produced my black velvet card bag from my dress pocket and pulled my chair closer to the sailor. He stank – they both did: Jordan of stale smoke and spilled whisky, a bitter scent tinged with a nauseating sweetness that permeated our linen, my dresses, our shop; whereas the sailor smelled like a man who'd not washed for twenty days and had spent every moment of them sweating. I tried to think of the buns I'd bought earlier from the Dutch bakery two doors down. I imagined the fresh honey scent of the dough, breathed through my mouth, and spread the tarot deck on the table between us.

'I heard about you down at McSorley's,' the sailor said. His voice was higher than I'd expected. Looking at him properly, I thought he might not even be eighteen. 'You're a real mystic, then?'

'She is.' Jordan's dark eyes followed my hands as I shuffled. 'Providence brought us together a long time ago.'

Providence could also be called a tall man with a loping stride and a slow smile picking a little girl who could read tarot out of a ragtag pack of foundling gypsies at the Old Brewery, and promising to take her away from the slums. Pity he didn't mention at the time that 'away' only meant adjacent. I stared at the back of his head as he bent to his work, hating the thinning, greasy hair that lay there. *Lying bastard.*

'Now you work for the Irish?' the sailor asked, shooting a wary glance at the clover stamped on the back of Jordan's hand. I had a similar one on the side of my right breast.

'Nah.' Jordan hated the suggestion he worked for anyone but himself. 'But they make good neighbours.'

Bullshit. The Irish gang, the Dead Rabbits, were not good neighbours and Jordan and I were as thoroughly in their pocket as every other business that backed onto Mulberry Street. He gave them gang signs, the dead rabbit or the clover, I gave them readings and they took a cut and chose not to bash our heads in.

'How's it work then?' The sailor watched the cards sailing through my fingers, mesmerised. Customers liked the sleight of hand. I cut the deck and laid the cards before him.

'Turn the top three.'

He did so. I read for him, saying the phrases I knew pleased Jordan the most. If I could work in that a tattoo would get this poor sucker a woman, so much the better. It barely mattered what I said, though. Now that I was sitting close, the sailor's eyes never left my skin, skimming the edges of the short-sleeved, low-cut dress Jordan preferred me to wear in the shop.

'You'll be lucky on Friday if you place a bet—'

His eyes found the tiger on my left shoulder.

'You've got a good chance at success for whatever you try your hand in—'

They travelled to the Chinese dragon on my right wrist as I pointed at the Sun card.

'You're going to draw someone to you, a lover of great desires and passion—'

They settled on the wheel of fortune below my collarbone. I didn't need to look up from the Page of Pentacles to feel Jordan's anger throbbing nearby. If the boy looked away from my chest, we might be able to move on.

'These all your work, then?' he asked Jordan.

I stiffened.

'All mine.' Jordan's voice was dangerous and soft as velvet. The sailor didn't notice.

'Never seen a girl with so many like that.' His eyes were still on my wheel. I started to sweat. 'Never seen a girl with any, apart from people in the West Indies. She lets you do it?'

'Of course. She likes it.'

I had liked it. In the beginning I would have done anything for him; he was so handsome and kind, and he worked so carefully and gently, whispering how the pain would soon be over and how beautiful I'd look. He'd followed it with kisses and caresses until I didn't feel the difference; pain and love, it was all together. Then, later on, he'd wanted to ink me in places people would see. That's when the problems had started.

'Likes it?' The sailor's eyes were wide. 'Good God, if I could find me a woman who liked pain!'

This boy doesn't know what he's doing, I thought, *he doesn't know what he's costing me*. If I could have, I'd have stared him dead in the eye and told him to shut his fucking mouth but looking at him was the worst thing I could do. I stared instead at the sweet-faced page boy on the card, his pink skin grubby now from my fingers, his cup yellow and the sea behind him blue as ink. I wondered where I would have to go to see water that blue.

'Say, you don't…'

4

I felt it before he said it, that this pause before he spoke would ruin my day.

'… lease her out, do you?' He sounded so hopeful, I could almost have laughed. He had no idea the man standing beside him had a gun under the floorboards and a fighting reputation. I held my breath.

'Not for sale.' Jordan's voice was so sharp now even the boy noticed. I felt his stiffening posture in front of me and stilled. 'Go upstairs, Florence.'

Didn't need to tell me twice. I grabbed my cards and my coat and fled up the sloping stairs, letting the bedroom door click behind me. I waited beside it, listening. He was either going to kill him, or take all his money and kick him out. He might finish up the tattoo before he did either; Jordan never liked to leave a job incomplete. I found I didn't care much what happened. For me, the end result was the same. It was always my fault. I sat on my side of the grimy mattress and closed my eyes. There was no way out of it. I had stopped trying to find one long ago.

I shivered. The late February wind was whistling through the window, the frame cracked and rotting away. It was always cold upstairs. Even when Jordan would finally heft his drunken, shit-smelling form under the blankets beside me after an evening of drinking, his boiling body wasn't enough to keep me warm. I pulled my coat on, tugging a squashed bun out of the pocket. I pressed it to my nose, the shiny brown surface of it silky on my skin. They were better fresh, when the hot smell of them was so thick you could taste it, but I bit down happily, the stretchy yellow dough inside melting on my tongue.

I pulled out my cards and cut them, staring idly out of the window as I felt the worn edges in my fingers. I did this out of habit, whenever I was on my own. Jordan didn't like it. It made me feel homey, or as homey as a child who grew up wild in Five Points could feel, the repetitive slice and shimmy of cards in my hands bringing my mind to a quieter place where the world slowed down. I let the tingling grow

5

at the back of my neck and my breath became unhurried. I watched the cards. The Two of Cups. The couple standing on the card lifted their tiny inked goblets to toast one another, the ink lines around them expanding to fit their movement. Partnership. Union. Then the little figures upturned their cups, spilling the golden ink to reveal the blanched white paper underneath. The Two of Cups reversed, I supposed, though I had not moved the card. A broken relationship. No guesses what that was about. I could see the shades of other meanings pressing into the corners of the room, spirits lingering in the crevices of the rotting window. The chill was intensifying, my breath growing shorter and the steam of my breath thicker so I tapped the card with a trembling finger. *Behave.* The figures righted themselves and warmth returned.

Even when I was tiny and saw older Romani girls turning cards, I knew what pictures were coming. They told me I had the Knowing. Things people didn't want anyone to know were whispers I heard or pictures I saw; I didn't know it was wrong to speak them out loud until I'd had a few beatings. The Knowing made me odd, even among slum orphans. I'd been easy pickings for a man like Jordan.

I heard the shop door slam downstairs. He was coming. I threw off my coat, stuffing the half-eaten bun and my cards underneath it as Jordan's boots stomped up the stairs. I heard the clink of his belt buckle pulled loose. No use in hiding or protesting, that had only ever made it worse.

'My Florence, my Flora, my little flower.'

Dangerously too many names. I followed his hands with my eyes. One closed the door behind him, the other swung the belt.

'Who do you belong to?' A soft voice, like snow that falls quietly and crushes all the flowers.

'You.'

Only one answer, but it wouldn't make it better. At this point, all I hoped for was to make it so bad.

'Only you, Jordan.'

'Very good, little one.'

He leaned forward, whisky breath sour on my face, and I could see every broken blood vessel in the slack, stubbled skin around his neck and jaw. He kissed my shoulder and the tiger that growled there, the one the sailor had examined so keenly.

'So then why was he looking at you, eh?' His voice was still so soft. 'Why was he looking at you?'

He always seemed to think I had somehow put the thought of wanting me inside the other man's head, as if I perversely ushered along what inevitably came next. I lay back and rolled over, pressing my left cheek into the mattress. At the first stinging strike of the belt, I stared at my cards, a few from the scattered pile poking out from under my coat. My fingers itched for them. The belt struck, again and again, and I rose above myself, seeing our bodies below. I watched Jordan drop the belt with a clatter, I saw him pull down his trousers and wriggle my skirt up. Dark figures stood on the edge of my vision, ominous witnesses whose faces I was too afraid to see. I felt their secret anger pressing in on me, as if the very fabric of the world was in my hands and if I only gripped tight enough, I might tear it in two. But I'd learned long ago that listening to the dead came with its own cost, just like everything else. I released my clenched fists and let all that power be wasted. I drifted back into my body, to the deep, dull ache inside and his slimy stomach against my back. I tasted sweet dough and bile and swallowed it down. Pain and love mingled together; if whatever this was could even be called love. I didn't want to think about that.

Instead, I thought about the half-eaten bun. It was a good thing I hadn't finished it. Now I had something to hold on to, something to look forward to, after.

Chapter Two

I met Minnie on a Friday. It was my day off, which was how I came to be there, dodging pickpockets and begging veterans around the Battery and trying to find a quiet bench where I could sit and watch the new immigrants coming through the reddish sandstone arch of Clifton Castle. I liked to watch them, imagining the places they might have come from, Italians and Germans setting their shaky, trepidatious boots on American soil. I'd never known anything outside Five Points, but watching the tall ships sitting in the docks, the gulls wheeling around them, allowed me to imagine a world beyond the frozen skies of New York. I stamped the cold out of my feet and pulled my coat closer around me. Manhattan winters were always brutal, but this one had been lingering on for months. It was the first weekend of March; my coat elbows were already thin and patched, and my boots wouldn't take another blizzard. I frowned angrily at the languorous clouds that pressed down on the horizon, all the way out to Brooklyn, and told the sky: *No more snow.* It responded by sending a sharp, chill breeze off the grey water. It was too cold to sit and dream. I turned my back on the miserable waters, preparing to walk back uptown to Jordan. As I did, I accidentally caught the shoulder of a tall, thin man.

'Watch it.' I sprung away, instinctively recognising the signature bump and grab of many of the desperate con artists who had been spilling into the city since the war, preying on the discharged soldiers and their pensions, but it seemed like he had the same idea about me. He snarled at me, a guttural sound in his throat like an angry bird, and grabbed the arm of my coat. I'd not buttoned it well enough and they were loosely sewn anyway, so it flapped open, buttons rolling off the edge of the harbour to plink like pennies into the water and exposing my tattoos to the world.

'Get off!' I spat at him, jerking back, but he gripped harder and growled at me menacingly. 'Let go, you shit-swine!'

I noticed a splattered pink and white scar splotching up his throat and chin, livid against his dark skin. My first, abstract thought was perhaps his voice box had been scratched out by a bear and I was just wondering how hard I would have to scratch to get him to let go when a voice interrupted our tussle.

'Hey! What the fuck are you doing?'

The voice came from below my line of sight, causing me to look down. There she was. She was about the height of a ten-year-old girl even though she was clearly a woman and had no lower arms to speak of save a nub below her right elbow that looked like half a hand. I'd seen foundlings in the slums without arms or legs and they mainly begged, and often made good coin from it whilst they were young enough to appeal to the uptowners. I'd seen soldiers who'd been crippled on the battlefield and they seemed to do everything the same as they had before, just made use of their teeth and feet to beg or work on the docks. I'd never seen a person dressed as finely, made so beautifully and staring so haughtily at me as she did now.

9

'What's your goddamn problem?' she snapped at me. 'You don't have to speak to him like that.'

I stared between the two of them, the towering giant of the speechless black man above me and the tiny blonde woman below me, and struggled for my words.

'He grabbed my coat!' I said, taking the opportunity of the man's relaxed body position now that the woman was speaking to rip myself away from his grip.

'Abernathy?' She immediately fixed her intense blue eyes on his face.

Abernathy bent towards her and I heard a weird assortment of sounds: barks, whispers and growls. Still, she seemed to understand and turned that piercing gaze on me.

'You tried to rob him.'

'Did not!' I exclaimed. 'I just bumped him.'

'Oh, the bump and snatch?' she snorted. 'I've seen it all. Cheap trick thief, are you?'

I was surprised. She was dressed like a lady – her gown was clearly made custom to fit her petite frame and the rich, velvet fabric had to be a dollar a yard – but she spoke like an urchin. She clearly thought me one.

My mind went in two directions simultaneously. Out of the corner of my eye I saw a copper standing at the edge of the railings, keeping an eye on the harbour. If she called him over I'd be done for. A girl like me didn't want anything to do with a night in jail. My other thought was of running. I was measuring the distance from here to Five Points, calculating the people I'd have to push past and how quickly Abernathy's long legs might catch up with me. I didn't like my odds. I'd just have to show her I wasn't to be pushed. I straightened my back and glared at her.

'No, I'm not,' I said. 'I'm a mystic and the only lady tattooist in New York City, at your service.'

I bowed sarcastically, but when I looked up she was eyeing me up and down curiously.

'Mystic, you say? And a tattooist?'

Her eyes flittered over my exposed neck and collarbone without judgement. I tried to stare down Abernathy over her head but his amber eyes were steady with boredom. Clearly, he was used to staring down more intimidating souls than me every day.

'Well, you've a fine hand,' the little woman said. 'Where'd you come from?'

She gave compliments and demands easily, as if she were used to being answered, so I did.

'The Painted Man, belonging to Jordan Whittaker. On the corner of Mulberry and Chatham. Five Points.'

I expected her to baulk at the address but she only nodded thoughtfully, her lips pursed together. I noticed how perfect her cupid's bow was and wondered if her lips were so red naturally.

'Do you take clients, girl?' she demanded.

'Yes, I suppose,' I stammered. I was surprised. I took whomever or whatever Jordan didn't want. No one had ever come in asking for me, but at the same time, work in a post-war New York was scarce. We weren't in the position to turn away paying clients.

'How's your afternoon?' she asked. 'Could you fit me in?'

Her tone was so imperious and the look on her face so commanding, I didn't think about the true answer to either of those questions.

'Yes, ma'am,' I said.

That made her grin. A row of teeth, a little crooked, but very white.

'No need to call me ma'am. I am Wilhelmina.'

She offered her half-hand. I grasped it and was surprised to feel her few fingers curling around my palm to grip me tight.

'Wilhelmina the Magnificent Armless Wonder. Let's go to your shop.'

At her words, I had the strangest sensation of the world around me suddenly re-starting, as if our conversation had been happening upon a small stage and the audience were as still as dark statues around us. As Wilhelmina began to walk towards uptown, I became aware of the people stepping aside to let her past. Some were laughing, some recoiling in disgust, but they all moved, and Wilhelmina the Magnificent Armless Wonder marched ahead. She was astonishing, sauntering like any fine lady three times her height, the purple feathers on her hat bobbing along jovially. She turned on the edge of Broadway, calling back to me:

'I'm not biding all damn day, girl!'

I jerked forward, obeying without thinking, and led the strangers into Five Points.

'This way.'

Five Points was sinking, everybody knew that. The shabby tenements of the slum leaned lopsidedly against each other as if, like many of their tenants, they no longer had the energy to stand. As Manhattan grew up around us, it felt like the only home I had ever known was rotting slowly into the ground. The smell of overused outhouses and too many unwashed bodies was as familiar to me as the scent of ink and blood. At the centre of it all was the Old Brewery, the derelict brewery that had once housed great, churning machinery and now played filthy home to a thousand of New York's poorest. I remembered how it felt to live in those stuffy, hop-scented basements, crammed into spaces divided by makeshift walls and sleeping with all of your worldly possessions under your head for fear of thieves. Until I'd moved into Mulberry Street, I knew no other home. It was a place where people were born and lived and died in the same gutter. It was unsurprising that their ghostly spirit remains lingered too, but the Knowing was no weapon against groping boys and girls who nicked my boots when I slept. My life with Jordan might not be a delight, but at least I was no longer roused by tussles taking place next to my head or a whore doing business inches away. I picked our way over drunks rolling out of doors and ducked under decaying beams. We passed the amputee soldiers, their frayed caps held upturned to passers-by, begging for charity.

'Fought at Antietam,' they croaked. 'I was there at Gettysburg, miss, spare some coin.'

I glanced over my shoulder, watching as Wilhelmina lifted her beautiful hem over stinking puddles with an unworried expression on her face. She didn't look at them with the dismay you often saw on the face of out-of-towners. She wasn't a lady, but she wasn't like any woman I knew either.

'Where are you from, miss?' I asked.

'Wilhelmina,' she corrected, passing easily under a ladder that Abernathy had to crouch beneath. 'Call me Minnie. We've been all over. I have my own troupe of performers.'

'Like Barnum?'

I had seen Barnum's Museum on Broadway and Prince Street, but never been inside. The posters outside were full of girls in skimpy outfits flying from trapezes, the famous little man Tom Thumb and freaks with strange bodies. Wilhelmina the Armless Wonder wouldn't be out of place in that cast of characters. Neither would I, I supposed.

'No, I am not like Barnum. I only work with girls,' Minnie sniffed.

'Oh.'

It seemed Barnum mainly worked with girls too, but I didn't say that. I sensed Minnie didn't think much of Barnum and the stacks of money he must have made from people like her.

'So you're a mystic?' she asked, falling into step beside me as we crossed a road.

'You could say that.' I hated the word but Jordan said we attracted more customers when he painted it on the window. 'Sort of.'

'Palms? Séances?'

She spoke so naturally, as if it were completely normal for a woman like her to be strolling in a slum like Five Points and talking about calling the dead. She didn't gawk and stare around her like the uptown snobs who came down for walking tours. They stumbled over shit and gasped and clasped scented handkerchiefs over their mouths. Minnie walked the slums as if we were strolling through midtown.

'Just cards. I don't do palms much, but I can do.'

As a child, scathing boys used to beat me whenever I spoke of ghosts. I'd learned to turn my eyes away from dark corners where spirits might lurk. The Knowing was like having a broken bone that never healed quite right. It twinged. Occasionally the world would slow and the shadows would lengthen, my breath would catch in my windpipe and my heart would lurch, but I would look away. Growing up in Five Points had knocked the truth into me: there was safety in not knowing.

'For customers?'

'And for the Rabbits.' I guided us onto Chatham, dodging the carriages that rolled along, relieved at least for Minnie's hem to be out of the sludge of the slum drains.

'The Dead Rabbits?'

Minnie's voice displayed no surprise, but I caught the glimmer of a glance between her and Abernathy.

'Yes, we do their marks. I do their cards, sometimes.'

I tapped the clover on the rise of my breast, now visible thanks to Abernathy's assault on my poor coat.

Minnie nodded thoughtfully.

'You're Irish, like them?'

'I'm Roma,' I said, 'but our shop is on their patch.'

I instinctively looked around me, searching for familiar gang marks, flat caps and watchful eyes among the passing New Yorkers. Speak of a Dead Rabbit, see one that minute, or so the superstition went. If they were lurking, watching me escort a woman in a too-smart dress and a black giant onto their corner, they were letting it happen.

'Is that it?'

Minnie pointed to the tattered sign of The Painted Man with its peeling lacquer and Jordan's name painted on the window. I stopped on the sidewalk, Abernathy pushing past me with a bump and a grunt. They drew closer, her bright violet dress lurid against the brown and grey of the street. Jordan was inside. I had never brought back a client, a stranger or even – not that I had any – a friend of some kind, but I knew in my bones he would not like it. When I looked at Minnie's small figure, her blonde head held high as she bobbed along, I knew there was something here not to like. I tried to breathe deeply, but just drew in a mouthful of foul air, hot with horse dung, and coughed.

'You all right, girl?' Minnie's blonde eyebrows produced a tiny crease over her nose.

'Don't tell him you met me,' I blurted out. 'Please. Say you're just coming in for some ink, not that you saw me or anything, please.'

Those eyebrows rose. I had never met anyone who talked so little from their mouth and so much with their eyebrows, but there was understanding there; a flash of something, woman to woman. She nodded slowly.

'After you,' she said.

I nodded my thanks and rushed forward to go back inside, feeling oddly like a spring being stretched, as if I were pulling away from something that would inevitably bounce back and hurt. The bell jingled on entry and Jordan looked up from his table. He was counting takings in between the untidy pots of ink, the smell of stale coffee filling the shop.

'Where have you been?' he grunted.

'Nowhere.'

I quickly sat down, distancing myself from Minnie and Abernathy, but I could already see that it would never cross Jordan's mind to assume someone had followed me anywhere. Jordan took one look at Minnie, snorted, and pointed down the street.

'Walking tour of Five Points begins at Chatham Square, miss. Though I doubt you'll be able to keep up with them.' He eyed Minnie up and down wryly and then his black eyes rested on Abernathy. 'Perhaps the kind gentleman can carry you.'

Minnie deflected his rudeness with a tilt of her chin and a flick of her blonde curls.

'I'm here for some art,' she said.

I saw Jordan frown at her business-like tone. Women never came in and he liked it that way. Women were for serving drinks and bedding, not inking, unless they were me. As if it knew I was thinking about it, my most recent tattoo began to sting.

'I heard you were the best needle artist in the city,' Minnie continued. It was a smart choice to flatter him. Jordan lit a cigarette and leaned back, appraisingly.

'Aye, it's true,' he nodded, 'but we don't get many of your type down here.'

'My type?' I heard the edge in Minnie's voice. Jordan did too.

'Uptowners.' Jordan blew smoke towards her. 'I've heard fine ladies were having art done, in secret, like, but I doubt they would come to the likes of me for it.'

16

'Well, I'm not from uptown,' Minnie stated.

She sat herself on a stool and I watched in amazement as she deftly removed her boots with her one hand and then, with her bare feet, right there in the shop, lifted her toes with unbelievable dexterity, to unbutton her coat and give it, clenched between her toes and the balls of her feet, to Abernathy who was waiting by.

'I'm a performer.' Minnie smiled.

I gazed at her white foot, so clean and pale with no red rubs on the heels, chilblains or dirty nails. What would it be like to touch it? Jordan did not look impressed by this performance at all.

'Seen better at Barnum's.' Jordan glanced at Abernathy. 'And what does he do? Hold your coat? Or is he a specimen from the Indies?' He smirked. 'Does he carry a spear and show the ladies his cock?'

Abernathy growled at Jordan, the same menacing sound he had used on me. Abernathy looked younger than him but he was two heads taller and maybe twice as broad in the shoulders. Jordan didn't move, simply puffing smoke towards Abernathy's imposing form. Regular entanglements with the Dead Rabbits made him difficult to scare and he liked a brawl. He wore a tarnished signet ring on his middle finger and enjoyed breaking teeth with it. I had a scar in the shape of it just behind my right ear.

'He doesn't speak.' Minnie pulled her shoes back on. 'He used to be a fire-eater and burned out a part of his throat.' Jordan's eyes flicked to Abernathy's prominent scar.

'Worse things, I suppose.' Jordan shrugged, uncaring. He clearly didn't feel the same nauseating anxiety I did when he saw that shiny skin amongst the dark flesh, imagining the searing heat required to melt it.

'So, what are you wanting, little lady? Just a little prick, is it?'

He grinned lasciviously, appreciating the scoop of her neckline as she re-set her dress. There was no one he wouldn't leer at.

'A little prod with something sharp?' He laughed at his own joke, smoke billowing out of his nose.

'Not quite.' Minnie's smile was sugary. 'I want your girl to do it, alone.'

'Florence? Why?' Jordan stopped laughing.

'Because it's what I want.'

Minnie's voice was sharp but calm. I had never heard a woman speak as she did. Abernathy dropped a stack of bills on the work table. I could see it was easily triple what a regular would pay, but Jordan sat back, suspicious.

'I thought you were coming for my hand, eh?' I felt the edge of his gaze on me and turned away, mixing my inks and trying to look busy. 'What are you wanting my girl for? She's no talent, I can assure you.'

Might not be, I thought bitterly, *but at least I can do fucking elbows, Jordan.*

'A precaution. I'm a woman, she's a woman; I'm sure you understand.' Minnie smiled at him, her white teeth shining. 'Why else do you employ her, if not for this?'

She was smart to use that tone; a little fancier than how she'd spoken to me, strolling up Chatham. She could clearly turn it on when she wanted and it looked to be working. I could see him calculating the risk in that dark mind of his. Letting me be alone with her, with anyone, letting me be given anything by someone else was something he hated, but there was also a fist fight tonight at McSorley's.

'It's only a small one,' Minnie said. 'Won't be ten minutes if she's good.'

That cinched it. The lure of gambling won.

'Fine.' Jordan snatched the bills. 'But your bodyguard sticks with me until you're done. That will be my precaution.'

18

'It seems fair. We have an accord.' Minnie smiled.

Abernathy did not look like it seemed fair. He looked at Jordan like he was horse shit and I could have sworn he rolled his eyes.

'I'll take him over the way for a brew.' Jordan rose, pulling on his brown jacket and crumpled hat. 'Like it dark, do you?'

Abernathy snorted and held the door open.

'Work quick,' Jordan commanded me, placing his hand on the back of my neck as he moved past. To anyone else it might have looked like a gesture of sweetness, a stroke of affection between lovers, but I felt the clamp of his hand and knew what it was for: to remind me of punishments delivered whilst he held me down.

'We'll wait outside.'

I nodded, trying not to let my breathing show my thundering heartbeat. A tingling had begun down the back of my neck, the same feeling I got before a storm came. The sense of something beginning. The door closed and Minnie and I watched through the glass as the two men crossed over Chatham, dodging carriages and other walkers, to duck into the Italian coffee shop on the other side of the road.

'He's gone,' Minnie said, quietly. She was watching me carefully. I tried to relax my shoulders. I had never been in the shop alone with a customer. I looked at her, admiring the way her soft features and curved outline set off the mundane bits of furniture around the shop so nicely. It all seemed cheerier without the harsh straight lines of Jordan's body and expressions, lurking over his table and filling the air with furious tension.

'Let's move these chairs, I want to sit with my back to the window,' Minnie commanded me. 'I don't want your husband to see me talking when they get back.'

Her eyes were flitting backwards and forwards between me and the coffee house. It felt like a clock had begun ticking somewhere and only Minnie was aware of how long we had.

'He's not my husband,' I said automatically, yet I did exactly what she told me to.

Later, I would wonder at what moment my allegiance switched from him to her, but I cannot pinpoint it. Somewhere in the walk from the Battery, stepping over drunks in Five Points, and the moment the door had closed on Jordan's back, I became tethered to her and I could not explain why.

'What is he then?' Minnie asked me, sitting in my chair.

'He's… he's Jordan.' I picked up my needle, hardly eager to elaborate. 'What tattoo do you want?'

'Can you do me a pair of wings on my leg?' Minnie crossed one leg over the other, pulling her skirts up. 'Right here.' She tapped her thigh.

I watched the white flesh wobble slightly, like milk curds. I was surprised by how much I wanted to touch it.

'Any type?' I asked, throat dry.

'You choose.'

I'd done a sketch last week of the archangel Michael for one of the Dead Rabbits, a huge back piece, but the wings were probably transferable. I pulled it out and traced it onto rice paper, before turning back to Minnie to show it to her.

'All right?'

'Perfect.'

She wasn't really looking. I got the feeling she didn't really care. I saw her eyes drift back to the coffee place. I could see that Jordan and Abernathy were walking back now, cups in their hands and cigarettes in their mouths. I turned to my work. Taking a deep breath, I dipped my cloth in the alcohol and washed the springy flesh of her thigh. I pressed the stencil on and rubbed it, her bare skin cool and slightly pimply under my warm palm. I peeled it away, inspecting the faint pencil marks. I stared at the downy blonde hair on her skin.

I had never tattooed a woman. My world was men, with their grab-bing hands and sharp shoulders. I picked up my needle, coughing to find my voice.

'You'll feel a sharp prick,' I said.

I set the tip against skin, feeling the bounce of resistance followed by the pop of the needle entering.

'I was expecting to.'

Her voice contained a smile and was warm on the top of my head. I couldn't think of the last time someone had breathed on me like this and I had found it pleasant. I tried to do what Jordan did, maintain a steady patter of conversation, but could think of nothing. I was too nervous.

'Why wings?' I finally managed to say.

'It's what they used to call these in my childhood in the circus.' Minnie waved her arm at me, the fine lace at the end of the sleeve trailing prettily over her half-hand. 'My wings. Thought I could fly for a spell. Soon learned different.'

I chuckled weakly but with each rise and fall of the needle, each dip in the pot, I was calming down. The world was shrinking faith-fully to the skin and the ink, and as she began to question me I began to answer, as inevitably as the breaking of flesh beneath the needle.

'He did all of yours?'

'Most.' I licked my lips. 'I've done some.'

I could feel her pulse through her thin, porcelain skin. As my needle passed over it, I imagined following one teasing blue vein all the way to her dexterous feet.

'For how long?'

'Years.'

I had been Jordan's so long I barely remembered life before.

'How old are you?'

21

I heard the sympathy in her tone and didn't look up.

'I don't know.'

I knew that the year I had come to Jordan was 1859. It was the year before war broke out, the year the city was filled with the sound of church bells mourning John Brown. I had only just started bleeding. That was seven years ago, but the rest of it was all guesses.

'Did you want every single one?' Minnie asked. 'Every tattoo he gave you?'

I sucked in my breath, trying not to let my concern show on my face. Jordan was only separated from us by a thin pane of glass. I could see the tight curl of his lip on the cigarette, the tense muscles of his neck.

'Don't worry, he can't see your face. I'm in the way,' Minnie reassured me. 'Trust me.'

I realised I did.

'No.' I let my breath out slowly. 'Not every single one.'

'I see.'

'Do you?'

I looked into her face. I didn't think anyone could see the dark and intricate bonds of blood and bruises that tied me and Jordan together. She held my eye for a moment but didn't say anything. Slowly she pointed to my chest, where my coat still flapped open from lost buttons.

'It's a tarot card, isn't it?'

I barely knew her, but I could feel she had an excellent way of seeing the darkness in people. My chest piece was the tattoo I hated the most. It was a brand, and both Jordan and I knew it. It seemed Minnie knew it too.

'Wheel of Fortune,' I said, dropping my eyes back down to her thigh. I wiped some blood away with my cloth. 'Card for change.'

She didn't speak and I was lulled again by the repetitive motion of the needle, the familiar cramp between my wrist and thumb knuckle as I held it steady. One wing done. The other was smaller, tucked behind the first.

'He can't hear us,' she whispered.

Soothed, I allowed myself to carry on speaking.

'When we met, I was flipping cards for coins.' The second wing was taking shape, the ink almost purple when it was fresh like this. 'He came up and turned the wheel. Asked me if it meant he could take me for a dance. I said yes.'

He had stood over me with those dark, smiling eyes and the most handsome face I'd ever seen. The great wheel on the card contained all of heaven and earth inside of it and the crouching demon that squatted upon it had eyes flaming red in warning. A card with infinite possibilities in the rise and the fall, but a heavy price.

'Living in the Old Brewery, were you?' Minnie asked.

'How did you know?'

My hand stilled for a moment, a little too much ink sinking under the skin, leaving a darker mark. Minnie gave me a small, knowing smile.

'Where else would a slum gypsy orphan live in Five Points?' she said.

'Oh.'

I didn't ask how she knew I was an orphan. I supposed it was written on my face, plain as day. An unwanted, tetherless child, adrift in the world. If it hadn't been Jordan, it would have been someone else.

'Why did you say yes?' Minnie's voice was soft, like sand trickling through an hourglass.

The honest answer was because I'd liked his face, and I was sick of the leery drunks who grabbed my blossoming body and the slobbery kisses from the street boys who were starting to look at me like I was prey to be caught. I sighed.

'Because I was dirty and lonely and hungry,' I replied. 'And I had no one else.'

I'd had someone, once. I was sure of it. Someone had warned me to keep quiet about the Knowing and put cold cloths on my swollen lip after one too many beatings. Yet it had been so long ago and Five Points was full of people who disappeared. Now they were nothing more than the memory of the smell of warm skin close to mine, a remembered gesture that felt like belonging. When I'd met Jordan I had just been one of hundreds of foundlings slowly dying in Manhattan. I couldn't see what lay ahead, even with the Knowing. *If I had*, I thought vehemently to myself, *I would have just carried on dying*.

'You're done,' I said.

I set my needle down and wiped her skin. The black ink left a bluish residue around the lines and I dabbed them with rum, feeling her flinch, before smoothing my witch hazel balm on. I could feel the inflamed edges of the wings under my fingers. I heard the sharp hiss of breath pulled through teeth.

'Sorry, I know it stings,' I said, 'but this will help with the swelling. Rub it with oil and don't scratch.'

'Thank you.' Her voice was close to my ear. 'It's beautiful.'

I looked up and caught her eye, suddenly aware that my fingertips were touching her, stroking her, and I pulled them away. Again, I felt that tingling at the back of my neck. The soft, ballooning sense of premonition. I turned back to my table, eyes blind to ink pots, paper, needles, overwhelmed by the scent of her body: a musky smell with a hint of flowers that reminded me of expensive fabric shops. The smell of wealth.

'If you can, wrap it with a dry bandage at home,' I said. 'You could use a garter to hold it in place if you want.'

I was rambling, but she didn't seem to notice. She sat in the chair, her blonde head tilted slightly to the side, her tall hat feathers quivering. She reminded me of an inquisitive bird.

'He called you Florence,' she said. 'Is that your name?'

'Flora.' The roof of my mouth was sticky. 'You can call me Flora.'

'Won't you read my cards, Flora?'

I didn't want to. The air was too close now, her breath was hot and sweet, and I felt shadows lingering in the crevices of the floorboards, awaiting whispers. They had words for me, I was sure of it, those spirits that lingered, but I did not want to hear them. I shook my head, glancing to the window, Jordan's hard profile visible through the red painted letters. Minnie's eyes followed mine but she didn't turn her head.

'If you don't want to do it now, why not come to me uptown?'

Minnie leaned her head closer, under the pretence of inspecting her tattoo, and I could feel her warmth filling the soft space between our close bodies and bent heads.

'I may have an offer for you, Flora,' she said quietly. 'I could use a girl with skills like yours.'

'An offer?'

'A chance.' Her hand tapped the wheel on my breastbone. I didn't move, though I felt that little tap reverberate through my bones. I swallowed heavily.

'A chance for what?'

She leaned in quickly. For a cold, blinding moment I thought she might kiss me and I couldn't move.

'To start again.'

Then, whilst my body sat quiet and still under her words, I felt the soft puckering of a dry kiss on the edge of my cheek, below my ear. The pressure of it carried in my blood and I felt a responding tug in my abdomen so sharp I wondered if it was women's cramps.

I stared at those lips, watching them turn into a knowing half-smile. I shivered.

'We're at the corner of sixty-sixth, Hamilton Square. Abernathy will be waiting for you.' Minnie shuffled her skirts back into place, wincing slightly as she stood up. 'Bring your cards.'

She never asked me if I would come. Perhaps she knew from the moment her lips touched my face and I didn't recoil that I was somehow hers. I sat in stunned silence as she left, nodded to Jordan, and she and Abernathy walked purposefully away towards Chatham Square.

'Uppity cripple bitch,' Jordan snorted, slamming his way back in before taking his new cash influx to the pub for drinking and betting. 'What did she have?'

'Wings.' I cleaned my pots and packed my needle box. 'She's got no arms.'

'Delusional.' Jordan lit another cigarette. 'I'll be back later.'

He left, just like Minnie had done, and I was left alone, wondering if any of it had really happened. I tidied the shop and washed up the coffee pot. I sewed fresh buttons onto my coat (ones scrounged off an old waistcoat of Jordan's) and turned the shop sign to 'Closed'. The sun was casting its sharp orange evening glow down Chatham, the puddles and piles of fresh dung glistening with it. That's when I felt it. A tingling in my spine, a thinning of the edges of my vision. Light pierced the window, bringing the smears and nicks into focus and illuminating the floating dust in a slow waltz around me. I closed my eyes and pulled my cards from the pocket of my dress. I shuffled them through my fingers intuitively, the worn edges as soft as feathers. When I looked down at the top card, my breath caught. A whisper of an invisible premonitory finger trailed down the back of my neck. It was the Wheel of Fortune. Sometimes, the dead find a way. I felt my resolve click into place inside my chest like a dislocated bone snapping back in its socket. It was time to leave.

I took my cards; I took some buns and a spare dress. I took my box of needles and ink and lifted up Jordan's secret floorboard with the knot the size of a chestnut. I tried not to disturb the prime leaf tobacco, the small revolver and the items Jordan had always used to stop pregnancy, including a particularly loathed bottle of brown 'women's tonic' that had made me bleed like I was dying. I grabbed his old knife and a small stash of cash and replaced the floorboards, wondering if he would be angrier I had left or angrier that I had stolen from him.

Outside, I locked the shop door behind me and then dropped my key down a drain. No going back now. As I trudged through the evening churn of mud, I felt eyes on my neck and back and wondered how long it would take the Dead Rabbit outposts to get word back to Jordan that his girl had walked out of his shop at twilight and not come back. The thought caused an unpleasant nervous tingling behind my knees but I didn't stop walking. I set my eyes on Fifth and followed it like a pilgrim. Beside me, in the shade of buildings and gaps of horses' legs, they came. I would not look at them and I dared not see their eyes, but they followed me as earnestly as they had done every day of my childhood. I took the spirits with me.

THE LOVERS.

Chapter Three

Uptown, the air smelled of other things. As I walked along the dark sidewalk, I heard trees whisper above me and inhaled deeply: the sharp, green smell of living things and the sooty finish of machinery, the ever-present smoke from the trains. Hamilton Square was robed in darkness and silence, an eerie quiet that I knew only came with money. Standing on a stoop, with curls of grey smoke furling up from his hat in the orange glow of the streetlight, was Abernathy. I coughed. He turned, cigarette hanging in his mouth and nodded towards the house. He'd been waiting for me. I stared up at the great door, towering above us both with its stone crown of carvings and flourishes. I thought of the tilted walls of The Painted Man. This house certainly didn't look like it was sinking. I followed him inside.

I had two thoughts on entering: that I hadn't known houses could be this warm; and that it had the most doors I had ever seen. They lined up, great oak faces repeating down the hallway. Before I could consider what I'd got myself into, Abernathy's hand reached in front of me to push a door open.

'Florence!' Minnie turned to face me, eyes bright and expectant. 'How nice of you to join us.'

Minnie looked like one of the dolls you saw in the winter displays in the uptown department stores. I'd stood outside them before, my fingers absurdly hot with itchy chilblains and my toes aching as freezing sludge leaked into my boots, mesmerised by the shiny things inside. The people I was faced with were arranged like a display too, with Minnie in the centre. Then I saw their shifting eyes in the flickering firelight, eyes that raked over my sodden boots and snarled black hair, their lustrous pearls and shining shoes rebuking my dirtiness. I flushed. I was glad I was wearing my coat and my tattoos were covered.

'Chester, wasn't I just telling you about the mystic I had found?' Minnie said.

'You were,' a tall, fair-haired man answered. He stood at the fireplace, one hand on the mantle. He tilted the glass in his hand from side to side, the golden liquid inside sloshing helplessly, as he looked me over. I didn't like his eyes: eager and hungry. That was a look I knew all too well.

'Mystics are a special interest of yours, aren't they, Mr Merton?' The woman sat to Minnie's left pursed her lips. I saw, queasily, how the white face powder she'd used had congealed with her sweat and now sat like mushed-up newspaper on her upper lip. *It takes a lot of money to be that fucking ugly*, I heard Jordan say.

'How intriguing!' she cooed. 'This child has the gift, does she?'

'Oh, yes.' Minnie nodded. She smiled at me encouragingly, but I clamped my jaw shut and glared at her. If I wanted to earn my bread in humiliation I might as well have stayed in Five Points. At least they didn't look at me like I was a stain on the carpet down there.

'Florence, come to the card table for me.' Minnie gestured to me regally with the nub of her hand. 'Abernathy will take your coat.'

My chest tightened. I was only wearing my work dress, designed for maximum exposure. I swallowed hard.

'If I could just change my dress...'

Just as when you wash a shirt clean and hang it back up only to see the filth of all the others, when I spoke I heard the common tone of my voice for the first time. I had thought that because I didn't curse so much and I was trying my level best to practise my reading now and again, I might pass as a bit educated, at least in a midtown way, but it wasn't true. The very lilt of my voice, its tone and bite, gave me away: Five Points, through and through. I could see them smirking. I swallowed back words, not wanting to say more, and instead tried to plead my case to Minnie with my eyes: *don't make me do this*. Minnie just shook her head. Abernathy tugged at the back of my coat with an urgent grunt.

'All right!' I whispered, tugging my arm away. I was determined not to tear more seams. 'Keep your damn hands to yourself.'

I slowly started to unbutton. My fingers slipped and bungled each one, as if my body was fighting against this inevitable revelation of skin. I had a small, relieving moment of distance when my mind detached gratefully, and I watched this poor girl undressing for these fine men and women and asked her what the hell she was about. There was every chance she had launched herself from one hard hand to another, the fool. Then the last button was undone and the coat slipped from my shoulders and I heard the gathered crowd gasp.

'Holy God in heaven.' Chester took a step towards me. He stared at my skin with the kind of reverence I'd only seen in the faces of church-going folk. 'Are they real?'

'Course they fucking are.' If they were going to think me a common slum girl I might as well play up to my role. 'You wanna check?'

That was the wrong thing to say, because his eyes met mine and

I knew with a jolt that he did. I looked hastily away, searching for Minnie. She smiled at me reassuringly and gestured to the card table.

'May I introduce to you tonight: Florence the Painted Mystic!' Minnie announced.

They all clapped obediently as I sat down, but they didn't approach. Instead, they talked to Minnie like I was an interesting dog she had brought in.

'Where is she from?' one of the older gentlemen asked. 'What are her people?'

'She is a Seer from Transylvania, the land of the dark arts,' Minnie lied fluently. 'She was given her gift in a mystical ceremony and wears their craft on her skin. Her mother was murdered for her knowledge and power, and now, her daughter wears her mournful legacy.'

It was such bullshit that I struggled not to snort with laughter, but I felt Abernathy's finger in my back, prodding me discreetly to stay quiet, so I bit my lip and tried to look sad for my imaginary dead mother. I hadn't been part of a con since before Jordan, when I used to tell intricate lies of lost parents and imagined woes to separate gullible people from their money. I felt a familiar rush at doing it again.

'So, who will dare to look into the beyond?' Minnie asked beside me, inviting the others forward. She leaned down to whisper in my ear.

'Nothing fancy tonight, just your basic tarot stuff... can you do that?' Her warm breath tickled my cheek. It was comforting. I nodded. It was not like I had too much of a choice either way.

'Good.' She gave me a soft smile and then stood up to address the room: 'Let the readings begin!'

She wanted cheap tricks, and I was happy to give them to her. Abernathy handed me my cards from inside my jacket pocket and stood behind me. Minnie stood beside me, occasionally squeezing

my shoulder with her hand. One by one, I read for them. I didn't
let my gaze wander to the edges where shadows sat and the voices
of the dead might linger. The arcana ran before my eyes, unspeaking,
as I simply told them what they wanted to hear: flattering ideas of
self and arrogance. It took an hour, maybe two, as one eager face
blended into another, and then it was over. Minnie sauntered away
from the table, thanking everyone for their attendance; Abernathy
moved silently through the crowd, menacingly collecting payment in
a silver dish. I leaned back in my chair, my stomach cramping hard
with a hunger I hadn't previously noticed. I thought with longing
of my buns, still tucked away in my coat and wondered when I would
get to eat them and where I would be when I did. Perhaps I'd be
back out on the streets, seeking a sheltered doorway to huddle down
into and praying I didn't freeze until morning. Or, worse, Jordan
might find me and drag me back by my hair. I did not relish either
prospect.

'Will you read my cards?'

I hadn't noticed his approach through the rustling gowns of ladies
and the stern coats of gentlemen, but there he was: Chester Merton,
standing in front of me. I nodded, warily. His eyes were strange.
They were grey as clouds and thin, as if he were narrowing them
all the time. They lingered on the patterns on my arms as I placed
three piles in front of him.

'This pattern here—' he reached for the crease of my wrist with
a feather-light touch. I twitched. *Only Jordan touches*, I thought '—is
it a Chinese dragon?'

I saw Minnie frowning over at us and wondered if she was jealous,
and of whom. I turned the cards automatically, hoping he would
stop touching.

'Yes,' I said.

'Fascinating.' His fingers curled around my wrist greedily, turning it upward to him to see the ferocious, snaking coil of the dragon's body. 'And how long did it take? How much did it hurt?'

'Now, Chester, we don't touch the mystic.' Minnie was at his shoulder, her half of a hand resting proprietorially behind his neck. It was an intimate gesture, one for lovers or wives. 'We pay for the cards.'

'And how much do we pay to touch?' Chester asked.

He had not let go of me. Despite Minnie's words, his eyes were glued to the dragon's face, his thumb tracing further up my wrist, seeking out the line of my vein under the ink. My skin prickled. I wanted to pull away but I didn't know what would happen if I did. My slum instinct was kicking in: play dead until it's safe.

'She's not for sale, Chester dear.'

Minnie's voice was light and fluttery but her blue eyes were as hard as marbles. Chester glanced up and saw her expression. He smirked.

'Not yet anyway,' he said.

A frosty coldness settled under my skin. I had a sudden flash of an unwelcome image in my mind; of my own body, raw and vulnerable, spread bare across Jordan's dirty sheets, but where Jordan's dark features should have been, Chester's light hair and grey eyes emerged. Whispers like the sound of ferry boats passing in the distance filled my mind. Just because I had trained myself not to listen to them, didn't mean that ghosts didn't press their lips against my ears and breathe. I winced and blinked, trying to shake the picture loose, but when I looked up, I saw Chester watching me. His eyes were lit with a cat-like glow from the fire behind him and I had the crushing sensation that he had somehow known what I had seen. He smiled, a pink tip of a tongue wetting his hard mouth, satisfaction lingering around the edge of his moustache. Though his fingers on my wrist were the powder-soft touch of a gentleman, there was a creeping, thuggish spectre of something stretching out to me across the table, dark and suffocating.

Stay in the room. That persistent, familiar voice without a face from my childhood in the Old Brewery, quick with fear, repeating a phrase I always used to hold on to reality when the Knowing pressed in. I tore my eyes from his and looked at the green velvet of the card table, the swirling red and yellow pattern of the carpet, noticed the black soot spots on the edge of the marble fireplace. These things were here; steady, uninhabited objects, and I breathed out slowly. The profuse sense of another world bearing down on me receded.

'Show's over, Mr Merton.' Minnie's voice cut through the residual whispers. 'It's time to say goodnight, Flora.'

'Goodnight, sir,' I said, my voice only a whisper.

Chester let go of me, leaning back in his chair. Immediately, he shrank before my eyes, the presence of him cut back to the slight, dandyish gentleman he truly was; a sallow-faced man in his thirties with a wispy moustache and limpid eyes. If he was a monster, he wasn't the kind I was used to.

'I'm sure you paid good money for her, darling Minnie, but she'll have to do more than this to impress.' Chester stood up and looked down at me. 'I'll be watching your progress.'

'Thank you for the suggestion, Chester.' Minnie crossed back to me and petted my hair. I didn't know if I felt comforted or patronised. 'We'll go up now.'

'Very well.'

He moved to an armchair and sat, staring into the fire. For the first time that evening, I realised that we must be standing in his house: Mr Chester Merton of Hamilton Square, New York City. A wealthy man who called Minnie 'darling'. I glanced between them both, trying to see the truth of their connection in their slight movements and looks, but Abernathy was pushing me out of the parlour and into the dark hallway, illuminated only by an old gas lamp, probably for servants to use, on the dark wooden dresser. Minnie sighed as he closed the door behind us, the click echoing against the marble tiles.

'Follow me,' she said.

Abernathy took the lamp and soberly led the way upstairs. I instantly thought of a serial I'd spent a week or two deciphering in the back of the newspaper, a story of a boy trapped in a castle with a mad uncle who was locked in a dark attic. I followed uneasily. The staircase was remarkable. It was a steep, bulky tree of oak and varnish that grew in its hard, twisting way through the very heart of the stone building. I walked up it as tentatively as I would cross a plank over a river of sewage in Five Points. I heard the soft disconcerting creaks of it breathing and sighing under our footsteps. I imagined that it must be the same sound that sailors lived and died with, drifting inside dark ships on black waters. Huge oil portraits hung on the walls, flaring in and out of shadows as we passed. I caught flashes of painted wigs, soft, flimsy dresses and austere noses. The whites of their eyes followed me and I tried not to look into them, hesitant to notice abiding spirits loitering nearby. A house like this could hold on to the past like cheesecloth. Finally, after more stairs than I had ever climbed in my life, Minnie opened a door.

'Come in,' she said.

It was the chamber of a lady of the house, not a guest. I stared around it, taking in the monstrous four-poster bed and the well-stocked vanity, the myriad of gowns and brightly coloured fabrics flung over the chaise longue.

'Are you his wife?'

I couldn't help my incredulous tone. I had only just met Chester but I already knew that men like him did not usually marry women like Minnie. She laughed, shaking her curls.

'No! Sweet Jesus, save me.' Minnie stepped out of her shoes and sighed. 'His wife lives in Europe.'

'Oh.'

I hesitantly walked further into the room. The closer I looked, the more I saw the evidence of another lady's life. I noticed the wedding photograph of an austere couple, the woman clearly older than the young, blond man. I saw the delicate embroideries framed on the walls, showing a progress of skill over years, and all of it sat like a rebuke to us for daring to sully this space with our presence. I could tell from the length of the gowns strewn around that Minnie had taken complete occupation without any qualms. There was only one type of woman who would do that in a married lady's room: a mistress.

'You'll stay here with me tonight,' Minnie said, draping her shawl over the chaise longue.

Until that moment I hadn't allowed myself to feel the fear that Minnie might turn me out on the streets to shift for myself, and the sudden relief drained me. I was suddenly inexplicably exhausted.

'Can you get my buttons?' she asked over her shoulder.

Minnie lifted her stream of blonde curls away from her neck and I crouched down obediently, fiddling with the delicate line of minute buttons that trotted down her back. It took ages and I wondered who on earth would want to dress like this. She raised her arms so I could pull the gown over her head. It was heavy, like a baby, and smelled comfortingly of roses, sweat and a little bit of piss. I inhaled it deeply, the scent of her natural body making me less ashamed of my own.

'Thank you.' She stepped out of her crinoline and, with one practised foot, unhooked the metal clasps at the front of her corset. She had clearly had it adapted for her needs. Once free of it, she climbed into the giant bed in her shift and stockings.

'You can have the chaise—' she gestured to the long, cushioned chair near the fire '—or you can come in here with me.'

She patted the mattress beside her.

'In with you?' I stared at her. 'In… his wife's bed?'

'It's not like I take up much room,' Minnie said, smoothing the sheets.

I thought of what Chester's wife might think, to see a little slum girl clambering into her bed with her husband's mistress. Had he fucked her in this bed, his hands digging into the intricate wood-work? Had he taken Minnie under this canopy too? The hungry, lingering look in his eyes when he relished my skin hadn't left me. Perhaps it was the lingering dread, but it felt like I was being asked to climb into bed with the whole lot of them and it was thoroughly unappealing. I hesitated. In my silence, my stomach grumbled angrily. Minnie smiled.

'Hungry?' She reached for a silver platter covered by a dome waiting on the bedside table and set it on a cushion. 'Take your dirty dress off and come and sit on the bed, at least. Eat something.'

My qualms melted away when she lifted the dome – the aroma was painfully tantalising. I wasn't like the girls who whored for bread, but there wasn't much that I wouldn't consider when faced with the chance of a hot meal. I immediately stripped off my dress and ripped off my boots and clambered onto the feather mattress.

'Thank you.'

I tried to show some delicacy as I took a piece of a white roll and pushed some of the syrupy meat inside it, but I couldn't stop myself gobbling it whole. Crusty, buttery bread and melting, fatty pork blended on my tongue. I noticed Minnie staring at me and tried to swallow meekly.

'He did not feed you then,' Minnie asked, 'Mr Whittaker? The man you say is not your husband?'

'Not like this.' I shook my head and licked my fingers. 'I say he's not because he isn't. I've never been married.'

'Worse than, by the sounds of things,' Minnie snorted.

I thought this was rich coming from an uptown mistress, but I kept my mouth shut. I stuffed more bread in my mouth. Minnie watched, her blue gaze steady.

'Does he know where you are?'

My cheeks were full of dough but I couldn't have answered even if I wanted to. I shook my head.

'You left him?'

I nodded. Had I not been supposed to? The idea that I would have asked Jordan for his leave to come uptown to visit Minnie was laughable. In the first few years, he'd locked me in. Minnie breathed out slowly through her nose, a hissing sound.

'Will he come looking for you?'

The bread had formed a solid lump and I swallowed painfully, feeling it bump down my throat.

'Maybe.' That was a lie. I tried again. 'It depends how much he's drunk, how he takes it, what he hears from the Dead Rabbits but... shit, yes, probably.'

I caught Minnie's guarded expression and knew that the possibility of Dead Rabbits knocking on her philanderer's door was definitely unappealing.

'I shouldn't have come.' I looked down at my greasy hands. 'I'm sorry.'

The bread and meat were turning in my stomach, the sickly taste of them working its way back up my throat. Even if she threw me out now, I could never go back. He'd kill me, for sure, or punish me forever. Maybe I could hide out in Brooklyn, work the piers for a bit. There was always work for a girl willing to sell herself.

'Don't be sorry.' Minnie's hand pressed mine and my panicked mind slowed. 'I asked you to come. I knew this might happen.'

'That I'd bring the son of a bitch down on you,' I said, 'and all those gang rats too?'

Minnie gave me a small, tense smile.

'Don't give yourself too much credit, girl.' She drew her hand away, its warm, sweaty residue lingering on mine. 'Even if those bastards look for you, I doubt they'll even think to look so far up this way.' She looked at me sideways. 'They'd never think you'd have a reason to be uptown.'

They would be right, I thought. The idea that someone like me had a reason to be sitting in this fine room eating this fine food was ludicrous. I reached unsteadily for a glass of wine, sipping gratefully at the sweet, stinging liquid. Then I had enough courage to ask the question that had been on my mind since I had left The Painted Man.

'You said you had an offer for me,' I said. 'A chance to begin again?'

'I do.' Minnie held her own wine glass and rocked the crimson liquid from side to side. 'I have need of a girl like you to join my company.'

'Your company of… ?' I stopped myself before I said the word 'freaks' but Minnie gave a wintry smile as if she had heard it anyway.

'I want you to come onboard as a mystic and as an… attraction.' Her eyes lingered at my exposed neck. 'I could make good use of you. I'll look after you.'

'Oh, you will?'

I clumsily set my wine down, feeling the warm trickle of it slosh onto my fingers and seep into my shift, but I didn't care. I felt a flicker of disgust at her words. I should have known that my value was in my ink here just as much as it had been with Jordan. Minnie

39

ignored my tone, dipping one of her fingers into the plum sauce and sucking it off.

'Yes, I will,' she said, calmly. 'I'm always looking for new performers and you have a talent that people want to buy—'

'Want to gawk at, you mean,' I muttered.

Minnie raised her eyebrows. 'They will pay to gawk, my girl. They pay for lies and do it happily.'

'You think I don't know that?'

Minnie looked at me in surprise. Perhaps it was the alcohol, but I had followed her every direction so far without a second thought. I took a sharp breath in through my nose, the vinegary scent of wine stinging behind my eyes. If there was a time to ask the question, it was clearly now.

'I've spent my life selling lies in a shithole. This sounds like more of the same. What's the difference?'

I glared at her, looking for tells even though I had never been able to spot a liar in my life. Minnie seemed to find it funny rather than abrasive.

'I'm the difference,' she chuckled. 'You are. You won't be making money for him; you'll be making money for yourself.' She prodded my knee, pressing the wine stain into my skin. 'Spiritualism is a big market, girl.'

'Spiritualism?'

I'd seen the letters on music-hall posters accompanied by pictures of old ladies with crystal balls and levitating girls. The Knowing was a mystery to me, an ability inside me ruled by anger and instinct and was thus essentially limitless, but I was certain it would never make me levitate.

'Yes, your cards and such.' Minnie waved her hand dismissively. 'Is that not what you call it?'

'No, we called it differently,' I said.

40

'We?' Minnie frowned. 'I thought you had no one.'

Even though she was right, I still flinched at the words. At the back of my skull, I felt the whisper of a memory of kind hands teaching me to shuffle cards, stroking my head before sleep on those nights when the Old Brewery was rowdy and terrifying. It was only a flicker without features or feelings, a memory of a memory. Not a parent, for I had never known anything but being an orphan, but someone kind.

'I had someone, once, before Jordan,' I said shortly, and tried to change the subject. 'So is that all you want? My skin and the cards?'

'Why?' Minnie raised her eyebrows. 'Do you have more?'

'No.'

I had spoken too quickly. Minnie's blue eyes narrowed and I picked at the loose thread and tried to calm a sudden feeling of being locked in. A faraway voice made of memory whispered: *Tell nothin'*. Memory assailed me. When I was still a little scamp, a solemn woman with pearly skin and a pretty red rose pinned to her dress had taught me hopscotch in Murderer's Alley behind the Old Brewery. She was kind and spoke to me softer than the other boys and girls. It was only when I was caught, when familiar hands pulled me away and shook me in rebuke so hard that my teeth rattled, that I realised the truth. The hopscotch girl was dead, her rosy dress dyed with an ancient bloodstaining, turning the lace purple. She was the first ghost I met and my first lesson that ghosts were not to be played with, and that day, the doctrine was handed down: *Tell nothin'*. Whoever the person was who taught me, even though they had left me behind, I still survived by their lore. The taste of the wine was leaving a lingering bitterness in my throat and Minnie was still watching me expectantly. I swallowed.

'Do you still want me to work for you?' I asked.

She looked at me for a long time, her head slightly cocked to the side, that perfect cupid's bow mouth slightly open in thought. My job was to root out the secrets of others but Minnie was watching me like she was trying to see my deepest thoughts. I held my breath and recalled the scent of her body when she had pressed her lips to my cheek that afternoon. I wanted her to say yes.

'Tonight we made ten dollars,' she said. 'Four are yours if you want them. Do you want them?'

I thought about all the things four dollars could buy. Selling my skill was better than selling myself and I needed to sell something if I was going to survive without Jordan. Minnie did not look like a woman to be haggled with.

'I do.'

'Good.' She nodded. 'We will talk more in the morning.'

She finished her own wine, draining it easily.

'Where would you like to sleep?' She set her wine glass down and the plate on the floor. 'You can take this pillow and blanket if you wish or bunk here with me.'

As she spoke, she flipped back the cover of the quilt next to her, making space for me. I stared at the vast expanse of fresh, white linen. My mind raced over my own stockings, grubby with slum mud and horse shit and my shift, grey with over-washing and marked with rusty bloodstains. Instinctively, I crossed my arms protectively over my body.

'Thank you.' I picked up the pillow and blanket and turned towards the chaise longue, my heart hammering. I wondered if she would command me back, and what I might think of to take my mind away if she decided to touch me, but she didn't.

'Goodnight,' Minnie said behind me. She extinguished the lamp and cast the room into a red dimness, the embers in the grate still glowing.

'Goodnight.'

I settled myself on the chaise, its firm stuffing unforgiving and hard beneath my back. I realised that this was the first time I had slept alone in my living memory. There had always been someone close by, Jordan's hulking form, another lonely child to curl against in the Old Brewery, and long ago, warm arms that held me in my nightmares. I rolled over to face the cushion, my back muscles tensed against possible intrusion. I listened for the quiet but stealthy steps across floorboards, remembering how it had gone with Jordan in the beginning. None came. After a few seconds of silence, I allowed myself to breathe out slowly. Maybe it would be all right. I turned over carefully and watched Minnie's body in the grand bed. Her shoulder was a dark mountain peak, dusted with her loose, golden curls that still caught the edges of the red light, and glowed. I wondered sleepily how one would feel if I dipped a finger up inside it or stretched a curl out and ran it under my nose to inhale the scorched scent of rolled hair. Then I thought of Jordan's hair, a splash of spilled oil across his forehead and reeking of tobacco. I clenched my hands against the rough wool of the blanket and fought in my mind against his grasping hands. With a dry throat I longed for Minnie's kiss again. At least then the raw thing inside of me could be quietened by the silent oblivion that expanded inside my mind when she did it.

'It's all right.' I jerked at the sound of Minnie's voice, my body suddenly stiff and waiting. 'I won't send you back to him. I'm keeping you now. Go to sleep.'

I tried to, but a whisper startled me from half dreaming. The fire's embers were low and smoking, the room astonishingly large and strange in darkness. I heard the whisper again, or maybe the hiss of a cat by the door. I felt a tickling sense of unease start in the soles of my feet, as if they longed to run. I could not move. Then I saw the bronze doorknob move. It twisted slowly and I held my breath,

43

imagining Jordan's slim fingers, a tattooed rune on each one, grasping behind. Then it stopped. Whoever or whatever was outside couldn't get in. Not yet anyway.

I looked at Minnie. She was still sleeping. I rose quietly, my feet cold on the floorboards. By the time I reached the door, the frail whispers had dissolved to nothing. Only the crumbling of charcoal and small huffs of Minnie's breath. I cautiously touched the handle, now inert, perfectly silent and ordinary. I twisted softly. It did not hiss or whisper. Whatever man or spirit that lingered beyond had gone away. I was relieved when I tugged the handle, feeling the hard press of the hammer against the lock, resisting opening. I scurried back to bed, plunging myself under the blanket that still held hints of warmth. It was only as sleep drifted around me that the creeping sense of portent manifested at the edge of my mind. I realised, with a dull, familiar sense of foreboding, that whilst no one could get in, I could not get out. *I'm keeping you now*, Minnie had said. In my dreaming eye, the words seemed to be a cage which had caught me and held me tight, too tight to move.

Chapter Four

For the first time in my life, I wasn't woken by the bells of St Philip's clanging out over Five Points. Instead, I was faced with a surly-looking maid glaring down at me.

'Up!'

I was blasted with cold air as she pulled back my blanket with a face that was clearly calculating how long it would take her to get the smell of my stink out of the fabric.

'Sorry,' I mumbled.

I automatically stumbled up, my feet chilled against the cold floorboards, and sought out a corner next to the fireplace.

'Morning, Flora,' Minnie said, rising from the bed and holding out her arms for a maid to slip a housecoat over her back. 'It's time to bathe.'

'Bathe?' Blinking against the bright morning light, I watched as maids rustled in and out of the previously locked door, one filling a giant copper tub by the fireplace and a manservant walking in and out again with steaming bowls of water. I wondered briefly who had the key before I caught a sharp elbow to the rib.

'Get out of the way,' the surly maid hissed at me. I was awake enough now to notice that the angry glances she was throwing me were more than irritation at a new inhabitant and were actually tinged with a sneering nastiness I was more than acquainted with. I raised my own chin, defensively, before elbowing her back. She looked to be a couple of years older than me but there was no need to give her the impression she could push me around. Her frown darkened but I quickly sidled over towards the windows and out of the way. The chimney pots raced away from me towards downtown, so far I might have almost seen the ocean if not for the great bulking red tower of the Cooper Union Building. I was high enough to see the endless stretch of sky with its dusty grey clouds. I didn't know if I had ever seen so much of it.

'Get in, Florence.'

I turned back around. Everyone was staring at me. The maid by the bed had ceased her folding, the other, smaller one stood with a towel and some soap, and Minnie, her blonde eyebrows raised, gestured to the tub. *Fuck.*

'Now?' I stammered.

'Come on—' Minnie jerked her head '—we've not got all day.'

I glanced towards the open door and, as if she was reading my mind, the surly maid slinked over and closed it with a definitive snap, eyes greedy. Apparently, it was to be a private show. *Get it over quick,* I thought, pulling my shift over my head. My naked skin puckered with the exposure and I clambered into the tub with a splash that sent water rolling over the edge. I quickly sank deep to hide myself. It did no good. The surly-faced maid added my shift to the pile of laundry in her arms with the same kind of enthusiasm as an unfortunate person who had dropped a scarf in the shithouses of Five Points. Then her eyes shifted to my skin and the familiar look came onto her face and she looked at me with gleeful, righteous disdain.

Bitch. I crossed my arms over my breasts, but it made no difference. After all, my naked breasts were hardly the most interesting thing about me. Minnie noticed.

'Get out, Hettie.' Minnie pushed the maid away with her shoulder, blocking her view. 'We'll manage with Polly.'

Hettie glared daggers at Minnie as she left, closing the door so sharply that the glass bottles on the vanity rattled. Minnie set her hand down on them to still them and rolled her eyes.

'Uppity bitch,' she said under her breath.

It seemed I wasn't the only freak that Hettie the maid disliked. I smirked, and then noticed Minnie was watching me in the vanity mirror. I looked away. I moved my knees, swirling the burning water into the colder water underneath me.

'I like your pictures,' a voice whispered above me. I looked up into a pair of silvery eyes, as glassy and round as marbles as she stared at the tattoos on my knees. I saw no malice there. Children tended to like me; they liked odd things. I relaxed my shoulders into the hard copper rim.

'Thanks,' I said. 'I'm Flora.'

'I'm Polly.' She smiled. She couldn't be more than twelve or thirteen and had the quick, crooked smile of a chipmunk. 'Is it warm enough?'

'Warmer than I've ever had,' I said honestly. I was rewarded with that smile again, and this time, a giggle, as Polly tipped more water in.

'Me too,' she whispered. 'It's fancy here.'

I watched her small hands grip the black iron kettle, and noticed the small, dark burns on the backs of her hands. Cigarette burns. I recognised those. Slum children all had them, a way that older children liked to rebuke. I was a child who claimed to speak to ghosts; I had more than my fair share. Mine were all covered with tattoos, except one. I moved my left hand forward and twisted it so the fat muscle of my thumb was upturned for Polly to see, the little patch of darker skin, healed a long time ago, but still distinct. Polly's shimmery silver eyes flickered over it and she smiled. There was a flash of something then, a mutual knowing between us of another world.

'That's enough, Polly.' Minnie stood up and crossed over to us. 'You can go.'

Minnie sat on a stool beside the tub. Polly didn't look at Minnie. Her expression became closed, her small smile disappearing as Minnie approached.

'Yes, missus.' Polly dropped into a clumsy curtsy and for a moment I thought I saw a flash of resentment in her eyes, but then she was gone.

'She's young,' I commented as the door closed. Minnie and I were alone.

'She's a scullery maid,' Minnie said, 'but Chester doesn't employ a full household since he doesn't live here all the time, so I often have need of her. Here—'

Minnie rubbed the bar of soap into my back and I jumped away, banging my elbow painfully on the edge, a tingle stretching all the way to my pinky finger.

'I can wash myself!' I twisted around to stare at her, but then, aware of my swinging breasts sloshing in the water, twisted back, embarrassed.

'Really?' Minnie snorted. 'Girl, you've likely never had a proper wash in your life.'

'I know what to do with a bar of soap,' I countered. I was naked and flustered and I didn't want to be touched. 'Why do you call me "girl" anyway?' I glared at her foot, the only part of her I could see as she sat behind me. 'You can't be much older than me.'

'I'll have you know I'm two and seven; you don't even know how old you are.'

'Around one and nine,' I muttered churlishly.

'So I call you girl because that's what you are—'

Minnie pushed my shoulders forcefully with her one hand, ducking me under the water in a pop of bubbles before pulling me up, that one half of a hand astonishingly strong, as I spluttered and coughed, my curls a heavy curtain of rain around my face.

'—and even if I had only one month on you in age, I know more about this world than you do. Have you ever left Manhattan? Ever ridden the Fulton Ferry? Look at me, Flora.'

I did, wiping hot stinging soap out of my eyes. Her face was intent and her one full finger and three little nubby ones gripped my skin.

'Have you?'

I shook my head, still breathing heavily. I could taste bathwater in my nose. My hair dripped onto my neck. Minnie nodded, satisfied with my answer.

'A slum girl has no idea how to exist outside of slum, not without whoring herself, or fucking upwards. You know what that is? It's when a working girl gets a wealthy man and becomes a pet to him; it's whoring all the same but it's safer—'

As she spoke, she was rubbing the soap into my hair, the hard nail on her longest finger scratching into my scalp, and then I felt something else: the cold, slightly moist skin of the sole of her foot against my cheek, the tangy smell of sweaty leather. She was making up for only having one hand by using her foot to bathe me. I said nothing as that firm, vigorous appendage washed me. It turned out, a well-used foot felt no different to a hand.

'I call you "girl" because you've got no clue, darling, of how to manage yourself in this world,' Minnie went on. 'You've had a man over you your whole life and he's kept you as a girl, so how would you know what it means to be a woman? How would you know how to do anything?'

Minnie did not come from the slums; I knew that much. She might have landed there for a time, she may know the names and the streets from her circus days but she wasn't made in Five Points like I was. The first clue was that the type of whoring she was describing was well above the level of whores I knew. Whores in Five Points flashed their goods in doorways and took a man in hand for a gin. The second was that wherever she came from there had been comfort there at the very least, because when you came from the slums, you knew what you knew and it was not nothing. Five Points taught me to steal, to beg, to sleep light and anywhere, and to fight dirty. I knew how to make pennies stretch for a week when I didn't have shit and how to survive a gang war. I knew how to do a lot of things but I didn't say any of them to Minnie, because one thing I knew for certain was how to keep my mouth shut when someone else had all the power and I was naked.

'Lean forward.'

Her hand and her foot brusquely rubbed the music-hall scene across my shoulders, the snake that writhed up my spinal column, and the pirate ship that rocked on the waves over my kidneys. She saw them all and said nothing. Despite the warm water, I flinched against her cold clinical touch, each tattoo trembling and puckering underneath it. It seemed that she might be finished telling me what I didn't know, so I risked asking a question.

'Why does Hettie hate you?'

I had hoped to smart her a little with that, perhaps even knock her down a bit since I was just a slum girl and she was so high above me, but she merely snorted with laughter.

'It shows, doesn't it?'

'Don't you care?'

'Not a damn.'

I twisted around to look at her. She flashed a sudden, cheeky grin. Not only did she not care, but she also perhaps took joy in not caring. That was an intriguing revelation to me. 'Hettie's like all Irish: she's got all the look of prayer and all the habits of sin.'

I didn't comment on that. I'd heard every bad thing a person could say about the Irish and they were all pretty much the same things people said about the Bowery B'hoys, or the Chinese or the black preachers at St Philip's.

'So why does she hate you?' I pressed.

'Because of her former mistress, Mrs Merton. Hettie's very loyal.' Minnie sniffed, as if loyalty to Mrs Merton was wasted.

'What is she like? Chester's wife?'

The pressure against my back had increased at that word. I held my breath. Maybe it wasn't my smartest move to make inquiries of the wife to the other woman.

'Old,' Minnie said, finally. 'It was an unequal marriage. Chester was barely one and twenty and had a good name; she was old and came from money. She practically hand-reared Hettie, from what I can tell, and Hettie hasn't forgiven Chester for insisting she stay here in New York and serve me instead of going to Paris with her beloved mistress.' Minnie snorted. 'As if that speck would know what to do with herself in Paris.'

'They don't have children together?'

Minnie barked in cruel laughter.

'Lord, no. She's over ten years his senior and was much richer than him. She had no idea he was a gadabout. Once the vows were exchanged, he made it clear he'd never visit her bed and she went to Europe. Gave him exactly what he wanted: freedom. The sly bastard – but then, he always was. Even twelve years ago.'

There was no love in her voice. If she was harsh in her critique

51

of Mrs Merton, it was not because she was besotted with her husband. I recognised the tone. It was the same one used by women all over the slums, including myself: hatred and brutal honesty, laced with exhausted resignation. She might not be in love with him, but they were bound together somehow.

'You knew him back then?'

Twelve years was a long time to be a mistress, but maybe she had merely known of him then. Time was a good measure of a woman's commitment, though I couldn't say exactly why it interested me whether Minnie had always been Merton's.

'I've known him a long time.' Minnie tapped my shoulder, shutting the conversation down. 'Turn.'

I obeyed reluctantly. Having her wash my back was one thing, but face to face was another. I set my eyes on the carved bedpost behind her and sent my mind wandering away from Minnie's wet foot with some quick calculations. By my reckoning, Chester Merton was in his mid-thirties. If she was twenty-seven, then she'd known him since she was fifteen. I wondered under what circumstances a young circus performer, even one as elegant as Minnie, had become the acquaintance of Chester Merton of Hamilton Square and had kept him for so long. I glanced at the shiny silk of her sleeve. If it was not affection, perhaps it was money. That kimono alone had to be worth a few coins. My head was too full of sums to care that my breasts were clearly exposed to Minnie and her foot was bumping the hard soap over the ridge of my clavicle. With a pitch of my stomach, I noticed Minnie's foot moving lower.

'Did he run out of ideas?' Minnie stared. It was one part of my body that Jordan had not completely covered. He had placed a wide-winged angel between my breasts, since I was not blessed with the same ballooning tits as the Mulberry cathouse girls, and her wings unfurled underneath my nipples leaving the space above them unmarked.

'No.' Minnie's eyes were questioning so I added vaguely, 'He liked it this way.'

He liked it because it made me more exposed, my naked flesh like a sudden window of exposure to the lewd parts of me. He had deployed the same technique downstairs, which I was thankful for.

'I can see why.' Minnie nodded. 'It is beautiful.'

Her foot pressed the angel's face for a moment, damp skin to damp skin. I swallowed hard. Last night, I had wanted to be kissed by her. This morning I didn't even want to be touched. I closed my eyes tight against whatever came next.

'You are beautiful.'

I opened my eyes in shock. Comments made to the ink on my skin were regular, but comments on my own person were as rare as clean stockings. Yet still she looked. There was something about the combination of that light pressure on my ribs and the hot water creeping into the unreachable places of me that made me tremble. Her blue eyes were like the dark ice that gathered on the Hudson River. A woman had never called me beautiful before.

'So are you.' I swallowed heavily.

She was, anyone could see that; in fact, she was probably the most beautiful woman I'd seen up close in real life. Unlike showgirls or bawdy girls, Minnie didn't try to whiten her skin with chalk, perhaps because she was already so damn fair: I could see the tiny dark spots on her nose, the dusky blue skin with its minuscule folds underneath her eyes.

'I may not always be patient with you, or kind,' she said softly. 'I will call you "girl" and I will work you hard because you need to learn and there's almost too much to learn in this business.' She shook her head. 'But I'll do right by you, I promise. I'll teach you how to get on, even to get away from it all, if that's what you want.'

'Did you have to get away, once?' I asked.

Her eyes fixed on my elbow.

'Yes.' One word with a million possibilities. 'But I had to come back.'

I didn't dare ask why. The soap was drying sticky on my skin. I wished I could pull away and wash it off, but I knew when to stay still when people were touching. Yet she wanted to teach me how to get away, maybe even from her. That was something. I nodded.

'We'll have séances here every couple of nights, and when I think you're ready I'll take you out to do a show with my girls. If you trust me, you must do what I say, all right?'

She looked at me, waiting.

I nodded. Inside my head, I imagined the locked door opening. If this was how it had to start then so be it. She smiled and began to rub my skin again, ignoring the tiny flinch I couldn't hold back. I saw her foot shake slightly. Had she been expecting me to deny her?

'Even when it seems hard or strange, you have to remember I'll do right by you,' she said quietly. 'I always will.'

I was eye level with an open triangle of pale skin at her throat. I saw a blotchy flush rising there as her foot rubbed wetly across my breastbone. I'd been listening so intently to her words that I hadn't noticed the signs but now I saw it and knew it immediately: desire.

I stared at her. I'd had women before. Not as many as her, I imagined, as I'd heard showgirls were fast, but there had been some. Jordan got bored. I wasn't much of a virgin when I came to him but I had been innocent enough in the beginning to hold his attention. When I grew tiresome he'd brought whores home, intent on wising me up. They'd come in two variants, these girls. Either they were the hard-faced and uninterested type who'd kick me off the mattress and steal all the blankets when they'd finished, or a friendly and teacherly sort who would make space for me under the sheets and provide concise, demonstrative instructions. Those girls gave me everything I would need to keep a loyal john: French tricks, how

54

to get a lobcock up, but most importantly they taught me how to manage myself. Once Jordan was slumped out cold, comatose from booze and satisfaction, they would coax my body to its own pleasure and then show me how to reciprocate. I didn't get a reputation exactly, but a secret among whores was that a night with the Dead Rabbits' tattooist and his gypsy was worth its coin. A thorough orgasm at the hands of a nimble-fingered girl who followed every damn word you spoke and gave you a warm bed in which to sleep it off was more than most of them got in a week on the walk. I couldn't blame them for making the most of it, and I'd learned something from it, at least. That when it came to pleasure, it mattered little to me if the giver of it possessed a cunt or a cock.

'Flora.'

She touched the side of my face. I looked at Minnie with a blank frankness, trying to see what type of girl she was and who she wanted me to be. Her blue eyes were wide, startled maybe, when confronted by a rough slum girl assessing her. If I hadn't been so aware of my own nakedness, if I hadn't been the poorer, uglier, more helpless of the two of us, I would have sworn that what I saw in her eyes was fear. Then she looked away. I saw the quiet chuckle, the shake of the blonde curls and the darting away of those powerful eyes. All of it amounted to this: she was embarrassed. I had never seen Jordan embarrassed. It was almost painfully endearing.

'All right.'

I didn't know if I was agreeing or conceding. Her damp finger traced my jaw and her eyes followed the inky leaves and vines that tangled there. I remembered Jordan's finger, his cold signet ring, tracing the same path. I felt it again as I had last night: that raw, screaming place inside of me that needed to be touched to be silenced. I took hold of her wet arm, tugging it. Her head moved towards mine as easily as a horse following a cracker. I kissed her, my dry lips rasping slightly against her soft ones. It was not the best kiss of my life – after all, the whores Jordan brought to bed were all excellent kissers – but it felt like something. There was a feeling inside me, like something small and fragile was unfurling. I pulled back and looked at her, waiting to see if I had passed muster.

'Flora.' She smiled again and huffed a little air out of her nose, as if I were an amusing puzzle – a knot on a gift, waiting to be undone. My body was chilled against her touch, my hair dripping icy trails down her back. I realised that this was the first time I had ever kissed someone without Jordan's permission. If I went back now, he would kill me. I shivered.

'Can I get out?' I asked. 'I'm cold.'

Chapter Five

'No, Chester, go away.'

'Come on, Min, don't be such a fucking tease.'

I looked up from the vanity table, where I was sitting with a pen and paper and trying to copy out the alphabet Minnie had written out for me, using her foot. Minnie was standing in the crack of the doorway to the bedroom having an angry debate with Chester. Ten days into my stay at Hamilton Square had made me abundantly aware of the reason for the locked door. They had been doing this once a day for over a week or so.

'Go down to Kate's and buy some cunt, Chester; you're not coming in here.'

I tensed my shoulders against Chester's muffled expletives on the other side of the oak door. If mistresses are meant to make husbands happy, to simper and fawn over them until they are sick of it, Minnie was not a mistress. She was something else entirely, though for the life of me, I could not figure out what. They were not like Jordan and me, for she didn't fear him (in fact, I sometimes thought he might fear her), but whatever the arrangement was it seemed to leave neither of them satisfied. She slammed the door on him, her cheeks flushed red, and locked it with a tiny key she kept in her shoe. I knew Abernathy had a copy but I had not yet been given one. I couldn't work out if it made me feel trapped or safe.

'Jesus.' She huffed air out of her mouth, causing the gold curls around her cheeks to flutter. 'He's gone for now.'

Downstairs, we heard the front door slam and the distinctive snap of well-heeled shoes and a gold-tipped cane on the porch steps. The sound of his footsteps was instantly lost in the patter of rain and the splashing of carriages trundling through the March deluge. Clearly, he had taken Minnie's instructions to heart. I curiously watched her evident relief.

'Don't you mind?' I asked.

Chester was a whoremonger, that much was certain, from the bite marks and cheap perfume smell that often came off him, but I'd never seen a woman send her man off to a whorehouse willingly. Especially a woman whose job it was to please him herself.

'As long as he doesn't bring home the clap and doesn't touch you, I don't give a fuck who he screws.' Minnie flopped down onto the chaise longue with a scowl.

I turned back to my letters and didn't ask any more questions. Since I had moved into Minnie's room, I'd found myself thrust into a war. Day after day, on every floor of the house, she seemed to be fighting a wordless battle to keep Chester away from me outside of the séances. We lived and ate in her suite at the top of the house and when I had asked on the first day if I could walk to the baker's, Minnie said no.

'I don't want to lose you, my sweet.' She petted my head, her finger tangled into my curls. 'The Rabbits might be on the hunt. Best to lie low.'

She tried to keep me busy by helping me learn my letters better and Polly kept me entertained by asking me shy questions about my tattoos when she emptied bedpans in the morning, but I couldn't deny feeling hemmed in. There was a persistent tickling of disquiet. I kept my eyes away from the shadows, but it wasn't only the creeping pressure of what the Knowing could bring that unsettled me. Whenever I glanced out of the rain-streaked windows, I found my eyes snagging on passing caps, on any man I thought loitered or glanced at the house. Over and over, I imagined I caught sight of a familiar dark head swaggering past the window or the recognisable stamp of a clover-leaf tattoo across knuckles and my insides stilled, like a rabbit spying a fox. But then the head would turn or the bare hand flex on the cane and I would be able to breathe again.

I quickly learned it wasn't only the Dead Rabbits I had to worry about. Inside the house, Chester's presence loomed. I'd become accustomed to the sound of the creaking floorboards outside of our room, and the way that Minnie would rise and lock the door when she heard them. I'd grown to expect to see an indentation in the rug outside our locked door, as if someone had stood for hours there, and smell tobacco smoke lingering in the hallway. Minnie said nothing about it, but the silence of it grew between us and came to be filled with unsaid words: he was used to having access to her room and everything in it. Now that included me.

'Wouldn't it be easier if I just fucked him?' I wondered, carefully tracing the curve of a letter with a shaking hand.

'Do you want to fuck him?' Minnie sat up abruptly, looking at me. We had not kissed again since that morning in the bath. I did not know what it meant when someone wanted to keep me so completely, wanted my company and my smiles and my conversation, but made no move to touch me. It was confusing.

'No, but it might be easier.'

'Easier?'

She looked surprised, but I knew that the buzzing silence when my mind fled my body was much easier to achieve when a man's hand wasn't around your throat.

'Yeah.' I set my pen down and turned to her, trying to understand those finely knitted eyebrows. I hadn't had her pegged as possessive but I supposed every mistress must be a little. 'Or you could fuck him and I watch, or the other way round if he wanted or—'

'Or we could make love and he watches?' Minnie shook her head in astonishment. 'Jesus, Flora, what kind of tattoo shop was he running? Why would you do that?'

I flushed and shrugged. I wasn't embarrassed by her surprise. She had said *we could make love*. Maybe she hadn't meant it, but the implication behind her words was that what we did together, if she ever decided we were going to do it together, would be different because we did it together. I glanced at the pink line on her bosom where the corset ridge dug in and wondered what that would be like.

'I'd rather give than have it taken.' I looked away. 'If it's going to be taken anyway.'

Minnie wasn't shocked by my words. Her blue eyes had softened, a glimmer of recognition dancing in them.

'It won't be.' She swung her legs down to the floor as she sat up properly, looking at me intently. 'I know Chester. Men like him, they collect special things but they quickly lose interest.'

'I don't care if he loses interest.'

I was rather counting on it.

'I do.' Minnie walked towards me in that magical, swaying way that always made her look like she was gliding. I breathed in deeply. I'd become used to her scent; a deep, musky floral smell that I found both comforting and distracting. She stared at me and I tried not to blink. We were the exact same height when I was sitting down.

'Because once his interest is lost, so is every other damn thing. He'll not let me keep you if he's not interested.'

It was the first time I had thought Minnie needed permission to have me in the house.

'And I want to keep you,' she whispered, like it was a secret.

I saw that glimmer of possessiveness again and realised with an uncomfortable thrill that it was for me, not Chester. She pressed her nose against my cheek, a cold brush of flesh, followed by a quick, stolen kiss that grazed the corner of my mouth. I tensed against it but tried not to show it. This was it, the moment when the bill for all this tenderness came due. I expected her to tug me to my feet, to pull me towards the bed, but she didn't. She just looked at me, breath so warm and smelling of eggs and coffee. Nothing happened. I swallowed hard, feeling a twist of anxiety in my belly. It had never been like this for me; this lingering soft affection interspersed with normal life that came with no demands or catches. I didn't understand it, but I didn't hate it either.

'What do we do then?' I asked, determinedly not looking at her lips.

'We hold his interest,' she said. 'We don't give it away for free. You're a performer now, Flora. We never give it away for free.'

So Chester's longing had to be endured, just as Hettie's scowls and Cook's bad attempts at Chinese buns had to be. There was a flash of anger through me, so quick I almost gagged on it. She might be offering affection without cost, but freedom still came with a price, and she was the one balancing the ledger. The rare kisses, the lessons, the soft comfort of her presence, it was all adding up to a cost I didn't quite understand. My fingers itched for my cards, and the shadows in the corners of the room twisted teasingly, offering answers.

'What about you?' I asked, emboldened by that fiery feeling of being manipulated somehow. 'With Chester?'

61

Her mouth tightened when I said his name. I wasn't stupid enough to ask for any kind of promise. Minnie might be kissing me, but she was Chester's mistress. The thought of her disappearing into bed with him made me inexplicably nauseous, especially when I thought of that ugly moustache against her pretty lips, but he was hardly likely to keep a mistress he couldn't fuck. I didn't know what I wanted from her right then; perhaps just to know that I wasn't alone in the cage she had made.

'I follow my own rules.' Minnie's voice was a door snapping shut. She kissed me on the forehead and turned away. 'Whatever he gets, it's never for free.'

It would have to be enough. Even without her strange, consequence-free kisses, in the choice between Minnie and Chester, I would always choose her. Men always lied.

*

'Have you ever tried poppy, Flora?' Chester asked.

I stared at the opium pipe. It was the last question I had expected to be asked in Hamilton Square, but here it was on the lips of a blond leering man who held out an ornate Chinese pipe to me with the same ease he offered whisky or cigars.

'Course I have.'

I watched the bluish smoke emerge, wafting in a cloud of musty, herb scent. It was the smell of customers who stumbled into the tattoo shop with glassy eyes and sallow skin. Even though I sat on a plump, velvet cushion in a parlour room surrounded by gilt and gold and pretty things, the smell of Five Points filled the air.

'Course she has,' he mocked. The gentlemen sitting beside him were already loosening their ties and chuckled appreciatively. I flushed and ducked my head away from their gaze. Minnie's chosen outfit for me for the séances left little less to the imagination than my short-sleeved workday dress. It was a silk and lace nightgown in cream with mid-length sleeves and a plunging neckline. Minnie said it was 'appropriately delicate'. Polly said it made me look like a ghoul, and I agreed.

'Here you are, then.' Chester handed me the pipe. I admired it, turning it in my palms. It was carved from ivory, light and smooth against my skin, with a perfect quartz stone set in the basin. The gold edges of resin lingered there.

'It's beautiful,' I said. It was certainly out of the run of the ordinary.

'It was a gift.'

Chester puffed his chest, exhaling smoke in a self-aware manner, as if he'd watched some poppy-head do it in a midtown joint and was copying them. The gentlemen around him stared, admiringly, taken in by this ridiculous show of 'downtown' behaviour. They clearly didn't know that where I came from, only ladies and dandies smoked. Real men shot the stuff straight in their arms.

'I bought it for my darling here, a long time ago. She used to like a puff or two, in her day. Didn't you, precious?'

Minnie didn't look at him. She sat, as prim as an Astor, the blue beads on her black gown shimmering like peacock feathers. She was in no mood to play. Chester grasped her arm, pulling her towards him as if she were a ragdoll, and slapped the pipe bowl into her hand.

'See? It is the perfect size for her limitations, is it not?' He landed a slovenly kiss on her hand. 'It was the devil to have made, mind you, and the chap who made it, some idiot from midtown, he kept asking, "Why does the good sir need a cripple pipe?" I just kept saying, "Well, my good friend, she is not crippled where it counts!"'

The gentlemen filled the room with raucous laughter. Chester Merton was a son of a bitch. He was a leering bullshitter, and no different to the Mulberry gang lords, excepting his finer waistcoat and tobacco.

'Leave off, Chester.' Minnie pulled her hand back from him, scowling, then she smiled beautifully at the gentlemen around her, the astonishing kind of smile that a man would drop fifty dollars on at once. I had never had the knack of it. 'Please do make use of my pipe, gentlemen. I would be so happy for you to do so.'

They stumbled over themselves then, these men with gold pocket watches and ivory cufflinks, to thank her and praise her and reverently kiss the hand they had just been mocking. She looked down on them, benignly, as if all their laughter at her expense was forgiven. She smiled at Chester too, with all the sugary sweetness of a victory. He merely shrugged and put the pipe to his lips again.

'*I saw a girl in a pretty blue hat*,' he sang to himself, eyes fixed on Minnie. '*A kitty cat who mewed and scratched…*'

Her mouth twitched angrily. Tension coiled in the back of my head, my body rigid between Minnie's silent fury and Chester's smirking. I waited for the inevitable explosion, just as I had always waited for the smack of Jordan's belt cutting the skin. I shifted in my seat, the scars on the back of my thighs itching.

'Have some, Flora, go on.' He was pushing the pipe under my nose, his face fixed on my wheel tattoo on my breastbone.

'She doesn't have to,' Minnie snapped. 'Not everyone likes it, Chester.'

'She's a slum girl, isn't she?' Chester grinned. His teeth were yellow. 'They love it.'

'That they do,' a gentleman called from the chaise longue, where he was horizontal in a cloud of smoke. 'Thank God for them!'

'No need for airs and graces.' Chester leaned closer, his breath a curdling mix of ash and whisky. 'Do as you would at home, little one.'

Little one. I heard Jordan's voice, smelled the stale beer on his breath. I shook my head.

'It makes me dizzy.'

That was a lie. Poppy made me see *them*. The spirits that lingered in shadows and gathered on the edge of the room already waiting for me to give them voice, but I refused to look in their faces. The burn and tickle would loosen my mind and the warnings that lived there. *Tell nothin'. Stay put in the room, little cub.* I wouldn't be able to keep silent.

'That's half the fun, little mystic,' Chester laughed. 'Come on, give it a blow.'

'No, thanks.' I shook my head again. 'There's better treats to be had than what comes of… blowing.'

I got a laugh at that and I saw Minnie smile proudly at me out of the corner of my eye. Chester was not pleased. I had one moment to register the tightness of the lines around his mouth before he had pounced on me, long fingers pinching my nose and the hard stem of the pipe bashing against my teeth as he forced it in.

'Chester!' I heard Minnie shout amongst the cackles of men's laughter. I blinked against the sting of it and fought a rising vomit, coughing against a vice-like hand that was pushing my cheeks together. I remembered a tattooed hand shaking my teeth.

'Breathe deep—' his voice was full of false gentility '—inhale slowly.'

I didn't have much choice if I wanted to breathe again. I took the smoke into my breath and body, giving in to whatever it would create and reveal. I closed my eyes and opened them slowly, and the first thing I saw were Chester's grey eyes, full of triumph. I spat the pipe out, my gums throbbing, and rubbed the bridge of my nose, eyes watering from the sting and the smoke.

He laughed. 'Good girl. Isn't she a good little thing?'

Little thing. Little one. Little cub. Names from the past blurred around me as he sat back down, resplendent in victory. Of course, he did not see the spirits moving over his shoulder, dipping their shadow faces in and out of the curtains. *Here we go*, I thought, my mind lazy with poppy. I reached for my cards; my fingers itchy for secrets.

'Oh ho!' Chester looked at my hands. 'Seems like a little flower makes the little flower blossom! Come on, little mystic, give us what you've got.'

'Do me first!'

The gentleman on the chaise longue rolled off it in a slump of good tailoring and crawled, God as my witness, crawled with his hands and knees on the sooty carpet as penitent as any laudanum nanny on the roll, over to sit in front of me like a child.

'Yes, do him.' Chester laughed. 'Then you can do us all.'

His eyes sparkled with his wordplay. I'd learned many things from my acquaintance with Chester Merton and one of them was that college education did not make a man witty. I looked at the gentleman at my feet. His secrets gathered around him. With a lurch of my stomach, I saw the shadows behind him; *turn our cards*, they whispered.

I turned the cards. Four of Wands. The happy couple danced under their bower, the golden ink swirling around them.

'Hey, how do the pictures move like that?' the man slurred, pointing to the cards.

'It's called opium, Martin,' Chester said, and the room laughed.

The bower broke and the secrets fell out, wisps of yellow ink bleeding into the grey smoke around us. Behind him, over Martin's shoulder, anger was taking form. The resentment of it was almost burning; I felt sweat on my brow. Still, I would not look. But when I will not speak, the cards do.

'You've played away,' I said. 'She knows.'

The room was quiet for a second, then laughter rose again like bubbles in a glass.

'This is what you get, Martin, for dipping your quill all over the slums!' Chester shook his head. 'Word travels amongst whores.'

Martin looked up at me, his face sallow. He didn't seem to hear Chester.

'She knows?'

'Eight of Cups reversed,' I said. 'She's walking away.'

I turned the card. The eight cups emptied their blue liquid of happiness out over the wanderer, spilling them on their way. I saw it rise like steam around us, colouring the watching faces. I wondered how they couldn't taste the regret in the air, wondered how they could breathe with the malevolence that filled the room.

'Walking away?' Martin gasped. 'She'll leave me?'

'Your wife can't leave you,' Chester snapped behind him, perhaps irritated at his friends' fascination, but his words were water on stone to Martin and I, trapped in the cards with their secrets. 'She's no money of her own; where would she go? Back to New Jersey?'

'She has to,' I said simply. I turned the final card over. The man juggled the many knives, speared from all sides by betrayal. 'The Seven of Swords. She knows about her father.'

The shadow behind Martin was tall now, a shape in the corner of my eye, looming and reaching for me. I refused to look at it. *I will not look at you. You cannot have me or my voice.* It was pressing, wrathful; my fingers trembled with the effort of not looking, yet still the secrets travelled on the opium smoke, angry words and fury from the long dead.

'She knows you stole her father's money. You betrayed her and bankrupted him to an early grave. She knows you bled him dry.'

The room was silent then. Only the blue smoke spoke, carrying its secrets away up the chimney, and the gold of the swords on the card, blue and gold together, as Martin sat in the devastation of his lies.

'What kind of bullshit is this?' Chester glared at Minnie. 'What kind of slut makes these kinds of accusations against good men?'

'She knows?' Martin stared at my Empress card with his hands useless in his lap. 'I was always so careful.'

'Men always lie.'

Minnie's whisper was too quiet for the ears of Martin but both Chester and I looked at her. She stared down at the card, face glowing with a hatred that had nothing to do with me.

'How did your wife find out?' another gentleman asked, shaking his head in bafflement. He looked at me then, and his eyes narrowed as he pointed at me: 'How the fuck did she know?'

When a room turns against you, you feel it. It became cold, despite the smog of the fire and poppy that hung in the air like summer mist. Their playful curiosity was quickening to suspicious anger even though their expressions had not changed and no one had moved a muscle. It had happened to me before. I had seen this same promise of violence in each pair of eyes. Deep inside me the memory of a voice spoke clearly: *Tell nothin.'*

'Flora, go upstairs please.' Minnie spoke into the silence. Their eyes turned to her. Their fury and dislike turned to her. I didn't want to leave Minnie alone with them, but she commanded me.

'Go. Now.'

I told myself I had no choice. Abernathy was dragging me up by the elbow and I was tripping over my housecoat, and it was true that I pulled back a little, protesting this abrupt removal, but I said nothing. I was relieved to be pulled away from the whispering shadows and I left her alone with the smoke and the secrets and the growing darkness in the men's faces. I left her with them.

When I arrived in our empty suite, I hesitantly undressed, my shaking fingers making a mess of the row of ivory buttons down the front of the uncomfortable fancy nightdress. I wasn't cold but I trembled as I pulled my familiar ragged shift over my head. Maybe I was just tired or lonely, but I turned away from my usual nest on the chaise to slip between the starched sheets of Minnie's grand bed. I sought out her scent on the pillows and pushed my face into them, trying to drown out the burning acrid smell of poppy leaking up through the floorboards. Nothing calmed the rapid thunder of my heart against my ribs, not until I fished Jordan's old knife out of my overcoat and stuffed it under my pillow. My mind was jangling with voices and words. *Tell nothin'*. I had not looked at a ghost, I had not listened to a spirit properly in a very, very long time. I averted my eyes, I closed my mouth and I kept myself safe, because that was the only way to survive living with a gift like the Knowing. That night I couldn't shake the feeling that I had broken a law or promise, given long ago by someone who had wanted to protect me. I fell into an uneasy drowse, the hissing of spirit voices clambering into my dreams. Half memory, half a dream. A dark face, a cloud of hair, speaking words I could not hear.

*

I was awoken hours later by Minnie stumbling into the room.

'Shhhhh, Chester, shhhhh!' Minnie whispered. 'Don't – don't wake up Flora.'

The room was dark, the red embers burned low and, at first, her shape wasn't clear to me. She looked significantly the worse for wear. Her hair was tumbled loose, golden curls losing their shiny ringlet form. She stumbled forward. She wasn't alone: he stood behind her, swathed in the dark of the hall, swaying in the doorway. His collar was open, waistcoat gone, shirt rumpled, an empty whisky tumbler in hand. They were both moving as if they were floating on water, with heavy, long steps as if each movement took effort. Minnie was fighting with her gown, trying to step out of her shoes, but it was Chester I watched. He walked towards me as if I was illuminated on the stage, one unsteady step after another, as if in a trance. He began to unbutton his shirt further. Even with the whole bed and several feet between us, I could smell the burnt herbs and ash floating off him.

'The painted mystic,' he muttered to himself. He was pulling his shirt down over his shoulders, tangling his hands like Jordan did when he was drunk. 'She's so beautiful.'

His skin was pale, paler than Minnie's, utterly untouched by work or sunshine. I glanced at Minnie but she was vacant, completely consumed by her attempts to unfasten her stockings, her usually excellent coordination fuddled by everything she had drunk and smoked. I had said nothing, I'd not moved a muscle and it felt like I had woken up in my little bedroom at Five Points and was waiting for Jordan to come home. I held my breath and watched as Chester dropped his shirt to the floor; I watched as the gingery blond hair on his chest shone in the low firelight, as he licked his dry lips, his eyes black as a wolf's, the pupils consuming the grey entirely. I watched as he pressed one knee against the foot of the bed, preparing to climb up and still I had not taken a breath, but as soon as his hand touched the blanket, as soon as I felt the pressure of his weight unbalancing me, tilting me towards him, I recalled the tight grip of his fingers over my face, unyielding, unforgiving. I found my voice.

'Abernathy!' I screamed, scrambling out of the bed to the furthest corner of the room with the knife held out in front of me. 'Abernathy!'

I heard the thump of him responding to my shout next door. Chester didn't seem to even see the knife as he continued to advance, crawling over the quilt, breathless, his eyes never leaving my skin.

Behind him, Minnie watched carelessly. There was a clenching inevitability to this but I raged against it, against her. Given not taken, I had said, and nothing about this scenario felt like giving to me. I didn't dare look into her eyes, knowing the painful indifference I'd find there. Then Abernathy was there, a silent giant, gathering Chester into his arms as you might restrain a small child. Chester let him do it. He flopped against him, emitting soft whimpering sounds.

'No, don't take me,' Chester moaned childishly. 'It's so beautiful, I want to touch it, she's mine!'

I winced. *Who do you belong to, Flora?* Abernathy responded with his own grunts, half carrying and half dragging him towards the door. He caught my eye as he left, glancing towards Minnie who still, unconcerned with all around her, sat at her vanity fighting her stockings. I nodded tautly. Despite her negligence, and despite everything she had sworn she would never let happen, he wanted me to take care of her.

I waited for the reassuring snap of the closed door before I peeled myself out of the corner. I approached Minnie cautiously. Poppy didn't tend to make people violent, but I didn't know everything they had imbibed together downstairs. And she hadn't saved me. I couldn't know her mind right now, if I had even known it before.

'Minnie?'

She was staring out of the window, through a crack in the curtain.

'The stars.' She didn't move as I crouched behind her to unlace her dress. 'They're beautiful, aren't they?'

I couldn't answer. My hands trembled as I drew the laces through the eyelets, undoing what had clearly been redone haphazardly by a man's hands earlier in the evening. She turned like a little doll as I lifted the gown over her head, filled with the stench of sweat, smoke and men, and I saw them. Red and pink indentations across the top of her breasts, pressed tight against her corset. Bite marks.

'They're very beautiful,' I swallowed. 'Let's get you to bed.'

There were other marks under the corset, red clench marks on her arms and legs that I stroked gently as I undressed.

'You're beautiful, Flora.' Her fingers found my neck under my hair. 'He thinks you're so beautiful.'

She wrapped her arms around my waist, nuzzling her face into the warmth of my stomach. With her head tipped forward, I could see a vicious red and blue bruise on the back of her neck. I remembered how bruises like that felt against the windpipe, the lumpy sensation of pain every time I swallowed. I stood, breathing tightly to hold back the prickling of tears behind my eyes. Maybe she hadn't stopped Chester because she felt she'd already done enough. Done worse.

'Come on, Minnie.' I loosened her arms at my sides. 'Come to bed.'

'Come with me?' Her eyes were suddenly alert, the blue rings on the edge of the giant, black pupils fixed on me. 'Come to bed with me? Please. Please.' She closed her eyes, swaying gently in place, rocking backwards and forwards. 'I want you.'

It was a wanting that I recognised, the wanting of a body rather than a person. There was a quiet but resigned devastation in it. Immediately, part of me wanted to be miles away, even back in my quiet bed in Five Points, rather than here in the middle of whatever mess this was, but I looked at the savage bite marks from downstairs that she had endured so I wouldn't and nodded stiffly. The last time I had shared a bed with a woman just for sleeping was before Jordan, when there were four of us on a mattress squashed into a sweaty basement in the Old Brewery, the bones of corpses left to rot underneath us. The experiences had nothing in common. Back then we had slept in a pile like newly birthed pups, in a tangle of sweaty limbs and knotted hair and blankets that were always damp with someone's fever or monthlies. This was crisp and cold and horrible. I helped Minnie under the covers on her side and then slipped in at the other side, knowing what was coming.

'Flora.'

'Yes?'

Her lips crushed against mine, a clumsy battle of teeth and sour-tasting breath, her hand grasping at my breast, quick and insistent. It reminded me of Chester, crashing the poppy pipe between my lips. I couldn't help it. I recoiled.

'Flora, please.' Her hand was groping for me, trying to pull me back, but the rage had returned. Chester was climbing over the bed to rape me whilst Minnie watched, eyes glassy, all promises of protection shattered.

'I thought we didn't give it away for free,' I said, voice trembling. Maybe she saw it as payment due for me leaving her alone downstairs with them, but I thought one narrowly avoided assault was enough to settle my ledger. Coldness was seeping into me, the terrible chill of disappointment. The bill is always due and it did not matter that the small, fragile thing inside me had started to bloom.

'I don't understand, Flora.' Minnie's blue eyes caught the firelight. 'I thought we were… Don't you want to?'

She was looking at me with such puzzlement in her face. I stared back, the sickly bile of anger rising and falling in my throat like the tide. I had no words for the turbulent fury that lived inside me, sometimes craving touch and sometimes snarling at it, like a dog. I took a deep breath and closed my eyes. Whatever it was, it wasn't her fault.

'I don't know,' I whispered back. 'I thought I did. Before.'

When I still thought she was different and not the kind of person who would grab and demand me when drunk or full of poppy. I had been a fool to think this would be different. She said nothing and I was glad, because there were no more words. I could smell the truth on her skin anyway, pungent and sweet, horribly familiar. They'd had her. Had her instead of me. Taken or given, maybe it was all the same. I had told myself that one more fuck with a bad man wouldn't hurt me but this did. The rip in my heart, like stitches popped in the underarm of a dress, filled up quietly with bitterness. Strangely, I remembered it from somewhere else, even though I had never had anyone to care who I fucked or anyone else to care for either. At least I thought I hadn't, but I recalled this feeling, this sorrow that bubbled up towards Minnie. Sorrow that someone had taken something I thought was mine.

'Please.' Minnie's voice was filled with quiet anguish. 'Stay this time. Don't leave me again.'

I did not know what she meant. Slowly, I extended my hand to her head. I had never done this before. Feeling no resistance, I petted her hair as she sometimes did mine, feeling the slickness of the grease that she sometimes used to set her curls. The fury inside me curled up on itself, a snake or a weasel nestling down for sleep. I held my breath, waiting for her body to slip into the easy rhythm of slumber. Then the tears came. I pressed my face into the pillow, letting feathers absorb liquid, snot and sound. Thank God for thicker, uptown walls where secret sadnesses could go unseen and unheard. In the dizzying red darkness inside my eyelids, I tried to stop seeing Chester's raptured face as he climbed over the bed. I tried to release my thoughts, let the untethering of the Knowing take me to distant, quieter places, but it wouldn't come. I was trapped, squirming and sore, inside my trembling body, too tight to sleep. I couldn't stop the feeling growing inside of me: the crushing realisation that, somehow, despite each of our best efforts, in the nasty turn of the cards that had made up our evening, Minnie and I had betrayed one another.

Chapter Six

Iknew it was a bad idea to go to the Bowery. Yet I found myself, two weeks after what I had come to think of as 'the night of the poppy', walking openly down the notorious street.

'We shouldn't be here,' I muttered, even though I had already been told to shut up. The end of March had brought wind instead of rain and I turned my gentleman's collar up against the gusts, staring nervously at the passing faces. 'I shouldn't be here.'

'Don't be dense, girl.' I flinched at Minnie's favourite unflattering moniker. 'Who's going to recognise you? You're just a boy looking for a show. Besides, it's not Irish down here.'

It was the opposite. The Bowery and surrounding streets were held by the infamous Bowery B'hoys, the enemies of the Dead Rabbits. They were firemen and butchers, anti-Catholic and anti-Irish working-class men who sneered at their neighbouring slum lords and those who lived under their grasp. I'd grown up knowing to run from the sound of their hobnailed boots; a stomp from one of them would leave you pissing blood for a week. They hated the Dead Rabbits and Jordan was as likely to walk down the Bowery

as he was to march himself into confession, but it was still perilously close to The Painted Man. The fraught territories were only
a street away.

Even being dressed like a young boy apprentice couldn't hide
my neck tattoos, and if the Dead Rabbits were looking for me, I
was sure as hell Jordan would have told them every identifying
mark I had upon me. Even in disguise my pulse quickened when
I thought about all the things I'd seen them do to other girls in
the past, some losing teeth, some losing eyes, some beaten so
thoroughly to death they were less woman and more meat. I'd lived
all my life under Irish rule. Setting my feet in the mud of the
Bowery felt like the most dangerous thing I could do, and Minnie
wasn't helping. She was too well dressed for the Bowery, a clear
cut above the dime-museum freaks that were so popular down
here. They were often gaffed; girls bound together to pass off as
Siamese twins, boys with their legs bound up masquerading as
amputees or their pricks pulled back in imitation pussies. Minnie,
with her silky hair and clean skin, could not pass in this arcade. I
tried to ignore her distinctiveness and focus instead on making
myself more inconspicuous. I watched Abernathy stalk along, so
masculine and confident, safe in his easy gait, and stuck my hands
in my pockets, trying to match his stride. I caught his tight smile
of approval. We stopped midway down the Bowery, Minnie looking
up at a tall townhouse.

'You both wait here,' she commanded. 'Let me check on him.'

The door of number 229 squealed shut behind her, and Abernathy
and I leaned against the sooty wall. A tingling sense of exposure
pulsed down my arms. My only solace could be found in the conviction of my disguise, so I copied Abernathy's nonchalant stance, arms
folded, the rough wool of the jacket bunching in pinching creases
at the elbows. Despite my fear of being down this way, there was

still tremendous relief in being out of the house. Every night I dreamt of the doorknob turning, or perhaps I heard it and awoke. I said nothing to Minnie and I averted my eyes from the shadows. If some spectre in Hamilton Square was waiting for me to look, they would wait a long time.

Abernathy offered me a cigarette from a crumpled pack of Philip Morris. I took one. All the men lounging outside the dime theatres and coffee joints were smoking across the road, and I wanted to fit in. The cheap, acrid fumes spiralled through my mouth, up into my nose, making me blink hard with the stinging heat. Abernathy nodded in approval, the long, pink scar stretching as he lifted his throat for a puff. I'd had many moments to examine it since arriving in Hamilton Square. Abernathy caught me looking and raised his eyebrows.

'How did it happen?' I blurted out.

Another raise of eyebrows.

'I know Minnie said it was fire-eating, but it doesn't look like fire.' I puffed again. 'I saw a man burned in fire once. It wasn't like yours; it was more...'

I stumbled for the right word to describe that melting, liquid effect on skin.

'... bubbly.'

Abernathy let out a rough bark of a laugh and shook his head at me, white teeth gleaming. Since the night he'd removed Chester from our rooms, he had been less of an annoyance to me. I found his lingering and grunts comforting rather than irritating now and had a better read on his expressions. At that moment, I saw a clear look of mischief.

'It wasn't, was it? You made that up together?'

The smile widened. He was clearly very proud of the lie he and Minnie had been circulating all over town.

'What was it?'

His lips moved. I thought he might be miming something, but then I heard it, a whisper of sound.

'What?'

He sighed angrily, and grabbed my lapel, roughly pulling me closer and bending down. He spoke the word against my ear:

'*Lynching.*'

The sound was a mix of the softest whisper and a scratchy, high-pitched whistle. It was so far away from the voice I had imagined Abernathy to have that I felt an immediate, sudden urge to cry. I blinked, staring at his throat. I'd never seen a lynching, though I knew they had happened in Manhattan during the draft riots. I remembered the orphanage burning on 44th Street, the black children torn apart by rioters. Abernathy's scar was older than three years ago and looked grown into, like a wound from childhood. When I looked at him, really looked at him, I saw the youthfulness in his cheekbones and neck. I remembered how angrily Minnie had defended him at our first meeting, thought of the secret language they had grown together that must have been years in the making, like an older sister and a younger brother. A window of knowledge opened inside my mind, the realisation that there was another life the two of them had lived, far away from Hamilton Square.

'You knew her before.' I blew smoke out through my lips. Abernathy shrugged with a wide grin. There were so many questions I wanted to ask, but my mind drifted to Minnie's words from the night of the poppy: *Stay this time. Don't leave me again.* 'Did she… have someone else before me? Someone she lost?'

Something desolate flickered across Abernathy's face. Before I could consider what it meant, someone elbowed me on their way down the street.

'Excuse you,' I said as a man pushed past us, jostled by the crowd of dock workers shuffling past from the train. He disappeared quickly, elbowing past sweaty faces, but I knew what he was. A Bowery B'hoy. The bashed stovepipe hat was a giveaway, and I saw the back of his ruddy red shirt. We were bound to see one, marching along, keeping an eye on their patch, but something about him unsettled me. Then I realised what I had seen – the familiar, blue and red curve of an inked dragon, snaring up the back and side of his neck. Jordan's signature. I gasped, inhaling a mouthful of smoke that sent me coughing, leaning into Abernathy to hide my face, his large hands thumping my back. Then Minnie was back, arm on the open door, frowning at us both.

'What the devil?'

I couldn't speak; the bristling smoke made the back of my throat itch, making it impossible for words to emerge. Abernathy bundled me into the doorway, slamming the door so the three of us stood in that dark cramped space between the door and the stairs as I spluttered and blinked back hot tears.

'What did you do, Abe?' Minnie said. 'You feed them to her?'

'It's not his fault,' I croaked. 'I saw someone.'

'Someone you know? Up here?' Minnie frowned. 'A Dead Rabbit?'

'No, a B'hoy, or he was dressed like a B'hoy.' I swallowed smoky mucus and winced. 'He had art by Jordan.'

His name fell out of my mouth easily but tasted like tar. I had not missed it.

'Why would a B'hoy have art by an Irish ink-man?'

'I don't know!' I shook my head. It was aching from the coughing. 'Maybe he's not a B'hoy; maybe he's a Rabbit dressed like a B'hoy.'

It was the sort of thing Jordan might do if he were looking for me. He'd hardly risk his own neck but he'd happily pay someone else to.

'Maybe it's just someone else's art,' Minnie countered. 'There are other needle artists in the city.'

'I know Jordan's hand!' I hadn't meant to raise my voice, but I felt Abernathy shuffle uneasily beside me. 'His dragon, it's always the same, it's always this one.'

I shoved up my right sleeve, displaying the dragon Chester had been so fascinated with when he'd first met me.

'Did you see him?'

Minnie looked at Abernathy. He shrugged his shoulders, grunted quietly. For once, I seemed to understand him. He'd seen a B'hoy, but not the tattoo.

'Maybe you imagined it,' Minnie said.

I shook my head. She didn't understand. The shapes he etched on skin, the lines he drew, they were the skin I lived in. It was like I had seen a part of myself climb out of the mirror.

'I think we should leave.'

I saw Abernathy's eyes dart to Minnie. Her face was blank. Since the night of the poppy, she had not come to me for a kiss. There had been no soft tangling of her finger in my hair, no brushes of her lips against my brow. It was hard to say that I missed it since I had been in possession of it so briefly, but a part of me felt as if it were starving. Another part of me was grateful she stayed away. I realised I had no way to truly compel her to comprehend the surety of terror that was seeping up my throat.

'No,' she said, evenly. 'I've already paid him. Mr Eisenmann doesn't come cheap. Come up.'

That was the end of it. If I had a notion of ignoring her, it was so small, so fleeting, that it didn't survive into a complete thought. I knew what it felt like to walk out of something now, how cold and alone I had been on the trudge from Five Points up and how warm the fires were in Hamilton Square, even if they came with the cost of Chester Merton. I wasn't about to start again, not if I didn't have to. I nodded and followed Minnie up the stairs, stepping in the path her crimson dress carved through the heavy dust on the wood. I'd made my choice in The Painted Man to pursue her wherever she went, whatever the risks. I couldn't stop now.

Mr Eisenmann was a plain, stocky man with a wife whose sneer could curdle milk. Whilst he and Minnie discussed what intricately painted set on canvas I would pose in front of (there was an ancient temple, a circus and even a jungle with a false rubber snake woven into the leaves of a potted plant), Mrs Eisenmann went to work on me. I'd had more gentle encounters with grasping drunks. She ripped me out of my boys' attire until I was pimply and naked behind the Japanese privacy screen and then pushed and pulled me into a cream wool combination suit. It was the kind you saw in ladies' magazines – no sleeves and tiny, short legs, decorated with ribbon. It may have been clean and fashionable once upon a time, but it stank of sweat and cheap perfume and the ribbon was yellowed from wear. I tried not to think about all the hairy armpits and damp groins that had stood in it to be photographed and concentrated on my breathing as Mrs Eisenmann strapped me into a satin corset with all the delicacy of a dock worker.

'Jesus,' I hissed through my teeth.

Mrs Eisenmann glared at me. The woman had no space between her eyebrows, the dark hair a continuous frowning line. I promptly shut up, holding out my arms for the gown to come but she stepped back, nodding efficiently.

'*Fertig.*'

I knew enough German to understand that and stared at her in bewilderment. She couldn't be serious.

'Minnie?' I called, ignoring Mrs Eisenmann's pokes in the back to push me out into the wide, bright expanse of the skylit studio. I wasn't going anywhere trussed up like this.

'What's the matter? Doesn't it fit?' Minnie stuck her head around the screen. She had removed her red hat and her blonde hair reflected the light magnificently. 'It looks capital on you; come on out and we'll get started.'

'*Fertig!*' Mrs Eisenmann repeated, her one, frowning eyebrow staring me down as if I would pay for denying her the satisfaction of a quick completion.

'No, this can't be finished.' I tried to glare back, but I was not nearly as proficient. I turned to Minnie. 'You want me to have my photograph taken, like this? They'll see everything.'

I held out my arms and both women glanced down at the dark swirls and patterns of my skin, then stared at me like I was simple.

'That's the point, girl.' Minnie tweaked the hem of the shorts. 'A cabinet photograph gives the buyer a miniature experience of the performer. Your skin is your calling card.'

Cabinet photographs. I should have put two and two together, but when Minnie had said I was getting pictures done I had stupidly thought it was a portrait for a promotional poster like the ones on the walls of Barnum's building. Cabinet photographs were something else entirely. All the famous freaks had them. It was something uptown folk did: they bought a little portrait of Tom Thumb in the Bowery for a dime and stowed it away in a nice book of memories; but cabinet photographs travelled further than uptown parlours.

'Someone will see me,' I said, instinctively crossing my arms. 'He'll see them.'

Even if Minnie trusted the Eisenmanns, I wasn't stupid enough to say Jordan's name out loud in earshot of anyone on the Bowery. If there was a B'hoy somewhere in Jordan's pocket then I had to watch my back. Minnie waved her arm at me dismissively, as if she saw my suspicions forming.

'Do you think I'm an idiot?' She shook her head. 'I have a very select group of clients. They'll not go below Broadway.'

That was an empty promise. She had no more control over the final destination of these portraits than she did over the stars. I thought of the wrinkled photographs Jordan kept in a box; lewd things of naked whores and showgirls. I imagined that someone had told them much the same thing as the camera light flashed: *Don't worry, no one will see it.* A familiar rage curled in my stomach, warnings stinging in my ears. *Tell nothin'.*

'It's bullshit.' I shook my head. Minnie raised her eyebrows and glanced at Mrs Eisenmann. The woman had lips pursed as tight as a cat's arse, but I didn't care: 'If even one of these gets into Five Points, then I'm fucked. You might as well invite the bastards up to Hamilton Square.'

'Leave us, *danke.*'

Minnie jerked her head at Mrs Eisenmann and the woman left, dropping my jacket on the floor as she went. Minnie stared at me. The seconds lengthened, but I wouldn't take it back.

'What was that?' she asked, voice low. I didn't answer. We both knew what it was. The taste of defiance sat on my lips, metallic with adrenalin. I couldn't speak. I had never before had to give voice to this feeling of being disappointed in not being listened to. I was far more familiar with never expecting to be heard. She stepped closer and I tried not to flinch back.

'What did I say to you, that first morning at Hamilton Square?'

I recalled the warm water, her firm soapy foot. My quiet acquiescence. The dry, odd kiss that had opened something raw and needful inside me.

'That you'd do right by me.' My eyes rested on her lips; the softness there had turned into a hard line. 'If I trusted you and did what you said.'

A lot had happened since then. I caught her eye without meaning to and then darted my eyes away. We'd not talked about the night of the poppy and my insides churned with anxiety at the thought of doing so now.

'And I will; if you trust me, then I will. Whatever it costs,' Minnie continued. 'Haven't I shown you that already?'

The night she had sent me from the parlour sat between us; the shared memory of the moment I had left and the moment she had returned, of bruises and an undone corset unfolded between us like the dark wings of a crow. The rush of the kiss and her hand on my body, my sudden rejection. I knew she remembered and perhaps had not forgiven me. She hadn't tried anything since then, even though I had continued to sleep in her bed. I looked down at my bare feet, the star on my ankle now almost completely healed. It had barely been two months and nothing about my life was the same, except this – the sensation of the ground shifting under my feet, being unsure of the person I shared a bed with, sensitive as a nervous bird to their every mood and gesture. I didn't answer.

'Sit down, Flora.' Her small hand was pressed to my breastbone, a forceful push to quiet me.

I obeyed, squatting on the low stool my clothes were draped over, knowing that sitting had less to do with trying to calm me down and more to do with Minnie needing to look at me eye to eye. She always held people's gaze, even men four times her height. It was what made her so compelling; she was an unreasonable combination of fragility and overconfidence. For not the first time in knowing her, I wondered how the hell she had gotten so much conviction. Even when I felt myself resisting her, she was still a damn marvel.

'Listen to me.'

She stood astride my knees; my legs trapped in the heavy warmth of her gown.

'You could be a big star, Flora; there's big money to be made here, and if there's safety anywhere, it's in money.'

The smell of her, soot from the Bowery, perfume from her toilette and the earthy, pleasant scent of her sweat, wafted over me. When she spoke, I felt the words in my legs, the vibrations of her voice box sending barely detectable movement through her skin to the places we met.

'Look at me.'

Her hand cupped my chin tightly, forcing my eyes to look at her.

'There is protection in fame, girl, believe me. If you can become loved uptown, become wanted, then he can't do shit about it. Do you think anyone ever took me seriously until I was a circus sensation? The Dead Rabbits can have your pictures, to hell with them, but if you've made it uptown then they can't touch you. If we don't give it away for free. Understand?'

Hearing her plan was like having a fairy story spun by a con man: the pictures were pretty, but it was like a tapestry of another life that came unravelled when I remembered Jordan's belt, Jordan's hands, Jordan's heavy black eyes. I thought of the tattooed Bowery B'hoy. I wished that I had my cards, longing for the surety I felt when they passed through my fingers. I closed my eyes for a second, trying to summon the feeling of them and the ethereal detachment that found out lies from truth, but there was nothing except the black and gold spots of light on the inside of my eyelids. *Can't summon the Knowing*, a voice reminded me, wickedly.

'Flora.' I didn't open my eyes. I knew what was coming. Last time I'd denied her, but the bill always comes due. She wanted to kiss me, and now I had to let her, otherwise she would undoubtedly send me away and I had been foolish to ever hope it was otherwise.

'Can I kiss you?'

'What?'

85

My eyes flew open. I stared at her. She shifted uncomfortably under my astonishment, but didn't move away from me, her fingers pinching my chin still.

'I wasn't kind about it last time. I... am not like him.' Her eyes flickered away from me for a moment and for a second I wondered who she spoke of — the man I had lived with who had forced me or the man we currently lived with who had forced her. Then her blue eyes caught mine with that familiar, rare intensity she possessed. 'Can I kiss you please, Flora?'

It was an apology, or as close to one as a woman like Minnie came. Those words said a lot of things: *I'm not like them*, they said, *I want you to choose*. I had been numbing myself, preparing for whatever she was going to do next, and now these words pulled me back into my body.

'I...'

Minnie moved her face a little closer.

'What do you want, Flora?'

I did not remember ever having been asked that question, either. I was trembling. I could not tell if it was trepidation or need but I wanted to be sure of her. I wanted to feel safe. I nodded, and then realised that I wanted to say it out loud, this first time of ever being allowed to give permission.

'Yes, you can kiss me. I... want you to kiss me.'

I kept my eyes open, wanting to see if it looked different. I saw the fluttering of her eyelashes, half-blonde half-black from lash colour, I saw the slight roll of the whites of her eyes before they closed. Then I felt her lips, slightly greasy and tasting like carmine from lipstick, against mine. It was mechanical almost, full of sound and scent; the crinkle of my chapped lips and the smell of sweet onion on her breath. Was this what it felt like to be kissed when you were truly inside your own body? To feel as if someone wanted to protect me rather than possess me? It was uncanny how similar the feelings felt, separated by the thinnest thread of hope. Then she pulled away and she was smiling. It was a smile I hadn't seen before, half sad and half tired, and yet, somehow, it was the most genuinely joyful smile I had seen from her.

'Thank you, sweet girl.'

I nodded in a daze, my lips tingling. I'd never been thanked for a kiss before. I let my mind make space for that new, small tenderness. Her hand moved to my neck, stroking the downy skin there and tangling her finger in the small curls behind my ears. I shivered, my skin rising in minuscule bumps all over my body, but I didn't pull away. We didn't speak. Minnie's hand was slightly clammy, I could feel damp skin in the creases of her flesh as she stroked my neck. For a flash she was Jordan, a firm hand on the back of the neck, fingers big enough to crush my throat, and then she wasn't. My bones softened slowly, wood slackening under rain. I was like a dog, lulled into stillness by gentle, repetitive touch. I watched her breath fall and rise in her throat, the flaring of her nostrils, and I felt it passing through me to rest in that aching, needful place inside me. The bubbling rage quieted. I did not kiss her and she did not kiss me, but we lingered there, the invisible threads of our shared breath binding us together.

'I don't want you to think of him with me,' she whispered. 'I can wait.'

I stared at her. That was something I had never had the luxury of before: time. Even though I thought there would probably never be a moment I did not think of Jordan. Yet the possibility of a future was tantalising; a future with Minnie, a future that was mine.

'Do you trust me?' she said, finally, as our breathing slowed.

I thought of the lurking figures I kept imagining on the corner of Hamilton Square, of the tattoo I had just seen that I knew in my waters had come from Jordan's hand. I thought of the doorknob to our suite, turning slowly in the dead of night, the creaking maliciousness of what might be waiting on the other side. I didn't know how to answer but then I looked into her blue eyes and saw I had not really heard the question. The question being asked, the only question she cared about was: Do you trust me not to hurt you? Like a fool, I said yes.

Chapter Seven

'What are you doing?'

I nearly jumped out of my skin, almost upturning my ink pot where it sat on the step beside me. I pulled my needle away from my forearm, cursing as I wiped excess ink across the old parrot. Polly stood in the kitchen doorway, one hand holding a wooden spoon and her little head cocked to her shoulder, like a stuffed bird captured in an inquisitive moment. I had sought a little quiet in the servants' yard, adjacent to the kitchen. I lifted my forearm for her to see. Her eyes fixed on where the skin was gently spotted with blood.

'Tattoos.' Polly moved forward, her face entranced. She stood over me and looked down at my forearm. 'It's a bird.'

I watched as she reached out hesitant fingers, reverently brushing those shiny, blistered pink fingertips against the raw, raised skin. She pulled them back in surprise, as if overwhelmed by the texture. She looked at me with utter delight.

'Did you do it?'

'Someone else did.' I dipped my needle in the ink and began again, hearing Polly hold her breath above me as the needle pierced the skin, as if she expected me to scream. 'I'm just refreshing where the ink is dull. See?'

'Yes.' Polly leaned forward, her little face screwed up in concentration. Short wisps of her hair fell out of her cap, so blonde it was almost white. 'Can I have one?'

'When you're older,' I said, even though I knew Polly was around the age I was when I first met Jordan. I gestured my hand to the rag sitting on the step and Polly handed it to me, watching me wipe the blood with a small, furrowed frown.

'Why aren't you doing it upstairs?' She turned the rag in her nimble fingers, examining the bloodstains. 'It's cold out here.'

It was certainly chilled. April had blown into the city with gusty winds that swept up and down Park Avenue, rattling the window-panes. My rear on the stone was numb and damp but I didn't care. Underneath the sweet decaying smell of potato skins that Cook spread over the tomato plants, and the dried horse dung from the road above, was the fresh, undefinable smell of free morning air. I felt as if I could breathe out there, whereas inside the house the dusty air felt heavy with expectation.

'I like the cold.' I shrugged. It was a lie. What I liked most about the servants' yard was that it was not inside Hamilton Square. Protected from view, hidden from the house, it was a place I went for brief moments of solitude. I could sit on the moss-covered steps and smoke or ink myself without having to think what every creak on the staircase meant. Polly stared at me for a moment and then sat down beside me, pulling her knees up towards her under her skirt.

'Do you think it's haunted?' She nodded upwards, her eyes fixed on the red brick that towered above us. I paused, the needle pressed under the first layer of my skin, letting the ink pool too long. I winced to withdraw it.

'Do you?' My voice was neutral. I did not want to tell Polly that, for me, everywhere was haunted.

'Sometimes it feels queer.' Polly frowned and tugged at the patched hem of her skirt. 'Like someone's watching but when I look, no one's there.'

I thought of how, deep in the night, I was still woken by the handle on the bedroom door being tested, the metal grinding carefully against wood and how the air in the doorway hung malignant and frustrated. *Tell nothin'*, a voice in my head whispered.

'Very queer.' I let the repetitive prick and sting of my needle calm me down. I pushed my shirtsleeve further up and pressed the needle against the tip of the parrot's tail. Polly looked at my shirtsleeve thoughtfully.

'Why are you dressed as a boy?' Her little finger brushed against the wool of my waistcoat.

'So people don't notice me,' I said, without thinking. It wasn't true, not exactly, but I liked the anonymity I felt dressed as a boy, and Minnie didn't mind when I lounged around our suite in a shirt and pants. After the cabinet photographs, something in the house had shifted. Everything in the last two weeks was the same in elements; I studied, I read cards, I avoided Chester, and at the end of the day, Minnie shuffled her small body backwards to curl against mine in bed. I let her, no longer tensing my shoulders against unwanted hands. I wasn't sure if I would recognise happiness if I had it, but when I woke in the morning to the warmth of Minnie's back pressed against my chest, I thought that I might have found something like it.

'Because they're looking for you?' Polly asked. I paused, the needle hovering over my skin, panic building in my blood.

'Who's looking for me?'

Polly instantly looked sheepish.

'Hettie says I'm not supposed to repeat rubbish and rumours,' she mumbled, tugging moss out of the cracks in the paving stones.

'Where did you hear it?' I thought of the way my eyes always lingered on men in caps I saw on the corners of the square. 'Here?'

'No, at the market, downtown. I've got friends down there, girls who beg and trick. Hettie says it's all silliness and they're dirty girls and people are always looking for whores like you.' Polly flushed. 'Sorry.'

I wasn't offended by Hettie's bad opinion, I thought no better of her, but Polly's words had caught my attention. It was the way slum children operated – we listened to whispers, we heard rumours – and I had a strong appreciation for its value. Hettie might be a maid but she had clearly grown up with bread on her table if she didn't know how much truth circulated at ground level in New York.

'Tell me what your friends said.'

'That the Rabbits are hunting for a whore with ink work, though they don't say how much work.' Polly's eyes darted over my arm. 'Could be you.'

I didn't speak and returned thoughtfully to my needle. It was quite something, the transformation that gossip had wrought upon my Five Points reputation – all the way from Jordan Whittaker's ink girl to nothing more than an inked whore. I couldn't help the swell of bitterness that this was my only legacy.

'Where are they looking for her?' I asked Polly.

'Downtown.'

Maybe Minnie had been right. Maybe the Dead Rabbits would never expect a slum girl to make it this far uptown. I let out a slow sigh of relief, because even if Polly's words had confirmed my nasty expectation that they were looking for me, they didn't know where I was. I vowed to myself, then and there, that whatever Minnie said, I would never go below midtown again.

'If you're really going to pretend to be a boy, you should cut your hair like one,' Polly said, interrupting my ruminations as her little grey eyes roamed critically over my black curls. 'Like mine.'

'Like yours?'

With the uncomplicated fearlessness of childhood, Polly pulled her cap off. Her hair was cropped so short, barely long enough to cover her ears and was so pale and white it reminded me of feathers. With her big, silver eyes and pointed nose, she looked like a ruffled baby barn owl.

'They shaved it off when I came here after the orphanage.'

I tried not to shudder at that. It was a common fear among foundlings that the people who took kids from orphanages would cut all their hair off and make them drink vinegar.

'Why?'

'Lice.' Polly scratched her head. 'Hettie said I was crawling with them and Mrs Merton told her to shave me.' She shrugged. 'I cried a lot, but Mrs Merton said it was the least they should do if they were bringing some guttersnipe into her house to slaughter her reputation.'

This was clearly a remembered insult direct from the infamous Mrs Merton herself, and I felt defensive on Polly's behalf.

'She sounds like a harpy.'

Polly shrugged. 'She hates me. That's why she's never here.'

That seemed like an exaggeration, but I knew how black and white a child's mind could be. If Mrs Merton had actively disliked Polly and made it known, then of course she thought her absence was her fault. Polly wouldn't know that Chester had banished Mrs Merton to Europe so he could whore his way down Manhattan.

'Which orphanage?' I asked.

'Randalls Island.'

It had a bad reputation.

'How was it?' I asked.

Polly shrugged. 'I had some friends there, but here there's only Hettie.' She wrinkled her little nose. 'She's boring. At Randalls, we played jump rope. No one wants to play here.'

I remembered being lonely too, watching the other girls playing hopscotch, missing someone who made me feel safe.

'I'll play,' I said. 'I can do jump rope.'

'Which orphanage were you in?'

'No orphanage.' I shook my head. 'I was in Five Points before here. The Old Brewery at the beginning, then Mulberry Street. I grew up there.'

I smiled at her astonishment. Randalls would be full of Five Points orphans, the unlucky ones scooped up by the mission houses and put away to work on the island.

'I was at the Old Brewery, too, before Randalls,' Polly said with a grin. 'That's funny. Hettie says all of Miss Minnie's friends are Old Brewery sluts.'

'I bet Hettie does.'

If Hettie was Irish but not from Five Points, she'd have a mid-towner's disdain for the Irish gangs. As if they wouldn't all kill their own mother for a bed and good pay.

'I don't really remember much of the Old Brewery, but I remember there was a witch girl there; everyone said she could tell the future.' Polly bit her lip reflectively and then looked at me, those sharp grey eyes full of excitement. 'Was that you?'

My stomach knotted painfully, like coiled rope in the pit of my gut. *Witch girl!* It had been shouted at me whilst I was beaten for knowing too much, for seeming too odd to the other children, deep in the slums. *Tell nothin'.* Whispers of memories of a friendly face and a cautious voice. Words had remained where features had been lost, a warning to keep my own secrets.

'Why would you ask that?'

'Hettie's been moaning down at market to anyone who'll listen that there's a witch in the house, crossing herself and going to mass twice a week.' Polly wrinkled her nose distastefully then looked at me brightly. 'I like witches. So were you? The witch girl at the Old Brewery?'

The relief I'd felt in hearing the Dead Rabbits were only looking downtown vanished, because a fat lot of good it would do me if loud-mouthed Catholic Hettie spread the word that there was a witch uptown. I tried to tell myself that they wouldn't put it together, to reassure myself with Minnie's promises that Jordan would never imagine I could rise as high as Hamilton Square, but I couldn't dispel the tightness in my ribs. I rubbed them with my spare hand and then noticed Polly watching me curiously, as if I might be performing some kind of magic gesture.

'No, I only do cards.' I glanced up to the road and away from half-memories of forgotten, kind eyes and warnings. 'Shall we play then?'

I dropped my needle in its box and screwed the cap on my ink.

'I have a game.' Her face split into a mischievous smile and her little knee jiggled with energy. 'It's upstairs.'

The library smelled of Chester. It was a deep, animal smell that hit right at the back of my throat; a combination of old cigars and too many leather furnishings, and it made me anxious. The heavy red curtains were partly drawn and shafts of yellow light split through the darkness of the room, bouncing off the sudden edges of the armchairs and glinting off the gold embossing on the books. I'd never seen so many.

'Mister Chester has a magic book he lets me play with sometimes.'

Polly dropped a tome onto the green felt of the billiards table, her little hands cracking its great spine without trepidation and flipping the pages for me to see.

'He says you do magic like this, at the séances. Is it like this?'

I stared at an illustration of an old woman, her huge, rolling breasts lolling out of her dress as her bony hands clutched a crystal ball. In the corner of the picture, a wealthily dressed man held an absurd, curved prick in his hand.

'No.'

There were bearded ladies with dangling, braided pubic hair. There were naked contortionists with their fleshy labias stretched on display. Then a tattooed woman, in the middle of being tattooed on one arm, and being fucked from behind by a gentleman with a wig but no pants. It wasn't the first pornography I'd seen, but it was the first time I'd seen a body like mine included. It had a title that, with slow whispering and tracing my finger, I could just make out: *The Joy of Freaks: Exquisite Pain.* This was what Chester thought of when he looked at me. This was why, on the first night he met me, he had asked if it hurt.

'Mister Chester says he taught his other girl this one.' Polly's fingers tapped against an illustration of a naked tarot card reader, lifting cards to the face of a man she was sucking. I stared at the cards in her fingers.

'He has another girl?' I murmured. For surely Polly did not mean Minnie.

'Used to, a long time ago.' Polly turned the page of the book and said no more. I wondered how many freaks Chester Merton had claimed in his time. 'He wants to teach me this one.'

The picture she tapped on was a small girl, bare from the waist up, apart from a ruffled collar like a puppet. She was painted up like a whore and lifting her skirts to reveal her naked, hairless crotch. I held my breath for a long moment.

'He asks you to do this?' I touched it for confirmation. The page was repulsively sticky.

'Well, no, because I wear bloomers underneath.'

I nodded, keeping my face expressionless. Polly seemed to be drawing in on herself as I stared at the pages, rocking backwards and forwards on her toes nervously.

'Does he do other things?'

I tried to speak as quietly as possible, as you might to a jumpy horse. Polly pulled her cap from her pocket and fiddled with it, her red, burnt fingers pushing and pulling the greying fabric.

'You can tell me,' I said. A coaxing tone, but also a little bit of a command. I'd seen older girls do this in the Old Brewery, when a young cub came back sniffling with hair rumpled and a cut lip. I'd seen their righteous, quiet rage and felt it building inside me. 'Does he do other things, Polly?'

'Sometimes,' she mumbled. She wouldn't look at me. 'He gives me sweets if I do as he says. Sit in his lap or kiss him or touch him in places.'

'I see.'

I was filled with a sense of cold recognition; giant, hairy hands grabbing my small wrists, a scream stifled in the dark. That old familiar face of an unremembered friend, dark eyes wide with fear. A frightened whisper: *Stay put in the room, little cub.* I closed the book with a snap.

'Polly, if you want sweets then come to me. I will give you as many as you want.'

Polly stared at me, eyes as round as bonbons. 'For nothing?'

'For nothing. Promise?'

'Yes!'

I extracted the twisted cap from her hands and set it on her head, tucking the short, straw-like feathers of her hair back in. She smiled, her crooked teeth showing, giving her the adorable look of a friendly squirrel. There was an unfurling need to take care of her, one scrappy orphan to another. Maybe because, a long time ago, I was sure there was someone who had taken care of me, and I was sure, in my bones, they had paid a horrible price for it.

'Enjoying yourselves?'

My chest constricted and Polly squeaked. We both turned around. Chester was standing by the door. His eyes flickered to the book on the table between us.

'Ah, Polly.' He tapped a finger on the silver head of his walking cane. 'You've been a naughty girl.'

I saw the hunted look on her face, knew it like I knew my own tattooed hand.

'Polly, go down to the kitchen,' I said softly.

'Polly, stay here,' Chester snapped.

'Go, little cub.'

It was a deliberately chosen word, a name used by older orphans all over the city to order young squeakers around. It was a command she'd known longer than the ones Chester had been giving, and she fled the room immediately, as if her little body had taken off before her mind had understood her disobedience. I waited for Chester's revenge, but he stood quietly as we both listened to her retreating footsteps down two flights of stairs and the heavy silence of the house settling back into place.

'It is strange to see you like this.'

He spoke calmly. He took a step towards me. His cane clicked on the wood floor and his hungry eyes sought out the patches of skin where the tattoos showed – my open collar, the cuffs of my wrists.

'The men's clothing: Minnie's idea, I suppose? It's very. . . compelling.'

He reached out a hand to my wrist and his favoured dragon tattoo there, but I pulled my arm back in denial. He smiled.

'I've been impressed with you,' he said. 'That was a neat trick you pulled a few weeks ago, using your riff-raff knowledge to put my friend in an almighty panic; why, it was quite the caper. We never had the chance to discuss it. I was sad you did not stay afterwards.'

In my mind's eye, I saw his lagging, pale body lurching towards me across the bed and stiffened. I watched him grin. He wanted me to remember.

'Minnie told me to go.'

Even here, with him, I was resistant to the idea that I had somehow left Minnie behind. She had sent me, I reminded myself. Chester shrugged as if the distinction was nothing.

'Well, you're here now.' He gripped my wrist this time. 'We can have our own caper.'

'I think I'll leave you to your caper, Mr Merton.' I tugged hard enough to prompt a release of my arm, but he only smiled playfully. I felt an impending sense of dread.

'Shall I call for little Polly to come up and join us? You seem to get along so well with my little pet.'

Minnie had sent me from the room. Had he taunted her with me, too? I looked him up and down, taking all of him in. I felt I had a sense of when a man wanted to take and when he wanted to buy, and I sensed Chester liked to deal and cajole rather than grab and conquer. *Rather give than have it taken.* The contortions of the universe were definitely testing my words.

'Leave her be, and we'll talk,' I said.

We never give it away for free.

He smiled and nodded. 'Talk away. What do you propose?'

'Leave her be, and I'll show you a tattoo of your choice, anywhere on my body.'

I swallowed hard. I didn't know why, but somehow bargaining felt more fragile and dangerous than simply surrendering. It was not my natural area of expertise. Chester tapped his long fingers against his chin, frowning in mock consternation, clearly relishing our exchange.

'One tattoo will not suffice. Let's say instead a certain area of the body?'

I hesitated, made a pretence of thinking about it, but I knew already I didn't have much choice.

'Agreed.'

'However—' he drew the word out, his eyes glancing over gleefully to see how my shoulders tensed '—I perhaps can get more enjoyment out of young, sweet Polly than I can of you. . .'

I tried not to show my disgust though I felt an immediate sickly taste in the back of my throat. I choked it down.

'Perhaps,' I said, coolly. 'But she does not have what I have. What only one other man has ever seen.'

He knew I was baiting him, but maybe he wanted to be baited. As he stared, small beads of anxious sweat formed between my shoulder blades. Maybe this was what he needed, to imagine that I tempted him to it. Then he broke his gaze and clapped his hands, a sharp sound that was eaten up by the stuffiness of the room.

'That sounds reasonable. Let's get to it then. Your front, please. If I am to be more specific, your décolletage and stomach.' He grinned with yellowing teeth, like a rat's.

I'd expected this but I still flinched inside, swallowing the urge to run. I told myself it wasn't something for nothing, that this was something for Polly, so I unbuttoned my shirt, letting it fall open.

'Won't you be taking it off?' Chester asked.

'No. You didn't ask for my arms.' I smirked at him. 'Tits and gut, that's all you get.'

I unwrapped the length of fabric binding my breasts, trying to look confident as I laid it down on the billiards table. Then I made a show of buttoning my cuffs. I wanted him to think I wasn't intimidated. It barely mattered. He dragged an armchair into place so he sat right in front of me, the wooden feet of it screeching across the floor. He leaned forward, so close I could feel his breath against my belly button, smell the lingering scent of whisky and sausage. My stomach tattoo is one of my oldest, since Jordan started with places that could be modestly hidden. There is a geisha, naked but hiding her face behind a fan, and standing in a koi pond. After a few minutes, I twitched my hand to redo my buttons but Chester grabbed my wrist.

'I decide when we are finished.'

'Our deal wasn't for touching!'

I twisted my arm, trying not to move my body, aware of how my naked breasts might be bouncing, but he held on, glaring up at me.

'I won't touch if you stay still.'

We stared at each other for a minute, then I capitulated.

'Fine.'

He leaned back and lit a cigar. Minutes piled on minutes. Despite being used to having strangers look at my skin, I'd never been stared at naked for so long, not even by Jordan. For Jordan, the excitement came in the inking, not the looking. For Chester, looking was clearly enough. I'd been around enough to know when a man was randy. His cheeks were flushed, his eyes glazed. He reminded me, queasily, of the rapturous faces of the gentlemen in his book. I tried not to look at him, counted the books on the shelves behind him and tried to read their titles from afar, and then found myself wishing he would just pull his prick out and have done with it. The light began to change, the sun dipping behind a cloud and I was chilled. My skin prickled and my bare nipples hardened, as naturally as a pigeon puffing their feathers against the cold, but Chester smiled. This was what he had been waiting for; a sign of my response. Of course he would take it as a signal of desire. Men like him always wanted to believe that.

'We are finished.'

I pulled my shirt closed, crossing my arms. Chester leaned forwards to stub out his cigar. I hated the smell of it.

'Do you remember our conversation the night you arrived?'

I looked down at him. His chair was in shadow now and so was his face.

'You wanted to buy me.'

I thought of the drawing of the small girl. I thought of Polly. I wondered where in the library I might find the stash of sweeties and bonbons he'd used to keep her quiet.

'Your skin only, your terms could still apply. No touching—' he pressed his palms together between his knees '—unless you asked me to.'

I could have rolled my eyes at his exhausting, typical response if I hadn't been planted to the spot. It was either nervousness or fear, but I felt I had taken root there.

'I already have a job,' I said.

'For now,' he chuckled. 'But Minnie has a way of losing interest. She likes to keep people for a time; she enjoys a curiosity but then she moves on. Then where will you be?'

His words were so similar to what Minnie had told me about him, that I listened. I think he took this for interest because he leaned forward and continued, speaking conspiratorially.

'You would have more freedom with me. Better pay, too, and no one would ever see your skin but me.' He smiled as if it was the most reasonable offer in the world. 'I'll take care of you.'

I had learned something from Chester's persistent hunting of me up and down the stairs of Hamilton Square. Despite my first impressions, he was not a man who fucked once and then took off. I recalled with a twisting pain in my throat the way he had looked at me the night of the poppy, the way he had said *it's so beautiful.* Minnie was right. He was a collector. I knew that if I let him have me now, he might never give me back.

'I don't think so, Mr Merton.' I stepped back from him, reaching to button up my shirt but my fingers were shaky. I only managed two before giving up and re-crossing my arms, trying to look defiant. 'As Minnie already told you, I'm not for sale.'

'Clearly.' He laughed nastily, gesturing at my unbuttoned shirt. I blushed but tried to maintain a little dignity by nodding my head politely and turning to leave. 'How much did she buy you for?'

I flushed for a moment, thinking of those rare kisses Minnie and I had shared, bodies entwined chastely night after night. I realised then we had fallen asleep and woken together every day since the Bowery. Minnie may still have been granting him access to her body, but only one of us was sleeping with her. I smiled with surprising triumph. Chester's eyes narrowed. I knew I'd regret it but I turned away anyway, moving towards the door.

'You know, I heard something strange last night. A drunk from Five Points told me that a gang down there has… mislaid an important whore.'

I didn't look back at him. I let the words fall on my back and dig their way in, a cascade of bullets. *Time's up,* said a voice inside.

'Shouldn't believe all you hear from drunks, but any girl who's got away from a gang is a lucky one.' I spoke to the door, refusing to look at him. I heard the creak of Chester rising out of the chair behind me and the groan of the floorboards under his expensive shoes.

'Excuse me, Mr Merton.'

I had misjudged how close he was. One hand grabbed my hip, as quick as a rabbit and the other had a shoulder. His words tickled my ear.

'You think you belong to Minnie, but you don't realise yet, little one: if you belong to Minnie, you belong to me. I can give you the world or I can send you back where you belong.'

I will admit, I did not struggle against his touch, but only because I was not really there. I know what it must have looked like from the outside, but as soon as his hand clamped on my flesh, my body returned to Five Points. Those were Jordan's hands and that was Jordan's breath against my neck, and, as instinctively as falling asleep, my spirit detached. The ringing in my ears grew to a screech and shadows lurched forward from the hidden corners, dark hands outstretched. For a split second, I thought I saw a face staring eagerly out of the shadows of the curtains, eyes that offered me a chance, a way out of this if I would only look and yield to their grasping reach. I would not look. Instead, I drifted above my body, looking down on the clutching, looming Chester Merton as he trapped me in his arms. I saw myself through a red veil, pliant and as yielding as snow in his hands, and saw the library door burst open. I only thought two things as Minnie's bright, angry face loomed and the shadows grasped closer. The first one was: *this won't be the last time*, and the second, most shameful thought was this: *take her instead*.

Chapter Eight

'**D**id he touch you? Did he hurt you?'

Minnie's voice, loud and demanding. Minnie's arm, pushing me down on the hard fabric of the chaise longue. A glass, forced into my hand, with a liquid drop of something brown dispersing in it. I stared at the swirling liquid, trying to bring myself back into my body, but it was like stumbling to find my footing in mud. The shadows lingered close to me, tripping me up with every step.

'Flora.' Minnie's face was in front of me as she knelt, forcing the glass up to my face. 'Drink.'

My teeth clanked against the rim of the glass.

'Answer me,' she demanded. 'What did he do?'

Who? I thought, *and when?* Memories sat on my shoulders and hissed like angry cats. I tried to find the words.

'He asked me to undress and I did.'

'He *asked* you to?' Her voice was harsh. 'And you did it?'

The water was chalky and bitter on my tongue. They always asked and I always did. I nodded.

'I left you alone for five minutes and this is what you get up to?'

Minnie glared at me. 'Christ, Flora! You can't be flashing your goods for pennies.'

'It wasn't for money,' I stammered.

I saw Polly's little face. I felt the shadowy hands reaching closer. I couldn't get rid of the ringing in my ears and Minnie was looking at me horribly; as if I were nothing more than a slum slut and she was only just realising it.

'I see.' Her little lip curled. 'This was your play for him then, was it?'

'No.'

I shook my head. The conversation was moving too fast for me; the library walls grew tall around me, the stench of Five Points stung my nostrils and my mind was far away, lost in those places where large hands grabbed small girls in the dark. The door to our suite was open and the shadows had followed me, impatient and eager, gnashing their teeth with my rejection. The Knowing was chasing my rage, so very tantalisingly close that I could almost feel its ashy power on my tongue. I closed my eyes tightly and tried to force myself back into the room. *Stay in the room, cub.* I knew what she must think, I could see it in her eyes – the girl she had welcomed into her arms and her home, to whom she had given everything and trusted, whom she had kissed tenderly and sweetly and shared secrets with, now found half naked and in the arms of her lover. I tried to catch up, to work out what Minnie needed to hear from me to stop her looking at me this way, but I couldn't get there in time. Her eyes had grown flinty and her voice cold.

'Don't lie,' she said. 'Girls like you are always after men like him; why wouldn't you be? He's walking cash for freaks like you.'

That brought me back, like a roaring train passing too close; a sudden rush of heat and soot that filled my lungs with breath and anger. Memories of scorn and blame gave me voice.

'Girls like me? Freaks like *me*?' I set the glass down with a slam, a wave of sticky water spilling over my hand. 'Not a girl like you, who has been living off him for years?'

If the only difference between her and Chester and me and Jordan was money, then it was hardly a difference at all. Minnie's back stiffened and her eyes widened at my rage.

'You don't know shit about me and him.'

'Really? You think I don't fucking know?'

I couldn't help but laugh, the sound cracking in my dry mouth. My lips were gluey and parched but I kept talking, despite the shadows reaching towards me. God, the ringing just wouldn't stop.

'You let him do whatever he wants here, to whoever he wants. You're damned insane if you think it's different.'

'So what, you saw some of your old bastard in him and ran right over?'

I had never had Minnie shout at me before, never imagined that such a loud, coarse roar would come from such a small, delicate woman. The ringing in my ears grew and I tried to turn my head away, but her hand was pressing against my face, making me meet her furious eyes.

'You promised you'd do what I said,' she hissed. Her eyes were chips of glass, flashing in the light. 'I told you what the terms were, and I come home to find you with your tits out for him. What happened to not giving it away for fucking free?'

'You're just mad that I didn't give it up to him on your terms, when you wanted!' I yelled back, eyes closed, flinching away from her rage. *Curl and hide*, said a voice inside and I obeyed.

'Is that what you think this is, me keeping you back as a reward?' Minnie demanded. 'Is that what you think I was doing, when I sent you away that night?'

I winced, hating her for bringing it up, fury finding flight on my tongue.

'I didn't ask you to do that! I would have stayed if... but you... you decided.'

I kept my eyes tightly closed, unable to say that I would have rather stayed and endured the hands of those men than have this debt hanging over me, but I could see her still. The Knowing could always see, and she stared at me through the shadows, lips white.

'I sent you away.'

Her voice was quiet and contained all the sorrow of whatever they'd done to her. I could feel it at the edge of the Knowing, like dark feathered wings made of regrets, the terrible secret events of that evening sitting so close to her skin.

'I sent you away so you didn't have to deal with more of the hell you've already been put through and you act like that's a fucking crime.'

If what I'd been through was hell then I hadn't been through it, I was still living my every breath in it. She presumed she'd saved me from something. When she had touched me, out of her mind on poppy, with her slovenly hands and groping mouth, it was the first time in Hamilton Square I had felt painfully, dreadfully used and it had been by her. My shame hardened to disdain inside me. *This woman don't know shit.* I opened my eyes.

'You sent me away, but then you came anyway.' I laughed drily. 'He almost had me; you almost watched!'

I turned my face away. It seemed suddenly absurd to be upset over that night, yet the betrayal didn't stop stinging.

'You said you would protect me,' I whispered. Minnie's face flickered through emotions too quickly to be caught. Perhaps regret but perhaps frustration, perhaps a deeper, gnawing sorrow I couldn't understand. Now, though, it was just passion curdling a cold fury.

'And this is revenge, is it?' Minnie raised her eyebrows. 'To fuck him for his protection instead? Switching players, are you?'

I saw his face. I felt his hands. I closed my eyes. I heard that old, gentle voice. *Stay put in the room, little cub.*

'No.' I thought I might be swaying, but I couldn't tell. The whole world was swaying.

'Why then?' Minnie glared at me.

The ringing shrilled nauseatingly in my ears. I shook my head and tried to laugh, but my throat was so chalky, so dry. I wondered what had been in the brown liquid. I wondered with interest if it was making the shadows stronger, but then I realised it barely mattered. This woman whom I had kissed because I wanted to, whom I had followed because I wanted to, was now a screeching bird cawing over a stolen man. The worst type of man, at that, and the man who knew the Dead Rabbits were missing a girl. An unsettling thought landed on me, melting into my consciousness like a snow-flake. She knew who he was and yet she still wanted to defend him. Telling her how terrible he was to little Polly wouldn't sway her now. After all, we were both just slum girls to her and I was a fool to think she would see me otherwise.

'Does it matter?' My grip on the room was slipping and I only had a few moments left to make her understand. 'I didn't throw away my whole life for him, did I? I didn't risk everything, the Dead Rabbits, Jordan, all of it for him, did I? I did it for you.'

'And why did you?' Minnie's voice was unflinching. 'Why did you follow me?'

We had exchanged no promises, she and I. We'd offered no words of love or sweetness, only a few kisses and the soft comfort of a shared bed. Yet whatever shivering thread of attachment quivered between us had burrowed its way into the flesh of my heart with the sharpness of a fishing hook. My throat was so dry but I had to say it, even if I hated myself for it.

'I wanted you.'

She stared at me.

'Well, you've got a funny way of showing it,' she said.

I lurched towards her, the floor tilting under my feet like the deck of a ship. I stumbled and kissed her. There were shadows in the corners and I was too weak to push them back. I was drowning and in need of an anchor. She kissed me back, an angry, possessive clash of teeth and hot lips, trying to punish me and teach me a lesson.

'I wanted you too, I still want you.' Her voice was lovely, velvety and soft. It should have kept me in the room, it should have kept the shadows at bay, but I could feel cold, feathered wings brushing against my face. I pulled away, my hands trembling.

'Flora, what's wrong?'

What the fuck did you do?

Sometimes, we are haunted by ghosts. Other times, we are more than capable of providing our own hauntings. I tried to ask her what had been in the glass of water but I couldn't. The memory was coming like a storm and I gave into it. The pull of the shadows and the coldness, I let them engulf me. My head thumped against Minnie's chest and I rubbed my dry mouth and nose against the hot skin of her collarbone. My body shook as violently as a morphia addict's. *It's been a long time*, I thought, abstractly. Funny how memories grew legs like spiders and spun their sticky webs across your mind.

What the fuck did you do?

'Abernathy!' I heard Minnie shout. 'Abernathy, come here. Carry her to bed.'

Everything was moving around me but somehow I was still, despite my falling, trembling body. It wasn't like the séance with the cards. It was worse. My mind flew away and perched above the fireplace and watched Abernathy rush into the room. It saw Chester's face outside the door, twisted into a curious sneer.

'What's going on?' he said. 'What did she do?'

'*What the fuck did you do?*' Jordan shouted at me, his face tight with disgust. He dragged me, bleeding and vomiting, to the shithouse at the back of the shop. I clamped my jaw shut, catching the edge of my tongue and feeling a burning sting, tasting blood. I tried to fight my way through the memory, to tense myself against the shaking but it did no good.

'Nothing,' Minnie shouted. 'Get the fuck out, Chester!'

'She's a hysteric, isn't she?' His voice was a sneer. 'God, Minnie, again? I told you not to go back to that shithole, but you didn't fucking listen! I'm not doing this bullshit all over again.'

I closed my eyes tightly as Abernathy's arms enveloped me, and breathed in his soft, smoky scent. *Stay put in the room, little cub.* I felt his large hand squeeze my shoulder, and then felt his bulky body behind me as he pulled my back against his chest. He was holding me close as he sat against the headboard, squeezing me so tight, squeezing the life right out of me, but oddly it was helping. Numbness spread.

'Go away!' I opened my eyes in time to see Minnie slamming the door on Chester and rifling through her vanity for a bottle. All was quiet inside Abernathy's vice-like grip. My rattling body was stifled and now just trembled like the downtown train crossing tracks. All I heard was the tinkling sound of glass bottles moving, stoppers being removed, and liquid being dripped into water. Then Minnie approached, holding out the glass of water again.

'Laudanum,' she said. 'Drink it. It will help.'

I couldn't speak to say no. Minnie tipped the glass to my lips as Abernathy held me. The bitterness of it made my tongue recoil, but I forced myself to drink, gulping readily. If the way in had been drugs then maybe the way out was, too. At the end of the water was oblivion. Maybe there the shadows and memories would recede and I would be strong enough to push the Knowing back.

111

'Well done,' Minnie muttered, setting the glass down.

I was suddenly tired, so tired that I lolled inside the safe, strong cage of Abernathy's body, and too tired to really notice the way Minnie tenderly petted my hair. Peacefully, I noticed her anger had abated. I didn't know why, but I was grateful, even as I felt sure it wouldn't last.

'Has it happened before?' she asked. 'The shaking? Like this?'

What the fuck have you done? Jordan said.

'Once,' I whispered. My throat was sticky. 'Maybe twice. I lost a baby. Or two.'

'Lost? Oh, sweet girl.' Minnie's eyes were brighter than usual. She climbed onto the bed beside us, stroking my hair. 'What did he do?'

I sighed deeply. My skin was heavy, pressing into Abernathy as if it was coated with lead. The shaking had all but stopped now, just irregular flurries of twitching in my fingers and toes, the places Abernathy's tight grip couldn't reach. The memory was less alive now, more like a stamp of words and images on the inside of my eyelids. As I spoke they grew bolder, stepping forward to be noticed.

'He gave me medicine.'

It came in a brown bottle, and he forced it down me. His fingers pinched my nose so hard and tight and clamped my lips until I swallowed.

'It made me sick. Made me bleed. Made me shake. Every time.'

Vomit on the pillowcase and meaty, clotted blood soaked into the bedsheets. Dragged, shaking and groaning to the outhouse and left in the bitter cold.

'How many times?' Minnie's fingers were lulling me again, just like they had at Eisenmann's. I sighed.

'I don't know.'

Three. Three horrible, terrible times. The third time I had done it myself and not taken as much and it had not been so bad, but then I had to follow it with a visit to a woman in the slums. A dark stairway rose in my mind, a dark room with a cold, metal bed. I groaned and felt Abernathy pulling away behind me so that my head rested on the cool pillowcase. Minnie nestled in close beside me, her arm tight around my waist and her breath gentle on my face.

'I can't go back,' I sniffled wearily. Exhaustion pressed into my bones and I couldn't possibly imagine how I would keep myself safe, especially if Chester was starting to sniff out the blood trail from here to Five Points, but I knew it probably started with keeping Minnie on my side. 'I'm sorry.' Minnie shook her head. Even slipping away into sleep, I could tell my apology had not been accepted, not for what I was asking.

'It was probably for the best.'

I couldn't tell what she was talking about. She pressed her lips against mine. The words she spoke fell inside my mouth.

'You'd have been tethered to him, you see? Your whole life.'

As she said it I saw it forming, a knotted cord, red as blood, stretching between Jordan and me in the dark. I saw its surface, rough and splintered as a Five Points wood beam. Then, between me and Minnie, I saw the thinnest thread, as fine as one of Minnie's own golden hairs or a shining fishing line, stretched between her own breast and a needle in my heart. I was drifting, the laudanum-edged dreams engulfing me in numb, slumbering clouds, but I still caught Minnie's soft words, whispered into my hair:

'A child is an anchor, Flora. Trust me, I know.'

I saw the sorrow in her voice, lit by the Knowing, blue with longing. I was not the only one who had lost things.

IX.

Chapter Nine

'You're late,' snapped the woman at the door, glaring down at Minnie, Abernathy and me. Chester stood a little way behind us, loitering by the carriage. It had been a tense ride from Hamilton Square with Chester 'accidentally' brushing a hand against my knee and Minnie sending him hideous glares.

'Show starts in forty minutes. Your girls are all here, all waiting.'

'Well, let us in then, Kate.'

Minnie brushed past her and we entered Hotel De Wood, the legendary brothel of Sisters Row in midtown. It didn't look like much from the outside, not like the bawdy houses I was familiar with where the girls hung out of the door, advertising their wares to passing drunks. It was a tall, clean brownstone on a respectable-looking street, all its floral curtains drawn closed and the only clue as to its real business one red lamp set in the fan-shaped concrete detailing above the shiny, green door. I'd been expecting a ragtag troupe in a saloon set-up or a pub with a little stage, not this feathery, genie's lair of fabulous silk furnishings of which the infamous Kate Woods was the gatekeeper. She was the most glamorous woman I had laid eyes on. She had dark hair, cherry-red lips and was dressed modestly in a high-necked black lace gown with touches of red piping on her collar and cuffs. The way she looked at you, as if you were made of dollars and dimes, was a disconcerting testament to the success of her business.

'Chester.' Kate Woods smiled at him as he entered. 'I didn't know you were attending our show tonight.'

'Didn't want to miss out, Kate.' He removed his hat, smiling tightly.

He'd dressed up for the occasion, a coat and tails and white gloves. I'd thought he'd been poking fun at Minnie, but now I saw that all the gentlemen Kate Woods entertained were expected to dress this formally.

'Been cut out of a lot of good fun, recently. Wouldn't miss this.'

He glanced at Minnie. She had cancelled all our séances since the day in the library. I hadn't been allowed outside of the suite for the last two weeks, not even to smoke. Polly had been sneaking in to play tic-tac-toe with me and give me gossip from Cook, which I was grateful for. I used every opportunity we were alone to ask for information.

'Has anyone called?' I asked Polly, dealing my cards for her. She liked the pictures. 'Any strange men with tattoos?'

'The flour man came but he's got no tattoos I've ever seen.' Polly shook her head and fixed her feather-grey eyes on my fingers as they shuffled cards through the air. 'Mr Chester has stopped giving me sweets.'

'Good.'

The fact that Chester clearly still thought the deal we'd made in the library was valid gave me hope. It was like Minnie said: as long as I held his attention, he was unlikely to search harder for where exactly he could send me back to.

'But he has been asking me things about you.' Polly looked at me nervously. 'Like where you come from.'

I felt suddenly weary with the predictability of his controlling machinations. He was just like Jordan, viewing every piece of information as a potential manipulation.

'I didn't tell him anything, but you should be careful tonight.' Polly stroked the face of the Justice card. 'Lots of Mr Merton's friends will be there.'

Polly didn't say the cruel thing: that whilst Chester had many friends who would happily help him hang me out to dry, I only had Minnie, and Minnie was barely speaking to me. She and Chester had been having hissing, whispered conversations in the corridor outside almost daily. I didn't need to ask what they were about. I could feel it. My actions had tipped the scales of an unmentioned balance inside Hamilton Square and now everything was dangerously off-kilter. I didn't know what the repercussions would be, but I knew they were coming.

'Is this her?' Kate asked, pointing a long finger with a ruby ring on it at me. 'Christ, Minnie,' she snorted. 'She's another street urchin.'

'She's a talent,' Minnie said. Kate rolled her eyes and I had the dreadful impression that this was not the first time Minnie had brought a girl like me in. Chester's words from the night of the library, sneered from the open doorway as I trembled helplessly against Abernathy, came back to me. *God, Minnie, again?*

'You seen her in action?' Kate asked Chester. 'Any good?'

'Yes. Very authentic.'

Chester smirked at me. My chest burned underneath my coat, as if he was seeing my tattoos all over again. I tried not to look ashamed.

'She made quick work of my chaps recently, had them all in a spin, and she's got something pretty special hidden under there.'

'She's got art?' Kate ignored me and looked at Minnie. 'Let's see it.'

'Yes, Minnie, let's see it.' Chester's fingers reached over to tweak my coat sleeve. I pulled it away sharply, and I heard Abernathy's low growl behind me. Chester snorted.

'Chester!' Minnie barked.

'Oh, I see.' Kate looked between us carefully, saying nothing. Whatever she saw, it was enough to light a glimmer of cunning interest in her face.

'Can we continue this upstairs, Kate?' Minnie's tone was taut. She wouldn't look at me. 'Away from prying eyes.'

Chester glared. Minnie stared straight ahead. The ebb and flow of their rage and frustration with each other was almost visible, bouncing between them like an unspoken argument, until Kate cut in.

'Fine.' Kate smiled at Chester, rubbing his arm placatingly. 'Chester, go and make yourself comfortable in the parlour. Lucy is working tonight and I know how you like her company.'

'Very well.' Chester inclined his head towards me. He ignored Minnie. 'Until later then, dear mystic.'

He walked off towards the sounds of laughter and drinks being made, leaving Abernathy and me watching Minnie cautiously as her blue eyes followed the back of his retreating jacket.

'Lovers' tiff, is it?' Kate asked. 'Did he bring some awful pox home with him? You'll know he didn't catch it here, Min; all my girls are clean.'

'Can we get on with it?' Minnie set off at a quick pace, marching up the stairs. Kate rolled her eyes and gestured for us to follow; our footsteps were muffled on the heavy, crimson carpet.

The stairway was flanked by two birds, so tall and terrifying I couldn't help but stare. They might have been like the fishing herons you saw at the pier, if not for the absurd plumage at the top of their heads: a thick cap of black feathers which then sprouted gold shoots that looked like dandelion clocks. Kate saw me staring.

'Oh, these,' she sighed. 'Gift from a client. He shot them on safari in Africa and had them stuffed for me, ugly great brutes. Can't imagine why he thought they'd be better than jewellery.'

As Kate talked, I stared at their shiny glass eyes. Like a tear starting in its corner, I could see the remains of a tiny smudge of blood. I shivered. Abernathy held a door open for me; light and sound were bubbling out of it in golden bursts. I hesitated but he jerked his head, eyebrows raised. *In you go.* I followed. At first, all I saw was skin and bodies and what seemed to be miles of floating fabrics and shining pots and bottles, repeating again and again forever. Then it became clear – many women of different types and shapes were dressing and the light was bouncing around the room, sending their reflections this way and that, due to the presence of about ten heavy, gilded mirrors. Before I could even really see the details of their many replicated faces, Kate was in front of me once again, arms tightly folded and frowning.

'All right, let's see it,' she said, gesturing to my coat. My stomach clenched.

'Here.' Minnie thrust forward a small card under Kate's nose. It was my cabinet picture. Her eyes widened.

'Christ alive,' she muttered, her strong fingers tracing the line of my exposed legs captured in light. I shivered. 'And she bares it all, does she? I've got a lovely Grecian backdrop some girls do nudes in front of. We could build a stunning tableau.'

Kate Woods had the calculating gaze of a butcher. My throat tightened. I did not want to be naked in front of her. I wanted to plead but my voice was gone.

'She's not a whore, Kate.' Minnie snatched the picture back, speaking over me. 'She's a mystic.'

'I have mystics.' Kate frowned. 'You've had mystics before. They're a dime a dozen. What I don't have is a tattooed girl; neither do you. What's the point of having her if she keeps her clothes on?'

I tried not to flick my shocked eyes towards Minnie. It was one thing to imagine Chester having another mystic – after all, I rather expected him to try to fuck everyone he met – but I had never considered that Minnie might have had someone before me. I immediately wondered exactly what Kate meant by the word 'had'.

'She's not a run-of-the-mill mystic,' Minnie said. 'She's a spiritualist. She calls ghosts, tells secrets. Your clients will love it.'

Tell nothin'. There was a flicker of static at the back of my neck, a sense of warmth and warning. I didn't remember the face that went with the voice, but I remembered what had happened when I'd spoken to ghosts in Five Points, before I knew better. I immediately felt a tightness around my face, as if my skin recalled the stretch of swollen skin healing from beatings. I had promised I'd never call ghosts like this. I tried to breathe deeply but my throat was closing. My eyes darted at the many faces of the women behind Minnie and Kate, but not one of them was looking our way or was even interested that Minnie was selling something I knew only led to despair.

'A spiritualist, eh?' Kate tapped a finger against her arm. 'Well, that's a hot market. We'll see how she fares, then we'll talk price. A word, first.'

Minnie hesitated. I felt her look at me for a moment, though I kept my eyes on the floor. Somehow, over the days and weeks living together, I had come to know her movements as if she were a play I had seen a million times. I could patch together snatches of her hair or her gestures in my peripheral vision and know exactly what she was doing or saying. What she meant was another thing entirely. Since the library and her subsequent baffling coldness to both me and Chester, I had begun to question if anyone ever had the measure of her intentions.

'Fine,' Minnie said. 'You two get on without me.'

Abernathy prodded me towards an empty vanity and I reluctantly removed my coat. I was already in my stage costume, and my skin felt warm under the sudden glow of the golden electric lights and the curious eyes of the other girls. I kept my head down and pulled out my cards, focusing on overhearing snippets of Kate and Minnie's whispered conversation.

'Seems like Chester has an eye for your girl,' Kate said.

'Chester has an eye for all my girls,' Minnie replied darkly. 'He's not having this one.'

'You be careful, Min. You can't afford to lose him.'

'You've been saying that for twelve years.'

I couldn't help jerking back slightly at the number. She'd been Chester's longer than I had been Jordan's. It was a long time to stay with the bastard without some other, unknown bond. The crushing weight of everything I didn't know about Minnie was squeezing the breath out of me. At least Jordan had never been a riddle.

'All right, duck?'

A tiny, dark-haired woman in a striped corset and stockings bent her face in front of me, blocking my sideways view of Kate and Minnie's dresses and obstructing their secret words with her loud voice.

'Yes,' I said, impatiently.

'I'm Myrtle, this is Hester.'

She gestured to another woman, sitting on the floor with both legs stretched out to the sides like a splayed doll. Hester waved.

'We're the Angel Sisters. Contortionists. You're Minnie's new girl?'

Myrtle had a flat, British accent and a hard, weathered face that seemed too old for her childish body. I shook her hand.

'Florence. Mystic and, well—' I looked down at my skin '—freak, I guess.'

'Nah, not a bit of it,' Myrtle said. 'Look around, duck. You're in home country now.'

Behind her, Minnie's voice rose, irritated, over the backstage babble.

'I'm not a fool, Kate. After all this time, don't you think I know what I'm doing?'

'He plays for keeps, girl, and he doesn't make concessions.'

'I got mine back, didn't I?'

I understood not a word of what they were talking about, but I recognised that tone in the way Kate said the word 'girl'. Now I knew where Minnie got it from and that only brought more questions. Then I saw Minnie glancing over to me and she winced.

'Hester, Myrtle, fix Flora's hair and face,' Minnie called, grabbing Kate's sleeve and pulling her to the door.

'Fix her how?' Myrtle grinned with a yellow set of teeth.

'If I gather everyone's powder I might be able to cover her marks,' Hester said, standing up. 'Maybe.'

I widened my eyes at Abernathy. *Help me.*

'Just get on with it,' Minnie snapped. 'Abe, come with me!'

Abernathy grunted behind me, lethargically hoisting himself out of his chair and clapping me on the shoulder as he passed by. I knew what that meant. *You're on your own, kid.*

'Show starts in twenty-five, girls!' Kate called, closing the door behind them.

Helpless, I turned to the Angel Sisters. They stood at the same height with their skinny arms crossed and both heads cocked to one side like seagulls. I worried that if I made any sudden movements they might pounce.

'Saw a lass like you once,' Hester said. 'Covered and all. In Liverpool. She was darker than you though, and pierced all over, even her teats.'

'You got your teats pierced?' Myrtle asked.

'No.'

'Thought not. Well!' Myrtle grabbed me by the shoulders and pushed me down on the stool in front of the vanity. 'Don't move.'

I sat as still as I could, worried what the fierce Myrtle would do if I didn't. Instinctively, I reached for my needle box, setting it out on the table and unscrewing my ink pot and rubbing alcohol. I cleaned my needle and dipped it in ink, pressing it into the pattern of leaves over the back of my left hand, just to calm my anxiety. The Angel Sisters pulled my hair and chattered with the other performers. Out of the corner of my eye, I saw a giantess in the corner, as dark as Abernathy but maybe a foot taller with the most luscious beard I had ever seen. There was a woman whose skin was as pale as a ghost and her eyes were pink; she had along with her a little dog with hair as fluffy and white as her own, whom she was making dance on his hindquarters. There was a muscled, intense-looking woman with only one leg and a huge yellow serpent wrapped over her shoulders. This, I realised, was Minnie's business. Selling freak girls, including herself. For someone who hated Barnum, she had a lot in common with him.

'Hey, you're good at that, aren't you, duck?' Hester said, twisting the front part of my hair back and fixing her eyes on my needle. It was sharp, unforgiving and always perfectly relaxing. I felt my shoulders begin to lower, the muscles unflexing with the deliberate, repetitive pain. I shrugged nervously.

'First show?' Myrtle asked pityingly.

'I've done séances before, but not the spiritualist performance.' I anxiously remembered the look on the faces of Chester's friends when they had asked: *How the fuck did she know?*

'Never?'

I shook my head. The two of them looked at each other in the mirror. They looked canny and sharp and the static at the back of my neck tingled in warning.

'What?'

'You ever seen a mystic show, love?' Hester's eyes were fixed on the white ribbon she was tying into my hair. I shook my head, wincing as she pulled my scalp.

'Minnie's told you what to expect, though?' Myrtle probed.

I shook my head. No one knew what to expect when you called ghosts and read cards, least of all Minnie. The tingling increased. My senses had been more painful since the day of my fight with Minnie. Every nerve seemed cut raw at the ends and now everything I saw, tasted or touched caught on the material world and snagged on them, hurting me. I looked at the sisters. Oceans of information were being exchanged in one glance between those identical almond-shaped eyes. Finally, Myrtle spoke.

'You'll know, though, that mystic shows are quite… drastic. Won't you?'

'Drastic?' I swallowed hard.

'Bloody manic, she means,' Hester said. 'The mystic will come out, all dressed funny and covered up and then they'll do odd voices and shake and throw themselves around like they're having a fit.'

'Sometimes their keepers will tie them up, like, or tie them to the chair,' Myrtle added, 'to make it more convincing. People go mad for it, but it can be bloody rough.'

I remembered being unable to stand or sit or stop trembling. I remembered Abernathy's arms holding me tight. Had Minnie witnessed me drowning in memories and decided that it was worth selling?

'Best you know now,' Hester said, squeezing my shoulder as I tried to bury the disappointment curdling in my throat. 'Pretending mad, or even just pretending to be touched mad-like, can be a heavy-going business for a girl.'

'What does that mean?' I asked.

They looked at each other in the reflective glass. Then they looked at me. Our mirrored eyes met, mine now perfectly lined with ashes and oil and as dark and mad-looking as any fortune teller on the circuit.

'Did you know they had another, a long time ago?' Hester asked softly. I didn't ask who she meant. There was only one 'they' in my life.

'Chester and Minnie had another girl.' I spoke slowly, voicing aloud the suspicion that had been chasing around my mind for days since I'd heard Polly's words in the library and Chester's afterwards.

'Effie, her name was.' Myrtle nodded. *Effie.* For some reason, the name mattered. 'Mr Merton pulled her out of Five Points – you'll know how he likes the Old Brewery lasses – and Minnie put her in the show for a few months, just turning cards, but he soured on her.'

'As he sours on everyone she beds,' Hester muttered. Myrtle poked her in the ribs.

'It was nearly fifteen years ago,' Myrtle said in a conciliatory tone, as if that would make up for the idea that Minnie was maybe using me to replace a lost lover. Inside my mind, I pictured Minnie standing in front of me in our suite, first explaining Chester to me. *He'll not let me keep you if he's not interested.*

'What happened to Effie?' I pressed my needle a little too hard against the tip of a leaf. It stung.

'Mr Merton said she was mad and sent her away. Didn't like her and Minnie either, by the sounds of it. Well, he's always hated that she likes a girl now and then.'

'Hester.' Myrtle silenced her sister with a glare and then looked at me. 'Let it be a warning.'

I almost laughed at that, the bubble of hysteria crackling in my throat. Oh, I had been warned before, little good that it had done me. The tangled web of Minnie's secrets and my place in it was spinning before my eyes. Effie, the girl from the Old Brewery who had played the mystic and gone to Minnie's bed. Effie, the girl whose shoes I had filled without realising, whose name was like a flickering flame in the back of my mind. Illuminating something I could not quite make out. Nausea was rising in me and I gripped the edge of the vanity. The static at my neck hummed like bees. I set my needle down, not caring to rub the blood from the back of my trembling hand. I didn't want to ask, not really, but the words were spoken before I thought them. If I was living the girl's life over, I had to know how it ended. The wheel of fortune was always turning and there was nothing to do but face it.

'What happened to her?' I asked. I remembered Minnie's words on the night of the poppy. *Please. Stay this time. Don't leave me again.*

'He got her put away in Blackwells, to the insane ward,' Hester said. 'She's dead.'

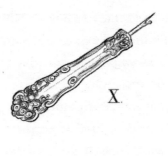

X.

Chapter Ten

'I need to speak to you.'

Minnie glared at me. I had tried to wait until we were alone, assuming she might pull me aside at some point, but the buzzing of bees in my ear, the sense of the small vibrations of the universe so close to my skin, had become unbearable. *Blackwells.* The name pounded around my head. Blackwells Island, the place inconvenient women were sent to rot. Perhaps it was all those hours lying in slumber together, our sweat and scent mingled and her breathless, longing mouth pressed against the back of my neck in the dark of the night, or perhaps it was only that she wanted to avoid a scene, but miraculously she nodded. She walked to the main door that exited onto the landing and held it open for me. I followed quickly, hearing the rise in the chatter of the other girls, and the door swung shut behind us.

'In here.'

Minnie opened a door to a closet and bundled me in, slamming the door and plunging us into semi-darkness aside from the orange triangle of light cutting in through the window from the streetlamp outside. The light fell on objects arranged on wooden shelves, casting weird bobbling shadows, and a strange-looking saddle on a wooden stand pushed against the wall.

'What the hell?' I blurted out without thinking. I had not seen a more absurd room in my life.

'It's Kate's store of bedroom treasures.' Minnie looked around, picking up an ivory cock and twiddling it listlessly.

I knew about these items, of course; the whores whom Jordan had brought to our bed had told me about them, but they were not working in the kind of establishments that provided such tools. They instead told me of daily objects that might as easily do the trick in a pinch. A bottleneck, perhaps, or a candlestick.

'So what's wrong?' Minnie demanded.

It was hard not to be distracted as she twirled the white and silver rod through her finger and nubs with admirable dexterity, but I brought my mind to the matter at hand – that she had somehow set me on a path that inevitably led to Blackwells Island.

'I don't think we should do this,' I said. 'What if something goes wrong, like last time, in the parlour?'

It had been the wrong topic to broach. Minnie scowled.

'It won't.' She pointed the hand-carved cock at me threateningly. 'Not if you don't say anything stupid, like you did last time. Just follow my lead, do exactly as I say. Don't bring your Five Points gossip up here; they don't want it.'

One of Minnie's great strengths was always her ability to employ an absolute tone of finality. Usually I admired it but today, taut with nerves and jumping at secrets, it only infuriated me.

'What do you want then?' I demanded. She looked surprised at my sharp tone and a bloom of unhappy satisfaction egged me on. 'You want me to shake and fall and re-live horrifying memories for you? You want me to collapse and play mad so well they cart me off to Blackwells? Like Effie?'

Minnie's face, which was often so unchangeable, a mask of professionalism and grace, blanched suddenly.

'You know about Effie?' she asked quietly. I didn't understand why her eyes were full of so much fear, as if she expected me to berate her. Unless she had played a part in the demise of the poor girl before me. My chest tightened at the thought.

'Hester told me there was a girl before me, that *you* had another mystic before me,' I said. 'He sent her to the madhouse.'

And you didn't stop him, I added inside my mind. Minnie's expression contorted into a sneer as if she had heard my unsaid accusation.

'Oh, what did those whores tell you?' She set the cock down on the shelf with a loud thump, accidentally knocking over many more in a crash of ivory, onyx and glass. 'That my old mystic went mad and it was my fault?'

'So it's true?' I wanted her to deny it, but she didn't. 'You and Chester shared another mystic?'

'No!' Minnie's tiny hand clamped into a fist. 'She was my friend! She worked for me! He just interfered, like he always does.'

I laughed to myself, pushing back the bitterness that was rising like acid inside me. Polly's words were a sliding poison inside my mind: *all of Miss Minnie's friends are Old Brewery sluts.*

'They said he pulled her out of Five Points, just like me! Did you make her promises?' My voice was ragged and I hated the grief in it. 'Did you tell her she was special and kiss her, too?'

'None of that is your business.'

Minnie's face had fallen into the shade of the cupboards, but her voice told me all I needed to know. The answer to every question was probably yes. The thought of it, of another girl like me in Hamilton Square, walking the staircase and climbing into bed with Minnie, was horrifying. I had been walking the path of Effie's ghostly trail all this time, and Minnie had let me. I stepped back from her, shaking, my legs bumping against the saddle on its stand. I noticed then the huge leather protrusions stitched into it and quickly took my hands off its sticky surface.

'Did he really send her away, or did you get rid of her when he got interested?' I sneered, throwing my fears at her as barbs. 'Will it happen to me? Now you hate me because he wants me so much?'

'I don't hate you because he wants you; I hate that you went to him.' Minnie stepped forward. One eye was caught in a shaft of streetlight and glowed yellow with a predatory gleam. 'Why did you do that, Flora?'

Why was he looking at you? I remembered Jordan's delicate touch and dangerous words. I closed my eyes and told myself it wasn't the same, but I was cornered nevertheless. Even at her diminutive height, when she was riled she was a forceful presence. I wished I could move further back but the damp leather of the saddle stopped me. My skin was itching. *No way out.*

'I did it for Polly.' I decided then the truth would have to do though I knew she would never believe me. 'I did it so she would be safe.'

'Safe?'

Minnie's voice was suddenly quiet. She had stepped back into the darkness. I wished I could see the features of her face but the orange light cut a clean line across her torso, right across her throat, so she looked like a beautiful, headless corpse.

'He's been... fiddling with her.' I could have used coarser words, but I wasn't sure they would be accurate. Polly hadn't been explicit. 'I think he has. Getting her alone and such.'

I didn't know what it was like to realise your lover had a penchant for young flesh, but I wasn't surprised that Minnie fell silent. After all, her goodwill with Chester Merton depended on her being his mistress. Perhaps she'd see little Polly as a threat. If a man fancied young girls and you were not one, there was nothing to be done, except perhaps remove the girl from the situation. Maybe both Polly and I were on our way to being rapidly removed, just like Effie had been. I let the silence dwell uncomfortably between us until it started to scratch at me.

'Are you going to get rid of me?' I asked. I tried to watch her carefully for a lie.

'No,' she replied quickly. Then I realised I had asked the wrong question.

'Is he going to make you get rid of me?'

Minnie sucked in a breath sharply. So did I. Then I felt her hand, fumbling for mine. I let her twist her good finger with mine, an absurd parody of a childish promise.

'Not if I have anything to say about it,' she whispered. Her face had hardened in the half-darkness. There was a tight, furious pain there and for the first time, I thought it might be sadness.

'What Kate said, about concessions,' I spoke haltingly, worried she would snatch her hand back at any moment, 'what did Merton take from you?'

'Everything,' Minnie snorted darkly. 'Nothing of importance.'

'Which one?'

'Both.'

She stepped closer so her face was illuminated. I was shocked to see her blue eyes were filled with glittering tears. They reflected the orange light, looking like golden pools. I had so many questions inside me clamouring to get out but before I could ask any of them, there was a hammering on the door, and a familiar, disgruntled voice floated through:

'You still in there, Minnie? Hurry up, goddammit!'

It was Chester. He sounded drunk. He rattled the doorknob, but

Minnie must have turned the key in the lock. She pressed her hand against my mouth, silencing me, and we both stood there, holding our breath, listening to his curses outside.

'Why are you always doing this?' His voice was plaintive, and he sounded like a schoolboy all of a sudden. 'Why are you leaving me out?'

Minnie's face was close to mine, close enough that I could see the way she closed her eyes against his words. Not as if they hurt her, but as if they tired her. She took a long, shallow breath out, an exhalation of resignation, but she did not move to open the door, as I had thought she might. She stayed right where she was, her hand pressed over my lips. He slammed his palms against the door and we both flinched. Then there was quiet. Minnie pulled her hand away, watching me carefully as if she was worried I might shout out or try to get away from her. I didn't. Instead, I looked at her and tried to answer Chester's question from wordless hints in her eyes.

'Why?' I finally asked, hoarsely.

Her finger rubbed over the ridge of my collarbone thoughtfully, then pressed into the hollow the skin created underneath it. It felt like she was trying to dig out my bones. With her finger there, under my bone, feeling my pulse, she looked at me.

'Because I don't want to share you. I don't have to share everything.'

Her face was full of a tentative, uncertain question for permission. I nodded slowly.

'I don't want to share you either,' I whispered. It was a daft thing to say to a woman who was a mistress, and who had just admitted to having a girl like me in the past besides, yet it left my lips. She stared at me. Perhaps she knew the truth. *I love you*, the words whispered. I knew she heard them. She kissed them off my tongue. She tasted of clean, bitter vermouth and of that odd, deeply satisfying taste of relief that comes when someone has been given exactly what they wanted. I was pressed awkwardly against the leather saddle and slipped a little, not realising there was nothing underneath it to support me, and we crashed to the floor, my skull bouncing and her body mashed against mine in a tangle of skirts and knees and elbows. Still breathless, her lips sought mine clumsily in the jumble and I understood that she needed to have someone that belonged only to her. Maybe someone to replace Effie, the girl who had been taken from her. It didn't stop me from letting it happen. There had always been an ache inside me, a wound that had been numb for so long that only twisting pressure made it hurt. I had learned long ago that it could be satisfied even when someone is thinking of someone else.

There was no startling revelation in it, but with her yellow hair glowing in the orange light, and my neck cricked painfully against the sweaty leather legs behind us, it was not as bad as I had thought it would be.

'You left him once,' I whispered into her hair. It tasted of burning. I heard her breath catch in her throat and then slowly exhale, like the squeaky rhythm of a pair of bellows.

'I did,' she sighed.

I said no more. I did not ask. For how do you ask a woman to leave, for your sake, the man who keeps her? I would not ask.

'Did you mean it?' I said instead. Her finger found the back of my hand, rubbed over the raised skin, the dried trickle of ink and blood. I felt her lips in the darkness, sucking the skin.

'I had to come back,' she said, 'but I... did not expect you.'

Her words were hot on my damp skin. They were not an answer to any question I had asked but the way she gave them, hesitant and stumbling, made me believe they were true.

'Did not expect me to be what?'

'No.' She twisted her face and kissed me. Her tongue tasted coppery, like blood and ink. 'I didn't expect *you*.'

The words delicately tore something inside of me, with all the careful precision of a stitch unpicker, opening me up.

'Me either,' I said. After all, I had never expected to be loved by anyone. Yet here it was. I smiled and stroked her cheek. It amazed me every time how soft her skin felt under my calloused fingertips, like the silk stockings she bought fresh from the paper box. Minnie smiled back and closed her eyes. I watched her black eyelashes, clumped with mascara, and wondered how long we could hide away. Not long, as it turned out, when moments later a crash on the door interrupted us.

'What the fuck?' Minnie gasped, pulling away.

The door splintered away from the frame and, blinking up into the bright light from the hallway, two figures became clear. I squinted stupidly up at Kate Woods, who was looking down on our tangled limbs and flushed cheeks with irritation. Behind her was the unmistakable looming form of Chester Merton. He stared down at us in silence. I didn't dare breathe.

'You're up next,' Kate said quietly. She looked completely unsurprised to find us this way. I felt as if I was on the deck of a boat, lurching with the knowledge of it: when it came to Minnie, I was not special.

Minnie scrambled up, pulling her skirt back into place. I thought she might leave me there, sprawled like a whore in the toy room, but she reached down and offered her arm to me. I took it and launched myself up unsteadily, nastily aware of the slickness in my bloomers. At least Minnie had a long gown to hide hers. I didn't dare catch her eye. Unfortunately, it was impossible to avoid the searing iron of Chester's glare. Our eyes met, and I felt a tremor of familiarity. Jordan had loathed me perhaps just as much as he did.

Chester puffed out a breath of cigar smoke and nodded triumphantly, as if he'd confirmed something to himself.

'You'll regret it,' he said, and disappeared into the parlour.

I watched him go, dread building in the back of my head like freezing rainwater. For a second, Chester Merton had looked like he wanted to take everything from me too.

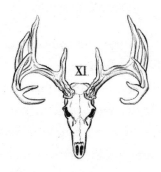

Chapter Eleven

The parlour was dark and full of smoke. It had the feeling of walking through a warm fog, as the heat of so many bodies and lit cigar tips filled the air. The stage had been set with small candles at the edge, making it glow magnificently, piercing the thick bluish smoke. I could see nothing as Minnie led the way through the mesh of bodies, stepping back to let me climb the small flight of dusty, squeaky stairs to the stage. I felt the gasp in the room rather than heard it. The creak of chairs as people leaned forward to stare at my skin, the movement of air around me as many mouths inhaled in surprise. Minnie stood up beside me, her teeth shining in the glow of the lights.

'Ladies and gentlemen, I am pleased to announce our newest act, our most remarkable performance of the evening: the Painted Mystic!'

I sat in the chair at the centre of the stage, waiting as Minnie pulled out an elaborate veil. She made a great show of attaching it to my hair and floating it over my face, leaving the rest of my body bare to the itching warmth of the light and the eyes of the audience.

'Tonight the mystic will take us on a spiritual journey into the world beyond for those who dare...'

As Minnie spoke, I tried not to fidget. Chester's words chased around in my head. The feeling was identical to the nights I would lie in bed, waiting for Jordan to return, knowing that some small look or tiny sin I had committed earlier would be leveraged over me for painful retribution. I tried to do what I had always done then, surrender to the inevitability of it, but I couldn't. The need to run was pulsing from my jiggling foot to my racing heart, but I was trapped onstage, staring back at a curious and indifferent audience. I tried to calm myself and pulled out my cards. Almost instantly, something settled in me. I might be trapped but I was not alone, not when I had the arcana at my fingertips. I sighed out a long breath as my hands fell into a familiar rhythm. I didn't care that the audience was following the flying cards with amusement. I half closed my eyes to better concentrate on the soft, repetitive slicing motion. Suddenly, beneath the semi-opaque veil, it was like seeing people through a mirror. It gave me a tiny thrill of power, that they were there but apart from me, entirely other. They couldn't harm me. I allowed my mind to drift and the gentle creep of separation to start until I felt that looseness in my mind, like my soul was a balloon only lightly tethered to my body. Blissfully, I stopped thinking about Minnie's tongue against my thigh, Chester's breath against my stomach as he stared at my tattoos, and the dead girl, Effie, whose life I was inadvertently living.

'Who will dare to ask questions? The mystic can reveal the deepest secrets of your heart. . .'

Minnie was walking to the front of the stage, inviting volunteers. A gentleman with a large brown moustache had raised his hand. When I set eyes on him, the world slowed. The prickling at the back of my neck returned, like unseen ant feet tickling across my skin, along soft, wet whispers from mouths no one could see. *Tell nothin'*. The remembered girl with the warning voice spoke softly into my mind but she could not help me now. Whoever she had been to me, she had abandoned me to the slums and was nothing more than a misremembered dream. Now I was alone. I shook my head, tasting panic on my tongue. Minnie didn't want it to be like the séance but the Knowing had not been this strong when I had read for Chester's friends. It had not been this audible since I was a child.

'The mystic will pull your cards, sir!'

I caught Chester's eye in the crowd, saw his taut features and fixed smirk, and there was a swooping in my stomach, like the sensation of falling from a bridge in a dream. The unexpected inevitability of pain was hurtling towards me and, this time, I could not wake up. *You'll regret it*, Chester had said. I thought of the girl he had sent away to her death but it was not enough to stop me. Something was coming, whether I liked it or not.

I pulled the man's cards. The Devil. Beside me, Minnie waited for me to speak but I couldn't. I was staring at a signet ring on the man's finger, a golden ball of pain and sadness. Minnie had begun talking, selling him some spiel about daring and adventures, but I watched his eyes. They were black as night and came to rest again and again on the small, flat-chested boys in petticoats at the back of the room: features only available to specific clientele. I didn't mean to look. I told myself I was looking for Effie but there it was, on the end of the line, knitting itself together out of shadows. It was pulling the dark fold in the curtain for its arms and the shadowed overhang of the bar for its skirt and I looked. I looked and I could not stop. I heard its whispered voice and did not turn my ears away: the thing coming that held the voice inside it was brimming with justice and rage and it chanted at me: *Hear me. See me. Look at me.*

Tell nothin'.

The thing about ghosts that no one will tell you is they are greedy. They ask to be seen but it is never just what they want.

Will you take my voice?

The viciousness of ghosts is they have too much to say and no way to speak it.

I'll tell you about Effie.

Hagglers, the lot of them, but they knew exactly what I wanted: I wanted to have a future with Minnie. I wanted to know how to survive. I could no longer hear Minnie's voice, the buzzing in my ears was too loud, like a bee struggling down towards my eardrum, and I could not take my eyes away from the hand, groping in the shadows of whores, trying to mould itself some eyes. So I took its voice. The taste of its anger was as rich as beef and blood on my tongue. Then I felt my mouth move but the voice was not my own.

'There is a secret, dark and deep, that young men and devils keep.'

In my peripheral vision, I saw Minnie's surprised but pleased expression. No doubt she thought that this was a good performance technique of mine, changing my tone to make myself more alluring to customers. She had no way to know the voice did not belong to me at all. Still it spoke, using my tongue, forming words of its own.

'There is a lock, blood and stone, that's spun in gold and worn on bone.'

The red flush of drink in the man's cheeks diluted. He twisted the stag ring on his finger. Minnie's mouth was moving noiselessly as I turned the next card. The Hanged Man. The little legs on the card danced on the air in a perilous jig.

'The stag roams free among the trees but falls when he sees...'

The last card. The Lovers. My eyes lifted to the back of the room, pulled by invisible string. Hotel De Wood had an infamous back door through which gentlemen entered when they had a very particular interest that disquieted the other patrons. They stood at the back of the room now, those objects of unsavoury interest, clearly shuffled in once the normal whores were seated, like a filthy secret, which they were. They called them chickens on the street and they looked like them, plumped and feathered and shining bright. My gaze roamed over each one, their boy bodies wrapped tight in corsets and their pretty mouths painted red. I didn't want to see him, freshly made from shadows and my voice, but there he was, on the end of the line. He stood aside from all the others, his bodice ripped and bloodstained, his plump lips bruised and very dead. On his neck was a pretty purple rope burn. He smiled triumphantly through his black and bloody lips and whispered a name into my heart.

'… Kennedy.'

The moustached gentleman erupted. The blonde who had been sitting on his lap, her buoyant breasts exposed and pale, was knocked to the floor as the young man's gold beringed finger pointed directly at me. Minnie was shouting placatingly, but it floated past me. I watched his moustache bristling, spittle catching in its hairs as it projected slowly through the air. Then a small boy's voice called out from the back:

'What happened to Kennedy, sir?'

'Boy killer!' another chirped out.

A row of little hard eyes and satisfied smirks. A hush descended. The gentleman was unmanned at the cry. He looked around him, like a man waking up from a nightmare and being surprised to find himself outside. He turned back to the stage and pointed the finger at Minnie. The ring on his finger sent its whispers over the air. Behind him, Kennedy laughed silently and I could do nothing but giggle. It rose on the air, a childlike trill. The audience pulled back from me, the man with the moustache glaring at Minnie.

'I don't know how you found this out,' the man said. 'But mark my words, freak, you'll pay for it.'

'Kennedy has something for you.'

He was a smart little ghost, I had to give him that, speaking in the third person as if he did not hold my tongue in his thrall. I spoke to the ring on the killer's hand, answering its golden questions. Silence fell and the man was struck dumb.

'Flora, stop it!' Minnie's hand was on my shoulder, her face tight with fear. 'He'll ruin us!'

'But Kennedy's coming.'

Minnie recoiled away from me. I didn't know what she had seen that scared her, but my eyes were pulled back to his face. It had begun now; there was nothing Minnie or I could do. The ghostly boy was moving forward, pushing through the crowd as if they were water. They shivered at his passing, the whores turning to each other and rubbing their bare eyes against his chill. When he pulled his bloodstained gown up to step over the candles, his footsteps knocked on the stage and the crowd's murmur grew with each one. Kennedy held out his hand to me. At last, the buzzing whispers ceased and my mind was filled with sweet quietness. Kennedy's hand was bleeding, the knuckle that had once borne a ring gifted from his lover now swollen and disjointed, blackened and broken. My hand rose to meet his, air and flesh. The man watched, his skull visible under his blanched, stretched skin. Kennedy smiled at him, with ring imprints stamped on his poor, sore mouth. Poor, vicious dead child.

'Kennedy wants his ring back, sir,' Kennedy whispered. My mouth moved and my arm gestured to the man's hand.

The murderer fell back from the stage, his arms stretched out to ward off Kennedy and me, tripping over tables and whores in his desire to run away. I wondered briefly if he could see his lover now.

'No, Kenny, no!' he moaned as he crashed away. 'I didn't mean it! I didn't mean it!'

As he ran, a booming wave of sound began, shouts and screams and cries, breaking over the stage with a fervour that made me wince. Minnie stepped back as if she had been knocked by a physical force. She looked at me helplessly, as if asking what we should do, but I could not answer. The stage was tilting away from me, a swaying deck of a ship. I tried to tell her with the pressure of my thoughts instead that I was ill, I must be, but nothing came out. *Stay in the room,* I tried to tell myself over and over but it did no good. Beside me, Kennedy grew stronger, his watery form taking on solidity and texture. He smiled pityingly and laid a hand on my shoulder. It couldn't be and yet it was. I could feel a tender, cold pressure there. The uncanny truth of it was an icy pebble, dropped into my belly: the spirits were trying to take me.

You wanted secrets, Kennedy shrugged. Ghosts are careless. They give no mind to broken limbs or fading heartbeats.

That's when I saw the Dead Rabbit. Struck immobile and dumb, his face was a flash in the crowd; dark hair, dark eyes and tell-tale tattoos: a four-leaf clover on his neck and Jordan's teardrop under one eye.

Tell nothin'.

I had broken a rule, the one rule I'd been given by the only person I could vaguely recall who had ever tried to keep me safe. This was the reward.

It's been a long time. Kennedy's grip tightened and my trembling heart rattled, quivering so hard I fell from my chair, though I felt none of it. For I was above it, looking at my quaking body from a great height, holding Kennedy's hand. It was starting to feel warm, though not yet entirely real, as if he were wearing very thick leather gloves.

Come. We followed the Dead Rabbit over the audience's heads, leaving my splayed body behind. I watched him walk slowly down the stairs to meet a partner at the open door, a man with a Chinese dragon tattooed on his neck – the watcher from the Bowery. He leaned against the doorframe as the Dead Rabbit handed him a card. He flipped it over to read something written on the back and I saw what it was. My cabinet picture. I could not move. I could not get close enough to see what had been written on the back of it before he slipped it into his coat pocket as the Dead Rabbit nodded, and the two vanished into the night. They were taking a picture of me, and knowledge of where I was, back to the gang, to Jordan, and there was nothing I could do about it. My arms and legs and mouth all lay useless on the little stage.

In the downstairs parlour, the murderer sat weeping. Kennedy brushed past me, a flutter of tattered skirts, and I knew I could not follow him either.

What about Effie? I thought desperately, pressing against the limits of my movements, feeling myself falling backwards as Kennedy ripped himself apart from my soul. Kennedy paused and grinned; cheeky and cruel.

You are the answer to your own question, he giggled.

Then he was gone and I was alone. Stuck. Weeping and dripping, that was all I could hear. On either side of the staircase were two growing pools of blood. It was the cranes. I could not back away. Slowly, with a sickly crunch of bone they turned their broken necks towards me. Their glass eyes were gone, and the empty black sockets filled with red, clotting blood. I was growing dizzy again, my body too heavy or too light to move, I could no longer tell. I could only watch them. *All the ghosts are awake tonight*, I thought. They lifted their crackling, varnished wings and took flight in a trail of blood.

Chapter Twelve

I had never died so I could not tell you if returning to my body after Kennedy was easier than coming back to life, but I had passed out before, one of the times Jordan had given me the dreaded abortifacient. On that occasion I had come to suddenly, gasping for air, violently assaulted by the cold daylight, the stench of the public outhouse I had collapsed in and the nauseating damp of my cheek against the wooden seat. Returning from Kennedy was like that, but in pieces rather than all at once. Sound came first.

'Flora! Flora! Wake up!'

Then a slapping sound, like wet feet on a stone floor. Then feeling came with it. A tapping at first, like a bird nudging at my ear, then firm and ringing, dry skin stinging my cheek and jostling my teeth. I opened my eyes. Black and yellow shapes loomed close and uncompromisingly bright, so I closed them again quickly.

'She's coming round. Abe, your flask.'

I heard Minnie's voice and smelled her scent above me. Then a liquid sloshing close to my ear. Cold metal bumped my teeth and the scratchy smell of cheap bourbon filled my nostrils, burning against my tongue. I recognised Abernathy's tobacco and the strength of his hands lifting me, sitting me up against a wall. I felt him sit beside me with a quiet grumble and wedge his shoulder underneath mine to keep me upright. I moaned and coughed, spluttering bourbon down my chin.

'Here you are, duck.'

Hester squatted in front of me, dabbing my face with a wet, dirty stocking. She smiled at me, but her eyes were concerned.

'You gave us a scare with your tricks,' she said quietly.

'A scare? Is that what we're calling it?'

Chester's voice. I could hear him but I couldn't see him, since Myrtle appeared too, breathless, her garish stage facepaint mask-like, right in front of me. The two of them were like a pair of absurd puppet heads, dancing before my eyes.

'That's what we're calling it, yes,' Minnie said.

'For God's sake, Minnie! She's bloody insane.'

My whole body jolted at Chester's words. The Angel Sisters gave one another sidelong looks. To be fair to them, they had warned me about the cost of playing mad. Foolishly, I'd not thought there would be a cost for not faking it either.

'Don't you dare. Not again.'

Minnie's voice was a low, deadly hiss and all of us flinched. I saw it on the twins' faces and felt it in Abernathy's arm. If Chester felt it, he wasn't deterred.

'I knew this was a bad idea, bringing another of these cheap girls into the house, but you persuaded me, said it was necessary—'

'Get fucked, Chester.'

The silence was a pool that Minnie's words dropped into. We watched the ripples extend out towards us. Hester and Myrtle moved slightly and I caught sight of Chester's profile. His jaw was tight, a shaft of dark shadow falling diagonally from his forehead to his ear.

His eyes swivelled to meet mine, the same way a dog's do when it is dreaming and feels a threat coming.

'This is all your fault,' he said.

I tried to open my mouth to explain, but I couldn't. I gaped at him, my mouth forming invisible bubbles like a fish drowning in air. He snorted and looked away.

'Madness.' He looked down at Minnie scornfully. 'This is all madness.'

'The police are here.'

We all turned to see Kate Woods standing by the door to the dressing room. It was then that I noticed the other performers were gone, only Hester and Myrtle had remained, and there was an eerie quiet to the building that I hadn't felt before. Kate was twisting one of her rings on her finger and she looked flustered. It was strange. I had not thought Kate Woods was the type of woman who could be flustered.

'Are they doing a raid?' Myrtle asked Kate.

Kate shook her head. 'They're here for her.'

She moved forward reluctantly, and it was then that I noticed how she moved like I was the centre of a circle she was drawing with her feet. She wanted to keep as far away from me as possible, but she looked at Minnie and Chester with irritation in her face.

'They want to speak to her,' she said. 'So you had better think of something quickly, and God forgive you for what you've brought into my house.'

'It wasn't my idea,' Chester said, but Minnie shushed him to be quiet.

'We need to get Flora out,' she said. 'Immediately.'

'And take her where?' Chester folded his arms furiously. Unlike Kate, his movements held no hesitation, only indignation and all of it was directed at Minnie. 'She's not coming home with us!'

'Where else should she go?' Minnie glared up at him. He shrugged, those grey, angry eyes resting on me.

'Damned if I know. Damned if I care.'

'You promised me, Chester.'

Abernathy stiffened beside me. There was a similar rigidity in my own flesh, as if somehow my skin knew that Minnie was on the verge of an important revelation, something that would open up her and Chester like the curtains of a play and all would be revealed, but she said no more. She simply looked up at him, her blonde curls in disarray over her small shoulders as she tilted her head to meet his eyes. He looked away.

'Well, we all made lots of promises, didn't we?'

Chester's words were clearly spoken to hurt, delivered with a disdainful curl of the lip. I wondered if they were about Effie. I wondered if they were about me. Minnie didn't move, but Kate did, stepping delicately between them.

'Is now the time?' Kate cautioned quietly, glancing between the two of them. Neither responded. Minnie's eyes never left Chester's face and he, in turn, kept his eyes fixed on a nearby vanity, fingers automatically twiddling his oak bowl pipe like a baton. Minnie didn't move, but Kate looked at the Angel Sisters.

'Can you take her with you?' she asked. 'For a few days?'

I felt like baggage being passed off to an unfortunate footman, and stiffened. Abernathy shuffled a little beside me, responding to my change in posture. He was aware that I was becoming more awake even if no one else was.

'Why are we trying to hide her?' Chester rubbed a long hand through his hair pomade, creating slick blond pieces that fell forward onto his forehead. 'She killed a man. When a dog is rabid, you take the bitch out and shoot her.'

'I didn't kill him.'

I found my voice, though it felt weak, as though I'd been screaming all night. They looked at me as if amazed I could be cogent after what had happened. I swallowed hard, the tang of the bourbon making my throat raw.

'I didn't kill Kennedy,' I said. 'It wasn't my fault; he was hanged by that man.'

'Jesus Christ.' Kate's face had blanched white. 'What the fuck have you been telling this girl, Minnie? All our trade secrets?'

'Kennedy told me,' I said before Minnie could respond. 'I didn't kill him; I just did what you told me.' I found Minnie's face, blank with her blonde eyebrows raised in dumb surprise. 'I'm sorry.'

Kate closed her eyes at my words, as if looking at me had become too much.

'Sorry? You're sorry?'

The fear was gone now, replaced by malice, and I was reminded of Chester's friends on the night of the séance.

'Sorry doesn't cut it, not with a dead man hanging in my parlour! And before you say another word, no, it is not Kennedy.'

Kate held up one finger with a ruby on it to keep me silent, though honestly, I was far too frightened to interrupt. I fixed my eyes on the ruby's red gleam.

'It could not be Kennedy, since Kennedy was found hanged in Bowling Green Park six weeks ago, but rather his lover, a very particular patron of ours and a close friend of the mayor, who is now swinging in my downstairs parlour. Unsurprisingly, his many friends who attended tonight fetched the police and are saying it is all our fault he is dead.'

'It was Kennedy,' I whispered. 'He went into the parlour, I saw him go.'

'Stop it, Flora!'

Minnie's voice was a surprising bark of outrage, making me jump.

Hester and Myrtle looked down at their shoes, shrinking away from me like I was infected. Only Abernathy stayed close, his quiet, measured breathing with a slight wheeze comforting me. I didn't look at him, but felt his hand squeeze the tips of my fingers as I pushed them into the scratchy hair of the carpet. *I didn't mean it*, I thought silently to him, furiously. He could not have heard me but he squeezed again and to me it sounded like: *I know.*

'The police want her, so give her to them,' Chester said and my stomach dropped. He shrugged carelessly. 'They'll question her awhile then drop her back in the slums.'

Just the thought of spending any time with the police made my guts cramp painfully so I couldn't help but emit the smallest of moans. Many of the police were Irish, and many took B'hoy bribes. They'd take an interest in me, and I didn't think I would enjoy the experience. I'd thought I had the measure of Chester Merton. I'd thought his punishment would be to send me back to Five Points to die, but now I saw that he didn't care too much how I stopped breathing as long as I did.

'We can't.' Kate twisted her ring again, spinning it on her finger. 'Those friends of his have said that for her to have such knowledge of the death of the boy, she must be involved. We must be involved.'

'Oh, it's "we" now, is it?' Chester sneered. 'I've naught to do with it.'

'Oh, you think so?' Kate grabbed him by the lapel, rumpling his shirt in her sharp fist. 'If you think you're gonna leave me in the lurch, Merton, you've another think coming. I'll tell them all about you, about which door you come in, shall I?'

Kate's voice became rougher in anger, and for the first time I heard her Brooklyn roots. I saw Hester and Myrtle's scandalised look at one another as they caught Kate's implication and looked quickly at Minnie. She didn't seem to care. Her face was blank, her eyes unfocused, just as it had been the night she had stumbled to bed in a poppy fog. If it bothered her that her lover occasionally fucked boys, she didn't show it.

'Now, now, Kate, let's not get nasty.'

Chester smiled sweetly, as if Kate had only said something very amusing, and the hairs on my arms stood up. I knew that look. Chester slapped his hand over Kate's and pulled her closer with that same disconcerting speed with which he had grabbed me. She stumbled into him and his other hand wrenched her dark curls back in such a tight fist that I winced.

'It's your whorehouse, sweetheart, and everyone knows it,' he sneered. 'What you offer to well-meaning God-fearing folk to corrupt them is on your conscience.'

'Oh, I see. On my conscience but on your cock, is it?' Kate leaned closer into his face. I was secretly impressed with her grit, but then I supposed standing up to men like Chester was part of her daily routine. 'When I gave you my best girl, all those years ago, let you take her and ruin her, you were more than happy to be business partners.'

'She picked me.' Chester's finger prodded Kate's chest and then pointed at Minnie. 'She chose to leave you. Everything would have been fine if your quack excuse for a doctor hadn't fucked everything up!'

'Shut the hell up!' Minnie said.

I saw the way she looked daggers at the two of them, and I saw the triangle of their relationship clearly for the first time. Kate, the madam; Chester, the customer; and Minnie, the best girl. I could see the years of bargaining and trading, the red threads of it tangling between them and the abandoned mad girl from the past. Effie, who had caught Chester's eye and been punished for it. What I didn't see was what had pulled it all apart. *I don't have to share everything*, Minnie had said.

'What are we going to do?' Minnie glared.

'Pin it on her,' Chester said, throwing me a nasty glance. 'We wouldn't be in this if she hadn't run her fucking mouth.'

'They'll blame her for Kenny's death,' Kate warned. 'As well as thinking she pushed that lad downstairs to take a short drop and a sudden stop.'

'So?' Chester shrugged, shoving his hands in his pockets. 'What's the punishment going to be for a little cocktease like Kenny? They'll probably thank her.'

I hated him from the top of his shiny, sticky hair to the tips of his freshly polished shoes. I imagined that he and Kennedy's lover probably had much in common. Maybe they were friends. I found myself wishing that the Knowing had led me to Chester's secrets, but then I remembered I knew about Polly and he had no shame. The likelihood of remorse taking him to the end of a rope was minimal, sadly.

'These friends want someone to blame.' Kate spoke slowly but I could see her fingers twitching and her eyes flicking to the door. She was worried about keeping them waiting. 'They'll likely push for the noose.'

There was a slight echo to that word, as if it was made of firmer air than the others and wafted between the mirrors, hitting their silver surfaces with a soft chinking noise. *Tell nothin'*. Somehow the words continued, a memory unravelling with the sound of a soft, Bronx voice:

Tell nothin' 'bout the Knowing. Oh, they'll use you awhile, tell you that you're special and the like, but it all ends sameways. They call ye mad or kill you.

I'd lived in Five Points for all of my life and avoided anyone trying to kill me for what I saw in the cards. That was the benefit in being a nobody: nobody was looking for you. This was the price for being seen. The urge to run was as instinctive and primal as the urge to cough or vomit, but I couldn't run; I couldn't even stand. I tested my weight against my feet, just to see, and my ankles shook like broken carriage wheels.

'What? Why?' Minnie sat heavily on the stool by the vanity in front of me. The edges of her skirts tickled my shins. 'He killed himself. It's obvious.'

'Course it's fucking obvious, but what's also obvious is she—' Kate pointed at me and I tried not to flinch '—stood up on my goddamned stage and told a powerful man's secrets! Course they want consequences! Didn't I teach you to manage girls better than this?'

She gave me such an intense look of dislike at that moment that I held no hopes of ever being permitted into Kate Woods' establishment again, if I could possibly escape it without finding myself in jail. She hated me. Not only because I had brought trouble, but because I belonged to Minnie, the girl she'd taught better. I was her failure too, by inheritance.

'God, Flora—' Minnie looked at me, helplessly '—why did you do it?'

Because I was told to, I wanted to say but I sensed there was no point. No one cared that they had got exactly what they'd asked for. No one cared that someone who deserved to die, who had tortured and used young sweet children, was now dead and some sort of justice had been done. For who wants justice for a poor dead boy?

'Well, better her than us,' Chester said.

He looked at me then, really looked at me as a person who he had spoken to and lusted after, not as a piece of shit at his feet. He had promised revenge and would make it happen if I didn't do something about it. There wasn't much fight left in me; perhaps about an inch of it loitering somewhere in my boots but I sucked it up, drawing it up through me like a dying plant and glared back at him. If he was throwing me under the train I was damn well taking the motherfucker with me.

'They might ask me questions,' I said softly, holding his eye. 'They might ask me where I've been. What I've seen.'

It was a wild swing and I think everyone in the room knew it. The Angel Sisters looked down at me like I was a little impressive but mostly like I was pitiable to be making such an attempt at a man like Chester. Kate almost rolled her eyes, but I didn't care. They didn't know what I knew. He'd gotten rid of Effie, but he wouldn't get rid of me.

He laughed. 'You think you've got something on me, slut?'

I blinked slowly. My imagination conjured Polly between us, and all the things she might say. His eyes shifted uncomfortably. I could tell he was wondering if Polly would actually speak out against him, and if it would make any difference. After all, many men fucked their servants.

'Pretty young though, and with the boys as well...' I whispered. 'Bad for a man's reputation.'

His eyes swivelled to me. The crushed and slightly fearful look on his face showed that, for a second, he worried I could read his mind. Slimy bastards like him always think they're unique. I couldn't help it, I snorted with irrepressible laughter.

'You little bitch!' His face was twisted up in a savage snarl and in a fluid motion the Angel Sisters had both stood up in front of me, facing him.

'Back off,' Myrtle said.

'Minnie!' Chester looked at her, expecting her to call her girls off but she didn't.

'We can't give her to them,' she said. 'Sit down.'

She caught my eye and I could tell from the widening of those blue irises that she didn't want anyone to know about Chester and Polly. It seemed odd to me since he had clearly fucked little boys too, but if it was keeping her from handing me over, I'd go along

152

with it. I nodded discreetly but he saw. His rage vanished as quick as a lamp turned off. Immediately, the suave gentleman's façade returned and he languidly took a seat on the edge of the vanity, smiling at the Angel Sisters politely.

'What are we going to do then?' he said. No one was fooled. It was like watching a fighting tom-cat retreat and prepare for another pass.

'She could play mad,' Hester said. 'They can't hang her if she's mad.'

'I've got a good mad doctor,' Chester said, warming to the idea quickly. *I bet you do*, I thought bitterly, thinking of Effie in Blackwells. 'He can see her and give her a—' he paused and his cheek twitched '—a treatment at Bellevue.'

I sucked in a breath. Everyone in Five Points knew of the hospital and feared it. Bellevue hospital was where people went to die, the only place in the city worse than Five Points, for at least in Five Points you might die in the privacy of your own bed. I saw the way Chester's shoulders straightened and the sharp, devious look he shot me. He might not be able to see me hanged, but he had a petty revenge to wreak on me somehow, and if he could deliver it through a doctor's needle or imprisonment in the madhouse, he would. I wondered if it had been the same for Effie. I never once imagined that there would be an occasion where I would prefer to return to Five Points. I began to sweat behind the knees.

'I suppose it might work...' Minnie sounded doubtful, reluctant, and for a moment hope soared in me. She wasn't sure. There was another way out, a way without Chester. I swallowed hard.

'We could leave,' I whispered.

'What, run away?' Chester's head turned to me so quickly I almost jumped, but I tried to hold on to Minnie's eye. It would only work if she trusted me, if she trusted us, whatever fragile thing we were.

'We could just go, Minnie.' I leaned forward and squeezed her knee. 'We could just get out, like you did before.'

'What have you been telling her?' Chester's words snapped through the air. Minnie refused to look at either of us.

'Minnie.' I shook her knee a little bit. I was close, I felt it, there was resolve in there that was melting. Twelve years with him; no one could tell me she hadn't dreamt of leaving. She'd left him once, after all. 'Minnie. We'll be fine.'

There was a chance here, but the space to take it was closing rapidly. Minnie didn't move. She stared at her dress, biting her bottom lip and then, slowly, shook her head. I sat back, cold disappointment seeping into my fingers. In her silence, I heard the quiet click of the door of our moment closing. Now we were both trapped. I didn't look at Chester but I could sense his smug, relieved satisfaction.

'No one's running anywhere and leaving me in the goddamned shit,' Kate said. She checked a silver pocket watch. 'They want to speak to you now, so what's it to be: is she mad or guilty?'

I wondered if I was both.

'Miss Woods?' a voice called. Irish indeed. 'Will you be ready for us now?'

I sank back behind my eyes, folding myself away until I was only the shell of a woman waiting for her judgement. Far away, deep inside, I curled up tightly and braced for the blow like I had always done when there were painful hardships to be endured.

'Flora, you have to choose.'

I opened my eyes. Minnie was leaning towards me, the vibrant purple of her silk gown enveloping my bare knees. I could feel the warmth of her skin like the heat surrounding a candle. She looked at me with desperation in the slight squeeze of skin between her eyebrows. Not quite a furrow, more like the pleat in a skirt. I knew she couldn't bear to condemn me, so she was asking me to do it to myself. I shook my head, snorting softly.

'You didn't expect me,' I whispered, ignoring Chester's frown. 'Did you mean it?'

Did you mean that you love me?

She looked at me briefly, eyes fluttering up to mine like a blue tit's wing and then away.

'Yes.' Her voice was nothing more than a breath between us, lost in the sound of shuffling fabric as she reached a hand down to press against my knee. 'What do you want to do?'

I stared at her. I wondered if this was love according to Minnie – letting me choose my own downfall. A pity or a mercy for a girl she had fucked. Or perhaps she thought we could still get out of this if it could only blow over, but when I thought of a future with Minnie now, I could not picture it. All I could think of was her standing in the half-light in Kate's closet, the light severing her at the neck, a faceless corpse.

'Flora?' she prompted.

Sitting on the itchy carpet with the cold wallpaper, I realised distantly I'd been making these choices my whole life. Reckoning between a series of non-choices where the future offered was as dark as any other. The answer was always the same: *they call ye mad or kill you.*

'I don't want to die,' I said.

Minnie nodded, turning to Kate. 'She'll play mad.'

Chapter Thirteen

She'll play mad, Minnie had said, and it was just like that: a play. What comes after is snatches of memory; my own ghosts, coming out in the dark over the longest and cruellest weekend of my bitter little life. The first part was easy. I was demure, submissive, distant and detached as they marched me down the long corridor of Bellevue hospital, squeezing me through a river of groaning voices and stinking bodies. People were laid on the floor, eyes vacant, waiting for death, as we drifted past. I kept my mouth closed, trying not to breathe their air. I tried not to notice or be noticed by the few battered stovepipe hats I saw, or the flash of a red neckerchief around a Dead Rabbit's throat. Like a hunted animal, I knew survival was often in being small and quiet.

The second part was simple, too. I sat on a metal bed with stained beige sheets. Minnie sat beside me, the concerned but generous employer of the mad girl, as a weasel-faced doctor spoke to Chester at the end of the bed and looked down at me like a scab to be harvested. I knew bad things would be coming, the same way I had known from the sound of Jordan's boots if a beating was in order.

So I was quiet and limp and let my spirit drift away, following on the currents Kennedy had left inside me. I still felt it when the needle went in. Minnie held my head to her breast, mouthfuls of her sweaty, damp skin against my teeth as I thrashed against the burn of something poisonous entering my body.

'The mercury creates a fever which helps sweat the lady's disease away,' the doctor said. 'That's most common for this type of madness. Inevitable side effect of the lady's disease.'

'Shhhh, love, shhhh darling.' Minnie's words were muffled against my hair, the sweet clean smell of her a blessed relief amongst the harsh tang of ammonia.

'Oh yes.' Chester's voice was cheerful. 'Most common among slum girls. Or so I've heard.'

My last lucid thought was that Chester would be the one to know how common syphilis was among slum prostitutes, but then the burning began. I realised he didn't just want to kill me; he wanted me to scorch out my mind until there was nothing but a shell and whispers. The shadows of the bedposts were stretching towards me, their ghostly hands made of splinters and claws.

Memories are like pearls on a string. When you touch one, the others tremble. Our minds are houses with locked trap doors, and when poison burns the building to the ground, the bones of hidden thoughts emerge from the dust. A face from my childhood, kind and familiar, cupping my cheeks and whispering, *Stay put in the room, little cub.* A beautiful girl, a cloud of black hair and a smile with a tooth missing, pushing me back into one of the basement rooms of the Old Brewery. *Stay in the room.* I recalled the illicit rush of disobedience, of opening the door the tiniest crack and setting my face against the stripped wood. I saw it all in the hideous darkness of the sludgy moat of trickling water and waste around the building.

A thrashing head, a small body held tight against a slimy slum wall. A gleeful, dreadful smile sharp as a fox, baring its teeth at me. A horribly familiar pair of nasty grey eyes, always greedy. A slick of blond, polished hair. He was the man we all feared, the fox man; he came and took turns with all the girls. His white paw giant against her dark throat, my friend, as she whispered fruitlessly: *No, no, no, no.* Then my own voice took the words, swallowing them whole like lemon sherbets, as my own face thrashed against a sweat-drenched pillow.

'No! No! No! No!'

'Wake up, Flora, it's all right.'

A cool hand with missing fingers pressed to my head, the familiar firm swell of the muscled palm blessedly soft against my brow.

'She needs water, she's burning up.'

Minnie's face swimming in and out of my vision, sometimes one of her, red hot and burning, and sometimes many of her, doubled and tripled like a cascade of cabinet photographs. Cabinet photographs. The Dead Rabbit had my cabinet photograph. I saw him trotting nonchalantly down the steps of Hotel De Wood; I reached out my hand to grasp the wool of his jacket but instead felt handfuls of slippery satin.

'No, she has to sweat it out, that's the treatment. The madness that comes with syphilis can only be treated this way, it's very progressive.'

More needles. Another thick, burning knot of fire in my arm. I clutched the satin in my hands, gathering it to me, pulling the soft-smelling centre of it closer and closer until my face was pressed against a warm hiding place. A heart beating, a stomach gurgling. A corner to hide as ghosts gathered close by. They could feel me weakening, wanted to press through, to use my skin like a cheesecloth to pass between worlds. A girl bony with a wasting disease, a soldier with an infected leg mouldering away beneath his knee. In between their spectral faces, the living were pale and broken in comparison.

'We should leave her here,' I heard Chester say. His mouth was moving slower than it should be, teeth yellow and black.

'She'll be all right soon.' Her face was slanted in my field of vision, pulled long like the hall of mirrors at the fair. I tasted the tangy air of the hospital; sweet ethanol and ammonia. Medicine and other people's piss. My head burned as my eyes turned – a blinding white-hot searing pain that produced a moan like a cow or a beast. I felt it pulled from me like taffy stretched between hands.

'Look at her, Minnie! She's clearly fucking insane.'

'No!' Her sharp voice, her red lips speaking close to my cheek. 'No, I won't do it, not again.'

A voice close to my cheek, speaking hot words into the burning shell of my ear.

'I love you,' it whispered. 'I love you. Survive, please; all you must do is survive and then… anywhere, I promise you.'

'What are you saying?' A sharp, male voice, as hard as the needles full of poison.

'Just calming her, Chester.'

'Maternal is hardly your colour, Min.'

I felt a warm body flinch against mine.

'Whose fault is that?' Minnie's voice smelled like coffee and sounded like glass. 'She's coming home with us.'

She's coming with us. Memories like pearls, dropping slowly to the floor and scattering across the boards. I stumble over my skirt and into a wet puddle. My paper doll drowns in mud. The fox man is back with a group of men with holes for faces and arms like houses and they drag her out of our small, shared bed in the Old Brewery. My screams die on my tongue, no matter how much breath I wrench up from my lungs. *No, don't take her!* There she is, my cloud-haired girl, the girl who taught me cards and brushed my hair, who named the ghosts and taught me everything I knew about how to live with the Knowing. *Tell nothin'.* Now her balled fists are cotton-candy balls pounding their leathery backs. I scramble to stop them, I scramble to hold on to her, the friend who knows about the Knowing, the only person who loves me as I am, but she kicks me away. Her dark eyes are wild with love. *Run, cub! Run!*

I ran. When I came back, snotty with tears and cold, she was gone. The fox man took her away and left me with the ghosts.

The next face I saw was small and pale, like a wide-eyed barn owl. My eyes hurt a little less and the shadows re-formed to their standard spaces, fitting perfectly under beds and behind cabinets. I smelled fresh bread and leather. Hamilton Square. I noticed that the room was different somehow, the wallpaper yellowed and the wood aged and for a moment I was afraid that I had grown old, but then I realised the owlish face was Polly's. She sat beside me, the soft weight of her against my hip with a wet cloth in her hand, and she was unchanged.

'Shhhh,' she whispered, her crooked teeth making a little whistle. 'You're at home, with me. It's Tuesday. Missus said to tend you. You've a fever.'

I nodded carefully, though I didn't understand the words. I could hear close by the humming of Cook and the clatter of pots. It must be Polly's room. Abernathy loomed above me, the creases of his face deep with worry. I wanted to know if it had worked, if playing mad had saved us and it was all over, but I was too tired. I sighed. He leaned close to me, his breath bitter with coffee and stale with cigarettes, and pressed something into my palm. The well-known ridges of Jordan's knife handle, the slightly rusted bumps on its familiar steel edge. I couldn't speak but it didn't matter. Abernathy's yellowy brown eyes and tight, slightly pursed lips told me what I needed to know.

You're not safe here.

I closed my eyes with a hiss. The past was tipping towards me like water cresting the bow of a boat but I fought it, swallowing back the film of bile and spit gathering in my mouth as Abernathy slipped the knife under the edge of my mattress. I nodded painfully, every moment holding my thoughts in this reality an effort like I had never known. My head was swaying, my mind loosening with the same kind of flying dizziness I felt in the Knowing, only now each swing was accompanied by a lurch of sickness and searing pain behind my eyes. I retched drily, gagging on air, and Polly pressed the damp cloth to my brow.

'It's the mercury sickness,' she whispered. 'Mr Chester wanted to send you to Blackwells. Said you were mad.'

Not surprising. It was more surprising he hadn't done it.

'Minnie stopped it. She yelled at him about another girl, long ago.' Polly lifted a cup into my field of vision. 'Try to drink something.'

She held it to my lips and my teeth chipped painfully against the china. I swallowed, the cold water a relief in my dry mouth. It felt like I had been screaming for hours. Through the swirling red circles behind my eyes, I watched Abernathy's hand press onto Polly's shoulder as he left the little room. The door closed with a click that resounded painfully in my ears and I winced, juddering water down my front. Someone had changed me into a nightshift, and the dribbles of water rolled down my breasts to seep coldly between the fabric and my belly button. I shivered, my skin puckering. I lay back against the pillow. If this was Chester's revenge it was ugly, but I had survived worse, and it sounded as if Minnie had wrestled back the upper hand. I didn't want to think about what the cost of that would be. Already, I could see the shadows furling together under the windowsill. I looked at Polly's door. There was no lock. If something was coming, something or someone like Kennedy, I wasn't sure I had the strength to not look. I tried to smile at Polly.

'Thanks, cub,' I rasped. 'Did you know her? The other girl?'

I didn't want to speak Effie's name aloud for fear I might summon her. I kept my eyes on Polly's face and did not look at the shadows. I wondered if this was how Effie had died. Her blood boiling, poison smouldering out the recesses of her mind.

'Minnie says it was before me.' Polly mopped my brow. 'That Mister Chester sent her away.' It was strange, I thought, to hear Polly call Minnie by her first name, but perhaps there were different rules downstairs.

'I'm glad you're here.'

'Me too,' I croaked, though I could not be sure it was the truth. My mind was full of the past, and ghosts lingered nearby. Not to mention that somewhere out there in the city, a Dead Rabbit had my photograph.

'Has anyone come?'

'No—' Polly hesitated '—but there's been some men watching the servants' yard. Cook shoved them off.'

'Tattoos?'

'I couldn't see but... I think so.'

I closed my eyes again. They'd found me. I was too hollowed out to feel anything but despair. The mercury had burned the core out of me. There was nothing I could do. Even lifting my head was agony. I could not possibly run away. Polly seemed to be reading my mind because she petted my sweaty face and said:

'You'll be all right if you stay inside. Minnie won't let anything happen to you. Just wait until you're better.'

Polly tucked the blankets around my shoulders and tears spilled from my eyes. Her tenderness was as sharp and deep-reaching as a blade between the ribs.

'Thank you, cub.'

Polly smiled down on me, her smile tremulous.

'You remind me of them.' She brushed sweaty tendrils of my hair away from my eyebrows. Her hands were deliciously cold and I sighed. 'Those lasses in the Old Brewery who watched my back.'

When one pearl trembles, the others follow. I remembered her face then, the kind and familiar face of the older girl who had protected me from violence, cherished the Knowing, scolded me and watched me and taken my beatings. *Stay in the room, cub. Tell nothin'*. I saw her dark cloud of fluffy hair, her yellowy brown eyes. The memory of her had been burnt out of the deepest part of my mind by the sorrow of her being stolen from Five Points and yet her name still eluded me. I closed my eyes, tearing up. Had I not remembered because I didn't want to, or because it hurt too much to have loved her and then, so cruelly, have lost her? I thought of Jordan's heavy scent, Chester's lingering gaze, Minnie's obstinate kisses, the heavy cage of my sickening body and the distant press of the Dead Rabbits, crowding around the house like wolves with my scent on their slavering tongues. All of the times I stayed when I should have run. Was it all penance for the time when I had?

'I ran away,' I whispered. 'I let them take her.'

'Go to sleep,' Polly whispered. I did.

*

'Wake up, Florence.'

A soft voice above me, warm and tender.

'Wake up, my little flower.'

There were moths in my dreams and their wings beat softly against

163

my neck. I reached up to swat them away, but my hand met hard skin. A finger. I groped in the darkness for the blanket to cover me up, perhaps it had fallen off, but it was trapped. The finger still roamed. The darkness was complete, but my eyes adjusted slowly. The little, windowless room of Polly's came into view, the floor mat she was sleeping on beside the bed illuminated by a chink of yellow light from under the door. Beside me on the bed, a tobacco- and whisky-smelling shadow loomed. A man was in the room. Not just any man. My nostrils flared against the metallic scent of ink. Jordan.

'Time to come home, Florence.' His fingers traced the tattoos of my breasts without sight, as only he could. 'Let's not wake your little friend.'

Polly was here. Polly was here in the room and had already suffered at the hand of one bad man. In the way that only people like us could, I knew she was only feigning sleep. Her perfect, rhythmic breathing had fooled Jordan but not me. Twelve years old was around the ripe age for a man like Jordan. Whatever I did, I needed to do it quick.

'How did you find me?'

My voice was hoarse, my words painful to produce. My back still trembled with lingering tremors of fever. I didn't know if I would be strong enough for this.

A flash of yellowy white above me, as Jordan's grin caught the light beyond the door.

'This, love.'

He held something up to my face. Its slippery surface brushed my nose. I didn't need to see it to know what it was. The smell of development solution was tangy in my nostrils. My cabinet portrait. Kennedy had shown me this would happen, though knowing it hadn't helped. The wheel of fortune turned in my mind, relentless and unforgiving.

'How did you get in?'

I tried to move my hand slowly to the bumpy edge of the mattress, feeling for the wooden knife.

'Special invitation.'

He turned the photograph over, just as I'd seen the Dead Rabbit do in Hotel De Wood. Someone had sent a message from there to Jordan.

'Imagine it, I'd had lads looking all over for you, even over with the B'hoys, and here I get a hand-delivered note telling me to collect what's mine.'

His lips were close to mine; I could see the sickly glisten and smell the cheap whisky on them. His words were gleeful.

'Seems you're not as popular uptown as you thought you were.'

I felt the hilt of the knife and pulled it out, pointing at him in the space between us, holding my breath.

'I'm not going with you,' I said.

We sat still as statues then, the velvet darkness wrapped around us. I begged for a sense of the Knowing, for a sense of what was to come, but only saw that old familiar face: *Can't summon it*, she whispered. If I could, wouldn't I have saved her?

'What are you gonna do with that, love?' Jordan whispered.

That tone, those familiar questions I'd heard most of my life that didn't require answers. His hand moved quickly. The knife clattered from my hand and onto the floorboards. Jordan bore down on me, his leathery fingers tight around my throat. Bright sparks burst inside my eyelids.

'You think you're gonna leave me, little flower?'

His whispered breath tickled my ear, in the same way it had done when he fucked me. So much of it was similar, I realised absurdly as my breath choked in my throat, my chest burning.

'You'll be fucking dead first, my sweet.'

There was only darkness and the dizzying reflections of his eyes. Then, the rustle of blankets beside us, and a sharp ringing jab over his shoulder. I felt the push of it ricochet through me. Jordan released me, growling like a slapped dog as he turned and I rolled on my side, coughing and gulping sweet air into my sore lungs. Polly's bare white feet glowed on the floor. The knife wobbled absurdly in his shoulder, barely pierced him, trembling there in maybe an inch of skin as he turned to Polly.

'Little bitch!'

Polly took a stumbling, frightened step back. I thought of the friend I had lost to the hands of men like him. No more. I gasped in breath and reached up, grabbing the knife out of Jordan's back. He roared in pain, it clearly hurt more in the removing than it had in the stabbing, and spun to face me. I didn't even need to move. He turned into it so easily that it was only the work of a moment to thrust his blade up between his ribs. The squeaking crunch of it – a sound like jointing a raw chicken – was unreasonably loud in the small room. He was sitting on the bed, one hand braced behind him as the other patted ineffectually at his chest. We were all shadows, made of soft fabric sounds and heavy breaths, but the knife held all the glinting light from the doorway, silver dipped in yellow and glowing. Whispers began around me, soft at first but then loud and keening, drawing close to his body as the puttering, stifled breath of him came slower and slower. We watched.

'Is it over?' Polly whispered.

I pushed him back with a nervous jab of my fingertips. He fell like a puppet with his legs skewed oddly underneath him. Just a dead body now, skin and blood and hair piled up on mattresses made of straw and feather that was piled up on earth and stone. I nodded. Polly jumped into motion behind me.

'You have to go!' Polly rushed past, opening the door and letting a yellow slant of light into the room. 'Mister Chester will blame you, but he won't blame me. I'll say I was attacked. You have to run!'

Run, cub! Run!

I was rooted where I stood, spirits hissing in dusty floorboards. The shadows climbed out of the cracks like steam rising from the pavement on a hot day. They began to build themselves but I would not look. Not yet. I stared at Jordan's face, his dark eyes open but dead, his mouth still open but dead, his blood still thickening on his chest and dripping onto the floorboards, but all of him dead. My cabinet photo was caught at the edge of his pool of blood, black oil in the darkness, smudging the white edges.

For you, the whispers said, luring me close. I turned it over. *Hamilton Square, Chester Merton.* He had not been able to have me hanged or sent to Blackwells but he could invite a madman into his house, uncaring of the child who slept beside me. I saw it then, the legacy of blood dripping from the man upstairs.

You can't summon it, my friend had told me, but you can, oh, you can. You can usher it in on the wings of death and blood; you can tempt it like a scavenging bird swooping low on a carcass. The Knowing sniffed blood and it came, how it came.

I pulled the knife out of Jordan's chest, ignoring the faint gurgle of blood bubbles on his lips. I was not afraid of who was coming in the shadows. I lifted my head and looked for their face. In the doorway a shadowed figure stood, a woman with ire and coal in her heart and a burning hatred for Chester Merton that couldn't be quenched.

It's you.

I didn't need to ask her name. I recognised her with my soul. Here she was, after all this time of waiting for me to look into the Knowing and see her, cloud-haired and ravenous. They had another girl, the Angel Sisters had said, but they were wrong about where she had ended up. With hollow eyes and cold bare feet, her spirit loitered in Hamilton Square, not in the madhouse. Effie tilted her head at me, the girl whose footsteps I had haunted, and licked her phantom lips.

Will you help me?

I nodded and let the Knowing take me.

Together we walked up the back staircase, reunited, a blend of air and flesh, following the dark feathers of spirit birds made of dust and bones.

I am a ghost, my heart whispered, *I am a ghost.*

The birds glided before us, leading the way to where we both knew he would be. Chester had had his revenge on me, he'd brought Jordan to my door, but he didn't know of the secrets lurking below stairs. We were coming.

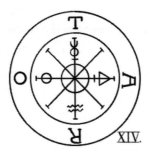

Chapter Fourteen

I smelled blood. I tasted it, under my tongue, on my lips.

'Flora! Florence, can you hear me?'

My eyes opened. The light was a dim, gold glow. Inside the black edges of my vision, I saw something small and muscular moving in front of my face. Coming close and then moving away, as if swaying like washing on a line. They were pink blistered hands.

'She's opened her eyes, Minnie!' a small, relieved voice called. 'She's following my finger!'

Minnie. I remembered Jordan. I remembered Effie. I remembered the knife in my hand. I remembered nothing else.

'We need to get her out of here.' Minnie's voice was oddly frantic. 'Now!'

I felt a firm, bristled surface against my face. It was the rug outside the suite I had lived in with Minnie. It scratched against the sensitive hollow of my ear and I turned my head to twist my ear away from it. The portraits towered; long bodies stretched towards the sky. The many eyes of the masters of Hamilton Square watched me pitilessly.

'You'll be all right. Mr Merton's hurt but he'll live and the tattooed man's dead,' the small voice whispered, its sound echoing from small, owlish blue eyes. Polly. *Who hurt Chester?* I wondered but then I remembered the sound of Jordan's last breath. I didn't know if I would ever be all right. I closed my eyes again.

Rattling. My teeth were rattling. My body trembled. I remembered windows shaking once, battered by clubs and fists in the draft riots. This time, there was no shelter. I felt slimy, slick with sweat. I remembered the burn of the mercury into my arm. I squirmed, sure that a needle was coming. Another needle, full of fire.

'Hold her tight, Abe, I don't want her to hurt herself.'

There was a grunt and then tight arms around me. I was a rabbit caught in a firm hand. I imagined a tattooed fist squeezing its throat, flat feet twitching, watching its long ears flop and still. I began to flop too. My tattoos were made of lead. They weighed me down. I had killed the Dead Rabbits' ink-man. They might already be coming for me. *I am a rabbit,* I thought as I surrendered to the red darkness behind my eyes. *I am dead.*

There was water. I could see it stretching in front of me, dark and endless, like ink. I knew I would drown in it so I thrashed against the arms that held me. I did not want to drown.

'Flora! Flora, stop! Let us get you onboard!'

I tasted salt on the air. The acrid smell of fuel made my nostrils sting. They were building a pyre, I was sure of it. *They call ye mad or kill you.* I thrashed more. The arms around me did not give, not even an inch.

'*Peace,*' the arms whispered with a rasping voice. Then I smelled it, the rough scent of stale smoke. *Abernathy.* I stopped thrashing.

My nails were painted red. I stared at them as they gripped a metal rail in front of me. When had I inked my own nails? I blinked.

'Red,' I croaked. My throat felt like crushed glass. I stared at my hand. I saw a little finger on a small, unusual hand delicately touching my wrist, hooking the sleeve of my jacket and tugging it forward to cover more red ink over my wrist. Not red ink, I realised. *Blood.* Hesitantly, I followed the finger along the familiar short arm draped with lace from a custom gown, up to a shoulder and beautiful throat hidden by a small wool cape. Then a face, taut with worry, blue eyes turned black in the darkness. *Minnie.*

'Flora?' she asked.

'Who else?' I whispered.

She didn't answer.

'Say goodbye,' said a sharp voice on my other side. I turned my head. I didn't recognise her at first out of her small acrobatic leotard but then I saw that she was doubled, another of her standing on her right side, like an odd mirror at the fair.

'Hester,' I whispered. She flinched and nodded down over the rail. I looked. Then I saw the dark water below us, the black peaks of the waves and the way the golden light of the ship's lamps spilled over them like flaming oil. Then I saw two figures standing on the dock below. One tall, shadowed. The other small, bright.

'Abernathy. Polly.' Minnie stiffened beside me, her small hand gripping my wrist.

'Yes,' she said.

My mouth was sticky.

'Polly helped.' The blood around my fingernails was crusted, like the rim of a pie. 'With Jordan.'

'Do you remember Jordan?' Minnie whispered.

'Yes.' I saw the knife in his chest, remembered the rough sound it had made. I winced. 'I killed him.'

'Yes.' Minnie let out a small breath and her finger traced the rose smeared brown with dried blood on the back of my hand. 'We have to leave.'

I nodded. I'd killed a man. It made sense. I remembered what had happened with Kennedy. It didn't matter if the dead man was a bad man; all that mattered was a woman had killed him. I swayed slightly, thinking the boat must be moving, but Minnie's hand moved to my back to steady me.

'Who hurt Chester?' I whispered.

I felt Hester stiffen beside me. Minnie didn't answer.

'Say goodbye,' Minnie prompted. 'You need to lie down.'

I looked at Abernathy and raised a hand. I looked at the peaks of Manhattan in the darkness. I looked at the island that had always been my home. If there was sadness or regret, I could not feel it. Someone had taken a scalpel to everything inside me. I was a broken egg, jagged and empty.

'Goodbye,' I said.

Minnie held my fingers in a china bowl of water. We were both swaying slightly with the movement of the ship. The bed was soft underneath me, the velvet of the blanket clearly worn down from past passengers, balding and thin in places. I stroked it and wondered absently at how distant it felt. How distant everything felt, as if the hot sweat of the mercury medicine had burned away the part of my mind that felt things properly.

'What... ?' I swallowed hard. The corners of my mouth were sticky, my lips cracked. 'What about Effie?'

Minnie stopped. With her half hand in the bowl of pink water, it looked suddenly like she had accidentally cut her missing fingers off there and then. I felt queasy.

'What do you remember about Effie?'

I watched the way the pink water rolled inside its little bowl and thought of the endless black ocean around us, rolling on and on.

'She was the ghost in the house. I saw her.' I remembered her cloud of hair, her fury towards the man who had killed her and loitered just upstairs. 'On the back steps...'

'Yes?'

Each of my nails were rimmed with blood. Minnie would need a brush to get it out, if it would ever come out. Dust. I remembered dust on the back stairs. I remembered the cold wood under my feet.

'I... climbed the stairs,' I whispered slowly.

'You remember nothing else?' Minnie pressed.

Inside my mind, I saw the door of Minnie's suite. I felt like Chester had been inside but, after that, all I could see was the bloody carpet I had woken up on. Slow, eking dread fluttered through me, as faint as moth wings.

'I hurt Chester, didn't I?'

I was surprised by the words that left my lips but Minnie didn't seem to be. She set the bowl aside and dried my hand with a towel. She said nothing. I looked down at the brown blood residue in my cuticles.

'Will he live?' I asked.

'Yes,' she said quickly, confirming my suspicions. 'Everything will be fine.'

If she tried to make her tone soothing, it failed. I didn't believe her. She looked into my face and must have seen my dull scepticism because she fumbled for something in her bag.

'Drink this. Just a sip.'

I looked at the small laudanum bottle. Jordan was dead. I had killed him. I had attacked Chester. I might be numb but one thing broke through the surface of my consciousness: there would be consequences. I took a sip, the bitter taste barely hidden behind a spicy hint of cloves.

'Where are we going?' My voice was drowsy. The roughened velvet was suddenly against my cheek. Minnie's finger stroked my nose.

'Away,' she whispered. 'Sleep.'

I slept. When I didn't sleep, I inked. I found my cards and my inkbox in my coat pocket with a small piece of paper folded in it. There were no words on it, but a crudely drawn parrot. *Polly*. I hoped she'd landed on her feet and her nightmares after Jordan were nothing like mine. My dreams were full of birds made of bone and bloody staircases that I climbed endlessly, searching for answers at the top that I would never reach. I ate little and spoke even less. When I thrashed awake from nightmares of knives and hanging rope, Minnie dosed me with the clove-tasting laudanum. I let her do it. I had killed a man. The truth of it sat like a fat tom-cat on my chest, heavy, soft, with claws sharp as pins when I tried to move it. I pressed my own needles into my skin and thought the words: *he's dead*. When the ink spread under my pores I thought: *I killed him*. Still, it did not feel real.

'Minnie says you don't remember much about Mr Merton,' Myrtle said. She was reading a ladies' magazine in our cabin whilst I tattooed a knife onto the inside of my calf, slipping it in a small thin space between Jordan's remains. I didn't care I had hurt Chester. I had no doubt he deserved it. But I had lived with Jordan half of my life; it made no sense to me but I carried a thorny grief in my abdomen. I nodded.

'You were in a bit of a state, catatonic like.' Myrtle clicked her teeth. 'But a dead man at Kate's is one thing. A dead man in Merton's house is quite another, especially when you left him in such a way.'

I nodded again. I had exiled myself and I knew it. It seems I had accidentally exiled Minnie too – or freed her, maybe. It wasn't quite clear, and I was too tired to work it out.

'Where's... Hester?' I croaked.

When Minnie could sit with me no longer, Myrtle did. I had not seen Hester since we came aboard.

'Ah, you'll likely not see my sister.' Myrtle turned the page of her magazine. 'Don't take it wrong, lass, but she's a bit put out about you.'

I raised my eyebrows in a question, needle lifted in the air. Myrtle sighed.

'Our cousin Thomas works this line; he's the one who got us our tickets home. We were only intending a little journey, like, but what with all this there'll be no jobs for us to come back to.'

I stared at her, not understanding. Myrtle rolled her eyes but went on.

'Minnie asked me to help the two of you get tickets for the voyage; don't misunderstand, I'll always help a lass out, but it does rather put us in your boat, so to speak.' Myrtle snorted at her own joke and shook her head. 'Naw, with a man like Chester Merton on the chase we won't be returning any time soon. Not that I mind much; I was a bit sick of Yankees.'

The needle in my hand started to shake. Even dead, it felt like Jordan was still with me, chasing me. I had been so preoccupied with it I had not thought that Chester would chase Minnie.

'Why?' I whispered, my voice chapped.

'You did wrong by him.' Myrtle's voice was oddly stern. 'Not that he didn't deserve it, but men like him don't take that kind of thing lying down. He'll be looking to settle his accounts.'

I thought of the bottom of the dusty stairs and the bristly rug outside the suite and the journey between the two that I could not recall. I wanted to ask exactly what I did to Chester but maybe it didn't matter what I did. As long as Minnie was with me, Chester would chase her, just like Jordan had chased me. I pressed the tip of my needle a little too hard into the skin. Blood ran. I watched it slide down the blade of the inked knife.

I woke gasping. The ship was lurching, the seas high.

'It'll pass,' Minnie whispered into my hair. Her body was warm against my back.

'No, it won't.' My mind was full of my nightmares, of eyeless birds who carried dead boys in their claws and Jordan's last, gurgling breath blowing in my ear.

'It'll have blown out by morning,' Minnie yawned.

'He'll chase you. Not just because I hurt him, but because he'll want you back.' The words brought a question into focus inside me, like a photograph curing in liquid. 'Why does he always chase you?'

Minnie stiffened behind me. I rolled over to face her, lifting the blankets slightly and letting the chill air in. We'd been at sea nearly ten days. The bed smelled like us now and I nestled closer, her warm, sour breath on my face. Minnie's eyes were dark and unreadable, the orange slip of light from the corridor outside stretching under the door and catching her hair. It glowed.

'Don't think about it.' Minnie lifted a finger to stroke my cheek, her movements sluggish. 'Please. Just let it be, Flora.'

I closed my eyes, allowing myself to feel the softness of her touch. It was delicate, as if she were stroking the trembling wing of a wounded starling. It was so faint I could have imagined it.

'Before the stairs, with the mercury, I remembered my friend,' I whispered. 'There was a lass, a girl like me. She kept an eye on me in Five Points. She was... my friend.'

'Do you remember her name?' Minnie whispered back. She sounded oddly stiff. I shook my head.

'It's for the best,' she said comfortingly. 'Don't dwell on the things that hurt you.'

That made me think of Chester, of how eager he had been to hand me over to the police.

'Will he find us?' I whispered. She said nothing, simply breathed. I was lulled by it, the drag and pull of her breath and the sound of the waves as they hit the iron side of the ship. Her invisible, barely there touch, tethering me quietly to this rolling, rhythmic world.

'Not necessarily.' Minnie's voice was soothing, as if she was trying to calm me. 'Which is why we're going far away.'

I remembered her words in Bellevue, whispered so rapidly under her breath I could have missed them if I did not have a mind made of many, tiny hooks, like a corset.

'Anywhere, that's what you said, if I survived...' My voice was becoming drowsy. 'In Bellevue, you said it. I heard you.'

I love you. I love you.

'Do you wish I hadn't said it?' Minnie's lips drew close to mine. I could smell cloves on her breath.

'I wish you meant it,' I said. Jordan was dead and Minnie was here, sailing the ocean to keep me safe. 'Because I meant it.'

She took a deep breath. I stared at the dark water outside the porthole window, the way the moon was swallowed by its rising waves. I didn't know if I would believe her if she said it. The soft, quivering part of me that had unfurled when I met Minnie had been drowned in blood and laudanum. I did not know if it would breathe again, but I needed to try. I needed to hear the words, especially now, with my ears full of the snuffled sound of Jordan's final breath.

'I love you,' Minnie whispered. 'I do.'

She kissed me. I kissed her back. She laid me on my back and touched me, claimed me again and all I could think of was Chester's words to me after the last time we had done such things: *you'll regret it.* I told myself I would prove him wrong as I held her against my chest, our rapid breathing beginning to slow. I would never regret Minnie.

'Do you want a sip?' she whispered.

I shook my head but she still rose and reached for the bottle. The last thing I heard before I fell asleep was the sound of the liquid inside it tipping towards her lips.

'It's time to get up,' Minnie said, trying to pull the covers from me. 'You need a walk along the deck.'

'I'm tired,' I muttered. My sleep was full of blood and my mind was thick with memories. 'Don't want to.'

'I don't care,' Minnie said flatly. 'Up.'

I scowled at her and instantly hated the small cabin that had become our home in the last nineteen days, despised the closeness of it all and the lack of privacy, and resented her cheeriness despite it.

'Work it up your arse,' I spat. Minnie's blonde eyebrows shot up and she squared her shoulders.

'Get up now,' she said sweetly. 'Come on, my little gutter-mouthed slum cub—'

'Up yours, you goddamned uppity wagtail—'

'Get up!' Minnie yelled.

'No!' I screamed back.

We stared at one another for an instant and then Minnie lunged. Before I could process what was happening, I felt her dexterous toes and limbs searching out every ticklish spot on my body. I screeched and twisted but it did no good, Minnie had one leg clamped over my hip, holding me in place with a wicked grin on her face and I yelled every insult, every ugly slander and rude jibe I had ever learned into the air until, finally, I could barely breathe and was forced to beg for mercy.

'Stop!' I gasped. Minnie let me go and I rolled out of bed, jumping to my feet and standing, a little unsteadily, in my nightdress. It was the first time I had risen since we'd boarded and, just as quickly, my legs threatened to give way.

'Watch it now, there we go.' Just as quickly, Minnie scrambled to hold me in place, her arm clamped around my waist. She smiled broadly as my trembling legs held my weight. 'There! Seems like we're on our way for a walk.'

'You're despicable,' I mumbled.

'So I've been told,' Minnie chuckled.

'Everyone all right in here?' a voice called with a gentle knock and Myrtle peered around the door. 'Only, well, you've got such a mouth on you for such a quiet lass, pet.'

'Oh, Flora's not quiet.' Minnie winked at me. 'Not when you get to know her.'

I stared at her, feeling something hopeful blooming inside my chest. I realised what it was as Minnie chattered away, carefully helping post my arms through the holes of my gown with her clever hand; it was the possibility of being truly known. Of never having to make myself small or quiet or unnoticeable ever again.

'There,' Minnie said, smiling as she turned me around to look at her. 'Better, isn't it?'

I squeezed her hand and smiled, the first smile since we'd sailed. It hurt.

'Much better,' I whispered.

The gulls screamed, wheeling above the bright, white stone of the Customs House on Dublin Quay. Rough Irish voices filled the dock around us and I winced. I closed my eyes and held my breath. I told myself these people didn't know me; they didn't know Jordan or Five Points or the small, unoccupied tattoo shop on Mulberry Street.

Yet the sound made me nervous. I bit the edges of my nails and fancied I could still taste blood there.

'We're off,' Myrtle said. They were catching a steamship to Liverpool. She handed Minnie a crumpled piece of paper, no doubt with her mother's address in England printed on it. 'Keep in touch, aye?'

'How will you make out for work?' Minnie frowned.

'Fuck knows,' Hester muttered, fixing her hat on her head and throwing me a dark glance.

'Our ma knows a foreman, plenty of factory work in the North.' Myrtle smiled at Minnie and Hester rolled her eyes.

'If he should find you—' Minnie began, but Myrtle put a hand on her shoulder with a knowing glance.

'We never saw you,' she said. She looked at me with an expression I didn't understand, half pity and half frustration. 'Keep a hold of yourself, lass.'

I had no idea what it meant. I nodded dumbly and we watched them walk away. Minnie's eyes were glassy. We had left a lot of people behind. The world was tilting slightly, the wood feeling oddly soft under my boots. I was still finding my land legs. I took deep breaths of salty air.

'What now?' My mouth was slow and cottony. I had let Minnie give me a dose of laudanum when I woke screaming in the night.

'Now we work,' Minnie sighed, her face set. 'Now we sell.'

I knew what that meant. I had skin to be bought, I had cards to turn and people to ink.

'Okay.' I nodded. 'We'll be all right.'

Minnie smiled at me and gently pressed her shoulder against me, darting her eyes around to check we weren't being noticed.

'Of course we will,' she whispered. 'We're together, aren't we?'

'Yes.' Under the cover of the press of our bodies, I brushed the back of my hand against her shoulder. We had been at sea twenty-four days. It was nearly the end of May and the blossoms were drifting from the trees. I might never see the August sun dance on the Hudson again, but somehow I had found my way through to the possibility of a future with Minnie.

'But Flora—' Minnie put her hand on my arm, her blue eyes wide and sincere '—no ghosts. Never again. You must promise me.'

I thought of the dusty back steps of Hamilton Square that led only to holes in my memory. I thought of the red haze of madness, which burned like a furnace through my mind. I thought of Kennedy's cold, unrelenting touch. I thought of Effie's eyes, filled with years of unspent rage. Even there, standing in the warm spring glow on the Dublin docks, I felt the pressure of shadows on me, shadows that could grow eyes. I'd been warned as a child. I wouldn't look in the face of the Knowing again, no matter how much a part of me longed to. I was terrified of what would come and get me.

'I promise,' I said. 'No ghosts.'

Chapter Fifteen

'What do you think?' Minnie asked.

I stared at the drooping wallpaper speckled with early dawn light and pale-blue mould. The boarding house in Spinningfields was not the best but it was the best we could afford on limited funds. I brushed the rain out of my eyebrows and blinked hard. Manchester was the dampest city I had ever been in. It seemed to be always either dripping with grey rain or soft and moulding, recovering from a downpour, and despite it being August, the sky was heavy and grey.

'It's...' I looked at the rainwater leaking through the cracked windowsill.

'There's a show here, run by a man named Shrew. Nasty little shit, but he's looking for girls,' Minnie said.

'For freaks,' I supplied. Minnie raised her blonde eyebrow at me but said nothing. We'd had this conversation once before, after all. *They will pay to gawk, my girl.*

'It pays pennies but it's enough to keep us in a bed,' Minnie continued. 'Besides, he can't manage his own arse. I'm sure he'll find proper use for me.'

I nodded and pressed my hand against the mattress. Even the cotton inside felt damp. I sat on it. It creaked horribly.

'Does he have any interest in a tattooist?' I asked. Minnie shook her head.

'A mystic, and, well...' She gestured to my hands. The wetter, colder air was making my skin pale. The ink stood out, dark on my fingers like spiders. 'He's running his show out of a pie shop round the corner.'

We needed the work. We had enough for our fare and a few weeks of living but nothing more.

'Right.' I nodded. I looked up at the ceiling and the soft balloons of water under the paint, like air in a girl's loose sleeve. It might not be Hamilton Square, but it was still a damn sight better than Five Points. 'I suppose we better take it.'

'Good.' Minnie nodded and smiled. She turned to the sour-faced landlady in a stained apron who loitered in the darkened hallway. 'Six shillings, is it?'

'Aye.' The landlady looked between us as I began to unbutton my coat. I was wearing a dress with a high neckline, something I'd bartered a tattoo for in Dublin, but she could still see my marks. 'You'll be sharing, will ye? Two lasses? Together?'

I flushed at the implication, but Minnie simply smiled wider. She pulled out two extra shillings and pressed them into the woman's raw, red hands.

'Will this suit?' Despite her height, despite our relative poverty, Minnie still maintained the bearing of an Upper East Side heiress. The landlady widened her eyes.

'It'll suit nicely.' She bobbed an absurd curtsy and left. 'Thank you, ma'am.'

I bit my lip and shook my head, trying to hide my own quiet amusement.

'Must you?' I asked.

'Defend your honour?' Minnie closed the door and turned the rusted key in the lock. 'Oh, I rather think I must, yes.'

I snorted and shook my head. It wasn't quite a laugh, but I was still getting used to the sound of my own voice, uninhibited. Minnie smiled her particularly smug and dazzling smile that she saved for when she made me laugh or smile and unpinned her hat. It was one of the few that had come with us from New York, the purple one with the feather she had worn on the day we had met. I looked at it fondly as Minnie nudged my knees apart, making herself space to stand between my thighs, trapped by the taut fabric of my dress.

'Who knew you were such a romantic?' I mumbled.

'Who knew you were such a wit?' she replied and again, I felt myself chuckling, the alien sound bursting from my lips. Minnie laughed merrily and held me close. She smelled of cheap perfume and wet velvet. I pressed my face against the front of her jacket, my nose bumping against brass buttons. As I moved my cheek, I could hear a crinkle of paper. The letter in her pocket. We'd been in Dublin two months before Minnie had received a letter she wouldn't show me and told me it was time to move on.

'Was it Myrtle?' I murmured. I pressed my hand against her hip, feeling the fragile crinkle of the letter inside. 'Was it a warning?'

'Oh, Flora.' Minnie shook raindrops off her head. Her curls had fallen in the rain and were sticking to her neck, blonde ringlets turned dark and slippery.

'Is he chasing us?'

Minnie did not like to speak of New York or anyone we had known there but fear was something that coiled in my belly, always ready to unwind and strike. I still couldn't remember how I had hurt Chester. The last memory I had, the carpet at the top of the stairs, constantly tripped me up.

'Hush.' Minnie's finger tried to untwist a knotted curl behind my ear but it only pulled. 'Don't think on it, darling; let it be.'

Darling. Chester had called her that. I wanted to ask for a different name, but I was too grateful for how it sounded on her tongue when she looked at me. There was a hint of the South in it, the way she didn't quite sound the final g. Could I live with not knowing, carrying the aching gap inside of me? Inside I wrestled with a familiar choice – accept Minnie's tenderness or push her for answers. The second was usually the quickest way to undo the first.

'All right.'

Tenderness won. I pressed a kiss against the triangle of skin exposed at the collar of her jacket. Her skin was chilled with rain and tasted like sweat. Minnie smiled, the small lines at the corners of her eyes crinkling under her damp powder. She petted my cheek fondly before pulling away. She reached for our trunks, pulling one open. I knew what she was looking for without asking. She pulled the bottle of Ayer's Pectoral out of its softened cardboard box and shook it critically.

'Almost gone,' she announced, sliding the bottle into her pocket. 'There's a pharmacy on the corner. I'll not be long.'

I watched her count out coins. In Dublin, my nightmares had been bad, but when I woke gasping in the night, Minnie was there with the little brown bottle. I often refused her, but still, the bottle emptied.

'It's raining.' I wasn't brave enough to look at her face. 'I'll be all right tonight. Go tomorrow.'

Minnie fitted her hat back on her head without looking at me.

'I'll fetch us some pies for a treat, for when we've unpacked. All right?'

She checked herself in the tarnished surface of the mirror that hung over the chipped washstand. I swallowed hard and bit down on the rim of my fingernail, tasting blood. I could always taste blood there. I didn't want her to leave me alone in this strange house, which creaked and dripped and sang with rain. There were shadows everywhere and I didn't want to look for ghosts. I had promised not to look but Manchester was a city full of death and the Knowing tickled insistently at my mind. I ignored it.

'Yes, love.' I lifted my chin slightly for a dry, soft kiss and then she was gone. I rose and looked out of the window, the slick window frame marking my dress. I saw her purple hat bobbing away down the street through what seemed to me to be a haze of grey, faceless people, identities being soaked away by English rainwater. I saw a stovetop hat and, for a second, panic rose inside of me as tall and fast as an incoming wave in the high Atlantic seas. I was always half convinced that someone was watching. Perhaps it was ghosts, new Mancunian ones, desperate to be seen, or perhaps it was someone more tangible. *You'll be fucking dead first, my sweet.* I felt itchy all over, as if I could feel blood drying on my arms and feet. I turned away and did what I always did when the memories pushed in. I pulled out my needle and ink and set to work.

It started with laudanum and then became pills. A wet summer turned to a wetter autumn. As the leaves began to fall, I noticed shillings slipping away from our earnings. I didn't need to ask where they went. Manchester was a city of pain; the mills churned around the clock, spewing out smoke to create a perpetual dusk and eating up the lungs and limbs of their workers. Every back-to-back tenement across the city had a bottle of Ayer's Pectoral, opium pills or lozenges. Show folks were no different.

'I'm off out for a tipple,' Minnie would say at the end of a show. She drank it, she ate it, she smoked it in the opium joints in Chinatown or popped pills coated in silver-leaf in Didsbury. I would always nod and say nothing, knowing she would roll into bed before midnight, her hair musty with poppy. Then, one night in November, she went for a smoke and didn't come home.

I had been dreaming of dark staircases and bloody footprints when I woke with a start to hear the sludgy combination of sleet and mill-smoke splattering against the window. No matter how much I tried to follow Minnie's commands and forget New York, I couldn't stop it invading my dreams. On these nights, it was even harder to ignore the Knowing. Since I'd called Kennedy, it was as if it finally knew what I was capable of, so it always pressed against the corner of my eye. I turned my head away so I wouldn't see shadows seeping out of the moulding wallpaper. I shivered in the cold and stretched in the dark, throwing my arm out, intent on pulling Minnie closer, but her side of the bed chilled. I thought, for a moment, she must have gone to the privy in the night. I waited and watched the orange light of the factory clock splinter through the raindrops on the thin glass. She didn't come back. Then, in the same way my abdomen cramped with monthly blood or the need to shit, fear climbed into my throat. *Minnie's left me behind.* I was abruptly awake and trembling with it, the need to verify as pure as the itch to scratch for lice. With my eyes adjusting to the darkness, I sought the shape of her trunk on the floor with the stamped letters, *C.M.* My clumsy hand scrambled against the crooked nightstand, feeling for the hard shape of the bottle of Ayer's I knew she'd never leave without. I flopped back against the pillow in relief, a fine dust rising around my face and making me sneeze. *Idiotic bitch*, I scolded myself. I told myself that she must still be down in Chinatown and she would be back soon.

I watched the hour turn from twelve to one and one to two. I let fear settle in my bones. First, I worried she had fallen foul of a fight, that she had stumbled into the canal on her way home. Then fear curdled into something sour and liquid in my belly. *Who the fuck is she with?* I rose and lit the gas lamp, the dim, orange light casting long shadows I deliberately did not look into. Instead, I turned out pockets of jackets, pulling out cotton fluff and ticket stubs. I could feel the ridiculousness of it, the compulsive urge to touch and know as my fingers caught on grubby opium pills and I scrutinised hair pins. I caught sight of myself in the greasy mirror, face half shadowed in the dark, and saw the desperation in my face. *You fool*, I thought, no longer able to look myself in the eye. *She was never yours. What did you expect?*

In the drawer of the small desk Minnie used as a vanity, my hands stopped against a parcel of crinkled paper. I set down the lamp, the light bouncing off her perfume bottles and hair tonics, and drew it out. I recognised it immediately. A yellowed bundle of letters, each one addressed to Minnie at a different post office across the city, some even in Liverpool, which had been forwarded, the original address scratched out. I flipped the top one over and read the return address, printed unsteadily on the back:

Care of Abernathy Siddles
Hotel De Wood, Midtown

I stared at the words and then stroked the name. I had never asked if he had a second name. *Abernathy Siddles.* I missed him. I didn't know why Minnie would keep his words from me but she had. My fingers paused on the envelope seal. It had already been broken, Minnie would likely not notice a second read and the lure of hidden secrets was strong. Those lost hours between Jordan's death and waking, delirious, on the carpet outside the upstairs suite still prickled against my consciousness. I thought of Effie, of the girl who came before me, the girl who had captured Minnie's heart and Chester's eye. The girl who didn't survive long enough to escape. *Does she wish I was Effie? Is that why she hasn't come home?* I bit down on the hard tag of dry skin next to my thumbnail, tugging it until the sharp sting of fresh flesh was pulled away. Jealousy was an odd, scratching, insidious thing. It was a sickening feeling, the anticipation of a wound that had not yet been dealt. I had never felt it with Jordan; I was his to be kept or discarded. As I stood in the flickering light of the oil lamp, the rain pattering against the thin glass, I felt a bizarre twinge of longing. Not for the man I had killed but at least for the surety of the cage he had kept me in. I sucked blood off my thumb.

Blood under my nails, blood on my dress, the ocean is endless in front of me and I cannot remember how I got there.

Tentatively, I lifted the edge of the envelope. It was addressed to the largest post office in Dublin. With shaking hands, I drew out the small slip of paper shoved inside. It was disappointingly brief, only two words, printed crudely and unevenly in the centre of the page: *NOT LONDON*. Before I could ponder its meaning, I heard a familiar soft tread on the staircase. I scrambled to shove the letters back behind Minnie's necklaces and slid the drawer closed, just as Minnie's key turned in the door.

'You're up late,' she said. I stared at her. There were grey blobs of sleet melting into her hat and hair. She was still wearing her wings from the evening show. They were made of real swan feathers and we strapped her into them under her biceps. They were soaked with rain, dripping water from the gold-painted tips.

'Where have you been?' I automatically moved to unbuckle the heavy wings from her small frame. She sighed in relief as I laid them down on top of her trunk like a fresh carcass. 'Jesus, these will take forever to dry. Why the hell did you walk in them?'

'It doesn't matter.' Minnie sat on the edge of the bed, kicking off her wet shoes. I looked down at the muddy water creeping up the hem of her gown, leaving a damp rim on the floorboards. It would need washing.

'Where were you?' I asked.

'Oh, out and about, you know.' I didn't know. Yet I was strangely calm, my earlier panic giving way to awkwardness. I kept staring at her as she rubbed her hand against her opposite arm, wincing at the tender skin. The leather straps always chafed her. 'Help me with this, will you?'

I numbly reached for the witch hazel balm I used for my tattoos. I sat beside her and as I came close, I smelled it: the ripe, animal smell of a man's sweat. I remembered, suddenly, the night in Hamilton Square when she had come back upstairs, high on poppy, with the smell and mark of Chester and his friends all over her. A dark, grubby voice whispered in a corner of my mind: *Did you really expect any different?* I unstopped the cork on the balm and rubbed the gluey liquid onto her skin.

'Why?' I murmured, fixing my eyes on the firm, red lines cutting into her pale flesh. Above them, I was sure I saw bite marks. Minnie snorted, as if my question was absurd.

'Why do you think, darling?'

She tipped open a small silk purse with golden birds embroidered on it. Three gold guineas fell out and with them a small, brown bottle. I stared at the coins. There was enough there to cover our expenses for nearly the whole month but I didn't understand why she had done it.

'I didn't ask you to do this.' I pressed my finger against the raised portrait of the young queen on the gold surface, my thumbnail drawing a line across her elegant neck, as if I were beheading her.

'I know you didn't.' Minnie's touch against mine was slovenly. I looked into her blue eyes. Her pupils were blown wide. I knew then that this had not been about money at all.

'What's this?' I picked up the bottle and shook it. It was unlabelled.

'Morphia,' she whispered reverently. She reached into the pocket of her gown and drew out a syringe. My whole body flushed warm as if my skin remembered the heat of the mercury, just on sight.

'Who gave it to you?' I don't know why I asked. Whoever had tousled her hair and left bite marks on her arm had given it to her; it was probably the reason she'd let him touch her in the first place, why she'd gone out dressed in her feathers. I remembered the title of the book in Chester Merton's study: *The Joy of Freaks*.

Minnie didn't answer. She deftly popped the cork of the morphia bottle, the scent of it oddly sweet and cloying on the air. She fumbled her finger to draw up the plunger and then flipped up her skirt, aiming the needle carelessly at the bulbous blue vein on her ankle.

'For God's sake!' I exclaimed, rushing to steady her. She smiled at me as she used the steadiness of my hand to pop the needle tip into the vein. I winced and wouldn't look at her as she pushed the plunger down. 'You're going to get yourself killed.'

'You'll still find me,' Minnie slurred, her sloppy hand brushing my arm. 'Little mystic.'

'You think you're funny,' I muttered. I scrambled for my tattoo rag with the other hand and, as I guided the needle away, pressed the rag against the bloody spot. My own hands were trembling. I remembered liquid fire in my veins, sweat on my lip and under my toes.

'No, you think I'm funny,' Minnie giggled.

I stared at her face. Her rouge had scrubbed up her cheekbones, giving her the look of a child in a high fever. All at once, I was unaccountably angry. Words that were six months in the making tumbled out of my mouth.

'Who writes to you?' I demanded.

'Flora,' Minnie sighed. She was beginning to sway gently from side to side, as if the hammering sleet was music.

'What do they say?' I pressed. 'Is it Polly? Or Abernathy? Is he chasing us still?'

'Please, Flora.' Minnie groaned and flopped back against the pillows. I pushed on.

'The night I killed Jordan, what happened upstairs with Chester?'

Minnie opened her eyes. With her pupils so wide and the angle of her face catching the sharp, orange light of the gas lamp, she looked entirely black-eyed. Like a cat in the shadows.

'We're here,' she said. Her voice was sharp; I could almost believe it was lucid if not for the slow and steady pant of her breath. 'We're here together. Nothing else matters.'

'What doesn't matter?' I said, daring and resentment rising in my throat like bile.

'Christ above, Flora.' Minnie shook her head. Her wet hair was seeping a dark puddle into the pillowcase. 'Can't you just forget it? Can't you just let it be?'

'How can I let it be when I don't know what it is?'

Minnie lurched up, her motion so jolting and uncontrolled, like a doll on strings, that I started with fright. *Jordan, slumping towards me like a drunk, a knife in his chest.* Her eyes were narrowed at me.

'Do you never think, girl, that there are some things that you are better off not knowing?'

Her voice was a soft whisper but it stung. *Girl.* She hadn't called me that since Hamilton Square and the word ushered memories with it. I recalled Chester's sneering face in his library a year ago: *Minnie has a way of losing interest.* I shook my head, trying to rattle the voice loose. There were painful tears starting in the corner of my eyes.

'Like whoever you fucked tonight?' I spat out, crawling on my hands and knees to my side of the bed and pulling the blankets up over me, like a child. I heard Minnie's frustrated sigh and didn't care. I was suddenly, violently and impossibly lonely. I felt her little hand stroke my curls where they lay on the pillow. There was a slight tugging to it, as if she were trying to smooth my hair to match the warp of the fabric.

'I love you,' Minnie whispered. 'I always come back to you, don't I?'

I swallowed back my tears. I rolled over to face her, my eyes fixed on her bare thigh where her dress had rucked up. I traced the outline of my tattoo, the wings. If I closed my eyes, I could still feel that dry, quick first kiss in The Painted Man, her lips full of promises brushing my ear.

'Yes,' I breathed. I heard Minnie's quiet snores. I opened my eyes. Her mouth was slack, drool gathering on her bottom lip, her body limp. I sighed and rolled away from her, reaching automatically for my cards on the nightstand. I had kept my promise, I only read cards for work and I never looked for ghosts, but the sensation of them sliding through my fingers was comforting. Tonight, there were whispers in the shuffle of paper on paper. I turned the top card of the pack and looked down. The herald of judgement floated in the clouds above earth, the beams of its yellow radiance sharp needles piercing the air. Flecks of fire drifted down upon the judged like feathers. My chest was tight. Our life was careening towards a future I could not prepare for. *All things come to an end.*

'What does it mean?'

Minnie's eyes were open, sleepily fixed on the card in my hand. The judged were raising their faces towards the heavenly herald, ready for the inevitable moment when all consequences of past choices are examined, ready to find out if they were in heaven or hell. I wasn't ready. I heard a distant, remembered voice whispering, the voice of the girl who had cared for me whose name I could not remember: *Tell nothin'*. The medicine at Bellevue had returned my scattered memories of her, the nameless girl who'd raised me, or as much raising as one orphan could give another. Then, almost as if there was a cosmic balance of things I was allowed to remember, the moments after the ghost of Effie appeared had been stolen from me. How could I protect Minnie from the future if my mind still refused to truly know the past? I turned the card over, hiding Judgement's face down in the deck. She had told me to let it be but I could not. I would find my answers. I leaned close and kissed Minnie on her morphine-flavoured lips.

'It means I love you,' I whispered.

Chapter Sixteen

I dreamt of birds with wings made of bone. I dreamt of eyes ripped from bloody sockets and hanging nooses. I dreamt of Jordan's face, flaccid and shocked in death. I dreamt of footsteps on a dusty staircase and my hands made of knives. I dreamt I was on the boat with Minnie, watching the New York docks disappear. My nightdress was damp with blood under my coat and my fingernails had a rusty-coloured rim I couldn't scrub off. I was leaving the only place I'd ever known, but I was taking Jordan's blood with me. He would always be with me.

'Let it be,' Minnie said, her hand squeezing mine. 'Don't think about it.'

I watched Minnie take flight beside me, stretching her wings over an ocean filled with enough ink to drown me. I tried to call after her but someone's hand was slick over my mouth.

'Tell nothin',' they whispered.

'Flora,' a soft voice in my ear. 'Flora, wake up.'

I moaned and rolled over to face her in the dark, unable to see her but feeling the shadow of her face close to mine. Blindly I dipped my head, knowing I would find the warm crook of her neck, where the scent of her skin, musty and sweaty mingled with the perfume of her hair. Dry, slightly toasted from curling, overlaid with a cheap rose fragrance we had bought from a vendor outside Victoria station. I sighed against her and shifted so that we fitted, perfectly. My head on her breasts, her knees tucked above mine in an almost foetal curl, and my knees lifted to press against her shins.

'It was the boat,' I whispered into the slight wrinkles in the loosening skin of her breastbone. 'I remember the knife and Jordan. I remember Polly was there and the stairs—'

'You came upstairs,' Minnie mumbled above me. 'Covered in blood. We had to run. Polly cried.'

I held my breath for a moment, waiting to see if more would come. When it didn't, I risked speaking again.

'We stood on the deck with Myrtle and Hester and you told me to wave—'

'To Abe. He took us down there, got our tickets,' Minnie breathed back. 'I miss him.'

Minnie only talked about New York and the people we had left behind when she was half asleep or under the lull of poppy. Her silence was like a rebuke. Despite the gaps in my memory, there were other questions that woke me, gasping from nightmares.

'Do you wish we could go back?' I whispered. 'That we had never left?'

It was a question that I held on my lips whenever we walked down to the quays, and I saw the way Minnie's eyes lingered on the ocean liners. The question that haunted me when I looked at the blue bruises on her ankles and the inside of her elbow.

'If I go back, I can't have you,' Minnie's soft lips, slightly cracked at the edges brushed against my forehead. 'I want you.'

Long ago, during my first night in Hamilton Square, she had said something very similar. *I'm keeping you now.* As I lay in bed in

Manchester, wrapped in her arms, I realised that she had not answered my question. I did not want the answer, not really. I wanted so badly to be kept.

As the birdsong of a March springtime chorus ushered in the dawn, I watched the sunlight climb the peeling paint on the ceiling of our lodgings and tried to remember my dreams. I rolled over and reached for a small notebook in which I kept my rough mentions of our accounts and, in the back, a different kind of account. My letters were still shaky and childish, but I painstakingly added to my list in the back pages:

I went upstairs covered in blood.
Abernathy bought our tickets.

It had been nearly an entire year and those missing hours between Jordan's death and our climbing onto the ship in New York harbour in May, bound for Dublin, were still unaccounted for, as was the name of my lost Five Points friend. I saw her cloud of hair in my dreams and sometimes I woke up thinking her name was just on the tip of my tongue, but it never came. Sometimes, I woke up breathless and frightened with everything I didn't know. So I tried to catalogue the moments of dreamy insight Minnie gave me, putting pieces of her memory into mine, like patches over worn sleeves of a jacket. It was the only thing that helped the constant feeling of missing, like carrying a small box of knives around near my kidney. When I woke from dreams, jostled, the pain in my stomach was instantaneous, as if the thing I couldn't remember was lost some- where else in my body, squirming and fighting to find its way back up to my mind. I stared at my own words and tried to imagine moments that I didn't recall. I bit at the raw, jagged skin around my thumbnail. When I woke, unable to get the tang of blood out of my mouth, it helped to taste it, to make it real and coppery on my tongue.

'Let it be,' Minnie said, calling from the other side of the room. 'You'll eat your whole thumb at this rate.'

I rolled over to look at her. She was sitting on the footstool in front of the vanity with her green leather box open. Since November, she had collected quite the accoutrement of morphine devices. The rubber strap was tight against the skin above her ankle. I watched the light-purple bulge of her vein and the slight pop of skin when the needle entered, held expertly in her teeth. I didn't offer to help, but I watched her carefully as the morphia slackened her. Her ankle dangled softly and then she lurched, eyes heavy-lidded, back to the bed. This was as much our morning routine now as dressing and washing. She shuffled her small behind against my hips. I tugged wayward blonde hairs out of my mouth where they pulled painfully against the underside of my tongue. That morning, there was none of the usual comfort in Minnie's warm, living body against mine. Instead, I stared at the back of her head and thought about my fragmented list. How close the answers to all my questions were, only separated from me by her flaky scalp and bony skull. Yet still somehow impossible to get to.

'I love you,' she breathed.

I softly kissed her shoulder and rubbed my nose against her skin. The first flush of morphine always made her soppy. I didn't say that I loved her back. Later, I would wish I had.

*

'He's lost his job,' Minnie whispered in my ear, the feathers of her wings brushing against the back of my bare shoulders. Forbidden from using the Knowing, I relied on glib tricks to please the customers. I shrugged my shawl further down my arms to show as much of my skin as possible.

'Come and sit with the Painted Mystic, gentlemen!' Minnie announced, gesturing with one of her wings. Two scraggly lads, one fair and one dark, sat down at the card table with me, stumbling in the half-darkness of the shrouded room. We worked out of the back of Mrs Piggins' Pie Shop in Spinningfields, an establishment owned and operated by an unpleasant baker called Thomas. He was, as far as I could tell, no relation to the fictional Mrs Piggins whose name hung above the door. The fabric over the windows was to create a candlelit allure, Shrew said. I reckoned it was simply to try and cover the evident flaws in shoddy performers with murky half-light. We were a variety of showmen, sat on chairs or wooden crates to demonstrate our tricks. Minnie and I knew very few of them well, since they changed so regularly. We'd seen men with skin that stretched, a girl with a tail, all manner of odd folk. Travellers would come to the city for a while, seeking bits of work and then move on. Only Magdalena, the bearded lady, had been in Manchester as long as we had. Minnie ran the tours inside whilst Shrew's people managed the street advertising. A show and a pie for a shilling and three pence. I tried hard not to think of the up to twenty dollars a night Minnie used to make at Kate's.

'Do you think she has half a cunt as well as half-arms?' the fair boy giggled to his friend, who snorted, spraying spit and chewed pie remnants across the cards.

I flicked it off with my nail. I felt a rough sort of vengeance inside me on Minnie's behalf and, for a moment, wondered what it would be like to reach for the Knowing and scare the shit out of them. *Tell nothin'*, a voice inside me whispered. I pushed it to the back of my mind. I'd managed to keep my promise since Dublin. It was second nature now, this casual swallowing down of a part of myself, like a ringing in my ears I no longer heard. *Let it be*, I told myself sternly, like Minnie always said. I cut the cards, deliberately pulling from the three decks cards that would weave an appropriate story.

'Don't you do ghosts?' the dark-haired boy asked, voice muffled with a mouthful of mincemeat as he dropped half-chewed piecrust over the table. 'I've got a word or two for my old da, the bastard.'

I hesitated, my fingers hovering over the Sun card. It held secrets inside it, desperate to spill forth and in the corner of my vision, the shadow of the boy stretched. I knew if I looked into it, I would see the eyes of his disappointed father. That day, something else made me pause. The golden face of the sun child with its curly hair reminded me suddenly of the feathery flicks of Polly's hair. A fleck of moisture from the boy's spittle had landed on the sun child's face, the perfect small darkening of the card making it look like a tear. The weeping child. I felt the same fluttering sense of unease I had when I had woken up that morning. *Polly cried.* The ringing in my ears intensified so sharply that I could have mistaken it for the wail of a newborn.

No ghosts. Promise me, Flora.

'No ghosts,' I said to the boys, flipping the next card. 'You'll find fortune in a new line of work…'

At lunchtime we sat down on the edge of the canal on our break, enjoying the slight breeze that came off the steady water. Minnie and I drank weak cups of tea with splashes of thin, bluish milk from the tobacconist she picked up her mail from. The arrival of letters always made me nervous. I watched a dark-haired man in a pork-pie hat on the other side of the water. He was resting nonchalantly against the lock and rolling a cigarette. There was something in the gesture, in the lean of his shoulder and the quickness of his fingers that was completely Jordan. I looked away, my heart pounding. It always happened like this. I remembered one thing and then other memories sprouted up everywhere I looked. I took a deep breath to push them back down.

'All right?' Minnie asked. She sat beside me, a tin mug hooked in her finger, blowing on the steaming surface so the greyish tea rippled. I nodded and glanced to where her latest letter was sitting in the pocket of her dress, making the fabric bunch slightly. After that fateful November evening with the morphia, she had kept the letters hidden away somewhere else. If she knew I had read one, she never said.

'Do we have to go?' I tried to keep my voice light, even as my stomach clenched. I asked it every time she received one, just in case this one, like the first letter in Dublin, would push us on to another city.

'No,' Minnie said, wincing as she sipped her weak tea. 'God, this is awful.'

'It is.' I smiled, trying to push down the persistent tingling of unease that had been building since I had looked at the Sun card. I leaned my head down against her shoulder and tried to reassure myself with Minnie's warm, musky scent. We were alive, both alive, and together. I struggled to let the miracle of it sink into my bones and comfort me. 'I like the city. I can see us here.'

'We are here.' Minnie sipped her tea.

'I mean properly. We could get a shop.' My fingers found the spot on her thigh where her tattoo sat. I stroked it through the fabric of her dress. 'I could ink.'

'Oh?' Minnie turned her face and quickly kissed my forehead, a movement so rapid anyone else would miss it, as they were supposed to. 'What am I to do in that scenario?'

'You could run your own show again.'

I knew she missed it, having her own enterprise, that she despised having to stand in front of working folk in a thrice-altered gown to be the subject of their ridicule, not their desire. When she spoke, all the delight was drained from her voice.

'It wouldn't be the same.' She shifted slightly against the damp stone. 'I have a meeting tonight.'

I paused, letting my lips rest against the rim of my mug just a fraction too long so that I felt the burn. Then I nodded, impassively. Minnie still pretended that the nights she came home in the early hours, ruffled and flush with both coin and morphine, were financial endeavours for our own mutual gain, but I knew better. Just as I knew better than to ask her not to go, for she would only go anyway and then I would be bitter. I ignored the sting of it, and instead I thought of the pages of flash designs I had accrued in a little sketchbook and the ten guineas I had squirrelled away, scratching the extra pennies away from our weekly earnings now that I was the one in charge of the budget. I thought of the ink I could buy and the future I could make for us. It wouldn't matter so much, then, if Minnie disappeared once a month. Perhaps she would want to less, when she had a proper home to come back to. Hidden from view of passing walkers by a black metal bollard, I let my free hand stroke her thigh.

'Are you happy, Flora?' she murmured.

'Of course I am, love,' I whispered.

I did not return her question. I already knew the answer: Minnie was happy, but only with me. Leaving New York had given me freedom, both financial and otherwise. I knew Minnie did not feel the same, which is why she would go out that evening, dressed in feathers with sparkling eyes that would be hazy with morphine when she returned, and I would let her. I was happy, but I could not make Minnie as happy as me. I told myself it was enough, despite the creeping feeling in my gut. Inside my mind, I saw the Sun card. The weeping child.

'Tell me more about the shop,' Minnie said and rested her head against my shoulder. I let her, knowing that any passing narrowboats would see us sitting together and assume we were a mother and child, not two women together. For a moment, we were safe. I watched the sun dance on the water, a rainbow of spilled engine oil reflecting a million colours back into my eyes until I could see nothing but white.

*

I was in the middle of a reading when I heard she was dead.

I had gone to work early, expecting to see her, and had an early client foisted on me by Shrew. I laid out the cards for a young girl from Withington asking a question about her family. She drew: the Queen of Pentacles reversed, the Hanged Man, the Young Lovers reversed... and then I heard her voice.

Flora.

Minnie's voice. The hair on my neck was tingling with the power of it, the skin there pimpling against an imperceptible breeze. Something that had been wordless inside me since New York suddenly spoke. My soul was still, my body trembling, waiting for more, not letting myself believe that this was happening, when Magdalena appeared.

'Flora, you must come. It's Minnie.'

We ran to the canals, fighting to blend in with our beard and tattoos and strange bodies. The police had her, surrounding her in a black box of wool and stern faces in the drizzling rain. This ending was her last act, her death a performance for match girls and beggars. They'd covered her with potato sacking and I saw the muddy edges of her wings. The policemen began to lift her and the sacking slipped. The wings slithered from her body to the cobblestones, revealing the bare, rounded end of her arm, marble white and streaked with mud. I remembered lying in those arms, her body pressed against mine. A great shout of disgust and surprise went up from the surrounding crowd but I stared, the world cold and slow around me. *You're going to get yourself killed.* I had said it, months ago, and now all I could think of was the vein in her foot, purple and ready for destruction.

'It's a child, is it?' a woman asked, standing on tiptoe to look.

A mill worker shook his head.

'A half-woman with no arms.'

'It's an angel!' a child cried.

'Like arse it is!' a fisherman spat. 'It's some freak who topped herself, is all! Bloody thing caught against the lock.'

'I saw her in the water,' a canal woman said, shuddering. 'It was ghastly. So tiny, all that blonde hair floating around and those great white wings.'

I pushed my way through, grabbing a policeman's shoulder. His eyes slid over my skin and hardened, as they always do.

'What?'

'She's my friend.' Everyone's eyes were on my marked neck. 'Where are you taking her?'

'Police coroner.' He wrinkled his nose at me, as if the stink of the black mould on the walls of the canal came from me alone. 'If you want her, you'll have to come and claim her at the station.'

He pushed me back with his baton, the firm hand of the law, not wanting to touch me.

I watched them place her body on a wooden stretcher and transfer her into the Black Maria. The crowd dispersed, dribs and drabs of people flowing away into the misting rain, leaving me behind with the bedraggled remains of Minnie. I walked over to the wings. They were dishevelled and brown, but yesterday they had been sparkling white and heavy with paint and glue. They would have dragged her down. I wondered if she'd fought them or let them take her, saving her from the slower, colder death. My gorge rose; coffee and bread and the poisoned bile of grief. I pressed my hands into the wings, the silky down mush between my fingers, the quills snapping under my palms. Yesterday we had sat in the sun and looked down at this water and today it had killed her.

'Here, *cariño*.' Magdalena dropped a shawl over my shoulders. 'Let us bring her home.'

Home. I remembered the streets of New York, the sharp needle tipped with ink, I remembered blood, warm and sticky on my hands. I blinked hard against the blunt sword of blame pushing against my ribcage. *I should have been with her.* I pulled my hands, wet with slime, from the soggy feathers. In my mind's eye, I saw the Judgement card. It was Minnie now, golden-haired and smiling, who lifted her face towards the oncoming reckoning with pure delight.

'We should never have come here.' My voice wasn't my own, a foreign keening sound that I heard distantly. It was as if I had been lifted outside of my body, rising towards the sky, striving upwards to wherever Minnie had gone because she was home and now it was ripped away. From a distance, I watched myself crumble and heard my own scream. The inside of me was as hollow as it had been standing on the deck of the boat, watching New York vanish. I felt nothing. Nothing at all.

Chapter Seventeen

'What do you mean, she's gone?' I stared at the red-bearded policeman behind the desk as I leaned on the grimy countertop. 'I've been waiting for her all day! This is a goddamned joke.'

The policeman instinctively leaned back from me. I gestured to the low bench by the station door that I had been perched on for the last six hours. The policeman winced as his eyes passed over Magdalena, who sat, tall and veiled entirely in black to hide her lustrous beard underneath, slow wisps of Spanish tobacco emanating from her mouth. Then he sighed and flicked ink-stained stubby fingers down his paperwork.

'It says here death were determined this morning, and the body were collected by relatives.'

'She had no relatives, she only had me, so what have you done with her?'

I pressed my hands into the wood, pulling myself up to my full height and glaring down at him, hoping the combination of wild hair and visible neck tattoos would be enough to intimidate him.

'I do not have that information, miss.' He eyed me up and down uninterestedly. Apparently, he saw scarier folk than me regularly.

'Then I want to speak to whoever does have it.'

'That'll be the coroner.' He opened his newspaper and leaned back, burying his face behind it. 'I shall let him know you are seeking an audience.'

'Now?'

The corner of the newspaper flapped down and a pair of bushy red eyebrows frowned at me. I glared at him. Grief was hardening me to everything and I was as sharp as a cuttlefish. I did not care if I was rude.

'Hopps!' he yelled, and a young, boyish bobby jumped up from the back room where he was stuffing his face with toffee.

'Mm-hmm?' the boy mumbled. His uniform was too long in the sleeves and the gold buttons swung merrily from his cuffs.

'Go and tell Biggins there's a...' The eyebrows considered me. '... a Yankee showgirl to see him.'

''Bout what?' Hopps coughed, crinkling toffee papers into his pockets.

'The half-lady fished out canal this morning.'

I rolled my eyes. Minnie would have decked him for that and the thought that she would never get the chance to do so pained me. Grief was like one of Hopps' toffees: hard and sticky in my throat, and threatening to choke me to death.

'A half-lady?' Hopps' eyes lit up with curiosity. 'Can I see?'

'Get on!'

Hopps sprang away through the heavy iron-handled doors, chivvied by a rolled-up newspaper and the bark of the desk sergeant who then looked at me, mouth set in a line, furious that I had dared disturb him.

'All right?' he said.

It was perhaps the Manchester phrase I detested the most, since they used it for absolutely everything and rarely ever for its intended purpose. In this instance, I understood it to mean: 'Have I done enough to shut you up, you nosey bitch?'

'I'll wait here.' I returned to the bench, squishing myself back in between Magdalena and a penny whore, folding my arms and fixing my eyes on the ginger policeman, daring him to try and slip one past me.

'They shall not return her body?' Magdalena asked, her thick Catalonian accent issuing from under her black veil. She was the only one of our colleagues who cared enough to come with me. The whore next to me shifted uneasily. Magdalena unsettled people.

'They say someone else has her. It must be a mistake.'

Magdalena patted my knee sympathetically.

'Are you all right?'

I nodded automatically and she frowned. Magdalena was Spanish; she grieved loudly and with all the performative ritual of her Catholic upbringing. In comparison, my silent numbness over the last few hours was becoming suspicious to her. I could not seem to pull myself back into my own body. It was as if I were standing just behind my own right shoulder, looking mechanically around the station. I had steadily memorised every single inch of the damned place to avoid thinking about Minnie. Her body shrouded in damp potato sacking, found dead in the water that morning, but, only yesterday, asking me if I was happy. I should have told her that I loved her.

There was a strange vividness to the ugliness around me; the dust on the dark, unpolished wood catching my eye, the pungent miasma of stale beer and vomit stinging my nostrils. Directly opposite the bench we sat on was a holding cell, grey bars housing slumping drunks and bloody-knuckled thugs. I examined the Scuttlers dispassionately as they stood close to the bars, their slim teenage wrists fed indolently through them. With their brass-tipped clogs and close-shorn heads with absurdly long fringes, a person could be fooled into thinking them silly lads caught up in a boys' brawl but Mancunians knew better. These lanky, spotty children with violent eyes were little gang lords and kingpins. They ruled the underbelly of Manchester's industrial beast with broken bottles and fists and fire. Refined masterminds they were not – a scrapping, gnashing pack of murderers they definitely were.

'Hey lady, show us your tats!' one of them called to me, a grin revealing barely four teeth. 'Come on, I'll show mine.'

He lecherously opened his own greyed shirt slowly, revealing a coarse, faded tattoo of an eagle across his pale moon of a chest. His friends jeered him on and pulled up their own skinny sleeves to show off bad renderings on young, hairless skin.

'Cheap work,' I commented to Magdalena, who snorted out smoke like a dragon. Somewhere nearby, church bells rang for six and she rustled, tipping ash on the dirty tiles of the station floor and slipping her pipe into her pocket.

'Going back for the show?' I asked.

'Yes,' she said, rising gracefully. 'I shall tell them why you are not coming.'

It hurt me to think that most would not care. They would shrug or gasp but move on with their day, this news merely an incidental blemish. It was baffling. I thought of the first girl ghost I had ever met, the lady with the knife wound in the centre of her chest like a flower. I thought this must be how it felt, to bear a wound that had ruined you inside for eternity.

'Thank you,' I said. 'I'm sure she would be grateful.'

I couldn't say her name yet. Not like this. I looked back up at

Magdalena. She stood above me for a second, a looming shape that was the spectre of nightmares, then lifted her veil.

'Jesus, Mary and all the saints!'

The whore next to me gasped and scampered away, crashing into the waiting woman with a baby on the next side, making the infant scream. Magdalena's dark eyes were brimming with tears. Her long, luscious beard was as black as soot and her moustache shiny and thick on her upper lip. The boys behind the bars drew back a few inches.

'May she rest in peace.'

She bent down and pressed her whiskery lips to my forehead; a sign of her blessing. This small tenderness was a chip in the window-pane between me and the world. It stung fiercely, a small fragment of the pain that was waiting on the other side of the glass, a grief that would drown me with this horrible truth: I was entirely alone in the world. Then Magdalena flipped her veil back down and swept out, opening the door with a thunk and letting in a blast of air full of the sickly waft from the tobacco factory.

'Who is looking for me?'

A small, balding man with rheumy eyes and a pair of round, buggish spectacles held open the door, peering into the station vestibule beside Hopps. Judging from his apron stained red like a butcher's coat, I supposed him to be Biggins.

'Me.' I stood up. 'I want to speak to you about my friend. Can we talk privately?'

I tried to keep my voice low. For some reason, the Scuttler boys were listening closely, their customary jabs and snipes silenced. Biggins stepped aside to let me through, and the swing doors closed behind us. On this side of the door, the sounds and smells were different. Male sweat replaced cheap, acrid tarts' cologne, and tobacco smoke hung like a mist over everything. Small rooms with wooden blinds held policemen working at desks, lying asleep on small cots, or standing smoking together. My heeled boots tapped sharply on the flagstone floor and gave me away. Eyes turned from whatever they were doing to follow the tell-tale sound of a woman walking. Biggins held open a side door and I gratefully slipped inside. The room was cold, the air that particular sickly scent of something rotten and animal, covered up with chemicals; formaldehyde and uncooked meat.

'Who was the deceased?'

Biggins crossed to his sideboard, dodging around the steel table in the middle of the room. It was a strange shallow bath with taps at the head of it and a rust-coloured sediment lingering around the plug hole. An odd sweating began on the back of my knees. This was the dead room. This was where he opened people up, found out their secrets.

Lots of ghosts here.

I shut my eyes briefly, grabbing the chilled edge of the steel table and trying to push back the shadows in my mind. I had promised Minnie no ghosts. *But Minnie's dead*, a cruel slippery voice whispered into my mind. Of course the ringing pressure of the Knowing had increased now she was dead. I pushed it away.

'Ma'am?'

Biggins was staring at me, holding a red-bound book in his hands.

'I'm sorry; her name was Minnie. Wilhelmina,' I said, pulling myself out of my memories. 'She drowned this morning.'

'Ah yes, the woman with dwarfism.'

He flicked a page of his book. I saw a march of names and dates, stamped out in black ink. So many names, so many dead. Their letters and syllables made my eyeballs itch, wanting to be read and seen and heard. I looked away, my hand wandering to the single white feather I'd threaded onto a necklace. A part of my mind was disbelieving numb, yet another knew. I had heard her voice that morning when I read the cards. I had heard her dead already. The realisation of that took the air out of my lungs and I had one, horrible thought: *how will I live without her?*

'It says here that it was a suicide.'

'A suicide?' I stared at him. 'That's unlikely.'

'Is it?' He raised his eyebrows and consulted his notes. 'From what I can make of it, a half-woman with only one hand would have more than enough reason to top herself. The lock is a good place for jumpers, too.'

He spoke lightly, as if all of this was only mildly interesting but there was a tension in the muscles behind his ears that made his neck tight. Something wasn't quite right. I crossed my arms.

'Minnie was a poppy-head.' I watched his eyes to see if he recognised the term and saw he did. 'She was well supplied with enough liquid opium to top herself in the comfort of her own bed, if that was what she wanted. So why on earth would she jump in a freezing cold canal and drown slowly?'

'That's not my area, miss,' Biggins sniffed. 'I only report what the body tells me.'

'And this time it was suicide?'

'Yes.'

His eyes slid away from me, a slow tilt like the deck of a ship. I knew he was lying.

'Who took her body?' I tapped my nails against the steel table. He watched them warily, as if each ringing click was threatening. 'I've been here all day, waiting for it. So who took it?'

'I can't tell you that.' I watched his Adam's apple bob in fear. 'It's against regulations.'

It's a foolish woman who walks through north Manchester without a weapon and it only took a moment for me to pull out my pocket knife. I was very fond of it; it had a feminine mother-of-pearl handle that made me feel dainty, and a curved, slender edge of the blade that always looked adequately sinister.

'Holy hell!' Biggins stumbled back, his book fluttering against his chest.

'Hush, hush!' I pushed him back against the wooden cabinet, his round bottom scattering papers and crushing glass vials. 'Now, you're going to tell me what I need to know or I'm going to put you down on that table and perform a live autopsy. Do you understand?'

The place you grow up never leaves you. In Five Points, I had developed the useful habit of being able to convincingly display the veneer of a person who could do harm without conscience. Minnie and I had lived and travelled as two women alone for the last ten months. It had given me plenty of opportunity to test it. Biggins' pinkish eyes flickered towards the door. He had a hunted look, as if he was just now realising that he was trapped in here with me.

'It'll do you no good,' he whimpered. 'They're looking for you. They know who you are.'

Those were never words I liked to hear. Instantly, I thought of Minnie's letters that had chased us since last June, each one carrying the potential warning to flee. *You'll regret it.* Chester Merton had made his promise. I pressed my knife against Biggins' waistcoat.

'Who knows?'

'They do!' His glasses trembled on his sweaty nose as he pointed to the door. 'Them in the cage!'

I remembered the leering glances of those Scuttler boys. Somehow, they knew me, and nobody wanted to be known by a Scuttler gang. There was a familiar feeling of a hot spotlight burning my face, of suddenly being found. I remembered what Kennedy had showed me, the cabinet photograph exchanging hands in the doorway of

Hotel De Wood. I'd been hunted by a gang before. I wasn't keen to go through it again.

'You're going to help me.' I pressed the flat side of the knife against his jumping carotid. 'You're going to tell me everything that's happened today or I'm going to stick you like a pig. Got it?'

'I can't, I can't!' He was shrinking away from me, curling up like a dead woodlouse. 'They'll kill me!'

'And so will I.'

A sudden smell of hot piss floated up between us. He kept his eyes closed, his muscles twitching like he wanted to cry. I nearly rolled my eyes. I sighed and flicked my blade back, lifting my skirts to step back and avoid the puddle of yellow liquid trickling out of his trouser legs.

'What's your name, Biggins?' I asked, trying to be kind. The man was standing in piss-filled shoes – he was already nearly dumb with fear.

'Leslie,' he snivelled, rubbing his nose on his arm braces.

'Leslie, here's what we'll do. You tell me what I need to know and I'll slip out of the back door, and you can tidy yourself up before anyone sees. If you don't tell me, I'm going to hurt you, quite badly, and then leave you tied up in here for all the good policemen to see you in your pissy slacks. Understand?'

His eyes widened. The threat of those tall, tobacco-chewing hardened police constables' laughter had done its job. He nodded quickly.

'This morning the girl came in,' he gabbled quickly. 'I did my report of her death and then Scuttlers showed up, wanting to take the body. They made threats that I was not to let anyone know who had her and to say it was suicide.'

'So it was not suicide?'

'I'd not time to see!' He shrugged helplessly. 'Usually we watch the body for lividity, see if bruises develop but…'

I clenched the table behind me, watching the piss from his boots make its slow, lazy way towards the plug hole in the middle of the cold tiled dead-room floor. Scuttlers didn't care about one dead freak; they were hammers of the streets, their brawls motivated mostly by alcohol and lust. Something about it made my jaw clench. A thought slipped into my mind: *he's used gangs to do his dirty work before.*

'Who threatened you?' I asked, and he flinched from my words. 'Who told you to call it suicide? Was it a Scuttler?'

'He was too big to be a Scuttler.' He shook his head. 'And dark… an African, I think.'

I frowned. A black man was a reasonably rare sight in Manchester, a city flooded with Irish and Chinese. He was most likely to be circus, or navy.

'Did he not give a name?' I asked.

'No.'

Those eyes slid again, resistant this time, as if he was starting to realise he had a tell that I had the number of and was fighting it with every last ounce of his will.

'Tell me.' I flicked the knife out again for good measure and he whimpered like a baby. 'Now.'

'He signed his name on the release,' he whispered, a trembling finger pointing to the red leather book on the floor. I scooped it up, holding it by the edge since the spine had unfortunately met with the yellow stream flooding from his trousers, and pressed it to his chest.

'Show me.'

He flicked rapidly, pushing his spectacles back against his eye sockets where they immediately slipped down due to the teary residue on his cheek.

'Here.' He turned the book around to me, one shaking finger resting against a name. 'That was him.'

I stared at it. Oddly, I thought of the cards I had drawn that morning for the girl from Withington: the Queen of Pentacles reversed for envy, the Hanged Man for uncertainty, the Young Lovers reversed for conflict. For avoidance of past choices. Now, the past had arrived and I stared at his name, those dark letters smiling up at me as if they were so pleased with themselves to be finally found. *Chester Merton.*

XVIII.

Chapter Eighteen

Flora.

Her voice rang loud in my mind like a warning bell. Caution from a dead woman. I stumbled out onto the street at the back of the police station and his name circled my brain, spinning like a top filled with images and memories that were too fast for me to comprehend. The quiet coldness of my grief was pierced by a roaring panic. I lurched through the back-to-back tenement houses filled to the brim with working families and strung with endless lines of washing that I ducked under, their rags drying grey in the smoke. My mind was its own rattling loom, churning out the same words and phrases: *He's found us; he's killed her.* I pulled my shawl over my head to protect against drizzle and soot. Rushing, I slipped and tripped in the unending muddy sludge that was churned up underfoot by a thousand pairs of work boots.

'Watch it, freak!'

The curse came from the bulk of a working man I had fallen against, a lurching mass of damp, stiff cotton and sweat-smelling tweed. His squat, gaunt face was yellowish in the fog, a dense, soupy green haze that descended from the trains and factories. He pushed me back against the slimy alley, the black mould on the bricks releasing that familiar musty scent. I let him shove me, my head slamming painfully against the damp stone and the world spun, dizzily, as I stared down at the puddle I stood in. It could have been churned-up crimson clay water or meat juice making its way down the furrows from the market, but it looked so much like blood to me that I was violently nauseous. The world tilted in a lurching pull and I tasted pennies.

Careful, Flora.

I closed my eyes. I didn't want to hear her. If I was hearing her, she was really dead. I stood, breathing heavily, trying to ignore the slippery succession of memories behind my eyes. A hospital bed. Chester's face. A knife in Jordan's chest. All of it was bundled together in a way I had never been able to untangle in the last ten months and now Minnie was gone and she would never be able to give me the answers. The city that yesterday had felt like home, or at least as close to home as I could feel, now felt alien and dangerous and I was alone. When Minnie woke me from nightmares, she would stroke my hair and surround me in the scent of her skin – sweat and rose, sour and sweet. Now, I could not wake up. I imagined what would happen if I simply refused to move. If I chose this muddy alley as my grave and stayed here, starving and freezing, until the cold, seeping mud in my boots climbed my legs and soaked up from my hem and swallowed me whole. Drowning me, just like her. Yet still I breathed. Still I was jostled by passing workers. The world refused my desperate need for it to stop turning and so did my mind; facts floated up into my consciousness like bloated corpses when all I desired was silence. Minnie's body was gone. Chester was back. Perhaps he had killed her. He could kill me, if I didn't outrun him. *Run, cub, run!*

'Flower for you, miss?'

I jumped out of my skin at the sound of a voice nearby. The alley had emptied, the footfall of factory workers vanished as quickly as it had appeared and now, from behind a couple of old barrels and crates, a hand hidden in shadow extended, holding a limp-looking yellow carnation. I couldn't see the face of the man behind it. I clenched my hand in my pocket, the comforting smooth handle of the pocket knife in my fist.

'No, thanks.'

He seemed too tall for a Scuttler, or even for a Mancunian. I flipped open my knife by my skirt, hidden in the fabric but ready if I needed it.

'Shame. Nice girl like you.'

He had an American accent, I realised, so couldn't be a Scuttler. The voice was worldly and amused, yet there was something in that voice, a gravelly scratch that was so familiar to me. Then I remembered Biggins' words: *Too big to be a Scuttler… Dark… an African, I think.*

'Abernathy?'

My voice was incredulous but there he was, stepping out of the shadows. Big boots, the same tall stature but his dark hair now further receded from his forehead, and the same wide grin, if a little more yellow, no doubt from tobacco. He nodded.

'You remember.'

I stared at him, not understanding, marvelling that he was here, standing in the Manchester mud with me rather than on the streets of Manhattan. Then, me slipping clumsily towards him, we embraced.

'You're here.'

My body juddered with the hardness of his elbows, his buttons, the jut of his chin. His arms clamped around me, stretching me to my tiptoes, almost off my feet and I breathed in the miraculous scent of him, still unchanged: cheap cigarettes and salty air. New York.

Squeezed against him, my lungs deflated. All my breath and the blow of Minnie's death stuttered out.

'Minnie's dead.'

'I know.'

He sighed, his arms relaxing around me as though our shared grief was softening our bones and we were fragile pieces, holding one another up. There was such relief in it, I realised, in finding someone who would grieve her with me. I put words to my worst fears.

'Chester's here. He took her body.' I stared at the sooty brickwork behind his head.

'I know that, too.'

I closed my eyes. It was a soft blow, the confirmation of my worst fears that I was once again on the same continent as Chester Merton.

'I know you do.' I pushed him back, glaring at him. 'You signed his name. Was that for me?'

He nodded, a little shamefaced. 'Needed to warn you. We've got a lot to say to one another, I reckon.'

He spoke more audibly than I had ever heard. His voice still rasped and squeaked a little, but it was like the real voice underneath had come back, strong as tar. It made him seem younger to me, truly a man in his mid-twenties. It was as if his silence had robbed him of his youthfulness, making him sombre and mysterious. For the first time I could hear the real timbre of his accent underneath – a rich, lilting baritone of the American South. I gestured to his throat.

'How did this happen?'

'Long story.' Abernathy looked over his shoulder. 'Let's go somewhere quieter.'

I hesitated. For Abernathy to have signed Chester's name he must have known he was here first. Months of lingering fear and paranoia stretched between us.

'Don't trust me?' Abernathy cocked his head to the side. There was a smile but also a gleam of warning there. 'It used to be you would always do anything for a warm bed and a hot brew. What if I promise to buy the tea?'

The words stung. In my mind's eye, I saw him that first night in Hamilton Square, crushing his cigarette under the streetlight and looking at me with pity and amusement.

'I can buy my own tea.' I shrugged. 'You're working for him now?'

I watched him for a lie. After months of watching Minnie descend into a morphine bottle, I'd finally learned to spot them.

'I came over with him.'

Abernathy looked at me intently, eyes the same colour as the red brick behind him. I heard the correction, but it didn't put me at ease, not yet.

'How did he find us?'

Abernathy sighed heavily.

'With this.'

He warily reached inside his jacket, fingers fumbling for a piece of paper he seemed reluctant to find. He handed it over cautiously. It was addressed to Chester Merton, Hamilton Square. I ran my fingertips over the letters, unable to halt the powerful scent memory that accompanied it; the dark tang of bitter leather and dusty varnished wood. I didn't need to open it to know who it was from. The wobbly handwriting and the slight smear of the ink as the prominent overworked muscle of her thumb followed. I turned it over. The return address, Minnie's favourite tobacco shop we had visited only yesterday. I tried to breathe through this too, this delicate but sudden rip in the tissue around my heart, sharp as a scalpel slicing dead skin. All this time, she had been writing to him. It made no sense to me; it was on the tip of my tongue to ask Minnie what the hell she was about before I remembered, crushingly, that I could not. I violently veered away from that thought, like a horse rearing from a snake, because there was more pain in that thought than I could possibly bear to hold in my body. I handed it back, resisting the urge to crumple it into my fist.

'Minnie told him?'

I had tried to keep the disbelief out of my voice, make it sound like a statement, but it hadn't worked. Abernathy nodded sympathetically, that gentle incline of his head too brutal to bear. Something was cracking inside me, as fragile as a bird's egg. *Minnie lied to me.* At that moment, the world was unrecognisable around me, like the mirrored fun house on the Blackpool Pier. *Why did Minnie tell Chester?* The question burned through me as if I was tainted with mercury again. It was a betrayal too impossible to comprehend. I would not let myself feel even an ounce of it. I bit down on my lip, tasting a burst of blood, and turned away, my head full of train timetables, of landing once more in an unknown city and disappearing into its darkness, only this time, doing it all alone.

'I… I should go.' My voice was thick, the urge to run building painfully in my limbs, as if all this only needed to be outrun to disappear. 'There are Scuttlers…'

'I can help you with your Scuttler problem.' Abernathy's hand gripped my elbow tightly, his eyes urgent. 'But I need a hand first.'

'You need a hand? Minnie's dead!' My voice bounced off the brick. I didn't know why I was shouting, or why my eyes hurt so very much. I just needed to go. 'Where the fuck were you?'

Abernathy blinked hard for a second. I wondered if I had hurt him, but then thought it didn't matter if I had. Minnie was dead. Nothing mattered.

'With Polly,' he said. 'Like Minnie told me to, but now Merton has Polly.'

'Polly?' I stumbled back from him, jerking my arm out of his grip. A small owlish face with crooked teeth and a fluff of white hair. Little blistered fingers pressing down on Jordan's knife. 'What do you mean?'

'Is he hassling you, hen?'

A rough Northern voice called out behind us. We both turned to see a cluster of factory workers looking down on us. Looking down on Abernathy, on his dark skin, with an eager look in their eyes. I could be on a train to London in thirty minutes if I said yes.

'Please, Flora, I can explain everything,' Abernathy whispered, his eyes darting between them and me with practised caution. 'He had Minnie all these years and there was naught I could do. Don't let him have Polly.'

I remembered standing in front of Chester only the year before, baring my skin to his ravenous eyes just so he would not touch Polly's fragile, young body. I calculated she would be around fourteen years old, the age that Jordan started holding me down rather than stroking my hair. I remembered vaguely my nameless childhood friend, her face clouded in those mercury-fuelled memories, who had fought to protect me just the same. I clenched my hand on my knife and felt a surge of bitter-tasting anger. Chester might have claimed Minnie's body but he wouldn't claim Polly. Not if I had anything to do with it.

'All fine,' I called over my shoulder to the workers, holding up the carnation. 'Just buying a bloom.'

The workers slouched on and Abernathy slumped against the wall, rubbing his damp face.

'Thank you,' he said. 'Let's go somewhere else. Somewhere I'm less…'

He gestured to his face. I nodded.

'Let's go.'

The only place in the city where a black man could stroll completely unlooked was Charter Street. Home to all kinds of street sellers, advertisers and performers, it was a noisy, smelly avenue of all the strange and wondrous things that the ships docked in Salford Quays brought forth from the exploits of empire. Knife-grinder stalls and carts fought for attention with Irish ballad singers, itinerant preachers shouted to be heard over Highland pipers and prize-fight squallers waved their match sheets alongside Russian knife-jugglers. No one even glanced at Abernathy down here. As soon as we stepped onto the cobbles, he opened a cigarette packet and offered one to me.

'Just like old times,' he muttered.

'Oh yes, fucking delightful.' I rolled my eyes and Abernathy grinned. I watched him take a drag, neck tipped back to the sky, noticing the newly scarred skin against the old. Curiosity battled with my grief and anxiety and won.

'Tell me then,' I said, gesturing to his throat.

Abernathy pulled down his collar. There was a thick, greyish line down the centre of his throat along his windpipe, overlapping the splotchy ring around his neck that I recalled from before. The damaged skin had started to resemble a twisted cross.

'There was a doc at Bellevue looking into voice restoration. Looking for subjects. I've never held much care for docs, or that place—'

Abernathy wrinkled his face in distaste. I tried not to shudder. The bloated corridors of Bellevue, constipated with the dying, were burnt on my memory.

'But the doc was a good sort. I was lucky, got about thirty per cent of my voice back. Some fellas got none. One poor soul died. It's not sore though, feel it—'

He took my fingers and pushed them onto the scar. The skin was perilously thin, almost indented into the flesh, and I could feel the firm bands of his windpipe underneath. The edges of the discoloured scar were clean, precise, and my palms sweated as I imagined cold steel so close to those warm, delicate muscles. If he only had thirty per cent back with this barking, fibrous baritone I thought wistfully what a strong, melodious voice he must have once had as a child. Minnie could have told me. It burned to think of all the things we would never discuss, like poking a broken bone.

'You could have died,' I said.

'Nearly did.' His voice was astonishingly breezy. 'Was in bed five weeks in the autumn. Hideous fever. Polly nursed me.'

I remembered a cool cloth in small hands, pressed against my crawling skin.

'She's good like that.'

I blew out some smoke and stared at the spiritual singer standing opposite, his cap held in his dark hands as his rich bass vocals floated over us.

'Why does he have Polly?' I asked.

'Why do you think?' He looked at me with all the desolation of a person who had seen what Chester Merton did to women, over and over again. 'He found someone to fill Minnie's spot.'

I winced and shook my head.

'He never waits long,' I said. Abernathy snorted appreciatively and nodded. I hesitated before continuing. 'So he came over for what? For Minnie?'

The words were sticky, I could barely speak them let alone bear to think what they implied. Minnie had been collecting letters from post offices all over the city since we arrived. It was unbearable. Abernathy nodded.

'He fancied them a proper family, now his wife's copped it. Consumption, in December. Hence the wanting to kill you.'

I frowned at him.

'A family? What do you mean?'

'Shit!'

Without answering, Abernathy pulled me behind an umbrella vendor's cart. Crouched, we watched a gangly pair of Scuttlers go by, their trademark clogs loud on the pavement.

'At least we'll hear the fuckers coming,' I whispered. Abernathy snorted and grinned at me again.

'She's got jokes.'

'Got more than that.' I flipped out the knife in my palm to show him. Abernathy chuckled.

'The more things change…' he said. I elbowed him and felt myself smile. Instantly, I regretted it with a nasty twist in my gut: Minnie was dead and my enjoyment felt callous. We watched the Scuttlers disappear into the crowd. The cogs in my mind, jarred and frozen since I'd seen Minnie's wings, were clanking slowly back into life.

'So you're telling me that Chester Merton hired a gang because he wanted to off me and take Minnie back?' I stared at Abernathy incredulously. It was absurd. It was also horribly consistent with Chester's character.

'No, this is a new development since he heard this morning. He went ballistic, took Polly, scampered off. He thinks you killed her.'

The implication behind these words was that Chester saw no need to kill me to regain Minnie's affections. I had seen Minnie wrapped in potato sacking, I had seen Chester's name written down, yet this was the thing that made me feel the most nauseous.

'Was she… was she leaving me?' Abernathy stiffened and looked genuinely unsettled. 'Just tell me.'

'I don't know.' Abernathy looked away down the street. 'He definitely had intentions but I don't know about her.'

You could find out. There was a fluttering in the back of my mind, as if someone was shifting furniture and dislodging moths. *The Knowing.*

226

'You don't think he killed her then?' I asked Abernathy, trying to ignore the idea of calling Minnie's ghost just to ask her what the fuck she had been thinking.

'We arrived the day before yesterday. It's mostly been gambling and whorehouses but he ditched me last night. I don't know what he's done.' Abernathy shrugged his big shoulders, his eyes resting on the bricks behind me. I wondered if Minnie had known, if the letter she had picked up yesterday had told her. I felt the flicker of something awkward in Abernathy's words. Something along the fault line of a lie. 'You'd know better than me if someone is capable of killing.'

'Subtle.' I glared at him. 'Thanks very much.'

'If the knife fits, chick.'

I snorted with laughter and quickly bit my lip to swallow it. *She's dead.* I would not laugh.

'So why do you need me?' I asked. Abernathy looked surprised.

'You'll help me?'

I didn't know if it was because the idea of Chester having both Minnie's body and Polly filled me with furious disgust or merely because the notion of going back to the boarding house alone and seeing all of Minnie's things laid out was simply unthinkable, but I nodded firmly. I checked the street for any other Scuttlers and stood up, nodding to the Chinese vendor in thanks.

'I will but I've got Scuttlers following me; what good am I going to be to you?'

Abernathy smiled ominously.

'To find a man like Merton, you've got to follow the money. He's paid Scuttlers, hasn't he?'

I stared at him shrewdly.

'If you're thinking of handing me over to them, I am going to fucking cut you, Mr Siddles.'

Abernathy grinned to hear his full name and shook his head, as we ducked behind an umbrella vendor.

'You know what they used to say to us when Minnie and I were in the circus as kids? Everything's a deal waiting to be made.'

'You'd have better luck making deals with circus monkeys than Scuttlers.'

'You've got something they want.' Abernathy looked down at my hands as if he expected my cards to appear in them. 'Your special skills.'

'I'm not a bloody compass.' I ducked out of the way of the organ grinder monkey and glared at Abernathy. 'The cards don't work like that.'

'Oh really? I had no notion of that,' he said sarcastically, slipping down an alley off Charter Street. 'This way.'

I smirked and followed. There was another version of me that would have left Abernathy here, turned tail, and run all the way to Victoria station to become a faceless, nameless wraith in another city, burying my pain in the past. *Run, cub, run!* Yet there I was, walking beside him, and I was not sure why. Maybe it was Polly, or the offer of protection from the Scuttlers, or even because now there was Abernathy, with his sharp wit slicing through the fog of grief. It was endlessly relieving, like a gasp of air in an infinite ocean of despair. If I left now, I felt sure I would drown. Besides, an hour ago I had thought that the only person who really knew me in the world was dead and now it wasn't true.

'Can you still do it?' Abernathy looked down at my hand. I hadn't realised I had even taken out my cards but there they were. I stared up at the cold sky, the hopeful shards of yesterday's sunlight forgotten. The tumbling clouds promised rain and Minnie wouldn't be there to see it fall. I closed my eyes and remembered her voice: *No ghosts, promise me.* Minnie would probably tell me to run, but Minnie was dead. Now it was my choice and my choice alone.

'For Polly—' I took a deep breath and thought of her little hand on Jordan's knife '—yes, I can.'

Dark wings fluttered open inside my chest at my words, as if my vocal assent made their icy feathers twitch. I shivered. The silence of the Knowing quivered expectantly, as if this was all it had been waiting for this long year since we'd left New York. There was an eager, painful relief, like a pair of bound wrists finally set free, bones bruised and aching. I felt power in my blood as well as fear. I told myself I had not missed it.

XIX

Chapter Nineteen

The End of Erin could easily be called the worst pub in Manchester. It was one of the ramshackle drinking holes that sat in Angel Meadows, the notorious Manchester slum. Between it and other buildings either side were areas that might once have been gardens in years past, but were now built up with squatters' cottages, the passages beside them heaped high with ashes and offal. That sweaty stench filtered into the streets with the unending waves of smoke and sweet decaying smell of waste. Five Points had been a pile of wooden tenements, freezing in winter and stinking in summer but Angel Meadows was a jagged brick hive of thievery, squalor and industry. Between the looming façades of the Strangeways prison and the Manchester workhouse were endless rows of brick three-storey houses, painted green to make them seem cheery or in other bright colours to indicate a bawdy house. But the dull shadow of the train line thundered above, the tracks suspended in the air belching soot and smoke down over the houses, staining those coloured walls and windows, blending with the yellowish spew from the tobacco factory and leaving a toxic smog that swallowed up the rooftops.

Accompanied by the meaty scents of pies and fish coming out of the End of Erin door, it was a thoroughly liverish combination.

'Are you insane?' I said, ducking my head and pulling my sleeves down to cover the tattoos on the backs of my hands, for sure as day, the Scuttlers looking for me would be watching for a tattooed girl. 'The End is a Scuttler hole.'

'Yes, and when trying to make a deal with Scuttlers, one has to actually approach Scuttlers,' Abernathy said, quietly side-stepping a couple of slum kids playing in the puddles, sooty-faced and sallow-skinned. 'I have a friend who can help.'

I glared at him. 'I could be on a train right now, you know.'

'God, gotten twitchy, haven't you?' Abernathy smirked. I glared at him, trying to remind him without words that my lover had been murdered not twelve hours ago. Twitchy did not begin to cover it. He rolled his eyes but gave me a conciliatory pat on the shoulder. He opened the door carefully. It was only hanging on by one hinge. 'Come on, we've been in rougher.'

He was right in a way. It wasn't any worse than the Old Brewery or the seedy music halls of New York, but that was not exactly a compliment. The bar was heaving with bodies exuding a soupy, sweaty aroma that caught in the back of my throat. The air was filled with smoke that hung low under the rafters, and nearly every piece of furniture looked like it had been broken and repaired again and again. The floor crunched as we walked on it – a carpet of crusted oyster shells. I watched my boots crumble them to sand as I walked, determined not to meet anyone's eye.

'Sit here.' Abernathy guided me into a booth at the back, glowering at a few young apprentices so they slunk away from his imposing presence and steely glare. I sat, obediently, the leather seat ripped and the straw stuffing inside leaking out. 'Get your cards out. Read for anyone who asks. I'm going to find my friend.'

I pulled my cards out of my jacket pocket where they always sat and shuffled them through my hands. The familiar motion instantly soothed my nerves. I sighed, cutting the deck over and over, remembering how I had done this very thing in Dublin. *Don't speak to anyone,* Minnie had always said, *if you do, they will realise you smoke your cigarettes rolled, just like the rest of us.* So I kept my head down, letting my hair cover my face until Abernathy returned with a plate of oysters and a bottle of vinegar.

'I've left word,' he said, slurping up an oyster. 'Eat something.'

'No thank you,' I muttered. Seafood was cheap and plentiful in Manchester and probably a safer bet in a place like Erin's than whatever greying, unknown meat was on offer, but I couldn't stand them. 'Minnie once told me they're alive as they go down.'

'Hah! I told her that when we were runts, and she believed me because I grew up on the water.' Abernathy grinned, sucking vinegar off his thumb. 'It's not true.'

'Where did you grow up?' I asked.

I'd asked Minnie this question once or twice since we'd left but she always snapped back 'Kate's' and shut the conversation down.

'Savannah,' Abernathy said. 'Then all over with the circus.'

'Until Kate's,' I said. I had so many questions but it felt strangely sacrilegious to ask them of Abernathy and not Minnie. Her absence made my hands shake as I slid cards into suits and out of them, dancing them across the table and turning faces.

'You do it differently now,' he commented as I shuffled my cards through my hands.

'Differently how?'

'Well, you don't...'

His hands waved in front of my body as if painting wiggly lines from the centre of my body outwards into the air. My stomach cramped. *The Knowing.*

'Y'know, it doesn't feel the same.'

'How does it feel?' I was curious. I had never considered that someone might feel something of the Knowing in a reading. Calling a ghost was very different; it was easy to feel a ghost when they were snuffing out candles and hanging men.

'I don't know.' He slurped an oyster noisily. 'Cold? Maybe a little like being drunk, but only when I look at you.'

'Even when I'm reading?' I shuffled mindlessly.

'With the big ones, yeah.'

I knew what he meant by that. The ones where spirits had something to say. In my mind's eye, I saw their pale faces and heard soft, insistent voices.

'Kennedy.' His name on my lips tasted like stage paint.

'Yes—' Abernathy frowned '—and... y'know, the last time.'

My stomach lurched. I didn't remember another time. I remembered the hospital in snatches burning through my veins, I remembered Jordan and the knife in Polly's tiny fist and a vision of Effie but nothing else. There was something deep in the back of my mind, soaked in laudanum, that fought the blankness of my memory. *Let it be*, Minnie's voice reminded me. I was less inclined to listen to her now. Inside my head, I found myself talking back, even though I knew it was utterly foolish: *Is that what you did with Chester fucking Merton?* Of course, there was no answer. Death was its own answer, after all.

'Well, I don't do that type any more.' I shook my head lightly and slid the cards neatly into three piles. 'No more secrets or ghosts, just... what people want to hear.'

'Oh?' Abernathy dropped his oyster shell on the floor, his eyebrows rising to make the smooth skin of his forehead crinkle up like paper 'Whose idea was that then?'

'I hear you're looking for a New Yorker in this dump!'

A hoarse, familiar voice interrupted us, travelling towards us through the bar crowds. I looked at Abernathy, who was rising, smiling in expectation. A woman burst through the clusters of dank-smelling shoulders and grinned at us, her mouth full of blackened teeth.

'Hester?' I stared at her.

'Hi, Abe.' She smiled at Abernathy and then frowned at me. 'So it's you, is it?' She looked me up and down and gave me leave to do the same. She did not look good. She had dyed her hair an orangey frizz that had the quality of carrot peelings and her skin clung to her like a skeleton. 'What are you wanting?'

'We'll need some drinks first.' Abernathy stepped out of the booth, giving space for Hester to slide into his seat. 'What can I get you, Hess?'

'Gin and water.' She looked up at him fondly. 'Thanks, Abe.'

It never occurred to me to call Abernathy 'Abe'. That was what Minnie had called him, and it had always seemed exclusive to her. The fact that Hester could use it too made me mildly annoyed, as if there was a club I was not permitted to join. I noticed Hester was watching me carefully, as if she could hear every childish thought churning around my brain. I looked down, avoiding her stare.

'What are you doing here?' I asked.

'You tell me, *mystic*.' She laughed derisively and then the laughter became a brutal cough. Close to, I could see the pallor; her skin was pasty with a sweaty sheen. She grimaced, swallowing hard and tapped the three piles of cards in front of me. 'Go on.'

I knew when I was being baited. I remembered her resentment towards me and Myrtle's words of warning on the boat: *Don't take it wrong, lass, but she's a bit put out by you.* Hester seemed more than put out. I wished Myrtle was there. Just to silence her, I flicked the top card without looking, instead searching out Abernathy in the crowd.

'Jesus!'

Hester's expression had paled. I looked down at the card. The Five of Cups. The figure on the cup shrouded in a dark cloak, face hidden as the cups around him spill out empty. *We mourn for what is lost.* I didn't need to ask who was lost when I turned the second card. The Sun reversed. The jolly faces of the child and steed inverted to strange beasts, the joyous toss of red fabric up towards the sun now a river of blood, pouring down. My ears buzzed insistently. I shook my head hard, trying to dislodge it and push away the red violence of the Knowing, but the words fell out of my mouth before I could think.

'Myrtle's dead.'

'Well—' Hester's lips pursed tight '—you've still got it.'

I felt a flicker of sadness for the woman who had sat and read magazines by my bedside onboard the ship for days on end. I looked at her sister. I could see the thinning of Hester's skin against her bones. It was more than malnourishment. I didn't need the cards to help me see the signs of lung disease ravaging her body. What had taken her sister would soon take her too. They would both be dead before they were thirty.

'I'm sorry,' I said. I had liked Myrtle. A lot more than I liked Hester. Her sallow face pulled into a sneer and she stood abruptly.

'You're not.'

'Not what?'

We looked up at Abernathy. He stood beside us, all three glasses held in a precarious triangle between his hands. He looked between us, saw the ravaged grief of Hester's face and nudged my shoulder with his hip, a familiar wordless injunction to make space. I did. He slid in beside me, the leather squeaking. I was comforted by his warm, smoky presence.

'I need your help, Hess,' he said. He pushed the glass of gin towards her and and she sat back down. Abernathy took a sip of his beer and pushed a short, watery Scotch towards me. 'Minnie's dead.'

'Dead?' I was glad when Hester spluttered and coughed, even though she coughed too long and went red in the face. 'Was it a john?'

'No, it fucking wasn't!' I exploded, turning a few heads from the group of men sitting nearest to us, emptying their take onto the table to compare. I was unreasonably offended at the suggestion. It was a little ironic that I should be concerned for her reputation considering how everything I had learned about her since her death had left me with a bitter sense of indignant fury. Grief, it seemed, was composed of a despair that threatened to burrow into my heart and feast upon it alongside a numbing hatred that left me breathless.

'Come on, Hess, you know what's about,' Abernathy said quietly. 'Who's about.'

'Merton again.' I wondered how she knew. Hester shook her head. A strand of wrinkly, lurid hair detached from her mop and floated into her drink. She didn't notice and sipped away, her eyes distant. 'She should have stayed.'

'Oh, should she?' I snapped. Hester didn't even look at me.

'Why me?' she asked Abernathy.

'We need some help with some Scuttlers.'

Hester leaned back in her chair, angrily crossing her arms over her grey shirt.

'You're the bloody limit, y'know that? Swanning up here, wanting me to ask Callaghan what the odds are, like he's a sodding bookie?' I tried not to look shocked. Callaghan was an infamous name on the streets. He ran the Scuttlers in the Meadows and often fought vicious battles with another gang called the Bengal Tigers in Ancoats.

'You're in with Callaghan?' I blurted out. Hester didn't even look at me, but if the Scuttlers had a job out on me from Chester, it explained how Hester knew about him coming to the city. She completely ignored me.

'Do you know what it'd cost me to do that?' Hester continued. 'For you? For *her*? After everything she's done?'

This was the trouble with New York people, they knew all the worst things.

The dusty staircase, the knife in my hand, the feeling of power that seeped through Jordan's blood and into my skin. 'Let it be,' Minnie said, her hand squeezing mine in the dark of our cabin whilst we rocked on the high seas. 'Don't think about it.'

'Not for her; for old times' sake. Look, for all of us back then.' Abernathy reached into his pocket again and pulled out a crumpled photograph. In the yellowy green glow of the gaslight I caught a glimpse of it as it moved between them. A wrinkled cabinet photo of a group of showgirls at Hotel De Wood. Minnie was sitting, smiling and resplendent, in the middle of it all. Something twisted at the top of my lungs and I had to look away. 'For Minnie, please.'

Hester shook her head, blinking away her tears as she clutched her slim body. It was as if looking at a picture of her younger self had punched her in the stomach and she doubled over slightly. Then I realised it must be seeing a picture of Myrtle.

'We had a good thing going, a good little family, before she showed up,' Hester choked out.

She threw me a sudden, venomous look. I simply stared at her. I wasn't sorry. The only thing I could think of that I could have done differently was to not have left Jordan and nothing could make me wish myself back to Five Points — not even, I realised with a lurch, if it meant Minnie would have lived.

'She's helping me; you're not helping her,' Abernathy said firmly, tapping the photograph. 'Help me.'

'Do what?' she snapped.

'Your man Callaghan has an interest in the mystical arts, doesn't he?' Abernathy nodded at me. 'That will be a boon for you if you're the one who gets him what he wants.'

'And for you too, I suppose, if you can stop whatever job he's got on her,' Hester snorted.

'We'll all play to our own stakes, Hess.' Abernathy smiled. 'You in?' She glared at me once more and then knocked back her gin.

'Come with me,' she snapped.

We followed her through the pub to a back door and then down some steps that reeked of piss. It was a cellar. A windowless, smoke-filled dank hole in the ground that no one would ever want to live in, though they were common enough in the Meadows. I would sooner have been buried alive.

'Jesus.' Abernathy touched the wall in disbelief, pulling his fingers away with disgust when he realised they were rolling with moisture and slick with black mould. He wiped his hands quickly on his trousers and reached for his cigarettes.

'Wait here,' Hester snapped. When the door closed behind her I took a deep breath and instantly regretted it. The air tasted like rot.

'We're deep in the shit, here, aren't we?' I coughed at Abernathy. 'We're waiting for a gang lord to come and have his cards read and we're hoping that'll be enough to settle whatever price is on my head?'

'He doesn't want cards,' Abernathy said quietly, puffing smoke into the putrid air.

I took great gulps of it, for at least it tasted a bit better. *No ghosts*, Minnie whispered. I stared around the dim, grimy room, feeling sick with the smell of piss.

'You don't remember, do you?' Abernathy looked at me with narrowed eyes.

I had the nasty feeling of being caught out. *Tell nothin'*. I swallowed hard and stared at the smoke leaving the end of his cigarette.

'I remember Jordan.'

The crunch of steel against bone. The blood bubble popping to a ring at the corner of the mouth.

'And after?' Abernathy prompted.

Let it be, Minnie whispered. I tasted remnants of laudanum. I inhaled and shook my head.

'Nothing after the top of the stairs.'

Abernathy considered me for a moment then held his hand out to me. I took it reluctantly. His fingers turned mine over, examining them, one calloused thumb brushing over the nail beds.

'They were red, like paint.'

My breath caught in my throat and I had to fight the urge to nibble on the dry tags of skin around my thumbnail, to taste the miniscule scabs that sat there. He dropped my hand and shook his head.

'That's why she kept you on card tricks, right?' he said. 'That's why she didn't let you call ghosts? Because she didn't want you to remember?'

I shrugged, tucking my hands under my arms so I wouldn't bite.

'I was drugged up most of the journey. I know I hurt Chester but when I asked, Minnie didn't want to talk about it. She said we'd be fine. By the time we landed it was all just… a fog. She just didn't want any ghosts. After Kennedy—'

'There are worse things than Kennedy,' Abernathy interrupted.

'Like what?' I asked.

Abernathy didn't answer. He stared at me for a moment, so long I could see the pupils in his amber eyes dilate as he tried to look at all of me at once. Then he let out a sigh and shrugged.

'Ah, it's probably for the best,' he said.

Minnie had said the same thing, repeatedly since last May. Now, I wondered if it really was best to move through the world with the screaming, broken part of you dull and sleeping. Surely it only burned worse when it awoke.

'I don't think it is,' I said, mainly to myself, but I saw Abernathy's eyebrows rise.

The sound of clattering clogs thundered down the stairs and Hester stood on the bottom step, her hair more rumpled than before, her shirt stretched up as a man's hand grasped it at the shoulder. Her eyes were streaming and her cheek was red, as if she had endured a stinging slap to the head. It did not bode well. Behind her, with a glowering look, was a man with a shaved head. He grinned at us with yellowing teeth.

'I hear you're looking for me. I'm Joe Callaghan.'

Chapter Twenty

'We've been looking for you, girlie.' Callaghan pointed at me with a battered police baton, the black paint scuffed off the wood at the end. 'Slipped my lads at the peelers, didn't you? Nice of you to drop in.'

I glanced at Abernathy, trying to convey how annoyed I would be if we didn't make it out alive. He smirked and nodded. I turned my attention back to Callaghan.

'I hear you're looking for a mystic,' I said lightly.

Callaghan was not an ugly man, at least for a young man running a gang of street thugs, but he had a dangerous bearing. Abernathy and I both stepped back to make room for him and his gang crowding into the room, but we both moved slowly, the same way a person skirted a rabid dog. We had known men like him.

'You hear, do you?' Callaghan laughed but no one else did. In fact, none of the Scuttlers had spoken. The rest of them were a wall of silence and violent eyes. 'And I suppose for your... services, you'll be wanting me not to have found you, aye?'

'And the location of the man who's paying,' I said. 'Chester Merton.'

'Lost track of him already, did you?' Callaghan looked suspiciously at Abernathy who nodded, slowly. Callaghan tutted, shaking his head. 'Slippery feck, that one.'

His Irish accent, buried amongst his Mancunian cadence, reminded me vividly of the Dead Rabbits. My jaw tightened.

'Give him to us,' I said, wishing my voice sounded more confident. 'And I'll call your ghost.'

Callaghan smirked, stuffing his hands in his pockets. Whilst all the Scuttlers around him were rigid as soldiers, their hands tight on various bottles, knives and batons, Callaghan was entirely relaxed, from the top of his shaved, nicked head to his bells, the flared edges of them damp and floppy with mud. He was clearly a man who loved violence.

'You come in here with brass balls, making offers, but I hear you do nothing but read cards.' He grinned at me, a lopsided, charming smile that reminded me of Chester.

'Maybe you should find out for yourself.' I shrugged, folding my arms.

Hester stared at me with wide eyes as if I were crazy, but I was not afraid. The absence of Minnie felt as if I was missing a lung or sporting a mortal wound. My whole being was twisting to protest the inevitability of it and that made me numb and reckless.

Callaghan nodded ponderously, his head cocked to one side like a dog before he strikes. Quicker than my eye saw, the punch came out of nowhere, a boxer's blow to the stomach that I felt in the back of my spine and my knees hit the damp floor, my vision blurry with pain. I fought the urge to retch as men scrambled and swore above me. I'd taken a lot of beatings in my life but this was my first gut punch. Now I knew why it was so effective. My eyes were swimming and my limbs were weak as my bruised intestines tried to work out what had happened.

'You're a two-bit whore just like your dead lass.' Callaghan bent down, his hand pulling my head up by my hair. Despite the ferocity of his grip, his voice was cruelly amused. Out of the corner of my eye, I saw three Scuttlers fighting to subdue Abernathy and heard his grunts and cat-like hisses as he ducked under the blows of the batons. 'You come into my house, making demands? Why would I listen to you?'

I tasted nervous panic. Blood and adrenalin. I'd not tasted it this way since Jordan.

'Because I know things,' I whispered, twisting to grab Callaghan's hand, holding his head close to mine.

'Aye?' He grinned at me nastily and I knew that if I didn't prove myself, there was a real chance he would kill me, to hell with what he'd agreed as payment with Chester. 'What things?'

Can't summon the Knowing, I had once been told, but that had been a lie. I knew in my bones, the knowledge of it leaking like poison from that deep, foggy, laudanum-soaked place inside me. In the fold of my skirt, I flicked my pocket knife open and in one wild, fluid movement I slashed it across Callaghan's face.

'Fuck!'

Blood calls to blood. It was warm and wet like piss and tasted like copper where it sprayed over my lips. I swallowed it eagerly.

'Fucking bitch!' Callaghan lunged for me, one hand pressed to his left cheek, but I flung myself sideways into the wall. My palms slipped on the squelching mould as the cold creep of the Knowing seeped into my mind. It followed the scent of blood. In the dark corners of the room, the lingering smoke took shape.

'Ghosts always follow the blood,' I said breathlessly, holding my knife out shakily. It was dripping onto my skirt.

I brought the knife to my lips and licked it slowly, tasting his desperation. It was part performance, part needful urge. There was triumph and terror rattling through me, making my teeth chatter and my knees tremble. A keening sound, like a distant baby's mewl, persisted in the hollows of my ears. The ringing inside my head that had been dogging me since I'd climbed onto the boat at the Battery ten months ago was finding voice, hissing and crackling, like someone whispering through a sheet of newspaper.

'She's a fucking witch, Joe!' one of the Scuttlers called, voice high with panic. 'We should do her in!'

'Shut your fucking holes!' Callaghan glared at them. They wilted, crossing themselves like the good Catholics they'd been raised to be.

'They're coming,' I whispered, pulling my cards out of my pocket. 'Time to choose, Callaghan.'

He hesitated. Abernathy had told me he could feel the presence of the Knowing. Callaghan could feel it, I could tell – his index finger took up a rapping beat on his police baton. Behind him, in the far corner, smoke assembled itself in grasping wisps. It was happening. I couldn't stop it, no more than I could stop fainting or purging. *Finally*, something inside me whispered.

'You call my gal and I'll let you go.' Callaghan pointed his baton at me.

'And tell us where he is,' Abernathy rasped, his voice even more papery since he was being pushed up against the wall by a big Scuttler with an elbow over his throat.

Callaghan nodded, distractedly. 'Deal.'

In the corner, unseen to them all, the presence was growing, knitting itself silently together out of their breath and warmth. It pulled at me, the same scrunching drag of monthly blood, but from my chest and heart and veins. I hissed through my teeth, short breaths, in and out. I sat in the wet puddle of the floor, my skirt pooling around me.

'Cut the deck into three.'

I put the cards on the floor in front of me, just out of my reach and set my hands flat on the grimy floor, so Callaghan could see I couldn't hurt him. He stepped forward slowly, lowering himself into a ready crouch at a distance. Then he cut the cards into three rough stacks, dirty fingers fumbling, and set them down. I eagerly turned the first card. My blood was on his fingers. His blood was on my tongue. I stroked the face of the card, watching the tumbled figures fall from the lightning-struck tower. Scratching, half-formed words crowded my eardrums and the blood on my fingers thrummed painfully. It was calling out and something was answering. Words came out of my mouth, languid ribbons of sounds, as if mumbled from sleep.

'The Tower,' I said. 'A terrible disaster. A man was stabbed. This is the man your father killed. Ted Gaunt.'

Callaghan stiffened. I turned the next card. It was Justice.

'My pa was put away,' he said.

Those Scuttlers standing near the corner were beginning to shiver, their breath clouding in the cold vengeance in the air. I could not stop its ascent. I turned the last card. There it was, the Three of Swords piercing the paper heart. A bleeding womb.

'Heartbreak,' I said. 'The Three of Swords. Three people. The woman you loved, Ted Gaunt, and you. Ted's girl.'

She stood in the corner, sewn together from mould and ash. The blood was dried on her arms from her sliced veins, rivers of black running up to her elbows. Callaghan's blood in my throat throbbed in recognition as I beckoned her closer. Her name was secretly written on one of the swords on the card.

'Maude Janeway.'

Callaghan's face blanched. The silent truth spooled out of him into the smoky air around him. I could taste it. I spoke it as fast as I ate it, my tongue stumbling around the words.

'Your father helped you kill Ted Gaunt. He took the fall for you so you could have what you wanted – Maude.'

I stroked the card, the swords trembling as if they were veins still carrying blood to a beating heart.

'Is she here?' Callaghan whispered. 'Will she speak to me?'

I looked up. Maude moved closer to Callaghan, her clogs making the faintest tap. Hester screamed, the Scuttlers yelled, their rough voices overlapping with accusations and shrieks. Callaghan crouched like a nervous dog, watching my face, his lip trembling as Maude came closer until we were bathed in her chill, the deep coldness of her bitter memories. Callaghan flinched. I held up my hand. Maude stopped but looked at me intently, eagerly. I knew what she wanted. My voice, like Kennedy had taken.

Let it be, Minnie has told me.

Tell nothin', the girl in Five Points always said.

So many voices inside my head trying to teach me to be silent. Both were dead and now I was alone and I couldn't deny it any more. I was the monstrous witch girl; I birthed secrets from my lips and ate them, like a rabbit feasting on her young. Minnie was dead and my body wanted nothing more than to surrender to the desire that was inside me, had always been inside me like a festering tumour, to sit with the ghosts and disappear from the vicious, stinging grief of this living world. I stared at Maude and nodded. Maude smiled; a mouth filled with teeth reddened by blood. In a rush of cold air she took me, her voice filling my lungs with breath that tasted deathly. Maude moved my jaw, tugging my heavy tongue to do her bidding.

'Had a babe,' Maude whispered.

'What – why is your voice like that?' Callaghan's voice had become higher, more afraid. I could feel the Scuttlers shrinking back away from us, nestling against the walls like the brick would save them. I

246

could not stop speaking her story and I relished my own silencing. I was gone and thankful for it.

'My Ted's babe, in my belly, and I lost him. Poor little blighter.' Callaghan was watching my lips move in terror. 'But the stairs was long and a hard fall and you pushed, Joe. You pretended you didn't but I know you did. You pretended you were sad, saying mass for the poor babe, but you never wanted it in me, did you? Not Ted's babe. Not in my belly.'

'No.' Callaghan shook his head like a worried horse. 'No, no, no.'

'That's why I did it,' Maude said.

'It was sin, Maude,' Callaghan croaked. 'To die by your own hand—'

'Was your sin.' Maude's voice was sharper on my tongue. It was hard to breathe, my lungs suffocating under the weight of her spirit but I did not care. Not when the story still needed to be told. 'Your sin, Joey, your sin of my Ted's death, of the babe's, of mine – all yours!'

Callaghan swallowed hard, his Adam's apple bobbing furiously. He didn't deny a word of it.

'I've atoned, yet I dream of you.' Callaghan's voice was wobbling. 'Jesus, Mary and Joseph, I still love you!'

He rolled up his sleeve quickly, showing the names of girls tattooed on his arm, a list ending with her name and a crudely drawn heart. I felt Maude's curling derision. Whilst her voice was inside me her form was not. She stood, staring down at Callaghan with murder in her eyes.

'I'm sorry, Maude,' he called into the air, his eyes swivelling around, wanting to see her. Her voice was not enough for him any more. 'God forgive me, I'm sorry! I've done my penance, Maude; what more do you want? Will you let me sleep?'

I looked up at Maude inquiringly. She was not becoming more and more solid, like Kennedy had; rather the shadows that made her were reaching out to caress me. She looked down at my body covetously.

You know what I want, her voice whispered inside my mind. *You always Know.*

I trembled violently, my hand gripping the Three of Swords tightly as if the inked blades could become a weapon. *No ghosts*, Minnie's voice whispered inside me. Part of me was leaning towards Maude with pleading desire but Minnie's voice held me back. I shook my head.

'Tell me!' Callaghan roared in my face, spittle flying. 'I have to know!'

I have gifts for you too. Maude lifted a bloody finger to her temple. *Memories. Answers.* My heart pounded slower and slower, but each thump was filled with thirst for what Maude offered. I closed my eyes and breathed out slowly, swallowing Maude to the back of my throat so I could speak with my own tongue again. She held my throat in a vice-like grip, as sure and crushing as Jordan's had been on the night he died.

'Where is Merton?' I ground out slowly. My teeth were sharp with Maude's vengeance.

'Sailing!' Callaghan gasped desperately. 'Tomorrow, nine o'clock. The *Dunlin*. Now tell me!'

Now, Maude stepped closer.

Flora, Minnie's memory seemed to caution, but I thought of the letter to Chester from the Manchester tobacconist. If I was betraying her now, it was nothing to how she had betrayed me, and I still didn't know why. Yet the knowledge it had happened, that Minnie had lied, released something in my chest, something furious and exhausted from always being pushed down. I would let it be no longer.

I looked deep into Maude's bloody eyes and drowned my whole self inside them.

Come.

I realised Kennedy had been soft with me, tender with my fragile head and heart as he teased my spirit out of my core. Maude ripped me from myself before I could even think. Suddenly, I could see through my eyes like through a steamed windowpane but could feel nothing of my body. I was pliant to her whims. I saw my own hands taking the knife, cutting shapes into Callaghan's arm whilst he screamed and prayed but I could do nothing to stop Maude's use of my hand. His blood spurted over my dress and he did not stop wailing until the cuts formed their sickly letters in his straining skin. *M.J. & T.G.* Maude was leaving her own mark of her sorrow and she was using my hands to do it. Her victory was sweet as honey, sharp as blood, and when it was done, I searched the prison of my mind to find a sliver of my own voice and make my short demand.

Answers.

Let it never be said a ghost does not honour her bargains. Even though she was still inside me, I saw her smiling face, her black teeth crumbling to ash as she complied. The memories were poison, a searing infection that spread through my gut and blood and bones, gnawing the ignorance out of me, completing me and damning me all at once.

Abernathy had said there were worse things than Kennedy, and now I knew: the worst thing was me.

*

The Gift of Maude Janeway

I am a ghost walking up the servants' staircase in Hamilton Square. My bare feet are made of glass and ice and leave no marks on the dusty floor. I see a light at the top of the stairs and follow the spirit birds of the Knowing as they rise to meet it, their dark feathered wings brushing along the tight, wood-panelled walls.

We are together, she and I, on the edge of that brightness, waiting to be heard. Effie and Flora, the girls Minnie wanted and Chester tried to kill. We are dust and air, we are shadow and corners. We watch and listen to the man and woman inside. Him tall as a demon and her bright as a daisy.

'Don't speak about Florence that way!' she yells. 'She's downstairs, probably dying, because of you—'

The man smiles, his long hands stuffed nonchalantly in his pockets. He's happy with the idea of death. The satisfaction oozes out of him like butter.

'Did you try and get rid of her, like Effie?' The woman shakes with rage.

A hundred memories are tumbling together, pearls drawn up on a string. Effie's memories as her spirit breathes beside me. I see her being dragged away from her bed in the Old Brewery, the small dark-haired girl in her bed screaming for her. I see myself and I know now. I know it is Effie who watched me and taught me. I remember her kind face as she protected and loved me in the dark of the slums. It's another lifetime. Her saddened spirit touches mine.

You weren't alone, wee cub, she says. *We're together again.*

Effie and I entwine even closer, flesh and air, blood and breath. The man leans towards the woman, his shadow is long.

'You're mine, Min. You always will be. Nothing can change that. No cheap slum bitch, no other girl that you take to bed just to rile me—' his smile is a gash of sharp teeth and red lips, ready to bite '—no one and nothing. You're mine.'

I am a ghost. I am a ghost and I watch from the doorway, blood-stained and silent with Effie as the man pushes the woman to the bed.

'Chester, no, not now – I said, no… No!'

Her repeated no's are incantations to us, nothing to him, but we are made of vengeance, and they pull us towards her like a hunter drags a carcass over leaves.

This is what he did, Effie hands me secrets, cutting and bitter. *This is why I left you.*

I see her memories of it, brutal and fast in the Old Brewery and then again in Hamilton Square, a large hand over a small mouth.

'I can't stay here.' Effie's dark hair was sodden against her head as she sat in the bathtub in Hamilton Square. 'I've a girl to care for back home. She's all alone, she reads cards like me, I can't leave her—'

'I'm sorry,' Minnie whispered, tears falling on her rounded stomach. She lifted the jug and poured water over Effie's head. She looked impossibly young, no more than fifteen. 'He doesn't want me when I'm like this, that's why he brought you here. He always gets what he wants.'

I am a ghost. I am made of sorrow and rage. I am Effie's hands, I am Effie's heart. The knife is dark with blood already and disappears into his skin so easily. He flops on his belly like a gutted fish. The birds circle. The woman wiggles out from underneath him, breathless and tear-stained as she gasps at us: 'What have you done?'

'Minnie!' The man groans. 'Help me—'

There is a clatter behind us. Another man runs in, rushes to staunch the blood from the wound. Abernathy.

'He's stopped now, Min-Min. I finally stopped him.'

Abernathy looks up sharply, his face creased in recognition. He hisses low, asking us without words... *Is that...* ? Effie waves in response, our hands light in heavy air.

'Min-Min?' Minnie takes a step back from us. 'What... *Effie?*'

Knowledge dawns in her eyes. We giggle, Effie and I, because she's understood now, she sees it. She's beside me, inside me, Effie who was mine before she was theirs, Effie who raised me and taught me and was ripped from me by his cruel hands.

'Not got long,' Effie whispers. 'It's time.'

Abernathy pulls the knife from his back. We watch the blood rush forth and are glad. Inside Effie's memories, I see different blood.

'It's time!' the midwife called.

'I can't do it,' Minnie gasped, flopping her sweaty and straining body back against Effie, legs spread wide.

'Yes, you can,' Effie said, squeezing her hands tight. 'You must do it, then you'll be free. You can leave him, we can leave him together, I'll get my Flora back and we'll be free—'

Minnie screamed. Blood flooded the sheets underneath her.

'Polly.' Minnie looks away from us, back to the man on the bed who she loves and hates and has never been quite able to leave. 'He promised he'd always look after her, but Abe—'

On the bed, Abernathy looks at her with infinite love, all the words he cannot speak floating on air from his scarred neck. He rises slowly. He is no ghost but some birds flock to him all the same. He carries memories of death. I can see them. The long view down from the end of the rope. The red gasp of a last breath of a lynching.

'Go,' he whispers to her, quiet and soft. 'He'll live. I'll look after her.'

Minnie's eyes are still on the stabbed man, his pool of blood, his sunken eyes and plaintive breath. We feel the pull he has on her, the dark ribbons binding her from her womb to his heart. Inside Effie's memory, I see the last time Effie said goodbye.

Effie was being pulled away, jostled down the stairs of Hamilton Square into a carriage with blacked-out windows. The name of Blackwells was stamped on the inside. From the upstairs window, Chester watched down, a malevolent ghost in his own home. Minnie was chasing Effie, body slim once again and her face aged with sorrow.

'No!' Minnie screamed, even as Abernathy tried to comfort her with his soft, clucking sounds. 'Don't take her; she's not mad, she's my friend!'

'Minnie.' Effie's older face was thin and urgent. 'The babe, they put her in the slums. She's alive, I'm sure of it. Men always lie, Min.'

Minnie staggered, gasping. Abernathy held her. Effie grabbed Minnie's hand, even as shackles were put on her other wrist.

'If you find your babe, find my girl too, Min,' Effie said urgently. 'Her name's Flora, she reads cards, she's — she's only little. Promise me. Keep them both safe.'

'I... yes,' Minnie wept.

'You promised,' Effie says, using my mouth to speak as Abernathy fights to staunch Chester's wound. Minnie stares at the two of us together, hating us for our Knowing, our truth cutting out her heart with its sharp, shiny edges.

'Let's go,' she says. She takes hold of my hand and leads me out of the room. Effie smiles. The last thought I have before she leaves my body and my knees buckle underneath me on the carpet outside is this: we are ghosts. We are all ghosts.

Chapter Twenty-One

'Polly is Minnie and Chester's daughter?' I asked, as soon as the door to our room at the boarding house was closed behind me.

I'd survived Callaghan by the skin of my teeth, coming round to my face pressed into the sickly damp straw of the floor to see Hester tentatively stitching up Callaghan's arm, the blood from Maude's improvised tattoo staining his skin a dirty brown. I had been listless and wandering, unable to speak and barely able to breathe, much like the last times I had let a ghost take my form. It wasn't until Hester had kicked us both out with a mumbled promise from Callaghan to 'drop' the job on me that Abernathy and I had made our stumbling way out of the Meadows and I had begun to recover my wits in the cold, night air. By the time we made it to mine and Minnie's rooms, a headache was starting and any trepidation I felt about returning to our shared space without her was slightly mitigated by a desire to lie down and close my eyes. In contrast, Abernathy was staring around the room with the reverence of a man in church. He smiled, reaching out nostalgically to touch the glass bottles and rabbit's foot puff on the vanity with a surprisingly dainty hand.

'Minnie.'

His throat was working intensely, the Adam's apple rippling visibly behind his scar. He missed her. I looked around and abruptly saw beyond the greying linen and metal bedframe to what it was now: a Minnie-themed curiosity shop. I sat on the bed, automatically taking my side and running my hand down her pillow, noticing the blonde hairs that clumped on the flat, lumpy mass. Everything was still the same. Grief, bitter and palpable, filled the unoccupied space between us. I took a deep breath.

'I haven't been back since this morning.'

I could not fathom how short a time it had been. When I had woken alone that morning, her absence was a familiar numb ache. Now it would be a permanent chill I would have to learn to live with. I stroked her pillow, fancying for a moment that it still held a fraction of her warmth.

'It all looks the same,' Abernathy whispered. He was right. Minnie had never stopped living like a maid would be along to clean up after her. Even in boarding houses like this one, where mice came in at night to nibble on her lace. Abernathy lifted a perfume bottle to smell it. I saw in the happy dimples of his cheeks that her scent conjured her back into being. Then he opened his eyes, and I recognised that unmistakable mournful flash of comprehension. We would always be searching for her now.

'Sit.'

I patted Minnie's side of the bed. He returned the perfume bottle carefully, as if that would be its place for evermore now, in a shrine to Minnie. As he sat, carefully keeping his heavy boots off the blanket, I got that peculiar rush of comfort from having Abernathy nearby. To have him back was so familiar, it was like Minnie being there. Except she wasn't, and she wouldn't be again. I felt a swelling wave of something too powerful to give name to, that tasted like the start of a fight and felt like falling. As I stared at the cracked ceiling plaster, the grey hanging threads of cobwebs, I felt myself teetering on the edge of sorrow; sorrow for her death, sorrow for Effie and Polly and myself, for all of us. I pushed it back down my throat. I would not drown in sorrow. Not whilst there were still questions to be answered.

'Polly was born when Minnie worked at Kate's?' I thought of Minnie's soft, knowing tone that night in Hamilton Square. *It was probably for the best.* Abernathy nodded.

'They tried to get rid of the baby, but Kate's doctor botched it.' I winced at that, remembering Jordan's dreaded brown bottle under the floorboards. 'So Minnie was stuck and Chester, well, he went looking for some fun to bring home and keep him occupied. He brought Effie back.'

He spoke in a whisper even though there was really no need, but perhaps it had been a secret so long it was just instinct. Inside my mind a young girl with a cloud of dark hair and a gaunt face formed and I named her, as I had never been able to do: *Effie.*

'When Minnie could go back to work, she took Effie with her, to read cards and the like, but Chester got sick of her. Put her away in Blackwells. She starved to death, I think.'

The inside of a room with no window. A mouth bruised and parched. Were Effie's memories now mine too?

'She stroked my hair and protected me,' I whispered. 'She taught me not to play with ghosts.'

I saw the corner of one of the big basement rooms in the Old Brewery that we had occupied; her cloud of dark hair that I followed everywhere. It was a twist in the gut, a breathless pain, to realise that the fox-faced man who had raped his way through the Old Brewery and taken Effie was none other than Chester Merton.

'What happened?' Abernathy asked.

I scrunched my eyes, trying to organise the new and old memories into a narrative inside my mind.

'Effie kept me safe from the other children; they used to beat me when I talked about ghosts. Men used to come down there, looking for girls. Then one day a man and his friends took her right out of our bed.'

'Chester,' Abernathy said.

'I never saw her again. I think I thought it was my fault, maybe, that she had vanished. So I... forgot her. I buried her. Lived by her rules, didn't talk about the Knowing. I did that right up until Bellevue. Even then, when the mercury burned some memories back into me, I still forgot her name. I didn't recognise her ghost until she took my body and then afterwards, I forgot it and... Minnie didn't remind me.'

I swallowed hard, breathing tightly through my nose. My insides curled with revulsion remembering Effie's memories of sitting in the bathtub in Hamilton Square, the same one I had sat in. How could Minnie have come to find me and not told me, not helped me remember the girl who had made her promise to care for me? I remembered how Minnie had stiffened when I spoke about the memories of the girl I didn't remember that had been shaken loose by the mercury, how she had asked me so hesitantly: *Do you remember her name?* How could she bear to not tell me the truth when all my memories of who Effie was to me had been swallowed up once more in drugs and trauma?

'They were friends.' Abernathy ran his hand up and down my arm, seeming to know what I was thinking. 'Minnie loved you.'

The word was simple and enough to bring tears to my eyes. I had worried that I was living a life that Minnie had longed to have with Effie. Now I knew it was what Effie had wanted for all of us. Maybe it was love, but maybe Minnie's love was tarnished by the promise Effie had held her to.

'As much as she could,' I sighed.

I had known every inch of Minnie's flesh, the mole with the hair in it on her left breast and the silvery rows of scars on her belly. I had never once considered they were the legacy of carrying a child and she had never reminded me of the secrets Effie had spilled and acted on. I winced to remember the knife in Chester's back. I'd not only stabbed him and stolen his mistress but she was also the mother of his child. *No wonder he's been fucking chasing us.*

Abernathy nodded sadly. 'As much as she could,' he repeated.

'She abandoned Polly. She ended up in Randalls.'

Even knowing Minnie, even knowing the incredible ability she had for always moving on, pushing forward, for fighting to survive, even knowing that the reason we had left Polly behind with Chester had been to save me from being hanged for Jordan's death and the consequences of attacking Chester, I thought it seemed like too much.

'No, it wasn't like that.' Abernathy shook his head, his hand gripping mine tightly. 'Minnie was only fifteen when…'

My stomach rolled. I had been around that age when Jordan had first forced his hideous abortion medication on me. I still felt a hideous tingle in my feet when I remembered it.

'Kate and Chester said they had rehomed the baby. Then Effie told her what they'd done, dumping the child in Five Points. I don't know how she knew it…'

Effie had been one of those older slum girls who taught me to read tarot. She may not have had the Knowing as I did but she was wise, and, just like Polly, she knew how secrets travelled among slum children. If a baby left Hamilton Square and ended up in the slums, she would know.

'… Minnie never forgave them that. She thought the baby would be dead.' I felt a flash of mourning for a part of the story I would never hear from Minnie's side. 'Minnie left Kate's, left Chester, but it didn't last.'

I thought of the letter to Merton from Minnie. Could it be as simple and horrible as she had just missed the father of her child, no matter how beastly he was? The thought made me want to vomit.

'We went back out to the circus for a while, but Minnie started to think Effie could have been right. The babe might be alive. After a few years we came back, worked out of Kate's and the other cathouses, running our show. All the while, we used our connections, kept an ear out and, eventually, Minnie found Polly at Randalls. She sent me to pick her up.' He grinned. 'Even at ten years old, she was such a tiny thing! Next thing I know, Minnie's made a deal with Chester and…'

'She's back in his bed and Polly's in Hamilton Square.'

She had saved her own child from Five Points, but not me from Jordan, and Effie had died of neglect, all alone. *Everything could have been different.* It was the dullest, deepest kind of pain. I closed my eyes against it. *No wonder,* I thought bleakly, *she proceeded to disappear into a syringe.*

'Yes.' Abernathy's head flopped back on the pillow. 'Minnie was fifteen, I thought that was the youngest. I never thought he would…'

Abernathy coughed, eyes wet. He hadn't known about Chester's preferences. I pressed his sweaty fingers with mine.

'You did what you could.'

We stayed silent for a while, Abernathy swallowing his tears and my thoughts churning as I stared at the white cross of healed skin on his throat. I stroked it gently, feeling him swallow.

'You never told me why,' I whispered.

Abernathy let out a slow sigh and closed his eyes.

'There was… a boy.'

In a Southern river town like Savannah, that would be more than enough. I did some quick sums in my head. He would have been only around fourteen. Suddenly, Kennedy's bruised lips came to mind.

'Oh.' I swallowed carefully. 'Is it... only lads?'

'Not only.' Abernathy gave me a sidelong look. Some secrets did not need the Knowing to be understood. 'I'm like you, I reckon. I don't discriminate.'

'Seems pointless to. Love's rare enough.' He smiled fondly but I did not feel fond. I had been loved romantically twice in my life and both of those people were dead. In that moment, I mourned both of them. I knew it was twisted and wrong and if Minnie were there she would scoff and tell me I had no business mourning how Jordan had loved me, but the perversity of being loved by Jordan was that, whilst I had been a prisoner, I had felt, at the core of my being, treasured. Wanted, at least. With Minnie too, I had felt it again, though softer and kinder, and now I was afraid that no one would ever want me again. Heavy with malaise, I lowered myself down onto the bed beside him, rolling onto my side to stare at his face. His eyes were glowing slightly orange in the yellow light shafting through the curtains from the factory clock face. He reached out a hand and touched the rose tattoo on my neck, under my ear.

'This one's new.'

It struck me as suddenly wondrous that he, like her, remembered the map of ink on my skin. He was the only other person in the world now that could. I remembered the first time Minnie had seen all of my skin in the bathtub, the strange and calculated kiss we had shared, less about lust and more a game of testing the fragile trust growing between us. I hesitated for a moment, then pressed the driest of kisses to Abernathy's chapped lips. Those eyes, the colour of a marigold, stared at me.

'What was that for?' He seemed to be holding his breath.

'I wanted to do it.'

What do you want, Flora? The memory of Minnie's words assailed me. Grief had made me raw all over, as if I was being fitted for a dress with all the pins still in, jabbed from all sides in unexpected places with sharp stings of the past.

'You just… do as you want now, don't you?' Abernathy watched me, carefully.

It was a revolutionary notion, terrifying and joyous and seemingly impossible. I had no idea what I wanted, only that I desperately needed to press something against every inch of myself until the stinging stopped.

'Maybe.' I shrugged softly. 'Maybe I missed you.'

Abernathy's lips lifted into a wry smile and I could breathe easier.

'I missed you too, chick,' he whispered. His thumb gently circled the rose on my neck and I sighed with the relief of it, to be tenderly touched when I needed it most.

I leaned over to turn the cheap oil lamp off. I quickly pulled off my jacket and boots, hearing Abernathy do the same. We wordlessly lay back down and I dragged up the light, holey quilt to cover us both in a puff of feather dust. In the darkness the odd lights of the edge of the city filtered in through the thin curtains and we both became shapes and warmth in the shadow. His knees fitted behind mine and his arm lolled over my shoulders, pulling me even closer, as if we had always intended to be there.

'I knew her longer than anyone and still I think I never understood her,' Abernathy whispered against the back of my neck. 'Now I never will.'

I heard the truth in his words, the frustration, love and grief. It resonated with me; I felt it twinge in my gut and travel down the back of my legs. I imagined I could see everything Minnie would never tell us unspooling like a length of wet rope, endless.

'It's all right.' Without thinking, I pressed a kiss against the skin of his forearm where it fell in front of my face. It was dry, slightly dusty. 'I'm here.'

I didn't know why I said it at first, why I thought that would be any comfort to him, but then as his breath evened out in relief and his hands cradled mine, I knew that it was. His lips found the back of my neck and kissed the flat trail of short, dark hairs at the nape. I nestled closer to him, feeling muscles that I had not realised were clenched as tight as piano wire relaxing into the softness of Abernathy's body, there, beside me, allowing me to comfort and be comforted. When I rolled over and kissed him, tasting my own grief on his lips, I realised why it was comforting. Minnie was dead but we were together, two thirds of something broken apart and drifting lonely on open waters. Out of the wreckage of all of this, there was something worth saving. We were something to save.

*

When I woke up to the cold light of the Manchester morning bleeding through the windowpane, there was a ghost in the corner of the room.

'Abernathy,' I whispered, nestled inside the warmth of his heavy arms as he slept beside me. The ghost was older, a man in his forties or fifties, and clearly a cotton worker. From his gaunt skin and mouth edged with blood from coughed-up matter, I could assume he'd drowned from the inside out, cotton dust souping up his throat. The quality of his body was smudged around the edges, any second he might be nothing more than dust dancing in the morning light. I nudged my elbow back into Abernathy's ribs. He grunted sleepily.

'What?'

'There's a ghost.'

'Oh.' Abernathy shifted, the cool skin of his chest pressing closer against my warm back. 'What does it want?'

He seemed neither surprised nor afraid. It had been a long time since someone had treated the Knowing as anything other than suspicious or lucrative. Not since Effie, in fact. Maybe this was what having my memories restored meant – the ghosts were back, just as they had been in my childhood. My reality, my air, my earth. I eyed the ghost warily.

'I don't know.'

'Ask him,' Abernathy yawned.

A simple solution. The ghost was seated by the window, content watching the street below. He seemed to have no interest in me. I stared at him, feeling slightly helpless. There was no tingling at the back of my neck, no dark bleeding into the edges of my vision, none of the things that pushed me towards that looseness of mind that enabled me to speak to spirits. Now I was just myself.

'I can't.'

'Then try listening,' Abernathy grumbled, dragging the blankets over his naked shoulder and rolling away from me. He was perhaps trying to be facetious, being a grumpy sod before coffee and tobacco, but his words dislodged a quiet memory in my mind. Sitting in the Old Brewery, watching a ghost in the corner, listening to them sing me a sea shanty: *The stars and bars they flew behind her, the stars and bars they flew behind her.*

I looked at the ghost expectantly, an eyebrow raised. *I'm listening.* The ghost smiled, bloody teeth loose.

Trouble's comin'.

His eyes drifted back to the window significantly and, with a sudden lurch of dread, I flung back the blankets, ignoring Abernathy's irritated groan. My naked skin immediately puckered against the chilled Manchester morning. The rain was beating at the window and sending that typical March mist through the cracks in the pane. Glimmers of splotchy, navy-blue sky rose into the inky blackness, the dawn streaking through it like dye running out of the hem of a black dress. Down in the street, I could make out the forms of several loitering Scuttlers.

'Shit.'

'What is it?' Abernathy came to my side, his bare feet slapping against the floorboards. We watched them carefully. They were striding back and forth, eyeing the door of our lodgings and twirling their batons expectedly. It didn't take a genius to see they were here for us.

'Callaghan, that slippery shit.' Abernathy's breath fogged up the glass. If Callaghan had broken his word to us, neither of us would be surprised, but it would make our journey to the *Dunlin* harder.

'We should go,' I decided, reaching for my clothes.

Abernathy nodded, throwing his shirt back on over his shoulders. I saw a flash of many criss-crossed scars. A flogging. I had felt them in ridges under my fingers last night, thick and bumpy, inflicted in childhood and hardened as he grew. I looked down at my corset, fumbling over the hooks, not wanting to be caught looking. It was one thing to uncover the story of a person's body in darkness, another in the cold morning.

Back stairs, the ghost whispered. I turned to him and he nodded to the doorway. I knew we were running out of time.

'Come on,' I said, scooping up my essentials – my cards, knife, my needle box, money, and a velvet flower that Minnie liked to wear in her hair – into my pockets and pulling a shawl over my head. 'Bring what you need. We might not be able to get back.'

Abernathy nodded, hesitating at the side of the bed as he pulled his coat on. His fingers reached out to delicately touch Minnie's perfume bottle, asking for permission with his eyes. I nodded.

Reverently, he tucked it in his inside pocket, and then set a cigarette to his lips.

'Hey, chick.' He grabbed my hand quickly. 'I know where Polly is now; I can take it from here. If you want to get away—'

'Get away?' I repeated blankly, my eyes on the ghost who was making a flapping gesture with his arms to hurry us on.

'Well, you did say you could have been on a train.' Abernathy smiled. 'You've been a wonder but you needn't stay, not if it's because we...'

He trailed off, eyes darting back to the bed. I stared at him for a moment. I had never even considered it. After all, a random coupling fuelled by grief and loneliness is hardly a good enough measure to judge a man's actions. The idea of leaving Abernathy now, of going to the station alone and disappearing once again, a nameless freak with nothing and no one to tie me to this earth was unthinkable. Besides, Effie's memories were heavy inside my mind. She had implored Minnie to save us both; she had hoped we would all be free together. I didn't believe in atonement but maybe this was something like it, reparation for the years I had forgotten the first person who'd loved me. Either way, it was my choice.

What do you want, Flora? a familiar voice whispered. I remembered sitting between her legs in Eisenmann's studio, those miraculous words warm on her lips before I admitted I wanted her to kiss me. The taste of her lipstick, fatty and perfect. What I wanted was Minnie back and I could not have it. I shook myself and unlocked the bedroom door.

'Trying to get rid of me, Siddles?' I raised my eyebrows at Abernathy.

'Not in the least.' He smiled, fondly.

'Well then—' I held the door open for him, decision made '—let's go.'

THE HANGED MAN.

Chapter Twenty-Two

The *Dunlin* lay on the other side of the Salford Quay, across the bridge on Huron Basin. It was barely dawn and, though the mills and factories were quiet on Sundays, the quay was still thick with great ships, their huge chimneys disappearing into the rain clouds above. We walked in silence, passing under the towering cranes, invisible in the dark air above us, and skirting the floating lifts for grain that bobbed precariously on the flat water, the metal fixings on them clinking musically as we passed them. Abernathy made quick work of bribing a guard in a burgundy vest and soon he was carrying a crate of oranges aboard, me slipping along beside him.

'Let's get Polly, get Minnie's body and get out,' Abernathy muttered to me. 'I don't like the feeling of this.'

I wondered if he was referring to the same dread that was threading through my body. Whether it was the threat of potential Scuttlers, the terror of seeing Minnie's body or the gnawing presence of spirits, I couldn't tell. It was a relief to step over the heavy black bolts of the hatch and into the iron belly of the ship, but only for a moment.

'You with me?' Abernathy frowned.

I nodded faintly. Boats hold many spirits. The iron leached the blood of workers who had lost their lives in the building of it, the timbers whispered the memories of those who had thrown themselves overboard, or quietly died on the voyage. I could sense their presence, almost as painfully as I had been able to sense Maude's arrival, my mind suddenly dizzy with a tireless ringing, secrets and souls clamouring to cleave the floorboards and slither into my consciousness, but there was one that was stronger, brasher, elbowing the others aside, and tasting distantly of musty poppy smoke. *Minnie*. There was a tugging at the back of my body through the centre of my spine and out into the world like a thrumming length of cheese wire. I tried not to groan at the rubbing ache of it but I had to follow it.

'Christ, we'll never find her,' Abernathy muttered under his breath as he read the signage on the wall. I fumbled for my cards in my pocket.

'Let me just—' I bent to the floor and split the deck.

'We do not have time for this!' Abernathy hissed. I ignored him, splitting three piles and then quickly, rushing to turn cards.

The Tower. Danger, that much was obvious. The Five of Cups. Loss and sorrow, deep in my bones but also, taking shape in the air beside me. Someone was trying to speak to me and I knew who it was.

Flora, she whispered. With shaking fingers, I turned the last card. The Six of Cups.

'Revisiting memories,' I muttered to myself. In my mind's eye, I saw the door to our suite the last time we had crossed the Atlantic, saw the brass plaque on the white paint. 'Room one hundred and six.'

Now, Flora.

I scrambled to scoop my cards up. Whispers buzzed in my ears and I was moving fast, towards something I didn't understand.

'What?' Abernathy was breathless, running to catch up with me whilst clutching the heavy crate of oranges to his chest. 'You told me it wasn't like a bloody compass—'

'It's not; someone wants us to know where to go.' *Minnie does.* My heart was thumping brutally, as if my body was preparing to flee. I didn't know if I would vomit or scream. I could hear her, I could feel her, I could almost smell her with that scent that was a combination of poppy and rose. I didn't know if I was eager or terrified.

'We don't have time for this, Flora!' Abernathy said, dropping the crate at our feet to grab my arm. I nearly stumbled over spilled oranges but I kept going. 'We just need to get Polly and get out—'

'What do you think I'm doing?' I wrenched my arm away from him and glared into his taut, worried face. 'Either you believe me or you don't, Abernathy.'

They call ye mad or kill you. Effie's words had been truthful for more than one reason. People did not react logically to the Knowing. They fought against it, pushing away the revelations it brought with both hands, even Abernathy who had never faltered, stumbled now.

'You know I do—' he pressed a heavy hand against my shoulder '—but these cards have got you into some tight spots. Are *you* sure?'

It was the first time in my entire life that someone had asked me if I truly believed myself. I could feel the frustration of the Knowing building impatiently, resentful at my hesitation, but I did hesitate. I had killed a man, slashed another, I had driven a third to his end by his own hand. Then I remembered all of their ghostly eyes, bright with deferred justice, hungry for vengeance. Had any of it been wrong?

'Yes,' I said. Abernathy's hand gripped mine, clumsy and meaty.

'Which room again?' he asked.

'Room one hundred and six.'

Abernathy dragged me along, my mind already foggy and the shadows ran with us, collecting shape and form as we went until we reached the correct door. He took a deep breath and tried the handle.

'It's unlocked,' he whispered. I swayed with the pressing feeling on my skull, the scent of poppy overwhelming and familiar. *Minnie.*

'This is it,' I whispered. 'This is where we're meant to be.'

Abernathy nodded but before he could twist the door handle, it opened. As it did, people appeared from the rooms opposite, Scuttlers with batons, and with an ugly crunch, Abernathy had taken a blow to the head.

'Abe!'

He was on the floor, eyes rolled back into his head, being dragged away from my scrabbling hands by two Scuttlers intently pulling his legs as the man in the doorway grabbed me. Inside, I looked at the face of Joe Callaghan again and glared at him.

'Liar,' I snarled, twisting against his grip as Abernathy was manhandled, heavy and barely conscious, through the doorway.

'I said I would drop it, witch; I didn't say I'd not pick it back up again.' Callaghan patted my shoulder in a conciliatory manner. 'He pays too well.'

I didn't need to ask who.

'Bring her in, Callaghan,' a voice called. I knew it well. *You'll regret it*, the voice had whispered over and over in my dreams. Callaghan dragged me over the threshold to face Chester Merton.

'Hello, Florence.'

The first thing I saw was the wheelchair. A giant, hulking beast of brown iron, wheels rusted and muddy from the streets outside that clicked as he rolled forward. I had tried not to imagine Chester during the last ten months, presuming only that he was out there, hunting us, as Minnie had always said he was. Not once in my imaginings had I conceived this. The man sitting inside the chair looked to be the same man in essentials, fair hair shiny with pomade, face taut with superiority, but now the impact of it all was entirely different. His smart tailoring and gleaming shoes now seemed sleazy, his curled lip more an unbecoming habit than a cruel sneer. I realised how much of my memories of him were made up of him standing over me, leering down, his height as much an affront as his words. The eyes, however, were utterly the same, with that familiar cloudy grey hatred.

'Chester.'

His name sat on my tongue like cod liver oil – a vile film that I had not missed.

'Florence.' His smile was the same too, still smug and dangerous. 'Are you proud of your work?'

He lifted his arms wide, the left arm trembling and tilting back down to the earth, as if it were heavier than the right. A result of Effie's knife in his back, no doubt. His hairline had receded. I imagined that probably annoyed him more than his evident palsy.

'Not really.' I swallowed hard. 'Should have stabbed you through the heart.'

Abernathy chuckled and was pushed onto the bed where he flopped, groaning, as one of the Scuttlers rolled him on his side to tie his hands together behind his back. His eyes flickered open. He saw me, saw Callaghan, and then those eyes flickered closed again. He did not look to be in a good way at all.

'Check her.' Chester nodded to Callaghan.

Callaghan smiled at me. He grabbed my waist and tugged me closer. His hand moved down, patting my hip, feeling for my pocket. I watched, impassively, as he pulled out my possessions, setting them curiously down on the table. When he got to my needles, he looked up, eyebrows raised.

'Do your own work, do you?'

'Why?' I glanced pointedly at his wrapped arm. 'Maude's not good enough for you?'

He ignored me and flicked my knife out of its mother-of-pearl handle, testing a large finger against the tip of the blade. He nodded approvingly.

'That will do nicely,' he said, and then he pointed my knife at me. 'Sit down. Get your cards out.'

Callaghan shoved me towards a small table and chair set beside a bed. The suite smelled strongly of the rich mahogany furnishings and the beeswax used to clean them, but Callaghan smelled of blood and smoke as he pushed me down, and I felt my own knife, the cold, silver tip of it, held softly against the spot of bare skin between my shawl and my ear. Just another knife. Just another bastard. Eerily, a chilly calm settled on me as I heard a door being locked behind me. In the shadows by the bed, I looked and saw form beginning to stitch itself together. They might have locked me in, but they didn't know what they had locked in with me. Not yet.

'Where's Minnie?' I asked Chester.

'Safe. In the cargo hold. I'm taking her home to be laid to rest where she should be, in the Merton plot, and you'll never be able to touch her again.' Chester smiled. I knew that smile. In the past, it had always preceded discomfort and humiliation. 'Now it's time for the show – I know you love a show, don't you, Flora?'

I said words I had waited a year to say: 'Fuck off, Chester.'

Abernathy snorted to himself.

'I don't think I will.'

Chester fumbled in the blanket on his inert knees, withdrawing a pistol. The tiny black hole of the barrel stared at me, an open eye of metal. I didn't move. Callaghan shifted nervously behind me and I winced as the tip of the knife pressed into my neck lightly pierced the skin. No more pressure than a needle but enough to show his discomfort.

'You didn't say you had that,' Callaghan said to Chester.

'It's not important.' Chester pointed at me, grinning away. I sat very still. I'd not been on the receiving end of many guns and I could tell Callaghan hadn't either. Chester had made himself the dominant power in the room and Callaghan didn't like that. I could feel it in the tension of his hand. Chester hadn't noticed. He also hadn't noticed the shadows. I looked around the suite for a hat or a pair of petite gloves but saw none.

'Where's Polly?' I asked. 'Hidden her away, have you?'

'Oh, you always were a jealous bitch.' Chester licked his lips. His eyes flickered on my neck and I knew he was hunting down my latest tattoos, wanting to see where the skin had changed. He was still predictably nauseating. 'But slum trash has never been my flavour.'

It was such an absurd mix of insult and ridiculous lie that I laughed, despite the knife at my throat.

'No.' I shook my head. 'I'm far too old for you now.'

Chester's eyes hardened.

'Hit her.'

Callaghan did. A ringing slap that knocked me forward onto the table, my chin painfully colliding with the wood and forcing my teeth through my tongue. A burst of warm blood filled my mouth. I turned my head to the side, spitting it onto the carpet as Chester wheeled forward to sit opposite me at the table, the gun aimed directly at my chest. He flicked his weapon down to the cards.

'Deal them,' he said. I caught my breath. Just as on the night I had left Hamilton Square, I felt it: a small resolve clicking into place, a bullet in the barrel of Chester's revolver. *A chance.* Yet I couldn't seem too eager, even as I felt the pressure of shadowed wings behind me.

'Can't you just shoot me?' I stared at the gun in his hand and fantasised what it would feel like to hold it to his cheekbone and pull the trigger. I imagined wet chunks of bloody matter on my hands and my fingers fluttered eagerly.

'Why would I give you mercy after what you've done?' Chester leaned forward. 'Do you know how long I was laid in bed, prodded and poked by damn doctors?'

I nearly snorted at him. Apparently he'd forgotten the women he'd left helpless at the hands of doctors. Myself. Effie. Even Minnie. This was probably not the moment to remind him.

'Can you even imagine living with this terrible pathetic infirmity?'

No doubt he didn't mean to, but his eyes inadvertently flickered down towards his own lap. With a flash of vicious delight, I realised he was impotent. Perhaps I was proud of my work. The world was undoubtedly a better place now Chester Merton's cock was terminally soft. I couldn't help smiling. Chester glowered.

'Hurt her.'

Callaghan was the type of man to relish such a vague order. His fist was in my hair before I could blink, his other hand grabbing my arm and twisting it back behind the chair. It was so reminiscent of Jordan, of the Dead Rabbit lads who used similar tactics for control of women, that I smelled ink and tasted salty air. I gasped, my breath leaving as an angry hiss through my teeth. Chester smiled as he took my cards in his free hand, spreading them messily across the table. My skin prickled irritably as he did so. Answers were spread out all around us and I could feel them spilling out into the air, calling in whispers around us. He didn't care. Finding the card he wanted, the Death card, he slapped it down in front of me like a challenge.

'You killed Minnie.' Chester inched the gun closer to me. If he hadn't, I might have rolled my eyes. 'I didn't believe that suicide bullshit when he fed it to me.' Chester jerked his head towards Abernathy. 'Utter horse shit, I knew then I had to cut him loose. You killed her, just like you tried to kill me.'

His version of our shared history was fascinating. Somehow, I had become the one in pursuit of Minnie when I had never felt

273

more like prey than I had under his roof. I looked down at my cards. Effie's hands had been my hands. I wasn't prey any more.

'I didn't do either,' I said.

'Oh, I just imagined you stabbing me in the spine?' Chester said, sandy eyebrows raised.

'That was Effie,' I said. 'Remember Effie?'

'Effie.' Chester grinned, but I saw his surprise underneath it: the smallest waver of hesitation. I latched on to it greedily. He hated to be on the back foot. 'No, don't think so. My memory is crystal clear.'

'Is it? I know all your little sins,' I whispered.

I flicked the card over with one finger, ignoring Callaghan's irritated hiss behind me. It was the Devil reversed. *Freedom. Release. Restoring control.* The whispers leaked out of the many drawn mouths on the cards, floating all around me.

'Minnie was only fifteen when you took her from Kate's. That's what you like, isn't it?' I said, staring into those eyes filled with silver scorn.

'No law against it.' Chester shrugged. 'They were both women. You all were.'

We were not. They were coming, I could feel it.

'Polly wasn't; she was only ten when she came into your house.' I could feel Abernathy wincing at my words. These were things he knew but not things he wanted to hear. 'She'd never bled; she wasn't a woman. She's your daughter.'

I heard a disgusted sound behind my head. The Scuttlers on the bed were looking at Chester in frank revulsion. These were Irish lads, some of the most violent youths in the city, but they had grown up under the shadow of St Michael's & All Angels steeple. They knew a mortal sin when they heard one.

'Your lies will die with you.' Chester's fingers twitched on the gun as he lifted it to point it at my head. 'Anyway, it's my fucking word against yours and who's going to believe a little slum slut?'

Not just your word. My soul stilled when I heard her. Behind me, beside me, always within me. I took a deep breath and looked. The shadows behind Chester were taking form, wings first. Enormous, damp wings dripping with blood and darkness. I felt a sting in my breast, as if someone had begun to tattoo the very muscle of my heart. I would not look away, not this time or ever again. Besides, I had never been able to look away from her. *You'll still find me, little mystic.* I turned the last card. It was like a hand over my mouth, unseen and stifling. Yet I could not stop myself from knowing. The Empress. The mother.

Speak, Flora.

'It's no wonder, really,' I said, 'that your daughter killed Minnie.'

Chester's eyes flew up to my face. It was an ugly kind of confirmation, halfway between a sneer and a scowl. This was the only thing up to this point that I had said that was any kind of real revelation to him. I glanced at Abernathy. I saw his big eyes filled with mourning. He hadn't wanted it to be true. He'd protected them both, loved them both like family, but he couldn't save them from each other.

'That's not true.' The fingers on Chester's free hand beat an angry tattoo on the table. 'You've always been a liar.'

'She's not lying,' a voice said from a small doorway I had taken for a closet. It was clearly the doorway to an adjoining bedroom and there she stood, her eyes fixed on her father. Polly Merton. Chester twisted in his chair, desperately craning his neck to look at his daughter. She stood in the doorway, like Minnie and yet unlike her in so many ways. The tilt of the head was the same, the slight sway of her grand purple skirt as she stepped into the room, the heart shape of her face that she had clearly grown into but she was so young, still. Her arms were too long, her gait uncertain, yet she looked at her father with venom. I could feel the spirit of Minnie leaning forward towards her daughter, urging itself into stronger form. I could not tell if it was malevolent or yearning.

'It's true, Chester... I killed her.'

'What?' Callaghan was shifting behind me, uncomfortable at the new intrusion. Abernathy was waking, becoming more alive with Polly's presence, and the Scuttlers were holding him down on the bed. Chester didn't answer. He was staring at Polly, the gun temptingly loose in his hand. I contemplated flinging myself across the table and grabbing it, but I felt the flat of my knife move to my shoulder blade.

'Don't even think about it,' Callaghan said.

He probably wouldn't mind if Chester was disarmed. He would sure as hell care if I had the gun, though.

'Why?' Chester's voice trembled with rage, the vibrations of his feeble body travelling up into his throat. 'I told you we would be a family again, that we would take Minnie home with us—'

'A *family*?' Polly cut him off, staring at him with his own grey, silvery eyes. 'You raped her! You – you made me do things too. How could you think I would ever love either of you? What father abandons their child only to do *that* to them? I knew she was my ma, knew from when Abe came to get me at the orphanage, but you! You knew I was your child and you made me do those things, touch you and – and let you touch me—' I was agonised to see the bright flush appear in her cheeks. She was embarrassed, when the humiliation was all his to bear. 'What love is that, when you forced yourself on me and she let you? What kind of mother leaves her daughter with someone like you? I hated her more than anyone alive. She left me with you!'

Her eyes were shining with tears, her young voice broken. I didn't know if the things she was saying were true, but I knew that she meant them. She wanted to hurt him, make him wild with grief. Wild men often make mistakes.

'And when I killed her, you know what I said? I said you sent me, Chester. She thought it was you.'

'You little *bitch*!'

276

It was working. He was becoming enraged, but not in the direction Polly wanted. He turned his fury on me, grey eyes glistening with infuriated tears.

'How do you always do this to me?' His face was red and his grip on the gun tightened. I remembered him whimpering through the door at Kate Woods' house, a year before. *Why are you leaving me out?* 'How do you turn them all against me?'

He was whining, red-faced, his gestures with the gun becoming wild as he screeched hysterically:

'Minnie was mine, dammit! She was mine!'

He was going to kill me. Then Polly. Then Abernathy too, probably.

I looked desperately for Minnie, for the shadows that had not yet dragged themselves into face and voice. I needed her now. *I don't know what to do!* I thought wildly to the half-formed shadows behind him.

You have the Knowing, they whispered back.

Before Chester could press the trigger or Callaghan could move, I flicked a card. I stared at it. The Hanged Man. *Sacrifice.* I saw the red of his stockings, red as blood, and I knew. *Blood calls to blood.* The Knowing can always be summoned. I held my breath and arched my back against Callaghan's knife.

'What the fuck?'

Callaghan stumbled back from me in shock. I fell sideways, painfully, as my arm jostled the table. Somewhere above me Chester still had a gun to point at me. I could hear Abernathy and Polly's voices underneath a persistent ringing in my ears. The knife was cold going into my shoulder, uncomfortable and sudden, but I knew it wouldn't be enough. I thought of the blood that had come out of me in agonising clumps when Jordan had fed me the medicine in the brown bottle. I thought of the blood that had poured from Minnie, staining her and Effie alike, bringing Polly into the world. Blood full of life, blood that could make things breathe. I scrabbled my arm around and pulled the knife out. A searing burn made me gasp, but I felt the blood. It was warm and full of their rage. Then I looked for her face.

Minnie.

Her ghostly eyes were no longer blue. They were black as the nightly waters of the canal that she had drowned in. The blood that left me seeped up to fill her, like a gown soaks up rain. As the life drained out of me, it filled her creaking, avian form.

'Minnie.'

I knew from the way he spoke her name that Chester had seen her. Minnie, dead and bringing death, shadowed wings and claws made of the dusty memories of Effie's death, of little boy-whores beaten and maids bent over the desk in the Hamilton Square library. Chester's history of violence caught like raindrops in her feathers, and when she beat them, smaller, skeletal birds took flight, their turbulent fury clamouring to find justice and purchase on his skin with their damp, inky claws. Chester only had eyes for her.

'Minnie,' he whispered, raising the gun to eye level. 'No, Minnie.'

He fired through her luminous, vaporous face. His hands dropped to his wheels, rushing to push them back. He was falling, or was he falling? Were there hands in the air, pulling him down? Were her wings gusting his head to lovingly crush it against the metal ridge of the doorframe? Minnie's feet, made real and strong again and dexterous by my blood, standing on his windpipe. Was he choking on air or the pressure of her weight? All I could see now was the water in Minnie's eyes, deep enough to drown in. It was my choice. It was my sacrifice and I let myself float into it.

I am a ghost, I thought. *I am a ghost.*

XXIII

Chapter Twenty-Three

In between death and life, there was a canal. Its surface was soft, the water slick like ink. Deep below, other beasts and people swam. The water drew stories out of my skin, turning them back into memory and thought. I wondered if death was becoming new again, but as I looked down at my body I realised I was finally dissolving. Becoming an ink blot. Was it right that in the end the tales etched on my skin drowned me? It felt right.

Then hands, small, childlike hands, were grabbing me and pulling my slippery, ink-stained body out of the canal. A voice, needle sharp and solemn, crying from a bird's beak.

'No, Flora! No! Stay awake! Stay awake!'

The stories in the water were mine, familiar skin and patterns, but the voice was unknown. A future, maybe. Where I carved more ink into uncharted skin. Where a scarred throat bore a lopsided smile. Silver eyes and rabbit teeth. In the water was the woman I had loved; in the voice, the girl who'd killed her.

I longed to stay in the canal, to sink and drown and never wake to the living world again, but she pulled me out.

*

Bright lights pulled me out of a penny-tasting dream. I couldn't feel my right side and I gasped for my breaths, pulling them into my lungs so hard my ribs creaked. It smelled like the dead room in the police station. I thought of the metal autopsy table. I retched, tasting meat.

'We're at the workhouse.' Abernathy's face floated in front of me. He was miraculously alive. 'They're about to stitch you up. Hold on.'

He vanished. I closed my eyes against the light. The only work-house where a person like me could get seen was the Poor Law hospital at the New Bridge Road workhouse. I could smell rotten straw in the mattress and hear the bustle and wail of people nearby. The scream of babies and the sound of vomiting. Someone was sitting beside me. Someone was holding me up, pressing something firmly against my back. Blinking hard, I saw a purple dress. Was it Minnie? No, Minnie was dead. Deep in the water, dragged under the soft waves of ink. I had left her behind there, or rather, been made to leave her behind.

'Polly,' I said.

'Yes?'

I couldn't see her. Only the cold black and white tiles underneath my feet. When I tried to turn my head it was too heavy and my peripheral vision was dark, but I could hear her voice, close to my ear. Had she always sounded how she had under the river? So reso-nant and commanding?

'Is he dead?'

It was the question I needed most to know. I thought of Chester falling back into darkness, his head crushed against metal.

'Yes.' I could hear Polly swallowing nearby. 'He bled out there. I watched him. I made sure. It looks like he fell.'

'Good.'

I glanced down at my skin. My tattoos were all still there. I rubbed my arms, watching to see if the slickness of the river returned but they stayed put, my skin raw. I was feeling dizzy now, starting to get cold. My legs were shaking and I felt a little hand press warmly on my knee. I thought to push it away but I didn't. My mind was a wearied jumble; feelings flittered past – rage and despair and relief and terror – but they were all fleeting, like snow I was handling with leather gloves, melting away before they could be felt. I did know this: Polly said she'd killed Minnie yet she had saved me. I didn't know if I was grateful yet. There was the sound of doors banging heavily, and then the presence of other people crowding around us. My dress was soaked with blood. They must have been waiting hours, hoping I didn't bleed to death before I was stitched.

'Let's have a look then.' A brusque nurse muscled in between us, pulling whatever Polly was using to stem the bleeding off my shoulder with a tug that made me groan. 'Nasty. Deep. But mostly clean. Few stitches; it will only be a moment.'

'You got something for the pain?' I asked, gripping the metal bedframe.

'No. We never do.' The nurse ripped the neckline at the back of my dress cheerily and I smelled the strong scent of iodine. Then I felt it, a burning searing under my skin. I sucked in my breath with a hiss, the edges of my vision blurring.

'Here—' Abernathy pushed his flask into my hand '—have some.'

I took it, the alcohol stinging the small cuts on my lips and then swirling into my stomach. Cheap Scotch. I choked.

'Just like last time,' I coughed, looking up at Abernathy with streaming eyes. 'At Kate's, remember?'

'We need to make better memories.' He smiled tightly at me, watching the nurse's hands carefully. She was likely an overseer in the workhouse, adept enough with cotton spinning to be thought good enough to sew human flesh. The needle burned as it went in and out. I closed my eyes against the pain, looking for a distraction.

'Callaghan,' I asked. 'Alive?'

'Yes,' Polly answered from behind me. It seemed I couldn't have everything I wished for.

'Shot in the arm,' Abernathy said. 'Gone back to the Meadows. Hester will patch him up again, I'm sure.'

'We need to get out of here before that happens,' I winced. Even in my slightly addled state, I knew Callaghan would hold a grudge.

'We will,' Abernathy said. 'Let's make sure you're in one piece first.'

'You're leaving?' Polly asked anxiously. Abernathy and I shared a look. There were things that needed to be said.

'All done.' The nurse put in the last stitch and there was a nauseating tug as she tied the knot with firm hands. 'I'll get you a bandage.'

She left, no doubt to scrounge up some vaguely clean fabric scraps to wrap me up in. I took another sip of Scotch and swallowed slowly. Polly walked around me until she stood on my right-hand side, her arms folded. In that posture she reminded me so intensely of Minnie that I had to shut my eyes for a moment. Minnie was dead in the river. Inside me, I could feel a deep part of me recoiling, like a wounded animal folding itself up. I wanted to withdraw the parts of me that were raw and howling so they no longer felt the sting in my shoulder, the lingering ghosts and the grief for the river I could not rest in, but it would not be enough. The ghosts were all here. Perhaps now they would never leave me. I was meant to be unravelled. Every card I drew now would show what should have been. The river of ink. The death I should currently be swimming in. I stared at my bloody fingernails. *Red, again.*

'What happened with Minnie?' I asked. Abernathy sat beside me and held my hand. Polly looked down at our held hands with a small frown and then caught my eye, blushing. She chewed her nails nervously. *Just like me*, I thought absently.

'She fell in the canal,' Polly whispered. The silence was taut and I was reminded intensely of the time I had confronted her about Chester, the same mute fear. I closed my eyes. Maybe it was an aftershock of the river flowing through me, or just the Knowing, tripping me up still, but I saw the two of them walking towards the water. Minnie was shouting, her blonde curls starting to straighten out in the damp air.

'You fought before that.' I ignored Polly's quick intake of breath. She didn't ask how I knew. 'Why?'

'Because... she wanted to see Chester.' Her words tickled my ears. 'She knew we were coming and I wrote her; I wanted to warn her that he was after her again. I hoped we would run away together, all of us, but she had no intention of leaving without seeing him. She said she was going to meet him. She wanted... money.'

I let out a long, heavy breath. I was filled with the urge to cry. I knew a part of me should have been grateful that Polly's answer hadn't been that Minnie had gone to Chester because she loved him, but I only felt desolate. Inside my mind I saw the morphine box still sitting in our boarding house, the doses that Minnie was no doubt tired of hustling for. I imagined her, perhaps already one dose deep, faced with a daughter desperate for something Minnie never had the capacity to give.

'She couldn't stop,' I whispered. I heard my own voice from months ago: *You're going to get yourself killed.*

'What happened then?' Abernathy's voice was harsh with despair and I squeezed his hand, forgetting my shoulder for a moment and wincing with the pain.

'I told her the truth: that he never loved her, that he was terrible, and she...' Polly's eyes filled with tears. 'It's like she didn't even hear me and… well, you know what happened. You saw it, didn't you? In the cards?'

Inside my eyelids, I saw Polly approaching Minnie, I saw Minnie's derision. I saw the cold stars bouncing on the dark, buoyant water.

'I want you to tell me.' I opened my eyes. The brightness hurt but I didn't want the knowledge that came from the river and the Knowing, whatever it gave me. Polly pulled me out. I wanted Polly's story. Her little lip quivered.

'She told me I didn't know what I was talking about, that I'd never know what she'd given up for me,' Polly whispered, her silver eyes wet like mercury. 'I was so angry, I pushed her a bit, I didn't mean to! But she fell. I tried to pull her out but the wings pulled her down, and I could only reach her neck, so…'

I closed my eyes again. The damned wings. Maybe she had worn them in a failed attempt to impress her daughter, maybe for Chester, I would never know. I looked at Polly. She was twisting her gloves together just the same way she had twisted her cap last year. Her blonde hair had grown enough to be curled but it was still the same feathery texture, the damp Manchester air making it fluffy, like a cloud. I jerked my head to my other side and she sat beside me, pressing her face into my shoulder. She no longer smelled of baking bread and sweat; instead, the scent of her was floral and musky. In a year, she had started to grow up. She was approaching the same age that Minnie had been when she was pregnant with her.

'I tried to get her out,' Polly's whisper was almost lost in the bloody mess of my hair. 'I really did. The walls were so high and the wings were so heavy and her arms couldn't reach me or grip.'

I looked up at Abernathy. Tears were coursing down his cheeks in slow solemn trickles. I raised a single eyebrow at him in a weary question: *do we believe her?* Abernathy nodded, fists clenched. He needed to believe her. I closed my eyes and I saw Minnie's wings, pure as snow and sprinkled with gold, dragging her down into the dark water. I could feel Polly's damp tears dripping down from my shoulder to my breasts, chilling my flesh. I closed my eyes again, beginning to shiver. *She's dead. She's really dead.*

'Come here,' Abernathy gasped between tears, pulling me close to his chest. His warmth and the strength of his arms stopped the trembling, just as they had done in Hamilton Square after Chester and I had bargained with my skin.

'She's dead,' I whispered. He squeezed me closer. He smelled of smoke and New York. 'I was there, I saw her—'

'I know.'

I looked into his face. I remembered what I had seen through Effie's eyes, through the grey veil of death. The way the deathly birds floated close to Abernathy. The long view from the end of the rope, a lynched boy walking through the waking world. Who knew what other world Abernathy had seen when he had danced on the air?

'The tree,' I said. He nodded slowly. We were both marked now. There was a strange kind of comradery in almost dying.

'Where's her body?' I asked.

'It's sailing back on the *Dunlin*,' Abernathy said, regretfully. I didn't blame him. It was too much to ask for a man to flee the scene of a crime with a woman mortally wounded and a stolen corpse. 'I sent a telegram to Kate in New York. She'll pick Minnie up. Give her a proper burial.'

I imagined Kate and the other working girls standing vigil beside a small grave. I was luckier than Abernathy in some ways; I only had to look in my cards to feel her close. He had to endure being an ocean away from her final resting place.

'I'm sorry.' We looked up at Polly. She was biting her lip with that same rabbity quality that she had done in Hamilton Square. Deep in her silvery eyes I saw hints of that same, icy blue determination that Minnie always had. It was the same thing I had seen when she had taunted Chester. She had hated them both with good reason, and maybe she hadn't tried as hard as she said to stop Minnie drowning. Maybe she had tried harder. Maybe none of it mattered. She didn't know what she had taken from me, but maybe it wasn't more than what Minnie and Chester had taken from her. She carefully pulled something out of her pocket.

'Can you tell me, please, just... I need to know.' Her voice was tremulous as she put my cards down on my knee. 'Am I going to hell?'

There was a prickling at the back of my neck when I looked at her face, at the numb resignation, the settling of shoulders under a horrible weight, the adjustment of posture to this new way of walking. I recognised it. My heart twisted as I recalled that feeling – the heavy burden of the death of Jordan, of watching his last gurgling breaths spill onto the bed. *Let it be*, Minnie always said. Polly was her only child. I had to try. I set my cards aside and pulled her into a one-armed hug.

'No,' I whispered against her ruffled curls, as fine as silk and smelling like curling irons, just like Minnie. 'No, cub. We've been to hell already, don't you think?'

'Too many fucking times, by my reckoning,' Abernathy said.

Polly snorted with laughter and pulled back, rubbing snot across her cheek with the back of her hand.

'But what do I do now?' she whispered shakily.

Debts must be repaid. Accounts come due. Nothing is for free. Poor girls know this better than anyone, but perhaps Polly's ledger had been settled. I imagined the Judgement card. The faces of all are upturned for the herald of endings and, in them, the universe sees the suffering of the endless girls who came before Polly and perhaps that it is enough. Perhaps there is justice in it. I thought of Effie, teaching me to read the cards and holding me close, of Minnie, making me laugh and kissing my tattoos. Kindness sticks with girls like us. I didn't know if I had forgiveness to give Polly, but I had kindness.

'You'll come with us,' I said, reaching out to let her sticky fingers grasp mine. Polly nodded with relief.

'But where will we go?' she asked plaintively.

'Good fucking question,' Abernathy muttered.

I hesitated. I felt something shift inside me, like the canal waters parting to make way for a voice that would never leave me. *Tell me more about the shop*, she whispered. I shook my head and swallowed my tears.

What do you want, Flora?

I didn't need to reach for the Knowing inside me for an answer.

'Well…' I smiled. 'I have this idea for a tattoo shop.'

Chapter Twenty-Four

Nine months later
Blackfriars, London

Abernathy winced and moved his shoulder carefully, peering his head back to peek.

'How is it?' he asked.

I shrugged and wiped it with an alcohol-soaked rag, nodding to the mirror.

'It's just like hers,' I said, turning away from the pair of wings I'd put on his shoulder. It was the first time since we'd started up that I'd hesitated before inking him. The giant tree on his back, the pair of swallows on his wrist, they had all been fine, but this request had given me pause. A tingling in the back of my neck that I did not enjoy. Abernathy looked at me closely in the mirror as he admired my work.

'It's only to honour a childhood friend.'

He gingerly pulled his shirt on. Behind him, whispers of dust and ink drawn into being by his words began to dance. The shape of her was clear enough, if I tried to see it. Spirits didn't just whisper to me any more, they were drawn to me like magpies to glittering rings. The ghosts were always close, and sometimes too close, but they no longer needed blood or violence to speak to me. They only wanted to be seen and heard, so I looked and listened. I did all the things I had been taught never to do: I spoke, I looked and I told the secrets, and Abernathy and Polly became used to walking into a room and finding me talking to the air.

'She'll be pleased,' I said and Abernathy smirked. The bell on the door rang and Abernathy craned his neck to the front of the shop.

'One for me.' He stood up. I nodded. He darted into the front and under the counter, starting to converse and lift tobacco jars down from the shelves. I sat still and breathed through my nose, waiting for the sensation of dropping slowly into black water to ebb away. I had to be vigilant after the *Dunlin*. Abernathy had taken to waking me two or three times a night, drawing me out of dreams filled with dark water and memory because my heart had stopped beating. The first time it happened he lay in the dark beside me, a trembling hand covering the angel on my chest.

'Your heart stopped on the *Dunlin*, before you came back.' His finger tapped against my sternum in the rhythm of the comforting beat he felt there. 'You stopped breathing, too.'

'I know.' I stared at the ceiling of our little flat above our shop, trying to not see churning currents. 'Polly pulled me back. The Knowing wanted me to stay there, in the river. With Minnie.'

'Tough shit,' Abernathy said, pressing his palm down as if I was about to drift off into the sky. 'I like you right here.'

'I just need to be careful.' I thought about how long life might be if I could never fall asleep. 'I'm not meant to be here.'

'If that's true then you wouldn't be,' Abernathy reasoned, pressing dry lips to the sweaty curls beneath my ear. 'Yet here you are.'

'There's always a cost, Abe.'

'Haven't we paid in full already?'

In the dark of the night when my heart stuttered was when memories of Minnie emerged to choke me. Instead of letting myself be strangled by it, I spoke to Abernathy.

'Do you remember how Minnie used to make everyone think she was practically an Astor?' I whispered. 'When we moved to Manchester our landlady was terrified of her.'

Abernathy laughed.

'Aye, even as a lass she treated everyone like she was above them,' Abernathy chortled. I smiled. The edges of my grief softened. I pressed a kiss to the branches I had tattooed across his shoulder blades.

'Are you happy, chick?' Abernathy murmured.

'Yes.' I smiled.

I was. Perhaps I shouldn't have been for we made next to nothing, selling tobacco and coffee and inking folk, but it was enough for food and there were no gang lords looking for rent and most importantly, it was ours. I drew boats on high seas and hearts pierced with knives onto rice paper and transferred them into ink and wove the stories of the ghosts I heard into bare skin. Then I let them march out of my door, each tattoo drifting into the wide world as mine, and mine forever. Abernathy had named the store 'Siddles and Flowers Tobacco and Tattoos', but it did not matter what we named it. Across Blackfriars we were known as 'the American store'.

'Look what I have!' The bell rang again as Abernathy's customer left and Polly blew back into the store in her usual whirlwind state. She no longer looked like a young copy of Minnie – the velvet gowns, curled hair and rouge were all gone. She was dressed top to toe in black like an undertaker's apprentice, with her feathery hair braided back from her face and tucked up into a cap. Luckily, our eccentric reputation as odd Americans meant most folks only watched her pouring their coffees and pricing up tobacco with a bemused, indulgent expression. She was always in motion, quick and loud, as if making up for long years of being unseen and unheard, and completely unlike her mother in every practical sense. Yet I saw Minnie in her every single day as she grew.

'You were meant to fetch sugar,' Abernathy scolded her lightly from behind the counter. 'What happened to that?'

'This is better than sugar, this is *grand!*' Polly gushed and I saw Abernathy smirk. Polly had made friends with some of the other merchant youngsters in Blackfriars and I often overheard them exchanging colloquialisms from across the sea.

'What is it?' I asked.

Polly sat down beside me at my station and pulled out a deck of cards, dropping them onto the table next to my ink pot with relish. I touched the tarot cautiously. I had not read for anyone, not even myself, since Manchester. I hardly felt like I needed to, what with the shadows of ghosts catching my eye on every street in London.

'What are these for?' Abernathy asked. He watched me closely from behind the tobacco counter, no doubt listening for my heartbeat.

'Well, I thought you might want to teach me,' Polly said awkwardly, shifting in her seat. I stared at her. I remembered Effie, sitting cross-legged across from me in the Old Brewery, laying the cards out between us.

'You want to learn?' I asked.

Polly nodded.

'Would that be all right?'

I didn't say anything. I picked up the tarot cards, fresh and sharp, and began to slip them through my palms until I felt a sudden slice at the tip of my index finger. *Blood.*

'Damn.' I quickly slipped my finger into my mouth but I was too slow. The edge of one card was lined with blood. I dropped it, feeling the cold water descend. I saw faces drawn into being at the windows, spirits clawing their way out of the river at the gateway of my slow-beating heart. The air chilled. I felt cold canal water against my skin, threatening to wash my tattoos away. I fancied I felt Minnie's wings unfold at my back and Effie's hair curling around my head.

'Shit,' Abernathy muttered, moving to duck under the counter but Polly's hand found mine. She pulled my finger out of my mouth and wrapped it quickly in a handkerchief.

'Breathe, Flora,' she commanded. I did. I took a deep breath and stared into her silvery eyes. Moonlight and smoke. The steam from the train as it passed over the bridge across Angel Meadows, leaving Manchester behind us.

'There you are.' Polly smiled, pressing her little hand with the blisters that had never healed against my cheek.

'You always pull me back,' I said. Blood and cards. It was still an overwhelming combination. Polly grinned, her little teeth just as rabbity despite her growing, lengthening face. She took the cards from me and shuffled, and I was relieved, suddenly, to have them out of my fingers.

'How do we begin?'

'A three-card spread is the easiest,' I said. 'Cut the deck into three.'

Polly did and set three piles out amongst my ink bottles and rice-paper designs.

'Why three?' She tapped her fingers against them. I noticed how her nails were like the few Minnie had; the same blunt, broad shape. I smiled.

'For the past, present and future.' I touched each pile in turn. 'Past events that have the potential to hold you back, present challenges and future direction.'

'So I just turn them and... what?' She frowned.

'Patience.' I caught Abernathy's eye and smiled. It was a skill Polly was not known for. Slowly, I told her of the arcana. I told her of the meanings and words that the images whispered and fielded her questions, as Effie had done for me. Eagerly, she turned her past and present cards in quick succession.

'My past card is Justice and that means... fairness? My present card is the Ten of Cups so that means... unity?'

I stroked the pictures in front of me. They were so clean, unlike my own cards, but still the Knowing whispered to me. Justice. *A warning for past actions.* Ten of Cups. *A union of opposites, of two hearts becoming one.*

'I don't think I'm made to be a mystic.' Polly shook her head. 'Are you sure you're not making it all up?'

'You're honestly going to ask that?' Abernathy looked up from where he was filling a jar of tobacco leaf.

I laughed. I heard Effie's whisper inside my head. *Can't summon the Knowing.* I could teach Polly but I couldn't give her what I had.

'What do you think it means, Flora?' Polly's eyes were fixed on me. She had Minnie's nails and hair and gestures but her eyes were pure Merton. I felt a tingle in my back, the wound that had healed a long time ago. The Knowing began to whisper, telling me all the things that these cards could mean for the slight girl in front of me, barely a woman and tainted by the blood of both of her parents.

'Nothing we can't handle.' I smiled, turning the two cards face down again. 'Did you want some ink today?'

I had kept my promise. Two months ago, I had given Polly her first tattoo and then her second.

'Can you add another swallow?' Polly's face brightened and she lifted her skirt to reveal the dance of the two swallows across her thigh. Just like Abernathy, Polly had been eager to have her own memories etched on her skin. 'One for each of us.'

I smiled and clipped my curls back in the old velvet rose pin that had once been Minnie's. I dipped my ink in my pot. I tried not to think of symmetry, of her mother being inked in the same place, of Abernathy having Minnie's first tattoo inked today. I tried not to see patterns and meanings where there was just skin and ink.

'Just to check—' Polly grinned, flicking over the final card from the third pile '—doesn't hurt to know.'

I paused. I stared down at the card. It was the one in the deck that had sliced my finger and now its fresh, clean surface was slightly bloodied. The Wheel of Fortune. It was the card that had brought me to Jordan and Minnie; I shouldn't have been surprised it found a way to wound me. I wondered if it did hurt to know.

What do you want, Flora? Minnie whispered, daring me to ask for more.

Nothing more than this, I thought, but the Knowing was a knife. It cut me. I closed my eyes for a brief second, but there is nowhere to hide when you are a living bridge to the precipice of spirits. The wheel of fortune shone inside Polly's silver eyes, promising rises and falls, promising change. I saw it turning.

Acknowledgements

As much as possible, I have tried to keep the historical world of this book equivalent to our own. For my Salford readers, however, I do ask your forgiveness for my lenient interpretation of when the Manchester Port and Salford Quays were built.

Many people helped shape this story into what it is today. Without my amazing agent, Alice Saunders, this book would still be invisible. Her constant kindness and honesty have kept me steady throughout this process. I count it miraculous that you found me, Alice, thank you. Your belief gave me self-belief.

I am so grateful to my wonderful team at Bedford Square, Jamie Hodder-Williams and Laura Fletcher, who believed in Flora and Minnie from the beginning. Thank you for answering my silliest questions and giving me the assurance I needed. Thank you also to Donna Hillyer, for your insightful edits.

Highest praise is owed to my fellow writer pals. Firstly, to my friend and mentor, the Venerable Doctor Rachel Mann, to whom this book is dedicated. Without your pastoring, both spiritual and literary, at such a critical time, I would not be here. I am also so grateful to my favourite dramatist and story maker, Sam Redway, and to my darling Andrew Miles, who has been reading my tales since we were eleven years old. All three of you were unfailingly generous with my sprawling first drafts. Every writer would be lucky to have artistic companions such as yourselves. Thank you also to my friendly pedant proofreader, Rachael Smith, who had the irksome task of managing my excessive use of an apostrophe with unfailing patience.

I am indebted to Mya Saracho for their wonderful artistry and exquisite tattoo illustrations. Thank you for bringing Flora's handiwork to life.

To my patrons, who have supported my work tirelessly in the last three years, thank you. Having readers like you is all anyone could ask for.

I owe a debt of gratitude to my Creative Writing tutors at the University of St Andrews, particularly Oliver Emmanuel – you helped me truly understand my wingspan as a writer. Thank you for guiding me and so many others at the start of our writing journeys.

Lastly, this book truly belongs to two people. To my friend Hannah MacDonald, the most voracious reader in the world, who cheered me on through this entire process and held on to hope when I had none. You are a marvel.

To my beloved Jonathan, who keeps me alive with tea and sandwiches and bemoans the lack of dragons in all my books – there are no adequate words of praise or thanks. So in lieu of them, this will have to do: *and then there was a dragon!*

Photo credit: James Melia

Emma is a queer playwright living in Manchester with a focus on telling untold feminist narratives. Her latest play, *PURE*, was featured in Turn On Fest at Hope Mill Theatre Manchester and she was the recipient of the Artist Development Grant at Hope Mill Theatre. She has written a few previous non-fiction books in her capacity as an academic (in another life she would have been a theologian) with an essay published in *Tarantino and Theology* with Gray Matter Books and her book *Ineffable Love: Exploring Christian Themes in Good Omens* published by Darton, Longman & Todd.

X @EmmaLouisePH

@elphreads

Bedford Square Publishers

Bedford Square Publishers is an independent publisher of fiction and non-fiction, founded in 2022 in the historic streets of Bedford Square London and the sea mist shrouded green of Bedford Square Brighton.

Our goal is to discover irresistible stories and voices that illuminate our world.

We are passionate about connecting our authors to readers across the globe and our independence allows us to do this in original and nimble ways.

The team at Bedford Square Publishers has years of experience and we aim to use that knowledge and creative insight, alongside evolving technology, to reach the right readers for our books. From the ones who read a lot, to the ones who don't consider themselves readers, we aim to find those who will love our books and talk about them as much as we do.

We are hunting for vital new voices from all backgrounds – with books that take the reader to new places and transform perceptions of the world we live in.

Follow us on social media for the latest Bedford Square Publishers news.

🐦 @bedsqpublishers
ⓕ facebook.com/bedfordsq.publishers/
🄾 @bedfordsq.publishers

https://bedfordsquarepublishers.co.uk/